JOEL N. ROSS

DOUBLE CROSS BLIND

Joel N. Ross studied history at Hampshire College and taught English abroad for a short time before writing *Double Cross Blind*, his first novel. His father served in World War II, along with all five of his uncles, and their stories provided some of the background for the book. Currently, Ross lives in Maine with his wife, Lee.

ANCHOR BOOKS

A Division of Random House, Inc.

New York

DOUBLE CROSS BLIND

JOEL N. ROSS

FIRST ANCHOR BOOKS EDITION, AUGUST 2006

The Library of Congress has cataloged the Doubleday edition as follows:
Ross, Joel N., 1968–
Double cross blind / by Joel N. Ross.—1st ed.
p.   cm.
1. Traitors—Family relationships—Fiction. 2. Military intelligence—Fiction.
3. World War, 1939–1945—Fiction. 4. Americans—England—Fiction.
5. Espionage, German—Fiction. 6. War neuroses—Fiction.
7. Brothers—Fiction. I. Title.
PS3618.O8455D68 2004
813'.6—dc22
2004049435

Anchor ISBN-10: 1-4000-7881-4
Anchor ISBN-13: 978-1-4000-7881-3

Book design by Gretchen Achilles

www.anchorbooks.com

Printed in the United States of America
10 9 8 7 6 5 4 3 2 1

FOR MY FATHER,

SGT. MARK ROSS,

THE FINEST MAN I KNOW

DOUBLE CROSS BLIND

CHAPTER
ONE

THE YOUNG WOMAN hitched her skirt to her thighs, revealing slender legs encased in lisle stockings.

"I do apologize they're not silk," she told the man in the shiny black waistcoat. "So *terrifically* hard to find silk these days, isn't it?" She lifted her skirt a fraction higher, and as the man gaped she brought the heavy iron piping down hard on his skull.

He fell to his knees and made a funny wheeze.

It was rather exciting. She hadn't been in London during the Blitz, but oh how she'd envied them the drama. The whine and clump of the incendiaries and ack-ack shells, the streams of tracers and the barrage balloons bumbling overhead. Now the Luftwaffe was raiding more heavily again, and she felt a glow of pleasure at being part of the grand sweep of things—a glitzy Berlin cabaret, with brilliant spotlights sweeping the darkened stage, but better for the real tears and blood and love.

And bomb sites were super places to trap and scrap onetime informants. The man in the shiny waistcoat was like a funny crab, trying to crawl away over the rubble. She checked that the message he'd given her was intact. She knew that *some* people in the SD—the Sicherheitsdienst, the security service of the SS—considered her flighty. They'd laughed that her code name should be Schmetterling, Butterfly. But she wasn't flighty. She was dedicated and smart and she did what needed doing.

She lifted the iron piping to finish the man but was interrupted by the gleam of a blackout torch pricking among the wreckage and an air warden calling out, "Hallo? Miss? You're within the danger area."

"Oh this poor man!" she cried. "Please—he's hit, he's injured. Oh, *do* help!"

She knelt as if to care for the man and put her knee on his throat.

"What? Is the gentleman hurt?" The elderly air warden hurried forward, babbling questions.

She felt the knobby bone of the man's throat crack and separate under her knee. She heard him wheeze and die, but it was nothing so climactic as a death-rattle. She stood, her hand to her own throat in horror, her eyes wet and wide.

The air warden became agitated, and she began to weep. It was curious, the lingering scent of a bomb site. Brick dust as thick as the London fog mixed with the smell of damp plaster and heavy clay and the bitter waft of domestic gas hissing from shattered pipes. The bouquet of an eviscerated building. She even imagined that the man in the shiny waistcoat had exuded a sort of fleshy-sweet fragrance, like narcissus, as he'd died.

She sniffled away from the air warden, murmuring that she simply *had* to leave, then rode her bicycle through the dark streets to slip into Mr. Pentham's house through the garden. She memorized the message the man had given her and destroyed it. Was it bad news? She couldn't decide. She was forbidden to contact Hamburg except once: the first and final time, when the mission was complete. The British had direction finders, and there was no reason to jeopardize the operation by using her wireless too soon.

The agent she called "Bookbinder" was in place. Not the place he'd intended, but in place nonetheless. He could not fail. Her faith in him was religious. The two of them together would ensure the victory of the Fatherland. It shouldn't be long now, ten days at the outside.

It was the most thrilling assignment of her career, and her satisfaction was complete—except for the occasional whiff of dead Mr. Pentham, who, she was afraid, was beginning to go off. But even *that* could be ignored, caught as she was in the excitement. She considered the message again. She'd never met a Yank, not really. Thomas Wall. Perhaps she'd call him Tommy.

CHAPTER
TWO

THOMAS WALL WOKE from what wasn't quite sleep. The bedside lamp smeared feeble light on the patterned tin ceiling and the scarred wooden bedposts. He sat up and the room reeled. He steadied himself against the mattress, his breath catching at the pain in his bandaged right hand.

The broken memory of a fever dream flashed and was gone. *England.* He was in London. The Rowansea Royal Hospital—a hospital dormitory, an asylum, once packed to the rafters with shell-shocked husks of the Great War. Now a new generation clamored at the gates as Churchill faced Hitler across the narrow Channel.

Tom had a bed in a semiprivate alcove, and the enforced company of hollow-eyed men stiff and brittle as scarecrows. All he needed was time, quiet, cool darkness. He needed sleep. Hadn't slept for two days and—

Someone was coming. He heard footsteps on the tile floor, sounding over the snoring, wheezing inmates. Tom turned his head, and the light of the hallway blinded him, shining like a deadly beacon on a deadly night. *The operation. The recovery. The airfield on Crete.* He lifted his bandaged hand to shield his eyes and heard the rustle of skirts.

"Harriet?" he said.

"Still awake, love?" a nurse replied, matronly and bustling.

"You and me both, Mrs. Harper. No rest for the wicked."

"The *weary*, Mr. Wall. No rest for the weary."

"Them, either—but what would you and I know about that?"

She clucked. "How you do go on!"

But he didn't go on. He stayed. He had recovered—except for his hand—but he stayed in the asylum, cutting paper dolls. All he needed was rest and sleep and . . . *Earl*. He needed Earl. Earl was a walking bomb only Tom could defuse.

". . . it's coming on seven," Mrs. Harper was saying, "and you have a visitor this morning."

"Seven? It's morning?" Another disorientation, the dawn obscured by the blackout curtains. Then he heard the rest of it: "I what? I have a *what*?"

She clucked again. "Hush, now. You'll wake the others."

He had a visitor. His family was in the States. In England, there were only Earl, Harriet, and Chilton. Not Chilton, never Harriet. Then Earl? He needed a gun. He needed his Colt. He needed his BAR, snap off the bipod and work it till the muzzle caught fire. He levered off the sheets. Beneath the white bandages, his right hand throbbed.

"Set yourself down, love," Mrs. Harper said. "Rushing's the last thing to heal you."

"What visitor? An American?"

"You know what the governor said, Mr. Wall—steady as she

goes." She drew the alcove curtains, and a mumbling moved through the room as light seeped in. "I told them, didn't I? No visitors. But do they listen to an old nurse who's been tending her boys since the Aisne River?"

"I'm steady," Tom said. "I'm four-oh. What visitor?"

"A gentleman from the Home Guard . . . or so he claimed. Called past midnight, if you please! I put him off, of course. He'll be coming at half eight, so we'll need to shave and dress, Mr. Wall."

"He *claims* to be from the Home Guard?"

"A Mr. Davies-Frank. Fire Control—or so his calling card said."

"Davis Frank?"

She hushed him and led him into the hall. There were doors every twenty feet down the wide institutional corridor, and buckets of sand—in case of fire—every ten. "Mr. Davies-Frank," she said. "Gentleman of your generation, and why he's not in uniform, I wouldn't presume."

"Not American, then," he said. Not Earl.

"English as the day is long, with an accent that could roast chestnuts. Nothing like—" Mrs. Harper shook her head. "I won't hear a word against Americans, but if you won't fight the Germans, I'm sure the king going on bended knee to your Ambassador Winant won't change his mind."

"This Davies-Frank mentioned Ambassador Winant?" Tom asked. "The embassy?" The embassy was where Earl worked—when he wasn't working elsewhere.

"There now, Mr. Wall," the nurse said. "Less of *that*, if you please."

She unlocked a door and led him past the chapel and the display of flags. Four flags were American, taken in 1814 when the Brits set fire to the White House. Some of the old pensioners

6

liked to twit Tom about the captured flags, so he pretended to think they were veterans of the War of 1812 and was rewarded with toothless and grizzled smiles.

Mrs. Harper led Tom toward the governor's wing and unlocked a final door. "Journey's end, Mr. Wall. Shave, bathe, and dress. I'll have Mr. MacGovern bring you a nibble. Is there anything else you'll be needing?"

"Scrub my back?"

She clucked in amusement, and was gone.

Beyond the door was a small, tidy bedroom. There was a suit laid out on the bed, and a narrow paneled door opening to an attached bathroom. There was a razor in the bathroom, an old-fashioned cut-throat with a handsome ivory handle. What the hell? Giving an inmate a straight razor instead of a safety?

He couldn't think. His mind was sluggish, exhausted as his body. He wanted sleep, he wanted Earl, he wanted Harriet—

Shaving left-handed was awkward, and with a cut-throat it was worse. There had been a girl who'd shaved him during the worst of it. He remembered that. He remembered her breath smelled of licorice and her front teeth were off-kilter, and she'd smiled at his gallantries as if she didn't suffer a thousand daily flirtations, a thousand broken men trying to prove themselves whole.

He cut himself on the chin, cut himself on the cheek, then stripped and stood under the shower until the stink of the dormitory sloughed off. The water was cold and smelled crisply metallic. It roused him and he realized he was still here, still going through the empty motions, when he needed to be gone.

He toweled dry and slopped a bowlful of sudsy water onto the tile floor, and left the razor at the edge of the basin.

He dressed. The suit was his—he'd bought it last year in Burlington Arcade, before it caught a Luftwaffe bomb. There was no wallet in the pocket, no money, nothing. An empty suit for an empty man.

The door opened and MacGovern entered. He was tall and bent, like Ichabod Crane, with bony shoulders and a gaunt face. He was stronger than he looked, and he ruled the men with a brutal bonhomie.

"Got yourself all prettied up, then," MacGovern said, putting a tray on the bedside table.

Tom ignored the tea and dry biscuit. "Mmm."

"You look a little sailor boy, at sea in your own suit."

"That's right, Mac."

"Audience with the king, I told the lads. What do they want with you, then?"

"My recipe for coffee cake."

Mac cuffed him. "Your bleeding lip, more like. I hear the man's calling from the War Office. Or is he the Yard's Special Branch?"

"Horse Guards. Want to come? They're in the market for a jackass."

"Better than a lame dog. Bloody one-handed Yank . . ."

Tom said "mmm" again and slipped his feet into the shoes. Nothing would placate Mac, not if he felt Tom's treatment was a challenge to his authority—being allowed a shave, a shower, and a mysterious meeting without Mac's permission. But he'd get his own back tomorrow, or the next day, or the day after that.

Tom crouched over his shoelaces, and MacGovern finally glanced into the bathroom, finally saw the straight razor on the counter.

"Stupid cow, handing that to the likes of you." His spindly legs unfolded like a stepladder and he was inside the bathroom almost before Tom knew he was moving. "Lucky you didn't give me a crisp new grin, from ear to ear."

Tom smiled and launched forward from his crouch. He hit MacGovern's waist with his shoulder just as MacGovern set his second foot on the soapy tile floor.

MacGovern buckled and windmilled his arms. He caught at the wet towel flopped over a hook and cursed and fell hard, his legs flinging upward.

"Bleeding fuck!" he yelled, splayed there like a stick figure come undone. "I'll see you get a week without—"

Tom dropped on him, his elbow hard into MacGovern's gut, and while Mac was gasping for breath, he took a handful of Mac's hair in his good hand and beat his head against the floor. Three times, and MacGovern stopped struggling. Four, and he was moaning in a semiconscious daze, his outflung hand clenching and unclenching.

Tom pulled Mac's arms around the water pipe, careful not to slip on the wet tile, and bound his wrists with the man's necktie. It was painful work, Tom's right hand flaring beneath the bandage, but he did it—tight as he could manage.

He stepped back. The exhaustion was gone, replaced with edgy euphoria. He'd done it. It was he and Earl in this lightless, ravaged city. He took MacGovern's keys and wallet, then closed the bathroom door and locked the bedroom. If luck was with him, the room was soundproof. If not, MacGovern's yell would raise the alarm.

Nothing he could do. Nothing but find Earl, and stop him.

TOM SLIPPED DOWN the corridor toward the kitchen stairs. He found himself in the front hall, what they called the Court Room, with its painted ceiling and dingy colonnades. A moment of vertigo, and then he knew where he was. He turned and—

Voices in the hallway. If they caught him now, with MacGovern bruised and bloody, no way he'd get another chance.

9

The voices grew louder, then faded.

He willed his heart to stop pounding. Sgt. Thomas Wall—Rosenblatt had called him "Tommy Gun," and the nickname caught on among the other men. That was him: fearless, quick, decisive . . . afraid of the echo of gossiping nurses.

No time for self-pity. He unlocked a set of double doors with MacGovern's key and walked twenty feet before a nurse came into the hall. He nodded without meeting her eyes, continued walking.

She said something behind him.

He said, "Yes, thank you," and didn't slow.

He turned a corner, opened a door, and slipped into a coat-room that stank of camphor. How soon before MacGovern was found? How long before Mrs. Harper returned? He rifled through the hangers, grabbed an old army greatcoat, and shrugged it on. The hall was empty. He went down the stairs and into the kitchen, past the sandbags and out the side door.

Fresh air.

Tom blinked, breathed, and made himself walk slowly across the wide windblown street. A pinprick of tension ached between his shoulder blades, as if he were expecting a bullet. He headed down the next street, trotted kitty-corner across the intersection. He boarded a tram, and fifteen minutes later he found himself on a common—Streatham, Clapham, where the hell was he? London somewhere.

The iron fence had been removed from the common, to be melted down into bullets and bombers. There were ruts where the railings had been, long, barren furrows. The front half of the green was divided into garden allotments, and there was a piggery built with bomb-salvaged timber, and Black Leghorns and Rhode Island Reds pecked at the dirt beyond. At a barrage balloon—

painted dull silver and tethered inside a wide wire circle—a mustachioed corporal and his crew trained their replacements, a dozen women from the WAAF, with a combination of efficiency and flirtation. There was a sort of domestic serenity to the scene, which made Tom slow, then stop.

The morning breeze blew the smell of pigs toward him, pungent and comforting. A handful of Englishwomen were digging in their allotments, arguing easily about Mr. Middleton's gardening broadcasts. A milk cart drove around the common, its horse clattering and nickering. Two office girls giggled together over a pack of cigarettes. They were plain girls, and beautiful.

He wanted to ask directions. He wanted to see them smile. But if he spoke, they'd know him for what he was—shocky and sleepless, an escapee from the Rowansea Hospital.

"Thirty-five girls!" the brunette said, lighting her cigarette behind the shield of the other girl's hands. "At three suitors per girl . . ."

"At Martyn's, it'd be three girls to one boy!"

They giggled again and the brunette looked at Tom, her eyes suddenly bold. "Care for a fag?"

"I'm lost," he said. "I'm looking for the train to the City."

"Canadian?" the brunette asked. "I can always tell. Except between New Zealand and Australia—they both *sownd abite like this*, don't they?"

He smiled. "American, actually."

"Eagle Corps!" the blonde squealed. "And wounded, to boot!"

She said it with such pleasure, he smiled again. The Eagle Corps was composed of American pilots who'd volunteered to serve in the RAF, in defiance of the Neutrality Act—and to hell with the isolationists back home.

11

"Just regular army, miss," he said. "Camel corps—infantry."

"An army of one, are you? Unless the States declared war last night."

"I drove to Canada and signed on the dotted line. I'm part of the Commonwealth now."

"So much for the American Colonial Uprising, then!"

"The Revolutionary War," he corrected sternly, and they all laughed, and his sense of dislocation was complete. The day was crisp and bright. The breeze was fresh on his face. He smiled at the girls and couldn't hear what they were saying. He had nothing but urgency left, and even that was fading. At least he was able to pretend normalcy, to pass without suspicion. At least they'd not raised the alarm. They told him to take the number 16 bus to the 88, or the 12 all the way in. They told him they couldn't buy Woodbines at the local tobacconist—he only sold to men—so they had to go twenty minutes in the morning for their Woodies.

They explained what they'd been giggling about, an article in the newspaper. "Thirty-five girls in the City went through their hatboxes and keepsakes," the brunette said. "And dug up all their old—"

"Dig for victory!" the other girl said, giggling again.

"—all their old love letters and donated them to salvage, and how many letters and how many *masses* of admirers must you have, even if there *are* thirty-five of you, before you're able to make a dent in the war effort? Why, even Daph here wouldn't be able to collect more than four or five. . . ."

Daph shrieked a protest and Tom smiled, disconnected. He watched from a spot ten feet above as the girls led him five blocks, then pointed to a bus stop.

"There's your bus now," the brunette said. "But it's traveling away from the Rowansea. Are you sure that's not where you're going?"

TOM GOT ON the train at Tooting Broadway. Someone suggested he change to the Piccadilly Line, so he did. There were crowds of mothers and children in the stations—ten thousand evacuees leaving London every week, and two thousand returning on the same tracks. They looked almost festive, and Tom caught himself smiling at a fresh-scrubbed face, a red ribbon tied in an elaborate bow.

Instead of schoolbags, they held cardboard gas-mask boxes. Already there were fifteen thousand dead in London, twice that in the rest of England. First the day raids, then the night. Hunger and fear and mothers sending their children to live with strangers, and it was nothing more than everyday life. But there were traces of desperation in the fond farewells. The stiff upper lip was qua-vering—it made Tom fonder of the Brits; he saw Harriet's strength in them, in their preference for the polite stupidity of courage.

He was back beneath the same ocean gray sky under which he'd arrived in London last year, shipped from Canada with the better part of his company. He remembered the air-raid sirens, the Moaning Minnies, the distant German bombers flying straight and slow, leaving hazy trails in their wakes to expand and disappear. He remembered the streaks of white caught by an interlacing cloud, the diving and climbing night fighters of the defending RAF. Faint blueprints sketched in smoke and exhaust, hanging above London's glow of fire. The distant geometry had seemed delphic, scribed in metal and moxie five thousand feet above the earth.

Tom had said as much to his squad, and they'd laughed with

an edge of unease, and called him "Quiz Kelly." They preferred "Tommy Gun." When Manny from Montreal had responded to an eruption of flatulence by shouting, "*Gas mask*," that was the pinnacle of humor. They'd laughed like children.

It had been November when he'd last seen this gunmetal sky. Was it November again? December? He bent forward in his seat to read the date on an old woman's newspaper. Monday, December 1, 1941. There. One solid fact: December 1, 1941.

He heard someone say, "Hyde Park Corner," and he was suddenly standing, swaying with the motion of the train. He was in the city proper now. The last time he'd been here, Harriet's hand had rested softly on his arm. He could still feel her fingers.

He walked up Piccadilly. He knew where Earl lived. Knew his home address.

He passed Apsley House. Passed a stately mansion with its windows blown out, roof gone, walls blackened and truncated. Beyond it, the In and Out Club was bloodied but unbowed, its structure shored up with wooden scaffolding. Tom paused. He felt a certain kinship. Then he took a left on White Horse Street, the tension back between his shoulder blades, his bandaged hand throbbing.

Shepherd Market was a narrow tangle of lanes. Between Curzon Street and Piccadilly, it was a cramped and shabby maze, with creaking old buildings and humble shops. The house was a pretty little redbrick mews, one step better than its neighbors. Two stories, with an angled roof, and no shop downstairs—two stumpy chimneys. *His and hers*. The front door sported a neat pile of sandbags for a welcome mat. The windows were crossed with sticky white tape against explosions. The blackouts were open, and the curtains were light and feminine.

The house sat behind a low iron fence. He swung the gate open. Just knock and enter? He didn't have a gun. It was knock or break a window, or go through the garden—he knew there'd be a garden, well tended, well loved. He lifted his left hand, and a woman's voice sang out from the patch of shrubbery next door. "Nobody home, I'm afraid." She was an elderly, elfin woman with a red kerchief tied round her hair and a tin watering can swinging in her knobby hands.

"Yeah." Of course nobody was home. Did he think Earl would be taking the day off? "He must be at the office."

"That would be the American embassy, then," the woman said. "He's second assistant to the undersecretary of piffledoggery, I believe. And she a FANY, of course." That was the First Aid Nursing Yeomanry, women who drove ambulances and supply trucks—and worked at the SOE, the Special Operations Executive, though few knew it existed. "Lovely young lady, and I use the term advisedly. Neither is here at the moment. She may be staying with his lordship. Lord Chilton has a— Pardon?"

"No. Did I say something?"

"I should think you did."

"Well, Chilton."

"Indeed." She set the watering can at her feet. "And he—I mean her husband, not her father—often travels on business. I've been keeping an eye out, because one can't be too careful in these days—except of course one *can*, don't you agree? Too much care is as dangerous as too little. God bless the king for refusing to retreat to Windsor—and the queen, too. They told her to leave, you know."

"Nobody tells me anything," he said, backing through the gate.

"Oh!" she said in sudden recognition. "You look quite like him. I'd have seen it before, but my eyes aren't what they once were."

"Nothing is," Tom said.

CHAPTER
THREE

RUPERT DAVIES-FRANK was sitting in the office of the governor of Rowansea Royal Hospital, trying not to kill the messenger. "He's gone?" he asked. "Between the time I rang last night and arrived this morning?"

"He was washing up for your visit," the governor said. "He accosted a nurse."

"How long ago did he escape?"

"Escape?" The governor's bushy eyebrows rose. "Not at all. Prisoners escape. But one's *patients*? Surely not."

Davies-Frank waited, his expression unchanged. If he didn't find Sergeant Wall today, the whole thing would come tumbling down.

"However," the governor said, "he did, hrm, depart. Or decamp."

"Exactly how long ago did he depart or decamp?"

"Not thirty minutes."

"Did he mention a destination?"

"Not that I'm aware. I haven't spoken with Mr. MacGovern, however—the nurse."

"His injuries aren't severe, I hope?"

"More startled than injured. He's under observation now."

"I'll need to speak with him. And with anyone else in Sergeant Wall's recent company." A thought occurred to Davies-Frank. "Did the news of my visit trigger his departure? He didn't leave until he'd heard I was coming?"

"It seems he simply took advantage of the break in routine. Your visit wasn't the cause, so to speak, but the opportunity. The last time Mr. Wall left us, he—"

"The last time?" That bit of information hadn't been in the hastily compiled report Davies-Frank had skimmed at midnight. "He's done this before?"

"Mr. Wall had a time of it in Greece. Rather torn up when he arrived, and not just physically."

"And he decamped?"

The governor nodded. "Not long after he arrived. He had six months of combat. Mr. Wall was a squad leader and the only surviving—"

"How long was he gone? No—where was he found?"

The governor opened a tabbed file on his desk. "Have to check. There was talk of returning him to the States after the general evacuation of Crete. But he's governed by the Army Act, and—"

"Governor." Davies-Frank's tone was mild. "I need to know where he went, and I need to know it now."

"Almost have my finger on it." The governor flipped through the pages. "You're aware of his fixation?"

Davies-Frank shook his head, but before he could speak, the

governor prodded the file with a thick finger. "Ah! He was appre-
hended outside Burnham Chase. Lord Chilton's home. He'd
already visited Shepherd Market, where—"

Davies-Frank didn't need to hear more. Wall's fixation, of
course. Tom Wall was hunting Earl. Well, he wasn't the only one.

"I need your phone, Governor. Your office, as well . . ."
Davies-Frank eased the governor from the room and placed the
call. "Is Highcastle in? . . . Find him and tell him Wall's gone.
Escaped less than an hour ago. . . . Yes, in fact I *do* know—he's
after Earl. No, catching Sergeant Wall shouldn't prove difficult.
But using him . . ." Davies-Frank shook his head. Using Wall
against Sondegger was using a housefly against a spider. "We need
to get him to Hennessey before our guest changes his mind. Bring
Mr. Tipcoe in. Tell him to jolly the guest along until we—
What?"

The case officer explained. More news. More nightmare.

"Tipcoe did *what*?" Davies-Frank's stomach turned sour.
"When?"

Good God. Sondegger was inhuman. Davies-Frank pressed
the heel of his hand to his temple. The Nazi's only trick was convincing them of his power; the rest was guile and artifice. Still, the
artifice was murderously effective. Though it shamed him,
Davies-Frank always spent two minutes in silent preparation
before entering the room in which Dietrich Sondegger was
chained, steeling himself to face the pale blue eyes and rhythmic
droning voice.

"Tell Special Branch to go easy on Tipcoe," he said. "Exten-
uating circumstances . . ."

He exhaled and loosened his white-knuckled grip on the
phone. He was a man who heeded his instincts, and his instincts
were telling him that everything was falling apart.

The call had come last night: Sondegger would reveal his

secrets, but only to one man. Davies-Frank had stood from dinner, put the phone to his ear, and turned from a husband and father into a dark priest in search of a virgin sacrifice. He tried to keep family time sacred; he treasured his evenings with Joan and the twins, not only for them but for himself, as well. Duplicity was his job, but the instant he let it seep into his home, he was lost. Sitting at dinner and listening to his family squabble was what enabled him to go on. Then the call came, and with it came the shrill, unsettling instinct: The center would not hold.

No. It *would* hold. He'd hold the bloody thing together with his own two hands. He told the case officer to forget Tipcoe. "We need Tom Wall. Inform the Yard, the Home Guard. . . . Just bring the bastard in—it's urgent. I'll stay here. I've a file to read."

He'd need to speak to the patients, too, and the staff. He was grasping at straws—and of all possible straws, Tom Wall seemed the most brittle, the most inclined to burst into flames at the touch of a spark.

TOM RECOGNIZED the buildings. Grosvenor Square—they called it "Little America," in honor of the U.S. embassy. He knew what he had to do, but he didn't have a gun. He could close his eyes and remember the weight of a weapon. He could feel the heat pounding off his BAR, scorching his face and his neck, his arms aching and sweat burning his eyes.

He zigzagged slowly toward the embassy. He knelt, and when he stood again, he was holding a shattered brick—three-quarters of a brick, with one edge sheared off. It was a red stone knife. He liked its heft.

He sat on a bench. He had to clear the cobwebs from his mind, but the cobwebs were the only thing holding it together. After a long, blank pause, he stood and headed for the embassy.

He nodded to the guards and glanced at the register. He couldn't find Earl's name, but he found his department. A frontal assault? Yeah. All he could manage was simple, and simple was always best.

Things turned complicated fast. He achieved the second floor without trouble, his ID a combination of counterfeit confidence and authentic accent. A woman was sitting at a long desk beside a flight of carpeted stairs. Tom said he was there to speak with Earl.

"Have you an appointment?" she asked.

"No—it's family business."

Something changed in her face. "You're his . . ."

"Brother."

She waved him toward an upholstered bench. "One moment."

"It's urgent," he said.

"Please. If you'd take a seat."

"Could you— Which office is his?" He tried an apologetic smile. "I'll be in and out before you know it."

She pulled a binder from her desk. "I'll ring up and—"

"That the embassy directory?" He grabbed the binder and found Earl's name as the receptionist loudly protested. Assistant to a special consul named Bloomgaard. Sure he was. Third floor. At least that was probably true. Tom touched the brick in his pocket, turned to the stairs.

At Bloomgaard's office, the girl said he was expected. It would've bothered him, but all he needed was five seconds alone with Earl. Five seconds, and for the sharp edge of brick to fall true.

"Go right in," the girl said.

Bloomgaard's office was plush for wartime. There was a red flower on the desk in a green glass vase. The flower had shed petals, like drops of blood, onto the glossy dark wood.

"Henry Ford, Charles Lindbergh, Father Coughlin." Bloomgaard gestured Tom into a seat. "Senators Wheeler, Taft, Nye, and Vandenberg. Square-shooting patriotic Americans, every last one against U.S. intervention in the war. Would you like to hear more?"

"I'd like to see Earl."

"How about a simple majority of Americans? And senators, too—even if they *are* too lily-livered to stand against Roosevelt. Hell, even he couldn't get reelected without his pledge: 'No American boys will fight in foreign wars.' That's what your President Rosenfeld promised. My job, the job of every thinking person in the diplomatic service, is to keep that pledge from being a lie."

What the hell was he saying? Did Bloomgaard think they were arguing politics? "I told your secretary I wanted Earl," Tom said. "Not a civics lesson."

"You wanted him before, and you know what it bought you."

But he didn't know. It was a distant blur. *Had* he wanted Earl before? When he'd returned from Crete, had he gone after Earl? He couldn't draw a line around his thoughts—the battles, the surgery, the hours spent praying for sleep. He remembered a bread knife with a serrated blade. If he'd come, he'd failed. Earl had walked away.

Maybe Tom should tell Bloomgaard what he knew. The airfield on Crete, Earl's treachery. The squad wiped out in a spray of blood, killed by a betrayal deadlier than the Nazi enfilade. Hanner the croot, Manny from Montreal. Rosenblatt and camphappy Lifton and O'Rourke and Tardieu.

Should he tell Bloomgaard? He knew the man was stalling, talking about President Rosenfeld and Charles Lindbergh, but didn't know why. Was it in preparation for Earl's arrival, or to cover his escape? More likely than not, Bloomgaard was in it with Earl. You didn't have to cast a wide net to catch a fascist in the U.S.

embassy. The rich appointed men in their richly appointed rooms, old-fashioned American patriots, pro-Franco, pro-Mussolini, pro-Hitler.

". . . least you fight your own battles," Bloomgaard was saying. "I'll give you that. Britons, Jews, and Rosenfeld, that's who want our boys in this war. Listen to William Regnery, listen to the America First Committee—hell, listen to the fucking polls. Seventy percent of our fellow countrymen say keep the hell out of the war."

"What was the question?" Tom asked. " 'Do you want your son to die in Europe?' "

"That's not me; that's Gallup—this June. Seven out of ten. Now, one out of five say Hitler's doing a fine job. One in three say the Jew gets what he deserves, and one in ten say *we* ought to give it to him, too."

"You're a dumb fuck," Tom said conversationally from behind a veil of fatigue. All he wanted was Earl. "You work for Winant, or Kennedy?"

Joe Kennedy, the previous U.S. ambassador, had denounced "Polish intransigence" against the Nazis and called Britain "doomed" and a "lost cause." Democracy was finished in England, he'd said, and probably in the United States, too. Roosevelt fired his ass, and none too soon.

"I'm a lifer," Bloomgaard said. "I work for lifers. Roosevelt can't lead America into a war nobody wants, so he drags us kicking and screaming. Unlike some, so eager to fight that they slip into Canada to serve in a foreign army, like a spade escaped from a plantation. Except spades are black—these men, they're Red."

So Bloomgaard figured Tom for a Commie because he'd enlisted with the Canadians. That's why he was stalling—at least why he was stalling like *this*. But if Earl wasn't here, why stonewall at all?

"Mr. Bloomgaard," Tom said. "All I want is Earl."

"You've been told he's not in."

"I've been told a lot of things."

"As have I, Mr. Wall."

"He's attached to your department. He's not in, you know where to reach him."

A flicker in Bloomgaard's eyes told Tom that Earl *was* there. In an office, down the hall? Had he been warned of Tom's visit? It didn't matter. Five seconds.

Tom stood. "I'll get him myself."

"Don't you dare—"

Tom reached over the desk and grabbed the front of Bloomgaard's shirt, a fistful of collar and tie. He yanked him against the desk, bent close, and couldn't think of a word to say. He shoved Bloomgaard back into his chair and left the room.

The girl was at her desk. She didn't look up when he entered. She was talking into the phone. "He's leaving right now. Yes, he—"

Tom went into the hallway and opened the next door down. It was a file room, and the one after that was Earl's office. It was half the size of Bloomgaard's. There was an uncluttered desk. A blotter. A paper cutter. A bookshelf with a handful of reference books. A lamp, a phone, a cigar box. A picture of Earl and his wife. But no ash in the tray, no jacket behind the door. A fine film of dust on the desktop.

Earl was gone.

DAVIES-FRANK EXCHANGED the governor's rooms for the humbler facilities of the goundsmen. The staff would be more forthcoming if he questioned them in a less formal setting. He wanted gossip, not obedience. There was a tap on the door and the nurse,

Mrs. Harper, entered. Davies-Frank stood from behind the cramped desk, gestured toward a chair, and invited her to be seated.

"It's disgraceful," she said by way of greeting. "Putting you in Kirrage's room."

"The move was my own request, Mrs. Harper," he said as the nurse perched on the edge of the chair. "I have questions about Sergeant Wall and was told you were the person to ask."

"Well, his doctors would know better than I about anything *clinical*. But it's true Mr. Wall and I enjoy each other's company. Always a gentleman—ready with a smile and a joke, and no harm in him."

"Mr. MacGovern might disagree."

"Mr. MacGovern is disagreeable."

He inclined his head. "I need to know about the sergeant's health—mentally, physically. I've read the reports, but events seem to be outpacing them. He's having a relapse?"

"All I have is my opinion, Mr. Davies-Frank. There are no fancy degrees on my wall, if you'd care to look. Still, some might say my opinion is based on more than air and notions."

"Yes—I'd like to hear it."

She met his eyes, then nodded in decision. "Mr. Wall isn't suffering combat fatigue—not now, not as his primary complaint."

"Combat fatigue—shell shock?"

She tsked. "You're a war late, Mr. Davies-Frank."

"A war and four hours, it seems."

"I'll not apologize," she said, bristling. "I hope I know my duty. Interrupting a patient in the small hours of—"

"Please, Mrs. Harper. There's no question you acted correctly. Combat fatigue *isn't* his primary complaint?"

She paused, considering. "I'm not saying that Mr. Wall doesn't have the symptoms—insomnia, paranoia, grief, and anger. . . . Well, I'm speaking psychology, and I shouldn't. I hope I know my place." The suggestion of a smile played on her lips. "Mr. Wall calls me his 'bedpan commando.' "

"Always ready with a smile and a joke," Davies-Frank said. "He has the symptoms, then, but his primary complaint is . . ."

"*Had* the symptoms. When he arrived, he had what I'd call a broad and shallow combat fatigue. But in my opinion, he was—"

"Recovering?"

"Recovered."

"Judging from today's behavior, Mrs. Harper, that's a trifle optimistic."

"You're not unlike him," she said. "You can say anything, can't you? But he'd rallied. He'd recovered. Until the recent surgery."

"On his hand?"

She nodded. "It hadn't knit together properly. His chest and leg healed, but his hand . . . The first operation was not a success. So back to the surgeon's table. The anesthesia, the operation—set him back terribly. He's not much better than when he first arrived."

When it had taken months for him to heal. Well, the Twenty Committee couldn't wait months—they couldn't wait until tomorrow afternoon. Davies-Frank felt for the American, fighting on the front lines, watching his men die. But Davies-Frank bore his own burden. His days didn't determine the life or death of a squad, a platoon, or a company—but a battle, a convoy, a city. It was less personal: He'd never see the faces of the people he lost, but still his burden drove him. Drove him to pity this poor bastard Wall, and drove him to care nothing for him except as a tool.

"How much better is 'not much'?" he asked.

"On the surface, very little indeed. Underneath? He's far stronger than he was. If he could get a single night's rest . . ."

"He'd snap to?"

"In my opinion." She brushed an imaginary crumb from her lap. "But you won't allow him that one night, will you, Mr. Davies-Frank?"

"If Sergeant Wall had not decamped, I'd have—"

"Decamped? If he'd not *decamped*?"

"The governor's word," Davies-Frank said, and smiled at her expression. "I promise you, once we find Wall, I'll see that he returns here as soon as practically possible."

This seemed to reassure her, though it meant nothing. *Practically possible*. He was on a fool's errand. All the hopes pinned on Thomas Wall were foolish hopes. Insomnia, paranoia, a broad and shallow combat fatigue. Thomas Wall against Dietrich Sondegger was grain against the scythe.

Still, it was that or face the possibility—the practical possibility—of losing the Twenty Committee.

CHAPTER
FOUR

THE TWENTY COMMITTEE started with "Sleet," a mechanical engineer in the employ of an Admiralty subcontractor. During the early thirties, Sleet traveled frequently to Germany on business, returning occasionally with technical information for the Admiralty and MI6. He was a casual spy, undemanding and hardly profitable. Still, standard procedure was followed: His information was inspected, his access was controlled, and his daily routines were surreptitiously investigated.

In 1936, the standard procedure bore fruit. Military intelligence intercepted a letter Sleet had written to a German agent in Hamburg; it became clear the mechanical engineer was buttering his bread on both sides. There was talk of detaining Sleet, but to what purpose? Under what pretext? He'd merely sent letters to a private citizen of a country with which England was not at war.

Patience paid off. Within months, Sleet contacted MI6 and

told them he'd been approached by the German Secret Service, the Abwehr. He'd agreed to work for the Nazis, he said, in order to penetrate the Abwehr as an agent of the British. And so from 1936 to 1939, Sleet played the double game. Or was it a triple game? That was a question without an answer—and Davies-Frank imagined it was a question nobody asked. Sleet had hardly been considered an agent of world-shaking importance.

Still, he plodded steadily along. He passed information to the British: false names impossible to corroborate, scraps of gossip, glimpses of tradecraft when he met his contacts. He provided his German masters with notes on British naval manufacturing, on popular sentiment. And, at the bidding of his Abwehr contact, he approached Sir Oswald Mosley's increasingly popular British Union of Fascists.

He was instructed to investigate the BUF in order to determine which members had sufficient influence, or access, to warrant a direct approach. He was instructed to arrange with the BUF for the establishment and operation of four wireless transmitters in England. Reports were filed. Information was assembled. Minutes were written. And Sleet continued to operate, under the somewhat-lackadaisical direction of both the British and the Germans, doing little good, little harm.

In January 1939, a bored junior operative, having exhausted the patience of his superior, was told to shadow Sleet. He spent two days tailing him from office to home and back again. On the third day, Sleet traveled to Victoria Station, where, in the cloakroom, he took receipt of a yellow houndstooth suitcase. Inside was a wireless transmitter disguised as a gramophone. Sleet installed the transmitter in his attic and established communication with Hamburg.

Another report was filed. It resulted in raised eyebrows but little else. Then war was declared—and Sleet taken into custody.

His wireless transmitter followed him to Wandsworth Prison and was installed in his cell. From the prison, he reestablished contact with Hamburg and began receiving orders and requests for information. Those, with the guidance of his British hosts, he contrived to answer.

THE TWENTY COMMITTEE hadn't been formed at that time, when the entire network of Abwehr spies under English control had simply been Sleet. But even then, during those first uncertain days, the overriding concern was the same: the truth.

The truth was the foundation of the entire framework of lies. It was the grain of sand around which the priceless pearl grew— and like a grain of sand, the truth was an irritant. It could be managed but not entirely controlled.

Still, the Abwehr inspected this cultured pearl and proclaimed it genuine. They believed Sleet was loyal; they acted on his reports. The double cross was successful—for the moment. The turning of an agent was delicate business. In the best cases, it was seduction: intimate, tentative, and impassioned. In the worst, it was rape.

Sleet, seduced and deemed loyal, was sent to Antwerp with an MI6 agent who was pretending to be a member of the Welsh Nationalist Party. They were given contact information for "Thrush," a German-born photographer living in Britain, who would aid with the development of microphotographs—pictures the size of a postage stamp or smaller, used for passing information. Thrush, despite being blackmailed by threats to her nephews in Germany, proved easy to turn. Next came "Bitters"— an ex–dope smuggler and confidence man whom Sleet recruited as an agent for training in Germany. Bitters took to espionage like a worm to mud, and he soon learned of three additional German agents to be parachuted into England. Two of them turned, and lived. One did not, and was hanged.

So it went. One agent led to another, to another, to another. As of late 1941, the Abwehr's entire organization in England was being run by the British.

It was a double cross of monumental proportions. A double cross: XX. The Twenty Committee, whose members were charged with designing a fabric of lies so consistent and convincing that the Nazis would never realize they were not the masters of their own spy network.

CHAPTER
FIVE

EARL WAS GONE.

Tom lifted the framed picture from the desk. Earl had sandy-blond hair, light eyes, a satisfied smile on his face. He stood with one arm wrapped tight around his wife and the other thrown wide in welcome. And his wife, her head turned slightly away, slightly down, the shadowed line of her jaw sharp against her pale face.

The picture crashed against the wall; glass splintered to the floor.

Tom heard men in the hall, coming for him. There was only the one door, and the window had bars. There was no time. Earl was gone.

He stepped into the hall. Two men on his right, three men twenty feet to his left. He opened the door to Bloomgaard's office. The girl was behind her desk; Bloomgaard was beside her.

31

Bloomgaard said something and Tom raised his arm and Bloomgaard flinched.

Tom went into the inner office, with the bloodred flower and the green glass vase. He locked the door and surveyed the room. There was the phone. There was the desk and the chair. The window was barred. Tom heard the men entering the outer office, speaking with Bloomgaard. He had to get away, had to get Earl. He couldn't think. He had to try Burnham Chase. He paced between the door and the desk. There was the bookshelf, the high ceilings—

"Mr. Wall?" A man's voice came through the door. He said his name was Knudson. He said he had the key. He said there was no harm done and he was opening the door and Tom shouldn't worry. Soon it'd be over, and all would be apples and plums.

The lock snicked open and the men burst inside, a solid mass.

NEXT IN DAVIES-FRANK'S dingy room was an old pensioner for whom Wall apparently had a fondness. Captain Bayliss was toothless and shrunken, his mind fogged and his speech nearly indecipherable. Davies-Frank warmed to Wall for befriending this broken old man, but he hadn't the luxury of indulging the captain. He dismissed him in favor of one of Wall's doctors, who was twice as voluble as Mrs. Harper, and nearly as well informed. He offered a discourse on insomnia, nightmares, postsurgical excitation, and Tom's reaction to morphia.

"Morphia poisoning?" Davies-Frank asked.

"I'd not say *poisoning*," the doctor said. "*Sensitivity* is perhaps more accurate. It seems Sergeant Wall had been dosed too highly in a field hospital, and the morphia given him here during last week's operation—"

Davies-Frank had read that in the file. "I heard that a night's rest could heal him."

"You've been speaking to the nurses," the doctor said. "Did they claim Mr. Wall has 'the screaming abdabs'? They often develop notions beyond their expertise."

So sleep would not knit up the raveled sleeve of care—not that it mattered, as Wall couldn't sleep. "I need the sergeant clear-headed, Doctor. For one day, maybe two. Is there anything you can give him?"

The doctor steepled his fingers. "Nothing."

"No drugs? No emergency actions?" Davies-Frank leaned forward. "Theoretically speaking, is there no way to ensure Wall's competence temporarily—at whatever cost?"

"There is not."

Davies-Frank quizzed him another ten unhelpful minutes before being called to the phone. He picked up in the governor's office, gazing over the placid front lawn. It was Highcastle, his gruff voice undermining the serenity of the view.

"He's caught," Highcastle said. "American embassy."

"The Yanks handed him over?"

"Happy to be rid of him. He's en route to Rowansea now."

"Good." Davies-Frank checked his watch. There was still time.

"Learned anything?"

"Nothing heartening. He's allergic to morphine, having a relapse of shell shock—"

Highcastle snorted. Highcastle didn't accept shell shock. In his fifty-nine years, Highcastle had never found reason to believe in the ills of the mind. Most likely didn't believe in ills of the body, either.

"Keep that opinion to yourself," Davies-Frank said, though

Highcastle outranked him. He allowed himself this liberty because Highcastle had no use for men who didn't speak their minds, and because Davies-Frank would not have been such a man in any event.

"I can keep silent," Highcastle said.

"Despite being such a chatterbox." Davies-Frank glanced unnecessarily at his notes. "Wall's relapse is possibly temporary, possibly not. He's an insomniac—definitely exhausted and probably delusional."

"Why'd he join?"

"The Canadians? He's an idealist, I suppose. Antifascist."

"Bolshie?"

"I've no idea. Nothing in the file—" He watched a white van pull into the long circular drive. "Ah, the prodigal son returns."

TOM GLANCED at the guard sitting next to him in the back of the van. They'd called the man "Ginger"—he looked like he'd been chiseled from a block of gray stone, his red hair an afterthought. On his best day, Tom could've taken him.

"Don't even wish it, mate," Ginger said.

"Not today."

Ginger inspected him more closely. "Fought in France, did you?"

"Greece and Crete."

"Mussolini, then."

"And after Mussolini," Tom said. "We fought with the Greeks until the politics went bughouse."

"Didn't know we had men there till Jerry stepped up."

"RAF and an interservice mission were all. We were dug into the Aliakmon Line. The Nazi Fortieth wiped up the Yugos, outflanked the line, and caught the Greeks shitting cinders."

34

"And you fell back, eh? I hear you mauled Jerry all the way."

Tom almost smiled. "Fuckin' Kiwis. Where'd they learn to fight like that?"

"You were evaced to Crete? Against the paratroopers?"

"The airborne Fliegerkorps." The Máleme airfield. Earl's betrayal. "A long time ago."

"Six months. Give it a chance, mate." Ginger's voice turned hearty. "You follow rugby? St. Mary's beat Oxford forty to three, you hear that? And what's Oxford supposed to do, with Colson's knee troubled like it is?"

The van stopped and the door opened. They were back at the Rowansea Royal Hospital. MacGovern was waiting outside, a plaster on his forehead and his eyes tinted pink. He greeted the redhead with an obsequious smile.

"Our wayward lad," Mac said, helping Tom from his seat. "Our beamish boy. You've a reception order to sign, sir?"

Ginger shook his head. "Not worth the paperwork."

"Whitehall, are you?"

"Mr. Wall is to be brought to the governor's office."

"I'll take him well in hand. Old friends, we are. Ain't that right, Mr. Wall?"

Tom looked at MacGovern. His neck was long and ropy.

"That's right," Tom said.

"If you've everything under control?" Ginger asked.

"You can be sure of that." Mac clamped a hand on Tom's arm. "Couldn't be more keen to welcome Mr. Wall home."

THE QUESTION WAS, How do you make yourself forget? The answer was, You don't. Forcing forgetfulness was impossible. You couldn't just blot out your ability to field-strip a rifle, erase your memory of a Glenn Miller tune. So you lived with the constant

35

clangor of your past—and if it grew too loud, if it stood an inch behind your ear, shrieking, you suffered with it. All Tom wanted was amnesiac silence, to be left alone by the world of things, the world of memory, to curl into his bunk and let the sleepless dark consume him.

MacGovern dragged him inside, pulled him past the dormitory, away from the governor's office. "Soap on the tile floor. Clever clogs, you are. But what of discipline, what of order? You think the old boys want to see MacGovern brought low?"

"I think—"

Mac shoved him into the wall. Tom's bandaged hand caught a hard edge and he gasped. "They want me raised high," Mac said. "Untouchable. Un-bloody-touchable. I may be a tin-pot god, but I'm theirs. What else have they got?"

Mac yanked on a door handle and dragged Tom outside, across a walkway and into what they called the gatehouse. They were alone. The air was cold. Mac shoved Tom into an empty room. It was tiled, there were spigots overhead, and one wall was lined with square metal basins. For shearing sheep? For slaughter? There was a moldering fox-fur coat draped over one of the spigots, hanging from a twist of wire.

"Off with it, then," MacGovern said.

Tom didn't understand. The room smelled of musk and mildew.

Mac cuffed him. "The clothes, your Sunday bloody best. Off with it."

Tom clumsily untied his shoes, took off his socks. He unbuttoned his shirt—the greatcoat was long gone, as was MacGovern's wallet—and eased it over his bandaged hand. He glanced at the fur coat on its wire-twist hanger. "Hang it there?"

"We've other uses for that."

Tom folded the shirt and laid it on his shoes. He stripped off his trousers and briefs and placed them on the pile.

"Cold yet?" MacGovern asked, his voice echoing against the tiles.

"I've been cold, Mac."

MacGovern unfurled one of his arms and cracked a window. December air seeped in. "You tell me, Mr. Wall, if you start feeling a chill." He turned a tap, the pipes knocked, and a needle spray of water burst out. "Keep your hand dry, now—bandage gets damp, no telling what'll be festering underneath."

Tom lifted his right arm away from the water. *Festering underneath.* He couldn't think about that.

MacGovern tossed the fur coat onto the wet floor and twisted the wire off the spigot, testing it for weakness. "Order. Discipline. Time you learned their value." He stepped toward Tom, and there was a sound in the hall.

The door opened. "Mr. MacGovern!" It was Mrs. Harper. An English gentleman stood behind her, with mussed dark hair and an air of genial inoffensiveness. Had to be Davies-Frank.

"Giving Mr. Wall a scrubbing," MacGovern said, "after his recent escapades."

"In the gatehouse?" Mrs. Harper said.

"Best hot water, once it gets flowing. Isn't that right, Mr. Wall?"

A long silence.

"That's right," Tom said.

"There you are, then." MacGovern's eyes flicked to the gentleman. "If you'll excuse us, sir? And you, Nurse."

"Mr. Wall can wash himself," Mrs. Harper said.

"I've the bruises to show he can't, Mrs. Harper."

The gentleman said, "Would you prefer to bathe here or elsewhere, Sergeant?"

37

There was no condescension in his voice. Merely polite inter-est, as if this were a situation in which one often found oneself, and he was simply doing the done thing.

"What I want," Tom said, "is to be left alone."

"I'm afraid I can't oblige, Sergeant. However—" He looked to Harper and MacGovern. "We will wait outside."

"I won't be responsible—" MacGovern began.

"That's quite enough," the gentleman said.

"You want something from me?" Tom asked.

"It's a private matter."

Tom spread his hands. He was standing there bare-assed—how much more private did matters get?

"Even so," Davies-Frank said.

"You want something from me," Tom told him. "I'll take my chances with Mac."

"You'll hear me out," Davies-Frank said. "You haven't any choice. Neither have I."

CHAPTER
SIX

TOM DRIED HIMSELF with the threadbare towel Mrs. Harper had placed on a milking stool outside the door. His suit had been brushed. There was a new tie—so loud, it echoed. He dressed and worked the tie until the knot was passable, then put the length of wire in his pocket. A broken brick, an old wire . . . he was turning into a rag and bone man.

Mrs. Harper knocked and entered. "All done, then? Let's have a look at your hand."

Tom turned his head away as she unwrapped the bandage. The cold air on his sensitive flesh sparked a shiver of revulsion. He'd never flinched from a battlefield injury, but he couldn't bear the sight of his own hand. Couldn't bear the thought of it—the knots of unclean scars, the puckered dead skin around the pitted wound, edged in ragged white.

"There," Mrs. Harper said, wrapping it firmly. "The pink of health. You must be gentler with it. And with yourself, as well."

"This from the woman who refuses me sponge baths."

She clucked and they stepped into the corridor, and Tom saw they were alone. Despite beating MacGovern's head against the floor, they'd left him alone with Mrs. Harper.

"Where's . . . anyone?" he asked.

"I told them not to be ridiculous," she said crisply.

"You're a marvel, Mrs. Harper."

"That I am, Sergeant."

She led him to Kirrage's room. Inside, Davies-Frank was reading a report at a small desk, his air of affability perfectly intact. He reminded Tom of a young bachelor in an Oscar Wilde play, the lead's agreeably dim best friend. But when Davies-Frank greeted Tom, there was nothing vacuous in his face. "Would you close the door, please, Sergeant?"

Tom closed the door and inspected the drab room. "This supposed to put me at ease?"

"Is it working?"

"Never been easier."

Davies-Frank nodded solemnly. "Excellent news. You're wondering, of course, Sergeant, why I—"

"Call me Tom. I'm nobody's sergeant."

"Then you must call me Rupert." He pushed the folder he'd been reading across the desk. "This is you."

"Yeah? You haven't caught me at my best."

"Neither have you caught me at mine." Davies-Frank leaned forward, intent. "I need your help. We need your help."

Tom almost laughed. "Me? You got the wrong man."

"Thomas Stuart Wall, born October 1912 to Farley and Eugenia Wall. U.S. Army from '32, served in Haiti and China, promoted, honorably discharged, and joined the Canadian armed

40

forces in early '40 and was made a sergeant by virtue of previous rank. Commanded a squad of mixed U.S. volunteers and Canadians in Greece and Cr—"

"Swell. Enough."

"That's the man whose help we need."

"You think that man can help you?"

"That's the question."

Davies-Frank patted his jacket, extracted a cigarette case, and offered it to Tom. Tom took a cigarette and leaned forward when Davies-Frank snapped a lighter. He bent the flame toward himself. English cigarettes, filled with nothing. Still, a lungful of smoke and he was calmer, clearer.

"What *do* I think?" Davies-Frank said. "I think it's not in your interest to help us, Tom. I think it may do you harm—it may even do *us* harm. Speaking candidly, the latter concerns me far more than the former. But I think you're the one person who can help us, and the only way to get your help involves deceiving you, playing to your illness."

Tom shook his head. "I'm tired; I'm spent. I can't even help myself."

"You went to Shepherd Market and the American embassy."

"Looking for a new tie."

"Looking for Earl."

"You know where he is?"

"I know where he isn't."

Tom snorted smoke. "Swell."

"He isn't anywhere he can be found. He hasn't been home; he hasn't been at work. As far as I can tell—and believe me, Mr. Wall, I have gone to some effort—he has simply vanished."

"This is the deception? Telling me Earl's gone?"

"No, this is true. He's been gone over a week."

How would Davies-Frank know? He was British intelligence,

of course—one of the many branches—and Earl was his American counterpart in the COI, the newborn office of the Coordinator of Information. But intelligence sharing between the two countries hardly existed. The United States had never had a central intelligence agency, unlike the Brits and the Germans, who were old hands at the game. Instead, it had dozens of scattered offices—in the State Department and the military, the navy's ONI and the army's MID—which scrambled for ascendancy. The offices were underfunded and understaffed, more engaged in bureaucratic infighting than intelligence gathering.

President Roosevelt, over the objections of a dozen lesser agencies, had recently appointed "Wild Bill" Donovan to head the new COI. Donovan was a stand-up guy, but the COI hadn't celebrated its first birthday yet. Relations with the Brits were more cordial than effective, and even the cordiality was strained. The COI wouldn't inform the Brits of a missing American agent, and the Brits couldn't have every COI officer in England shadowed, either. Or could they?

"I don't see it," Tom said. "What's between you and Earl?"

"Nothing—he's gone. And you won't find him if we could not."

"He's not your man to find."

"We worked with the Americans," Davies-Frank said. "They had less luck. I suspect your brother's engaged in COI business without COI knowledge."

"Earl likes to run his own show."

"Wouldn't be the first time he's flown solo, from what I was told."

"He's gone?" Tom said. "Earl's gone?"

"He has absolutely evanesced."

Sounded like the truth, and it tallied with the vacant house and the vacant office. But gone where? Why? And how could Tom find him if the Brits and the COI could not?

"Are you ready for the deception, Tom?" Davies-Frank asked. "If you help us, we'll find Earl and bring him to justice."

"But you're lying?"

"Oh, yes. We'll find him—you have my word on that. But bring him to justice?" Davies-Frank ground his half-smoked butt in the ashtray. "No. He had nothing to do with Crete."

"You know shit about Crete."

"I know you lost your squad. I know Earl wasn't involved."

"But you'll lead me to him?"

"That's right."

"So spill," Tom said. "What do you want done?"

WHAT DID HE want done? Davies-Frank could hardly answer. Other than Poland uninvaded, Hitler unelected, and dinner with Joan and the twins uninterrupted?

He met Tom's restless eyes. The American was detached, wounded—still, there was something solid at his core. Perhaps only an echo of the man Tom once had been, but Davies-Frank trusted his impressions. He wanted Tom: first to extract information from Sondegger, then to kill the Nazi agent. Davies-Frank was fascinated and repelled by Sondegger—and frightened. A thousand men he'd never know would die if he failed. So he wouldn't fail, not with Sondegger, not with Tom.

But recruiting from the sickbed required a novel approach—unlike the approach that had been made to him. Davies-Frank's father had been a dean at Oxford. A man of enormous intelligence marred by an equally enormous ego. Upon his retirement, he'd declared that nothing would again move him from his library.

43

When Highcastle had approached him about the XX Committee, he'd been true to his vow and declined. But he'd offer something better, he said: his son.

So Rupert Davies-Frank was paid a visit. A knock on the door, and Highcastle had stood without. He'd removed his hat and scowled—a stout middle-aged man with salt-and-pepper hair.

"Rupert Davies-Frank?" Highcastle had asked, though of course he'd already researched him exhaustively.

"Yes. May I help you?"

"The dean sent me."

"My father?"

Highcastle nodded.

"Pity, that."

Highcastle's scowl deepened. He stared at Davies-Frank and said, "You'll do," and through some alchemical impulse transcending class and generation and disposition, they had almost immediately bonded into a partnership.

The task of the Twenty Committee had grown exponentially with its continued success. Each additional agent added another factor of complication. If a single agent contradicted one forgotten report on one trivial point, it would undermine the whole system. Every message, every fact and opinion, had to be not only believable but compatible with all other fabrications—past, present, and future. They had to feed the Nazis a jumbled but perfect puzzle, with the assurance that the Abwehr analysts would assemble it themselves and trust in their own work.

The Nazis could never suspect the integrity of their British network. Even if it meant missing an opportunity to mislead them, even if it meant the loss of soldiers and civilians, the loss of matériel and morale. They must never suspect. The XX Committee would not win a battle today at the cost of the network's integrity tomorrow.

The motivating belief behind the Twenty Committee was this: There would come a day when the entire network, acting with a single mind, would strike a crippling blow against the Nazis—would tip the scales so dramatically, with timing so impeccable, that all the lives and opportunities previously lost would be not only redeemed but honored.

The men and women who risked their lives in the field could not be told the truth. In Germany and France and Poland, they polished the false pearl until it shone. They were trained by the Special Operations Executive—the SOE—not only to infiltrate and sabotage, not merely to build networks and gather information; they were trained to unknowingly disseminate falsehoods, to provide a framework upon which the Twenty Committee's work could easily be hung.

They lived and died. They valued themselves more cheaply than their ideals. They were not afraid of death, but of failure. And if Thomas Wall could not extract the information from Sondegger, they would die by the score . . . for nothing.

TOM FIDDLED WITH the length of wire in his pocket. His brother had snowed them all. Davies-Frank believed Earl wasn't involved with Crete, and Earl had walked away from the betrayal untouched.

"I need hardly say this is sensitive information," Davies-Frank continued.

"Then don't. I've been through that wringer already."

"Quite. The Americans vetted you, of course," Davies-Frank said. "Owing to your relationship with Earl. And your . . . uncle, isn't it?"

"Yeah," Tom said. His father, a doctor, had wanted his sons to follow him into medicine. They'd followed his brother Sam into the military instead—Earl into intelligence, Tom into the army. "My other Uncle Sam."

"We vetted you as well, because of your brother's wife." .

Harriet. His brother's wife. Tom felt the undertow of memory dragging him down, but he shook himself, focused. This was the man who might lead him to Earl.

"Plus, you have the security benefit of . . ." Davies-Frank paused. "Of being considered a not entirely reliable source . . ."

"Of being bughouse," Tom said.

"Precisely. It lessens the security risk if nobody believes what you say. Another fag?"

Tom took the cigarette. "You'll spoil me."

"I well may. Now, then. The Twenty Committee started in 1936, with a man I'll call Sleet. He was a mechanical engineer. . . ."

Davies-Frank spoke softly, fluidly, and Tom felt the veil of exhaustion sluggishly recede, observed the quickening of interest in his own mind. How long since he'd been briefed, been engaged, been advised?

. Sleet, Thrush, Bitters, Reindeer, Cardigan. The entire network of the British-based Abwehr wrapped up in a tidy package: a turned paymaster leading to another cell, a double agent escaping, stealing a canoe, being narrowly prevented from crossing the Channel to return to Nazi territory. Secret writing and wireless transmissions, and dead-letter boxes in Oslo, Paris, Brest, the Iberian Peninsula. The War Office, the W Board, Home Defence Executive, and MI5 and MI6 all participating, though usually unwittingly.

Tom was more aware than most of spies and counterspies— his uncle Sam had been Military Intelligence—but an entire network turned? And Earl, somehow involved? Too incredible.

Davies-Frank caught an expression on Tom's face. "Yes?"

"I'm waiting for you to say, 'Brought to you by Blue Coal dealers . . .'"

"Blue Coal?"

"Finest anthracite in America," Tom said. "'Who knows what evil lurks in the hearts of men? The Shadow knows.'"

Davies-Frank half-smiled. "Used to be quite the comedian, didn't you? I'm glad I didn't know you then."

His tone sparked something in Tom, some ember of fraternity. He'd been too long away from men who weren't afraid he'd shatter. "I'm a regular Jack Benny," he said. "How's Earl involved?"

"There's a man who calls himself Dietrich Sondegger. A Nazi agent. Sondegger is—Sondegger is . . ."

"Abwehr?"

"No, SD. Sicherheitsdienst. You've heard of it?"

Tom shook his head.

"The RSHA?" Davies-Frank asked.

"Himmler's new secret police?"

"Not so new. The RSHA combines the Gestapo, the Kripo, and the SD—the Nazi Party security service."

"What about the Abwehr, then?"

"That's precisely what Admiral Canaris—the Abwehr chief—wants to know. The SD has domestic and foreign arms, and they despise the Abwehr, a sentiment that is ardently returned."

"And Dietrich . . ." Tom remembered the name, but he wanted to check if he'd imagined the stress in Davies-Frank's voice when he said it.

"Sondegger."

Couldn't tell. "He's SD? He's the link to Earl?"

"Yes. And he's here."

"In England?"

"In London. In what we optimistically call 'a safe house.'"

"So he's already caught?"

"He turned himself in—"

"Ready-made double agent, just add water."

"He allowed himself to be captured, I should say. I don't pretend to understand his motives, or his goals, or the bottomless pit he calls a mind."

"What's the problem? You have him in custody."

"Why did the SD send an agent? To evaluate the Abwehr network? Do they suspect it's turned? Worse, Sondegger arrived with another agent—who's still free. His wireless operator, code-named 'Duckblind.' "

"He admitted it?"

A wistful glint appeared in Davies-Frank's eyes. "He was that close to hanging. He mentioned his partner only to save his neck. Duckblind could destroy the Twenty—one transmission and the whole thing collapses. And Sondegger is our only lead to Duckblind."

"So follow the lead."

"Sondegger has been . . . unhelpful."

"Ask him nicely. Then ask him again."

Davies-Frank was suddenly old. "Wait until you meet him."

Tom would be *meeting* him? "Every man breaks."

"So I'd always thought."

"This is all—this has nothing to do with me."

"Sondegger won't tell *us* where to find Duckblind. He'll speak only to Earl."

"Earl?" Tom shook his head. "He knows Earl?"

"Claims he's been in contact for some time. Not personal contact—they've never met—but letters were passed, a good many, judging by his knowledge of your brother's life. He claims he's here with Earl's consent."

"And Earl's gone."

"Indeed."

"So you're stuck."

"Which is why it's an excellent thing," Davies-Frank said, "we have you."

PRETEND TO BE EARL. Tom had the accent, the background. He had the look. Earl was three years older, but they'd sometimes been taken for twins. Pretend to be Earl. Find Earl. Stop Earl. It was spinning beyond his comprehension. Could he trust Davies-Frank? Probably not, but he did. Could he pass himself as Earl? Probably not . . .

He let the idea wash over him. Pretend to be Earl. Smile and laugh with careless ease. Walk like he owned the street. Walk like he was going home to Harriet. Could he pretend to be Earl?

No.

"If this Nazi is Earl's contact," Tom said, "the COI has the record. Why isn't this an American job?"

"This isn't America," Davies-Frank said.

"If you're asking me to work against the States—"

"The Abwehr has a functioning—a vibrant—network in the United States. You are now one of half a dozen Americans who know of the Twenty Committee. Telling the Americans is telling the Abwehr."

"You told me."

"Because it was necessary. Because you occupy a unique position in the spectrum of believability. Because you're subject to the Commonwealth Army Act—we can throw you in a cell if need be."

"So ask the COI what Sondegger's doing here, and don't mention the Twenty Committee."

"We did. They've no idea. Earl keeps his own counsel, and

49

the COI is not entirely . . ." Davies-Frank gave the impression of a shrug without actually shrugging.

Tom understood. The COI was not, entirely. The U.S. military was currently ranked nineteenth in the world—even the Royal Dutch Army was larger—and the COI was even lower on the list. Wild Bill Donovan had Roosevelt's backing, but the COI was still in nappies, as Mrs. Harper would say, and the Brits had no reason to trust an infant.

"If Sondegger's not lying," Tom said, "this is Earl's personal initiative?"

"Earl has that reputation."

"I'm supposed to go in empty? I know shit about this; I get lost between my right hand and my left."

"Earl probably doesn't know much more. Contact was made—Sondegger's proven that much—and perhaps a rendezvous was set. But if it progressed further, I'd be surprised."

"You think Sondegger set up a meet with Earl?"

"It's an educated guess."

"Why risk coming to England? Why not a neutral country? Doesn't make sense. Why turn himself over to your custody? Why not—"

"Tom, I don't know. We're operating blind. I expect nothing of you—not success, not insight—but that you'll try. Will you?"

"It won't work."

Davies-Frank made a noise in his throat. "There's a man in Berlin, one of our most highly placed assets. He has a wife and three children, two boys and a girl. His code name is 'Whiskbroom,' and if Duckblind transmits, if the double-cross system falls, they kill his wife, they kill his children, and, if he's lucky, they kill him." He was silent a moment. "What are you, Tom? An invalid or a soldier?"

"There's gotta be another option."

"Not for you."

"If I fall flat with Sondegger," Tom said, "you'll still lead me to Earl?"

"I will," Davies-Frank said.

"No way this will work."

"Let me ask you, Tom. That bit of wire?"

Tom shook his head.

"In the showers. The bit of wire."

"You saw that?"

"I saw you." Davies-Frank extended his hand across the desk. "May I have it?"

It was some kind of test. Check if Tom was planning to escape, was crazy enough to be pocketing trash. He reached into his pocket, dropped the wire in Davies-Frank's palm.

"You're a soldier, Sergeant," Davies-Frank said. "What's an invalid doing with this?"

There was that spark, warming him again. Tom looked at his hands, the one whole and the other bandaged. Pretend to be Earl. With Harriet and Chilton on one side, his squad on the other. Pretend to be Earl. He lost himself in the thought for a long moment.

Then he lifted his head and smiled—a reckless, confident smile. "Lead me to him, brother."

CHAPTER
SEVEN

HARRIET WALL BRUSHED a wisp of fine brown hair from her forehead and knelt in the cold dirt of her garden. She dug her fingers into the earth to rouse its scent, inhaled, exhaled: the first breath she remembered taking since she woke at dawn. Her knees ached with cold as moisture seeped through her skirt and stockings. Her back ached from ten hours at a desk—with four more still to come, at home. Her mind ached from the flurry of details, the awful proximity of death.

This was her time. Between Baker Street and Shepherd Market. She wasn't home yet; she was in between. She'd stepped inside, drawn the blackout curtains, discovered Earl hadn't returned, and shot outside before the stack of paperwork could entrap her. She'd not even changed. She'd forked and bonemealed the cramped bed by the rambler trellis and was now ruining her crepe de chine skirt planting bulbs.

Still, she needed the time, the scent and surety of her preposterous kitchen garden: a thumbnail of a yard, mostly paved over, converted from the approach to the adjoining stable block. It was why she'd taken this particular house. Rare thing, in Shepherd Market, to have even a single stitch of earth—but it kept her sane.

She cupped a handful of the dark soil in her hand. Her hands were her best feature, well-proportioned fingers, a graceful wrist, unvarnished nails with slender crescent half-moons. Her hands didn't allow her to forget.

She dug into the earth. It was too late in the year for anything but tulips and accents of seedling forget-me-nots. She'd try the daffs, as well. Better in the ground than the bag—if they didn't flower well next spring, they'd recover for the spring after. A rough start, but they would blossom. Some things were reborn after dying back. Others were not.

It was her hidden ritual. In a world of secrets, this was hers: She planted bulbs for the women she sent into the night. She tried to believe that if she tended the bulbs, if she sheltered and nourished them, her agents would return alive. They would not be captured by a traitor, by a mistake or a misfortune. They would not be taken to a basement cell.

Harriet turned a wrong-shaped bulb over in her hand, an anemone hidden among the daffs. She'd soak and pot it, then place it in the bedroom window. She put it aside and stopped, her gaze caught by her best feature. Her fingers outstretched, her nails dirty but unmarred.

The first agent Harriet had befriended was code-named "Governess," a working-class girl, twenty-two years old, with impish green eyes and a short bob of dark hair, a faint echo of an American flapper. She had the build, too, lissome and boyish—and the boldness. But in Essex, in 1940, the bob only meant she didn't fuss, and the boldness only meant she needn't.

Her mother was French, and she spoke the language as perfectly as she understood the people. She had the quick wit of a successful agent, the engaging manners, the ability to flirt and the wisdom to flee. After the lessons—the weapons, the documents, the codes, and the cyanide pill—she'd flown east. Harriet had stood alone on the grass airstrip at the Moon Squadron base at Tempsford and waved her droning Lysander into the night sky.

An hour later, Harriet had been back at her dining room table, doing the sort of paperwork one was allowed to take home—on Inter-Services Research Bureau letterhead, it could have been for a bank or a shipping company. She'd been unable to focus, watching the clock: Now Governess's pilot was watching for the flare path on the ground, the inverted L of the drop zone. Now waiting for the signal lights. Now Governess would be sitting, her slim legs dangling through a hole in the plane's floor, waiting for a red light to turn green. Now she would be falling through the air, now yanked upward as the static line engaged. Harriet prayed the parachute would open. Prayed the drop would be easy. Her prayers were answered: Governess had parachuted safely into France.

Directly into a tainted network.

Two months later, a man code-named "Aubergine" escaped from a dank Nazi cell. Harriet had read his report in Mr. Uphill's office, the door locked behind her. Governess hadn't had time to swallow her cyanide. She'd lost her ten toenails, then her fingernails, in a period of ten days.

Yet she'd revealed not a single scrap of information the Nazis didn't already know. She was killed with a bullet to the neck. She was the first of Harriet's women to die. She was not the last.

HENNESSEY GATE WAS a two-story farmhouse beyond the outskirts of London, squatting on what Tom figured were thirty or

54

forty acres of hill and pasture. There were a handful of outbuildings along the pocked dirt drive—a long, low barn, an off-kilter chicken coop, and what was maybe an old milking shed or collapsed granary.

The farmhouse itself was a neglected hodgepodge—faded, rain-streaked shingles hung above new wide boards haphazardly whitewashed and hammered to the walls. The front doors, flanked by sandbags, had once been red but were now a fleshy pink. There were no chickens, no geese, no farmhouse dogs.

"Lovely to have a place in the country," Tom said.

"Isn't it?" Davies-Frank said. "Our charming rustic hideaway."

"Reminds me of Burnham Chase. Except homier."

"Never been invited to Chilton's heap, myself."

"Weep bitter tears, Rupert. You've missed cold floors, cold food, and the coldest company." Tom could feel Earl within him like the flu, a swirling black patch of virus, guiding his words and his gestures.

During the ride, Davies-Frank had briefed him on Earl's life in the COI, the interdepartmental struggles and the personnel. Tom learned Earl had traveled to Cairo and Lisbon, had joined a cricket team. Tom memorized the new names and places, and was utterly unprepared. But he was Earl—he'd fly by the seat of his pants and land with a flourish to great acclaim. Earl always did.

They stepped out of the Daimler. The afternoon sun was yellow and round behind a wispy gray cloud, like a child's new toy with a smudge of grease. A lone cricket chirped halfheartedly and the air smelled of fallow fields and mud, and Tom saw two sentries in the shadow of the barn.

"Not open to the public?" he said, gesturing toward them.

"Kew Gardens during the Blitz," Davies-Frank said. "Closed up tight and guarded, because a bomb at the palm houses would cause a rain of broken glass—a thousand guillotine blades slicing down. And that would still be less dangerous than what we have at Hennessey." He turned as a man stepped from the house. "Ah. Highcastle. This is Mr. Wall."

"Earl Wall." Highcastle was a bull. Short and solid, with a bullet head and a pugnacious jaw. He was wearing a brown suit and a brown hat and a yellow tie. He extended his hand, scowling. "You came."

Tom lifted his bandaged hand to show why he couldn't shake. "Now I've seen. Next I'll conquer."

Highcastle grunted. "I'll finish Wall," he told Davies-Frank. "You call Special Branch about Tipcoe."

"Tell them what?"

"Invent something."

"To what end?"

"Have him released to our custody."

Davies-Frank nodded. "I'll speak with Illingworth. . . ."

"Come," Highcastle told Tom.

Inside, the farmhouse was a warren of small dark rooms, cramped with furniture that had once been colorful and frilly. Highcastle glared at the stairs, said, "He's up," and led Tom to a sitting room, which had been converted to an office, at the far end of the house. He closed the door and crowded Tom into a chair.

"Rupert and I know who you are. We're the only ones."

"The rest think I'm Earl?"

"Right."

"Because you don't trust me, or because you don't trust them?"

"It was decided."

"No," Tom said. "You're afraid."

Highcastle balanced a pair of wire-rimmed reading glasses on his nose. He opened a desk drawer and considered its contents.

56

"You reek of it," Tom said. "You and Davies-Frank both."

Highcastle closed the drawer, lifted his head. His eyes were almost yellow. "Heard you were a patient at Rowansea, not a doctor."

"I'm not the one asking for help."

"No?"

"You like swing, Highcastle? Benny Goodman? If you lead like you're all wet, that's how I'll follow—you follow?"

"Week and a half ago," Highcastle said, "two auxiliary firemen heard a commotion over Grand Union, behind the stables. Thought it was a tart having a quick one. The firemen gave it a moment—always polite—then found the Hun sitting on a bench, sucking a cheroot, singing opera."

"He turned himself in to firemen? Keystone Kops were busy that day?"

"Don't look for sense. You'll find none. He'd been in-country for at least two days. Probably more."

"You have no point of entry?"

"Nothing. Except he'd taken a nasty swipe to the face." Highcastle lifted a hand to forestall Tom's question. "No idea how. Still trying to backtrack."

"For a man who gave himself up, he doesn't sound forthcoming."

"He were forthcoming, we wouldn't need you. Hun claims he'll feed us Duckblind—his wireless operator—if we give him Earl."

"*Give* him Earl?"

"For conversation. I don't know his business with Earl. Don't care. All that concerns me is the Twenty."

"You think turning himself in—to a couple firemen—was his best way to Earl? He couldn't have taken the sixteen to the twelve to Shepherd Market and knocked on the front door?"

"Don't know, don't care. Long as he gives us the wireless operator."

"And if he does?"

A grim smile. "Then we address the deeper issues."

"I'm supposed to get the wireless operator's contact information without knowing word one about Sondegger's business with Earl?"

Highcastle grunted. "You fail, people die."

"That's swell," Tom said airily, feeling Earl uncoil within him. "Long as it's just for kicks."

"People die and you return to the basket factory. I will personally see you never find Earl. Personally ensure you never leave the Rowansea. You signed the Army Act. Your country's afraid to fight—but you signed, you're mine. Treated for shell shock. You know the names for it. Combat fatigue, cowardice, desertion." Highcastle lowered his head as if he were going to charge. "Don't much care that you're a faintheart nancy. Don't much care you haven't any guts, hiding behind 'shell shock.' All I care is that you walk up those bloody stairs, soldier, and you talk to that bloody Hun and you get the bloody rendezvous information. Then scurry back to your hole, and I never see you again."

Tom stretched his legs through the deep weight of fatigue. Let Earl handle it: "So the answer is no, you don't like swing."

"Want to know what scares me?" Highcastle asked. "There's a man named Simon Tipcoe. He was to be reckoned with, in his day—thirty years ago. He's bone-skinny now, rheumy eyes." Highcastle's forehead furrowed. "We put him in overalls, had him push a broom in the safe houses. Sharp mind, good ears. Nothing threatening about old Simon Tipcoe."

"You dressed him as a janitor to check the after-hours gossip? The agents didn't suspect he was reporting in?"

"Even if they did." Highcastle shrugged a burly shoulder. "They talked."

"Then you set him on Sondegger, rheumy eyes and all."

"Late in the Blitz," Highcastle said, "an air raid sent Tipcoe's wife and daughter down to the public shelter. They'd been shopping. Ended in the Balham Underground when the bombs struck."

Tom knew the rest of the story—they were allowed newspapers at the Rowansea. A bomb had landed in Balham, dug a hole into the earth, and exploded with a muffled thump. It caused so little damage on the surface that rescue workers thought it was a dud. Until two hours later, when the road caved and the water mains exploded and flooded the station below. Seventy people drowned in the thick London silt, buried by the rush of water and the slow creep of sludge.

"Balham," Tom said. "So you took him on?"

"He moved to a boardinghouse. A sociable man, Mr. Tipcoe, he adjusted as well as can be expected. Not one to complain. Not like some, find themselves on the front and realize for the first time the Huns shoot back. Run home pissing they can't sleep."

Tom raised his bandaged hand. Fuck Highcastle. It wasn't shell shock. It was shrapnel. He'd caught lead, and maybe he had trouble sleeping, maybe they put him with the head cases, but it wasn't shell shock. Lots of men had trouble sleeping once they started hauling bits of metal inside their skin.

"No, Tipcoe's not one to complain," Highcastle said. "Only thing that bothered him, the landlady didn't manage like Mrs. Tipcoe used to do. You think we can excuse the man that one complaint?"

"I don't judge what I don't understand," Tom said.

Highcastle grunted. "Don't judge much, then, do you? The

Hun got Tipcoe talking, or the other way around. Tipcoe would spend a few extra minutes with him, then a few minutes more. Hun speaks English perfectly—Russian, French, Latin, Greek. Hun has a way with words."

Finally, the answer. They were afraid of Sondegger's words.

"Four days ago," Highcastle said. "The Hun starts on about Raskolnikov. Familiar name?"

"*Crime and Punishment*. The man who—" Tom stopped. The man who kills his landlady.

"The call came this morning. Tipcoe listened to the Hun too closely—he was talked into bloody murder."

TOM FOLLOWED HIGHCASTLE upstairs, into a hallway that smelled of mildew and bacon fat. The green-and-white wallpaper was dull and curling at the seams. Bare bulbs hung from the ceiling and sand buckets lined the walls. Two paneled doors faced each other across the worn brown runner creeping down the middle of the hall, and there was a narrower door toward the end, imperfectly camouflaged by the wallpaper—a broom closet, maybe access to the attic. A fourth door faced the stairs. It was painted bright white.

A bulky desk blocked most of the hall, leaving an aisle two feet wide. Nothing on top but a cup of coffee and a bell button. A skinny young man stood behind the desk, wearing a blue jacket and a sidearm.

Highcastle glared at him. "News?"

"Nothing, sir. He's kept on all morning."

"About the key?"

"And everything else."

Highcastle puffed air through his nose. He opened the door on the right and Tom stepped inside. At a cluttered desk, Davies-

Frank looked up from a stenography notebook and asked Highcastle, "You'll be joining us inside?"

"Your decision."

"I'd rather you didn't." Davies-Frank took a fat manila envelope from the top drawer and explained: "Sondegger doesn't enjoy Highcastle's company, if you can imagine."

"You've dealt with Tipcoe?" Highcastle asked.

"He'll be remanded to our custody." Davies-Frank turned to Tom. "Need anything before the security brief?"

"What could I possibly need?" Tom asked.

"This." Davies-Frank tossed Tom the overstuffed envelope. "We couldn't match your brother's diplomatic passport, but the rest is good."

Inside the envelope were a watch, wallet, and wedding ring. There were a few bills in the wallet, and an ID card in Earl's name. Tom slipped the wallet in his breast pocket, laid the watch across his left wrist but couldn't buckle it.

"You'll have to explain that." Davies-Frank took Tom by the elbow, turned his arm over, and strapped the watch on his wrist. "Your hand."

"Earl doesn't explain." He dropped the wedding ring back in the envelope. "Or wear a ring."

Highcastle grunted and Davies-Frank nodded, and Tom figured that was as close to a pep talk as he'd get.

"Security is in a constant state of flux," Davies-Frank said, handing Tom a pack of Capstans and a lighter. "We begin with class one, a new agent, usually in prison, treated as hostile. We end—it is our fondest hope—with class five, an agent entirely loyal. We send fives to neutral countries under no supervision but their own conscience."

"What's Sondegger?"

"Zero," Davies-Frank said. "And there's a perimeter in his

room, which we are strict about enforcing. One must stay beyond the—"

"Not Earl," Highcastle said.

"Yes, of course." Davies-Frank shook his head. "Sondegger demanded proximity and privacy with Earl. We'll start with proximity, ignoring the perimeter. Work toward privacy."

"No time," Highcastle said. "Give the Hun privacy, too."

"Too dangerous," Davies-Frank said. "Speed cannot be—"

"Highcastle's right," Tom said. "Some things can't wait."

CHAPTER EIGHT

THE STAGE UPON which Sondegger performed was not measured by a length of iron chain. The sweep of his emotion was not arrested by the shackle on his ankle. These things were props: the chain and the ankle it bound, the wooden chair and the desk, the microphone expertly concealed in the lighting fixture above.

They were porous and penetrable. He ranged through and beyond them, with his mind, with his will, with his words. He was speaking. Seducing a man whose presence he had only recently confirmed. A tentative tapping on the wall yesterday night, and he knew the object of his attentions was succumbing. The content of his monologue didn't matter—the words were only hosts for the warmth of his tone. "Let us examine this notion, the 'duration of time,' shall we? The author said that if a critic resolved to take a pendulum—"

During the fluid pauses between his words, he heard footsteps

63

in the corridor. He recognized the distinctive clumping of High-castle, bred like a hound for loyalty and tenacity by a class both softer and stupider than he. The second man's footsteps were unknown to Sondegger. A new warder? A janitor, a replacement for Tipcoe?

"—and measure the true distance between the ringing of the bell and the rap at the door, and upon finding it to be two minutes and thirteen seconds—"

Poor Mr. Tipcoe, with his bucket of tepid water, deserted by wife and daughter, his moist eyes reflecting his shame at the past and his dread of the future. Sondegger had breathed life into Tipcoe's insipid performance. Should a man live and die without once taking destiny into his own hands, wrapped in homicidal ardor around the haft of an ax?

"—more than two minutes and thirteen seconds, perhaps . . . but come now!" A disembodied chuckle arose. "Surely that is close enough for our purposes!"

Could the second set of footsteps be Wall, the one man whose presence was essential? Wall, the carrier. Wall, the catalyst, waiting in the wings. Sondegger considered the corridor outside his door. Painted white, so that he would provide a silhouette if he escaped during a blackout. But if he slipped his chain, he would not be shot so anticlimactically upon his own threshold.

Should he slip his chain?

"Let us agree two minutes and thirteen seconds exactly had elapsed according to our pendulum, twixt ring and rap—"

Not yet. Highcastle was too cautious. Within the bounds of his apocopated half-world, he was proficient. Davies-Frank was far more promising, quick and contained, a lick of flame inside the scalloped glass of a lantern. Davies-Frank was afraid. He had children, discerned from a smudge of treacle on his sleeve and the quickening of his pulse when subjected to Sondegger's extemporaneous fiction regarding his imagined family, an inspired recitation of revenge tragedy.

"The idea of duration is got merely from the train and succession of our ideas. There is a true pendulum, which abjures the jurisdiction of all other pendula." The room filled with the rich baritone of his laughter. "If you'll excuse the word. *Pendula*. But the point, my friend, is—"

The third man in the office must be Wall. Excellent. Sondegger had demanded he arrive today, and they'd delivered. He prized obedience when directing such an intricate show. However, how to proceed? The intelligence he carried was not secure with the British. The British were infiltrated by the Rote Kapelle, the Soviet "Red Orchestra," and crippled by their ridiculous schoolboy sense of fair play. He needed Wall. But he could not yet trust Wall with the delivery of his parcel. A new script was required. He'd had to improvise; the circumstances of his mission had, in an instant, irrevocably altered.

"—that our perception of time, of what is commonly considered the inflexible and given duration of time, depends upon the rapidity of our train of ideas. Thus . . ."

Fortunately, he enjoyed improvisation. Despite the paucity of information, the blow to his face, and the footsteps approaching, the third act was clear: Use Wall. Wall must learn his part, must suffer for his art. How to direct him? How to force him to struggle—and, finally, to succeed? It was upon Wall's performance that the success of Sondegger's production depended—his primary production. He now had a secondary: exposing this sham of a *Funkspiel*, this radio game in which captured German agents were turned to traitors.

How deeply compromised was the Abwehr network? Sondegger had been given the cover names of three agents to investigate: Digby, Gerring, and Kruh. If they'd turned, the bankrupt Abwehr network would be replaced with one loyal to the party, the Führer, and Amter VI of the SD.

"—through the employment of much and multifarious thought, we can travel across Flanders into England in the moment between footsteps; we can—"

A muted conversation sounded in the hallway. The door opened. There was no fluctuation in his voice. His lidded gaze did not waver from the ceiling. He smelled a Capstan cigarette and Bardil sticky plaster. He felt the brush of air on his neck and heard the nervous stutter of Davies-Frank's steps.

"—lengthen the duration of our days."

Two performances, then.

The lesser: Inform the SD if the Abwehr network had been subverted.

The greater: Thomas Stuart Wall.

CHAPTER
NINE

TOM IMAGINED THE white door brightening as they approached, glowing white-hot. Sure, he was steady. He was swell. He shook his head, and the door dimmed.

Davies-Frank reached for the knob, and Tom said, "No lock?"

"He's chained."

"Then why the door?"

"So his voice won't carry to the sentry. Do you know what spread the Black Death?"

"The plague? Rats."

"Fleas. Insignificant pests, annoying but harmless. Listen."

Tom listened. A conversation sounded inside the room, a deep baritone rumble. "He's being interrogated?"

"He's alone."

"He talks to himself?"

"If you call it that."

"What do you call it? Tap dancing?"

"I call it annoying but harmless. He speaks hours without pause. Reminds me of nothing so much as the *Odyssey*."

"Never read James Joyce."

"The other *Odyssey*," Davies-Frank said almost apologetically. "Odysseus wanted to hear the song of the Sirens, who lured sailors to their death with their singing, lying in the flower-strewn fields, surrounded by corpses. He packed his crew's ears with wax so they couldn't hear, and sailed past. He was the only man to hear their song and live."

"How'd he work it?"

"He lashed himself to the mast. Shall we?"

Davies-Frank opened the door and Tom stepped inside.

It was a long, narrow room set perpendicular to the hallway. To the right were two upholstered armchairs and a hard-backed chair, with a low coffee table on a threadbare carpet between them. A bare bulb hung over the table and a barred window was at the far right. Beyond the bars were pine planks, assembled into a screen to allow light while still blocking the view.

On the left side of the room, there was a mattress on the floor, and a tidily folded blanket. A chamber pot sat in one corner and a bucket of water in the other, under a shelf with a ceramic jug. A chair and plain wooden desk were bolted to the floor against the far wall. There was a stack of paper on the table, and a waxy wooden plate and cup.

The man in the chair was in his fifties and plump, with a pleasant moon face and thatch of unruly blond hair. He was staring at the ceiling, his hands clasped on his stomach, a pencil held loosely between his fingers. There was a shackle around his ankle, and the chain was secured to a bolt embedded in a wooden beam. His feet rested on a coil of the iron chain as if it were an ottoman.

He was speaking. His voice hung in the air, still and sweet and thick. It was butter yellow and butter pure. It was Tom's father's voice, tucking him into bed the night before Christmas.

"Mr. Sondegger," Davies-Frank said.

Sondegger sat straighter in the chair, and Tom saw a purple bruise on his temple. "My wife and I had four daughters, Rupert," he said. He had blue eyes. They were nothing special. "Have I mentioned that?"

"You haven't," Davies-Frank said.

"And not a single son."

Davies-Frank sat in one of the upholstered armchairs. "What are their names?"

"Only one survived childhood," Sondegger said. "Hannalore."

Tom strolled forward, rested a hip on Sondegger's table. Took the pack of Capstans from his jacket and opened it with his thumb. "Cigarette?"

"Earl Wall, I presume?" Sondegger extended his hand to shake. It was pink and smooth, and Tom ignored it.

"I'm Wall."

"Finally we meet." Sondegger waved away the cigarettes. "I don't smoke. Did I never mention that?"

Tom's first slip. He covered with Earl's sarcasm: "You want me to check my diary?"

Sondegger's blue eyes rested briefly on Tom's face. "Still, I thank you for the offer, though I can't return the kindness." He gestured to the wooden cup. "Unless you'd like a sip of what they call rum?"

"I'm a lager man." Tom lifted the pack to his mouth, took a butt between his lips. "I ever mention that?"

"They drown me in overproof rum in the hopes of provoking drunken confidences." He lifted a wooden pitcher from the floor to the desktop. "Despite knowing I prefer brandy."

69

"Brandy and opera."

"Opera is a balm upon the mind, Mr. Wall. If you permit a crude metaphor, it is oil in the crankcase of consciousness."

"I permit the metaphor, and the pun."

"The pun?" Sondegger's eyes drifted beyond Tom, and he chuckled. "Crude oil. Very good, Mr. Wall, though of course the pun is the lowest form of wordplay."

Tom returned the cigarettes to his pocket. The man's voice was a bass saxophone blowing a low oleaginous note, but there was no time to let the words wash over him; he needed the rendezvous schedule with the wireless operator, Duckblind. Get the information, get Earl, and . . . And what? He was fogged by fatigue and memory and Sondegger's opium-den voice.

"You think because I am a National Socialist, I must appreciate Wagner?" A twinkle appeared in Sondegger's eyes. "I hope my tastes aren't so parochial as that. Though I do regret I was unable to attend the first performance of *Der Ring des Nibelungen* in Bayreuth. Born too late to see Wagner conduct—in January of the year of his death. However, I have seen his work performed at the Magdeburg and the Festival. I admire poor Siegfried's ambition, but genius is so rarely passed in a direct line."

Tom turned a sheet of paper on the desk toward himself. It was a pencil sketch of a young girl, four or five years old. A pretty child.

"My youngest daughter, Cosima—she died of blood poisoning. Siegfried was Liszt's grandson, you know, as well as being Wagner's son. His bloodlines are impeccable. But *Der Bärenhäuter*? It is too hard and too soft, like a mussel that has been cracked underfoot. Are you familiar with *Der Bärenhäuter*?"

Tom didn't answer, the drone of Sondegger's voice smothering him.

"I imagine," Sondegger said, "you would find *Tristan und Isolde* more to your taste, Mr. Wall. Poison becomes love potion; agony transmutes to bliss—it is the third most intensely erotic opera ever written." He deepened his voice and sang: "*Was ist? Isolde?*"

"I prefer," said Davies-Frank, "I prefer *Das Liebesverbot.*"

Tom had forgotten Davies-Frank was there. He snapped back to himself from a state as near sleep as he'd achieved in days.

Sondegger swiveled toward Davies-Frank. "Forbidden love, family man? Do you escort your children to the opera? Your daughters? Does the elder not tell her little sister— Ah, I see. Of course. They are twins. They are ten? Eleven years? They will be women soon, like my Hannalore. And your wife—Jane? June? Joan?"

"So tell me," Tom said. "Where the fuck are you meeting Duckblind?"

Sondegger's laughter poured into the room like cream into a bottle. "You must pardon me, Mr. Wall. I am allowed so few diversions here. I subsist on rum and speculation."

"And the sound of your own voice. Where's Duckblind?"

"I'm not sure I'll tell you."

"Talk business—I don't give a fancy fuck for opera."

"We do have business." Sondegger divided his stack of paper into two stacks, then four stacks, lined precisely on the desktop. "It grows geometrically."

"You know the deal. First the Brits want a location—then we talk."

"Intra-articular fracture?" Sondegger's eyes flicked to the bandage. "How did you injure your hand, Mr. Wall?"

"Playing clarinet. How did you injure your face?"

"A man betrayed me. Your hand became infected following

71

surgery? Surgeons. They cut you open and watch you bleed. Do you ever peek at what they've left behind? . . . No? Fear, Mr. Wall, is an obstacle to healing. You must not allow fear—"

"You have three minutes," Tom said. "Tell it or the hell with it."

"You will wait upon me." His smooth voice became a whip crack. "As you know you must."

"You taking odds?" Tom let him see a hint of Earl's recklessness, of his own instability.

For a moment, Sondegger hesitated. Only for a moment. "I am a man of many concerns, Mr. Wall. I am a nervous, worried, anxious man." Sondegger's voice was rock-steady. He slid his pencil behind his ear. "May I unburden myself?"

Tom checked his watch. "Two minutes thirty."

"I am concerned about being immolated during a raid, as the warder doesn't have a key to unlock my cuff. I am concerned about the contents of the cupboard in the corridor outside. I am concerned"—Sondegger lifted the pitcher of rum, topped off his cup—"that if I do not give the location of Duckblind, I will be hanged—and if I do, I will be shot."

"Give them the wireless operator," Tom said. "You prove yourself valuable, they'll keep you around."

"I am concerned about"—Sondegger's voice became a whisper—"a surprise attack against the United States." And louder, swelling with righteousness: "I am concerned we will not be able to speak business after I reveal my rendezvous with Duckblind."

He upended the pitcher. Rum burst onto the desktop, soaked the stacks of paper, splashed Sondegger's arm and chest—it smelled of molasses and musk—and he flicked Tom's lighter, which appeared somehow in his hand. He set the flame to an edge of paper, and it spread like a ripple in a pond.

Tom startled away. "Bastard!"

Davies-Frank yelled something and bolted for the door.

"They cannot act against me, Mr. Wall, until they confirm the information." Sondegger remained perfectly placid as the paper puckered and blackened and the desktop was consumed in a fireball. "Until tomorrow night at ten-fifteen."

Davies-Frank, in the hall, was yelling, "*The buckets, fire, the buckets.*"

Sondegger stood, his chain rattling. The fire consumed his sketches, wafted ash into the burning air. His left sleeve was engulfed in flame as he softly said, "The next meeting, the *treff*, is at All Souls Church—with the damaged steeple. Ten-fifteen tomorrow night." A black smudge appeared on his sleeve as the fabric burned through. The smoke was thin and bitter and the burn mark grew, a widening stain. The man had to be in pain, but his voice was a whisper, a kiss. "The clear to approach is vertical white tape in the zero of the three oh nine of the Polytechnic's address. Visual confirm outside the church, recsig is a white umbrella, secondary meet in the shell of Queen's Hall."

" 'The clear to approach'? Wait—"

"And if you want Earl, Thomas, I recommend you try the Rapids."

"I—what?"

"Your brother's home away from home." Sondegger's face glowed with reflected orange light. "The Rapids."

THERE WAS SHOUTING and the clang of a bucket and the slosh of sand. Tom couldn't breathe. He couldn't see. The smoke choked him. Sondegger knew he wasn't Earl. Sondegger had called him Thomas.

It was impossible. Should he tell Davies-Frank and Highcastle? Did they already know? No—if he told them, he'd never speak with Sondegger again. His one path to Earl would disappear.

Sondegger knew he was Tom, knew he was looking for Earl. The Rapids? That wasn't Earl's club. The contents of the closet in the hall outside? A surprise attack on the United States? Sondegger was playing games, and Tom didn't know the rules. He was too exhausted to struggle, too aware that if he stopped struggling he'd burn.

He'd burn, then. But not before he laid hands on Earl. The Rapids.

Tom stepped out of the room as Highcastle charged inside. Ash clogged the air, hung in the doorway and the hall. The guard called for a medic while the prisoner recited lyric verse.

Five steps down the hall, Tom put his hand on the narrow wallpapered door—to the broom closet or the attic, to what Sondegger called the "cupboard"—and pushed. Locked. He knocked and the door swung open.

"I heard— Smoke?" A short man stood there with straight black hair plastered to his forehead. He was in shirtsleeves, blinking like he'd been asleep. "Is there—"

"There was a fire," Tom said, and stepped inside.

It was a small room with an angled ceiling. There was a small desk and a small window, and a black wire dangled from the ceiling to the desktop and ended in a pair of heavy black earphones. A stenography notebook lay open on the desk.

"You write it all down?" Tom asked.

"Must we evacuate?"

"It's nothing; it's over."

"Has someone fetched the stirrup pump?"

Tom kicked the door closed. "You transcribe it even when he's talking to himself?"

"Are you certain—" The man saw something in Tom's face. "Oh, yes. Yes, every word."

"That's a lot of words."

"Three notebooks a day. One never knows when he'll say something significant." The man blushed. "Not that I judge significance. I simply write."

"You get the last bit?"

The man glanced at the open notebook. "The final audible words were Mr. Davies-Frank calling for a bucket, and Herr Sondegger requesting that a key be made available. But I really should . . ." He pulled out his chair, where his shiny black waistcoat was hanging. "I ought not miss anything, if the fire is . . . out."

"Write this down: Duckblind's next meet is All Souls Church, the one with the damaged steeple. Ten-fifteen Tuesday night. To clear the approach, you need a line of white tape in the zero—of the three oh nine of the number of . . . Shit. I can't remember. Whatever's three oh nine, nearby—a public building, I think."

The man's pen scratched as Tom spoke.

"That's a vertical line in the zero," Tom said. "Visual verification outside the church, the contact has to be carrying a white umbrella, and the backup meet's at Queen's Hall."

"Anything else?" the man asked. "No? Then if you'll excuse me . . ." He slipped the earphones on and his pen immediately started scratching at the notebook, as if he completed an electrical circuit between the wire and the paper.

Tom reached for the door and it banged open. Highcastle glowered inside. "Bloody hell are you doing?"

"Research," Tom said.

The small man said, "He obtained the information, sir."

Highcastle pulled Tom into the smoky hall. "Let's hear it."

They went over it four times and confirmed the details: All Souls Church had lost its spire in the Blitz; 309 was the Polytechnic Institute; the Queen's Hall, a concert hall, had been bombed into a shell.

"Recognition signal a white umbrella," Highcastle said. "Nothing more?"

Tom said there wasn't.

"Your last recorded statement was 'Bastard!' Then what?"

Tom told it again. Didn't mention Earl, though. Didn't mention the Rapids.

"Nothing more?" Highcastle said.

Tom shook his head and glanced at Davies-Frank, who was sitting beside Highcastle's desk, taking notes. Davies-Frank was still shaken—not from the fire, but from Sondegger's words. His daughters were twins, his wife's name was Joan. And the Hun was inviolable. Even being on fire didn't unsettle him.

"Nothing more, Wall?"

"You want to hear it a sixth time?" Tom asked.

"If necessary."

"Nothing fucking more. Oh, except . . ."

"What?"

"You know the Suzy Q?"

Highcastle scowled.

"The jitterbug, Highcastle. The Hun said maybe you can show him the Shim Sham Shimmy." Tom felt the fatigue draining off in a torrent of words. "Nothing more? Nothing fucking more? Did I mention the fucker set himself on fire? He's standing there—on *fire*—and he's telling me shit, and I'm supposed to be taking dictation? Your man, the microphone man, he missed maybe ten seconds because of the fire—how much you think the Nazi told me?"

"Why speak to Mr. Melville?"

"Melville? I had a question about the great white whale."

"The transcriptionist. How did you know he was there?"

"I told you. Sondegger mentioned the closet, the cupboard."

"What else did he mention?"

The Rapids, Earl. "Ten-fifteen, three oh nine. He called the meeting a 'treff.' All Souls Church."

"You stay away from there," Highcastle said.

"There's one thing I want from you, and it's not playing footsie with a man named Duckblind."

Highcastle grunted.

"We done?" Tom asked.

Davies-Frank spoke for the first time in a half hour. "When we find Earl, I'll send word to the Rowansea."

"Nix that," Tom said. "I'll call you."

"Intending to decamp?"

"Nothing for me at the hospital but bedbugs and bandages."

"You won't find him, acting alone. I assured the staff I'd return you—"

"What chance is there that Duckblind'll be at this rendezvous? Ten to one the Hun's twisting your wig. You'll need me again—you'll need Earl. You think he's not playing a game?"

Silence, and Tom nodded. The Hun was a puppet master; Tom could feel the strings looming over them.

"Arrest him," Highcastle said to Davies-Frank, meaning Tom. "When we need him, we'll know where he is."

"Sure," Tom said. "When you need me, I tell Sondegger who I really am."

A glance passed between the Englishmen, the two like an old married couple able to communicate in silence with blank faces.

"You've a few pounds in your wallet," Davies-Frank said.

"You've a suit and that horrible tie and . . . Return to the Rowansea for three days, Tom. Three days. Get some bloody sleep; you're a catastrophe."

Highcastle snorted his agreement.

"My advice, Tom?" Davies-Frank continued. "Forget Earl. You've a bad case of nerves. Return to the Rowansea and fix your bloody head."

"You're done with me, then?" Tom asked.

"Not quite," Highcastle said. "First, we check all the Hun gave you was information."

Tom didn't understand, until they made him remove his jacket, turn the pockets inside out. His shirt, his pants, his socks. They inspected the lining of his cuffs. They examined the soles of his shoes.

"Don't forget to check I washed behind my ears," he said.

Highcastle folded his ear roughly forward. "All wet."

Wet behind the ears. A joke, from Highcastle? He turned to respond, and Highcastle was running his fingers over Tom's loud necktie. Turning it over, checking behind the label.

"You think he hid something in my tie? The man never touched me."

"That reminds me." Highcastle reached in his pocket, handed Tom the silver lighter. "This is yours."

THIS TIME, the car was a Morris Bullnose, far cry from Davies-Frank's Daimler. The driver was one of the sentries from Hennessey Gate, blond, clear-eyed, and silent. Silence was good with Tom. He closed his eyes. Sondegger said the Rapids was Earl's home away from home. A club? But not his usual, which featured after-dinner exhibitions of Victorian plays in the attached theater.

That always seemed too sedate for Earl, too square. A place called the Rapids sounded more characteristic.

Should Tom wait three days in the Rowansea? In three days, he might have forgotten about Earl, the betrayal, his boys on Crete.

The car slowed and rattled, and Tom opened his eyes. They were on a narrow road. They passed a crooked sign that said SEDGEWARE BURY. He'd tried to memorize landmarks on the drive in—a leaf-bare oak, the rise of a shallow hill, an old white church. He thought he could find Hennessey Gate again.

He grinned at his reflection in the window. He *thought* a lot of things. What he *knew* was more limited. It was December 1, 1941. Early evening. He had to find Earl, and the only lead was a Nazi agent saying the Rapids . . .

They were in the City. Heading south. The Bullnose stopped at an intersection. A group of office girls walked past, chattering about the Scarf Room at Jacqmar's. Office girls and Kiwis—Tom's heroes. These girls, during the worst of the Blitz, they'd wake every morning and pencil their brows, fix their faces—rouge and lipstick, whatever the hell they did—and they'd choose a dress and a hat and shoes and they'd grab their bag and pick their way among the wreckage to the office, past gutted buildings and anti-aircraft batteries, careful of their permanent waves, to take dictation, to make tea.

"Office girls," Tom said.

"Hm?" the driver said.

Tom gestured. "She's a live one. Could be Penny Singleton."

"Hm?"

"Blondie in the green hat."

"Mmm," the driver said.

"Walks like she's stirring July jam," Tom said, trying to

remember his squad's pet phrases, to keep the driver looking. "Puts the burn in Hepburn."

A horn sounded behind them. The traffic light had changed beneath its blackout hood.

"What she is," Tom said, "is out the door—"

The driver put it in gear.

"—and over the roof." Tom worked the handle and stepped into the road.

"Oi!" the driver said.

Tom was gone.

NOBODY HAD HEARD of the Rapids. Not the stall holders, not the railwaymen, not the bookseller's wife or the butcher or the Poles. Not the top-hatted old gentlemen.

Not the Oliver Twist children playing in what Tom first thought was an overgrown garden. Turned out to be a field leveled when the rubble of bombed buildings had been cleared—five houses, of which nothing remained but crumbling foundations and waterlogged cellars. An acre of the country growing between tiny yellow-brick houses, reclaimed by nature's vanguard: blackberry snarls, brittle stalks of nettle, and creeping jenny veining the ruined walls with vine.

"The Rapids?" An owl-eyed child said at Tom's question. "I dunno."

"Here," a grimy boy said. "Give us a prezzie?"

"A prezzie," Tom said.

He was lost. Been lost a long time. He'd never find the Rapids—if it existed. It wasn't a nightclub, wasn't a pub, wasn't a neighborhood or a show. He'd have to walk back his brother's movements. Earl must have left *something* behind. The first step was clear.

CHAPTER
TEN

HARRIET DUG TWICE as deep as the tulip bulbs were tall. She picked through the bulb fiber and chose the varieties she wanted. Flair for those soon to leave, Electra for those in the field. Peach Blossom for those missing in action, and Brilliant Star for the dead.

She patted the peat tight. She wouldn't allow herself to cry, not even here, not even alone with her hedges and her holly. In France, in Norway, in Poland and Germany and Belgium, her women could never relax their vigilance. If they betrayed themselves with a single misspoken word or ill-timed tear, they would die.

Her unwillingness to cry—for them, for herself—was as ludicrous as planting her bulbs. Yet it was all she had, once the Lizzie trundled down the grass airstrip and took flight. She broke apart a clump of dirt. Too late for tulips, the first of December, but life

81

was hearty. Life would prevail. This spring or next, green shoots would push through the heavy earth.

"Tucked in tight," she said. Cyclamen, bluebells, the humble snowdrop—with wallflower and polyanthus, they would create messy drifts of color, messy and vibrant. Harriet had no patience for a tidy garden. She stood from the bulbs to harvest berries from the holly before the redwings and robins did it for her. She brushed her fingers on her skirt.

She was officially the coordinating officer of WIT Section of the Special Operations Executive—which meant, in SOE argot, she was the chief's secretary. Mr. Uphill was a kind man, an affable man, and not a very bright man. Happily, however, he was a man secure within his limits. If Harriet was slowly encroaching upon his duties, he wasn't a whit offended. So long as she kept his appointment book in good order and fetched tea, he was entirely willing to depend upon her discretion in other matters.

Particularly in matters feminine, about which she had become the unofficial conducting officer. It was understood that she'd brief female agents about those matters the male instructors preferred not to discuss, those matters about which they preferred not to know.

More officially, she maintained files of the rules regulating daily life in five European countries—travel, curfew, rations, paperwork. Files of fashion, music, food, slang. The details one hardly thought of but was required to know: when to apply for bread or tobacco rations, which days alcohol was not served in the cafés. She had her bijoux: local bus tickets, sales slips, matchbooks, scraps of local newspapers, photos of putative relatives. She had the duty of ensuring that all vestiges of England were gone from the agents' possession—no English coins or cigarettes, no jewelry or ticket stubs. She checked every chemise, every watch strap—even hairstyles and table manners. She collected every scrap of gossip from returning agents and refugees, from newspapers, underground publications. She was called upon—unofficially, again—to recommend which woman should be sent into the field as a radio operator and which as a courier, which, in the rare case, as an organizer. Couriers were almost always women—less conspicuous than the young men subject to army service—and women were almost never organizers. But there were no rules: That was the first rule of covert operations.

It was her hand that posted their prewritten letters and postcards to family. It was her hand that drew up the wills. It was her hand that waved good-bye.

Harriet snipped a cluster of holly berries. Almost done. She ought to dig the borders, such as they were. Perhaps she had time for—

She paused, scissors motionless. She'd heard something from the house—not the slamming of a door or the drawing of water through pipes. No, it must have been from the street. Had she locked the front door? She couldn't remember. Housekeeping wasn't her strongest suit—she'd been brought up to manage a housekeeper, not a house.

There was another clatter, this one definitely from inside. Harriet lowered her face to the basket of holly berries, hiding her glow of pleasure. It was Earl, finally come home. He'd toss his overcoat over the banister, and she'd scold him for it, laughing. He'd kiss her breathless and run his hands down her waist to her bottom.

She pushed a wisp of hair from her forehead and felt dirt smear across her skin. Lovely. She must look dreadful, disheveled and muddy, her skirt and blouse in complete ruin. Hardly fit to welcome her dashing husband home. She never was, quite.

Earl once overheard her deny that she was beautiful—for she wasn't—but admit that she was perhaps not unhandsome. He knew it was her conceit that she'd age well, as handsome women did, and be more striking at fifty than thirty. He'd laughed and called her his "handsome girl"; still, there were times when a jot of offhand beauty would have been quite welcome, thank you, and a romantic homecoming was one.

She slipped through the garden door to the sink and splashed water on her face. It was past time he'd returned.

SHE'D BEEN MISSING HIM since last week, when she was called to Ashwell to speak with the girls in Signals on a matter of some urgency. One of their duties was writing poems for agents, as messages were encrypted in the field using memorized poem codes. Original poems were much preferred to classics the German codebreakers might recognize, but some of the girls were proving a little *too* original:

> If Stalin's prick
> Were twice as thick
> As Hitler's arsehole was wide,
> He'd shriek and cry,
> "Oh, Joe, I die!
> Quickly—another ride!"

Harriet had spoken sharply to the girls responsible, though she suspected her censure appeared as counterfeit to them as it felt to her. Still, they'd spare their poor CO any further embarrassment; another crisis of national significance averted.

If only her personal crises were so easily dispelled. From Ashwell, she'd gone directly to Burnham Chase, and a bitter argument. She and Father had never been *au fait* politically, but their disagreements had always been polite . . . until Churchill. Father despised the man, while Harriet—though her eyes were not closed to Churchill's faults—considered him unquestionably the man of the hour. The private man had private faults, which in the public man were virtues.

"I don't nominate him for sainthood, Father," she'd said at lunch. "But I'd rather have him for PM than any other man."

"Churchill," Father had said, "is a half-breed mongrel. He is unstable, unsound, untrustworthy—and not a gentleman."

A half-breed mongrel, because his mother had been American. "Your grandchild, should you be so blessed, will be a half-breed mongrel."

Father's color deepened. "Churchill's mother is a woman with more than one past. Churchill is a cad and a gangster."

"He is—"

"An adventurer and a dipsomaniac."

"Whatever his personal qualities," she said, "he has certainly proved prescient in his objections to your Mr. Hitler, in his opposition to appeasement and—"

"Appeasement was simply the—"

"And his opposition to the fascist Mosley and his trained buffoons."

Father slammed his glass onto the tabletop. "*You will not speak—*" he began, then realized the glass had shattered in his hand, though he was not cut.

The footman at the sideboard hesitated, and Father had lashed at the man's vacillation. *Was he not employed to clear the table? Was he not able to discern the glass was broken? Was he not competent to gather the debris?* This from her father, who did not acknowledge the help during meals.

Harriet had placed her napkin by her plate and excused herself. She'd had Charlotte pack her bags, and been back in London by sunset.

HARRIET DRIED her face. Earl had been gone when she returned from Burnham Chase, but there was nothing unusual in that. His business was such that his days were unpredictable. She'd called the U.S. embassy and been told her husband was unavailable. She'd asked for more information and been given bland and evasive reassurances.

She accepted them. Ignorance—and the Official Secrets Act—was the price of her marriage. Earl had disappeared once, without notice, for almost two weeks. He'd returned gloatingly self-satisfied, and she'd imagined he'd cast mud in the eye of the isolationists and fascist sympathizers in Kennedy's embassy. He enjoyed nothing more.

Well, perhaps there were *some* things he enjoyed more. She smiled. There was a dashing man in the front room, to be greeted by his handsome girl.

CHAPTER
ELEVEN

"BLEEDIN' PEA SOUP-THICK." Rugg spat on the pavement he couldn't see. "How the fook are we meant to find the Yank in this?"

"Chilton said"—Renard's footsteps quickened beside him—"find him, deal with him proper."

Rugg cracked a knuckle. "Don't see Chilton paddling through this gloom and—oi! Where the fook are you?"

From behind: "Here, wait."

Rugg was a head taller than Renard, and twice as wide. His stride took him farther and faster, and since the day they went off the tit, he'd been slowing for the little squit. "Speck the Yank in this? We'd 'ave more luck digging in your arse for a brass doubloon."

"Chilton was particular."

"We're supposed to find a scrap of white bandage? A Yank in the dark with a crabbed hand and a mad gleam in his eye."

"He ought be at the club, back in lock hospital, or at the Market."

Rugg grabbed Renard for a chin-wag. "Shepherd Market. Where the fook are we now?"

Renard said he knew, stared bug-eyed into the dark.

Rugg waited for a pause, then dragged Renard over the road toward voices. ARP wardens. Screeched at him once for looting, when all he'd done was slip a few bobbins off a pair of cold birds. Didn't need them anymore, did they? Wasn't theft. Was fat of the land.

The voices sounded closer, maybe a lightening of the gloom.

"Oi," Rugg called.

The wardens stopped, their torch pissing match light.

"Shepherd Market," he said. "Where the bleedin'—"

"Simply can't find it," said Renard, putting on a poncey accent. "Have rather an appointment."

"Shepherd Market? You're all turned about." The warden was a man with a redbrick face and white hair that showed better than a bandage would.

"Continue straight," the other warden said, a woman with a face like a hen. "Until you come to Vincent Square. From there—"

"Shepherd Market," the man said. "*Shepherd* Market, Miss Dodd."

The wardens bickered. It set Rugg off. All he'd done was slip a few bobbins, from nobody who'd miss them.

"And then west," the man said. "Four, five, six streets and you will—"

Rugg heard himself make a low noise. He wanted to hook behind the man's head, turn his face red and splattered under the white crown of hair. Then the woman with her peck, peck voice.

Renard elbowed him. "Six streets, then right and . . ."

Rugg kept himself still as they prated on. But it set him off.

"Much appreciated," Renard said, and they punted away. "We're one blinkin' mile off, Rugg. We'll find the Yank soon. Keep it in the cupboard till we do."

"If he's there."

"If he ain't, he'll be at the second place, or the third."

"So Chilton said." But Rugg felt a tingle on the scruff of his neck. Good to do some good again. Been too long. Find the Yank, fix him proper.

CHAPTER
TWELVE

HARRIET HEARD EARL clatter in the drawing room. Was he lifting her picture from the sideboard? Was there a smile on his strong, handsome face? She touched her hair—too demolished for easy repair—slid off her shoes, and slipped to the drawing room. What she lacked in oomph, she'd achieve by surprise.

His overcoat was not upon the banister. The blackout curtains were drawn, but only the wall lamp was lighted. He was rustling in the darkened parlor. She paused in the doorway to watch him. Earl was tall and broad-shouldered, but the shadows made him thinner. He was moving with uncertain deliberation. Why would he be skulking?

She almost laughed. He'd bought her an extravagant Christmas gift and was hiding it! It was unlike him, but less so than skulking. Earl was never uncertain. He did not enter a room; he commandeered it. He did not creep; he strode. He also didn't question, didn't dig beneath the surface. He didn't have her self-doubt. No regrets, no fancies. No dead agents stood at his shoulders; no bulbs were planted in fantastical hope. He was perhaps without as much depth as she—and she loved him for that as much as for his self-assurance, his utter, unthinking confidence. But the shadows made him appear erratic and unsure.

"Earl?" she said.

He turned. He didn't say "my handsome girl."

She reached for the lamp chain, and he said, *"Harriet."*

HARRIET. Tom's world stopped.

She filled the doorway; she filled the house. There was no room for air, for light. No room for Tom. Her storm gray eyes danced. Her face shone and her hair was disheveled, her hair curled in disarranged tendrils at her long, long neck. Her hair, which smelled of lavender and sage. Her classic, inquisitive nose. Her buttermilk skin, the arch of her naked back, the curve of her spine with the two dimples at the base.

Then she saw him, and everything changed.

Harriet.

"TOMMY?"

He was wearing his good suit, now a size too large. Standing at the escritoire, one of her envelopes in his unbandaged hand. The window behind the settee was broken, the frame splintered.

He didn't speak. He was so much like Earl, and so little. He had his height, his eyes, his voice. He used to have Earl's presence . . . but no longer. Instead of calm command, he radiated intensity, his eyes feverish and his color high.

"You smashed the window," she said.

"I thought you were away."

"Do they know you're gone?"

"I'm looking for Earl."

"Again.".

"If at first you don't succeed . . ." His eyes were too bright. There were marks under them, the dark of bruises.

"Tom," she said. "You look dragged through a hedge backward."

"Well, in this tie. Can I borrow one of your husband's?"

"Don't do this. You can't do this."

"Do you remember the last time we met?" He smiled distantly. "You were drinking chocolate."

Of course she remembered. "No, Thomas, I don't. I've been busy."

"At Glynn's. The cup was white; it had a blue rim. There was a smudge of lipstick when you put it back on the saucer. You told me good-bye. You said you were leaving."

"Yes."

"You stayed in town," he said.

"You resigned your commission." Keep it factual. Calm Tom and ring the hospital to retrieve him. "You drove to Canada."

"I stopped in Philadelphia for a cheese steak. You knew I left?"

"Your mother told me. You should write her more often."

"Your mother-in-law."

"Stop, Thomas."

"She tell you I was itching to fight the fascists?" He dropped the envelope onto the desktop. "I was, you know, even before '39."

"She knows why you left. I know why you left."

He didn't say anything, and Harriet wondered if he'd heard her.

"I was on Crete," he said. "When it fell."

"Tommy—does the hospital know you're gone?"

"They treated me like some kind of hero. The Yankee volunteer. Fighting the good fight. But I wasn't, not like my men. Manny and Rosenblatt, Tardieu, O'Rourke—those kids were world-beaters, Harry."

"Whilst you are . . ."

"You know what I am. You know why I signed."

"And it's *my* fault? Is that what you want, to hear that I'm to blame? You drove to Canada on my account? It is my fault that you're"—she gestured to his hand, to his heart—"injured? That you hurt? Did you come here to show me what *I've* done? Is that why you're here?"

"It's not *your* fault," he said.

"Stop hiding behind Earl, Thomas. You're a child no longer."

He cringed at the tone. Good. If she could lash him back to the hospital with her words, she would. If the only way to compensate for the cruelty she'd done him was with more cruelty, she would be cruel.

"Look at yourself." She turned on another lamp, then another as she approached. "You're three years younger than I, but you could be Father's age. Do you know what your mother told me? Yes, my mother-in-law. She always preferred you—Earl was such a healthy young animal."

Something sparked in his eyes, and she said, "You know precisely what she meant. As do I. She said the wrong brother went to Annapolis, the wrong brother to Amherst. She'd have you a professor, Tom, a poet or a priest. Look at yourself. You've the eyes of a refugee. No country, no home, no family. You—you're injured. I'm sorry and I—"

"It's not shell shock." Tom put his hand on the back of her slip-satin chair. "I'm steady. I'm—"

"I'm sorry, Tom. It must be very hard. But you can't continue in this fashion. Do you understand me? This cannot continue."

"Earl's gone." Tom lifted a snap-brimmed fedora from the chair and turned it over in his hand like a jeweler with a gemstone. "He's vanished."

"He has his work, as I have mine."

"They don't know where he is. Bloomgaard doesn't know. Nobody knows. He's gone. Evanesced. He had a meeting with a Nazi agent—in London, an agent of the—"

"I won't hear this. Don't speak of his work."

"He's gone to ground, Harriet. They don't know where."

"Do you imagine Earl punches a time card? He's a cowboy, in the company of cowboys. He does what he likes."

"Ever hear of a place called the Rapids?"

"No."

"I need to look through his papers."

"You certainly may not."

"Harriet."

"No," she said.

"I need, I need—"

"Thomas, no."

"Earl," he said, and there was something terrible in his voice.

It became very silent and very still. Harriet put her hand on his arm. "It's nobody's fault, Tommy. It's war. People die."

"You used to love me."

THE FIRST TIME Tom saw Harriet, she'd been seated across a snowy expanse of tablecloth. The heavy crystal glasses sparkled, the silver gleamed, and the waiters had been so resplendent in their jackets and gloves that Tom wanted to salute.

It was the sort of affair he hated. Dinner party for sixteen

94

guests, with enough conversation for four. Maybe he'd been good at it once, under his mother's amused tutelage. He knew which fork to use, and not to spit in the gravy boat. But he'd been most recently under the tutelage of the Fifteenth Infantry, the "Can Do" regiment, in Tientsin, and they didn't much care where you put your elbows.

He'd been in China that December of 1937, when the Japs launched a surprise attack on the USS *Panay* in the Yangtze River. Dropped fifty bombs in an hour, then strafed the crew who'd waded to shore. But the U.S. had stuck it to them. Demanded a couple million for the gunboat—the first U.S. Navy vessel ever lost to enemy aircraft—and a sincere apology, too. Yeah, stuck it hard.

Not long after, the Fifteenth had been withdrawn from China. Late spring, Tom found himself on leave in D.C. and his uncle strong-armed him into a monkey suit for the evening's bacchanal. A new British security coordinator had been appointed, and was doing what he could to heal the rift between the Brit and U.S. intelligence agencies—including dinner parties. All one happy family.

Earl was in Antwerp, which was why Uncle Sam had tapped Tom for dinner duty. Tom said he was on maneuvers, but Sam scoffed at *"skirt patrol,"* and there Tom was, trying not to salute the waiters. Been as much fun as a toothache, until he'd seen her across the table, halfway down. Wearing a white traveling dress. She'd been seated next to a thin-lipped man who spat when he spoke. She fiddled with a silver napkin ring, and didn't flinch. There was nothing but pleasant attention in her generous gray eyes, and maybe a hint of humor if you knew where to look.

She was hardly a beauty. She was an Englishwoman of the type who is drab five days out of seven and stunning the other two. Tom never understood it. She'd be mousy on Tuesday for dinner. Wednesday lunch, she'd be luminous. She had perfect glowing skin, purebred English accent. It didn't matter. None of that mattered—what she looked like, what she sounded like. Harriet was Harriet. There was no standard against which to measure her.

After dinner, Tom rescued her from the thin-lipped man and they'd stood on the porch. It was chilly, but his fingers were hot on the silver napkin ring in his pocket—his first keepsake of her.

She and her father were on a three-month tour of the United States. She'd seen the sights—Boston, New York, Washington. Tom later learned that her father had been attending quasi-diplomatic meetings, enjoying long lunches with newspapermen and industrialists. Always wondered if Chilton had met Edward R. Murrow, who at that time was CBS's director of Talks and Education—and whose coverage of the Blitz later swayed more Americans toward the British than anything else on earth.

Chilton had been a representative member of the pro-appeasement Cliveden set. He'd held firmly to the majority opinion: peace at any price. There'd been no shame in that then. Hell, it was *still* the opinion of the majority of Americans, despite Ed Murrow's broadcasts during Nazi raids, with explosions and sirens in the background.

There'd been a different sort of explosion on that porch in the Washington evening. It took Tom three hours to fall in love with Harriet. Three months to woo her. Three days to lose her. To Earl, who had betrayed him . . .

SHE'D TURNED THE switches on two lamps as she'd approached—bathed in illumination, an onrushing radiance. Harriet didn't wear perfume, but there was nothing Tom remembered so clearly as her scent. It engulfed him. He drowned. Years without seeing her, he knew every line on her face.

Her accent was so refined, there was nothing she could say that didn't end up poetry. He'd once had her recite his filthiest army vocabulary, just to hear the words rendered pristine. She was speaking and she laid a hand on his arm. Her fingers were strong and firm. When she was angry or aroused, her face would go blotchy. It was blotchy now.

There'd been a hat behind the chair, Earl's hat. Not a porkpie—he'd have expected a porkpie—but a good snap-brim felt fedora. This was the hat Earl wore. This was the chair he sat in. This was his table and this his wife.

Tom's lips moved and his mouth made sounds.

"Oh, Tommy," she said, and he wanted to believe it was kindness in her voice, not pity. "What shall I do with you?"

"Fox-trot?"

She removed her hand from his arm. "I ought to place that call."

"You never visit."

"I was told that would be best."

"Would you come if I ask?"

"No. No."

Tom nodded. He remembered her playing "Autumn in New York" for him on a glossy black piano somewhere, off-key and radiant.

"No, Tom. I will not visit you."

"I'm getting the picture, Harry." Why was he here? What was he doing? He needed information. He needed to leave before he lost himself. "Earl's gone. You think I'm crazy, fine—but he's gone."

"That you believe it," she said in her gentle polished voice, "doesn't make it so."

"It's true."

"And your squad on Crete?"

Earl had betrayed them. He'd known the Nazi gliders were landing in force at Máleme, six thousand Fliegerkorps. He'd done nothing. Tom's men had died to lose a battle.

"I lost them," he said.

"We heard you were recovering. The injury, the morphia . . ."

"I'm swell now. I'm four-oh. All I want is to talk to him. All I want is to ask. I can't—I don't sleep anymore, Harriet. The good news is, I finally have time to learn the clarinet."

She said something, but he missed it. He wanted to take her in his arms.

"All I want is to look at him," he said. "Look in his eyes and see what's there."

"No."

"A peek at his papers, maybe I can find him."

"No."

"You owe me."

Her eyes held no mercy. "I owe you nothing."

"You owe me a quarter for that cup of chocolate."

She brushed a lock of hair from her forehead. "The Waterfall."

"What waterfall?"

"The Rapids. It's what he calls the Waterfall."

"It's a club? A nightclub?"

"Of a certain kind. I've never been, myself."

Ah. A nightclub with fan dancers and exotic nude tableaux. Women welcome, but wives not received. Many such clubs had closed during the Blitz, but they had reopened now. The solid dark of the London night was forbidding and inviting to different degrees. He pictured Earl in a nightclub, inspecting the girls on the stage, Earl in a nightclub while Harriet waited at home. . . .

"Earl's a regular there?"

She gave a short nod.

"Regular lady-killer," he said. "Regular Don Juan."

"It's work, Thomas. I trust my husband."

"I trusted him, too."

She didn't respond. He would never rouse her to passion again. His touch would never please her. His breath would not catch in her hair.

"You don't know where he is," he said. "You don't know what he's done. He tells the embassy, 'If my wife calls, I'm on business. I'm at the Rapids, a bit of charity sitting on my lap.' Any sacrifice for the home team. You think he sleeps alone? He doesn't recognize a bed unless it has a skirt attached. Does he come home smelling of perfume? Does he—"

She slapped him. "I haven't time for your wretchedness, Tom. I'll tell you this once. You're not yourself. You cannot trust what you think. You're exhausted and deluded. Listen to me. You know nothing—nothing at all. Go back to the hospital. Go—and don't come back."

She walked to the front and opened the door.

The imprint of her hand was raw on his face. He went.

OUTSIDE THE DOOR, the moon was feeble behind the sooty clouds. The city was flat black and Tom's eyes couldn't adapt. He couldn't trust what he thought; he was exhausted and deluded and—

No. No, he was swell. He'd been hurt, he'd been doped, but then he'd recovered. He strained his eyes to catch the light, but he felt the looming buildings more than he saw them. He was fine. He was four-oh. Harriet was wrong. . . .

The streets were black and cold. He heard a cane tapping,

hushed voices; the dark city swallowed noise like a grave swallows a coffin. There was the growl of a car engine, the faint glow of hooded headlights. Shapes rose before him—a bus stop sign, a brick wall, a surface shelter. He stumbled into a mailbox and excused himself, then said, "Shit."

He heard the clanking of a cart and saw a tongue of blue light hovering in the blackness, caught the scent of something that made his stomach hollow. A man was selling fish and chips from a wagon, the covered flame burning to keep the food warm. Tom bought a serving, took three steps back, and the darkness engulfed the wagon, leaving nothing but the scent of fish and the clattering of the wheels.

Tom ate, then followed a man to a big Victorian pub with mahogany furniture and engraved glass. He sat at one of the three bars, ordered a brown ale, and asked his neighbor about the Waterfall. The man gave him a knowing grin and clear directions. Another man overheard, said the first man was off his head. They finally came to an agreement Tom didn't understand, then started talking about Mr. Tanner and the AEU's demands for wage increases for shipyard workers.

Tom finished his ale and returned to the black streets.

They'd said the Waterfall was half a block off Trafalgar Square or Piccadilly, or on Coventry, maybe down an alleyway. Not far from Hatchards—maybe between a cinema and Tudor's Dry Cleaning. Tom blew into his hands to warm them. His right hand smelled of bandages and iodine. Harriet was wrong, telling him he couldn't trust himself, when it was *she* who shouldn't trust. If only he could prove Earl had betrayed—

There was a muffled squeal of protest, a woman's voice, and Tom spun. She was sobbing, more violent than tears. He jogged across the street to an alley. There were shades of darkness—the glossy black of a raven's wing, the dull black of soot—and the alley was a muddy gray. A diffused light picked over the walls and out-lined a writhing shape, a Jack the Ripper shape. A blackout torch wobbled in the air.

Tom moved in, and the torch swiveled and a face sprang from the darkness. A woman's face, oval and ivory against the velvet darkness. Her eyebrows were tweezed to nothing, her red lips a slash. She was keening. The black shape swarmed over her—an army greatcoat swinging loose like a cape. She was hidden but for her agonized face.

Tom took two steps. The woman screamed when she saw him; the man started to turn, but Tom was already there. He caught the man in the kidney with his left fist, swung him gasping away from the woman. The man fell to his knees, panting and swearing.

The woman said, "Bugger off!"

Tom kicked the man in the side and realized the woman was talking to him.

"Wait yer bleedin' turn," the woman said, rearranging her skirt. "You cracked bastard."

Tom felt blood rushing to his face. The man was on his bare ass, pants around his ankles. No wonder he'd fallen so easy.

"Seven shillings sixpence," the woman told Tom. "But first you learn to queue."

A knee-trembler in an alleyway. Swell. Tom was recovered. He was fine. Sure he was.

HE WALKED TOO QUICKLY through the treacherous dark. Ought to be back at the Rowansea, cutting paper dolls. Ought to give MacGovern a jingle, have himself locked away, but his boys had died and the island had fallen. Earl was a turncoat and a killer and in bed with Sondegger. . . .

The sky lightened as Tom entered a square. There were

voices, laughter. He smelled the chalky scent of the river, heard the jingle of a bell, saw dark patches of movement. A shape towered over him, resolved into a man not much bigger than King Kong.

Tom stumbled against him. It was like stumbling against poured concrete.

"Oi," Kong said. "Bleedin' berk." His voice was high, almost womanish.

"Sorry," Tom said, and stepped past.

Kong muttered and receded into darkness; then his high-pitched voice came louder: "The fook are you?"

"Here, wait, here," another voice said.

"You speck that? Gotta be the . . ." Kong's voice faded as a group of young people chattered past: "Wasn't Miss Durbin smashing in *Eve*?" . . . "Hardly good as Lana Turner in *Honky Tonk.* . . ."

Tom made it across the square without breaking any laws. He stopped under an awning, lighted a cigarette. Enough glow leaked out to read the sign: TUDOR'S DRY CLEANING AND PRESSING. Tom checked next door—a cinema. And between them was a nondescript alleyway. Halfway down, under a hooded lamp, a set of double doors stood beyond a half moat of sandbags. A chalkboard listed half a dozen names—comedians—and a discreet sign said THE WATERFALL.

Tom opened the door and stepped into a handsome foyer with lofty ceilings, ivory walls, and red-and-gold carpeting that ran down a wide flight of stairs ten yards in front of him. A faint tinkling of piano and a murmur of voices ran back up. There were two closed doors on the left wall and a narrow stairway to his right with a thin chain across it.

There was a doorman at Tom's elbow, halfway behind a polished wooden pulpit. "Member or subscriber, sir?"

"Earl Wall," Tom said. "I'm his guest."

"Have you an invitation?"

"He's expecting me," Tom said. "I'm his brother."

The doorman's eyes flicked at Tom. "Pardon me. I didn't see the likeness at first. How is Mr. Wall?"

"Don't tell me he's not downstairs."

"We haven't seen him for several days now."

"Said he'd be here."

"It's unlike Mr. Wall to miss an engagement." The doorman stroked the gold braid on his jacket. "Perhaps Flight Lieutenant Inch might know. . . ."

"Inch?"

"Inch Rivere of the RAF. They often share a table. He's downstairs now."

Tom thanked the doorman and left his hat and coat with the cloakroom girl. Down the stairs was a landing that opened into a narrow balcony. A row of linen-draped tables followed the brass balustrade in a semicircle around the room below. Half the tables were occupied—men in uniforms or dark suits, and young women in velvet bridge jackets and silk dresses that whispered encouragement as they pooled around slender ankles.

Past the landing, Tom went downstairs to the parquet floor of the main club. Everything was dark wood and brass, except the high, arching ivory walls. The tables around the dance floor were set with silver and the same snowy linen as on the balcony. The customers were male, with the occasional flash of color showing a woman among them, like a spray of flowers on an undertaker's tux. The women were more than one step above their sisters on the balcony—fast upper-class girls who couldn't be bothered, and fast upper-class girls who could.

There was a big mahogany bar with a big mirror and a big bartender with a chin like a shovel. There were a dozen girls serving dinner and drinks, wearing long white gloves and what could pass for full evening gowns—if Mata Hari were doing dress inspection. There were cigarette girls wearing less.

One of the serving girls drifted past with a tray of food. She had the face of a mischievous child and the body of a bombshell. A tendril of black hair crept from behind her ear, caressed her neck, and headed south toward her décolletage.

Tom caught a whiff of grilled fish, another of roast mutton, and a third of something subtler, floral and light. It made him hungry, and he watched the girl walk away. She cast a lowered glance over her bare shoulder at him, and there was a devil-may-care swivel in her hips—but in her eyes was a kind of tomboy innocence. Or maybe he'd been away from women too long.

He stubbed his butt in an ashtray at the foot of the stairs. Across the room, there was a wide stage with a recessed bandstand and a fat man at a grand piano, hitting the right keys at the right time. A strawberry blonde in a red dress swayed next to him, singing from deep back in her throat, standing close to the microphone.

> I've got a cozy heated flat,
> There's a rack to hang your hat.
> Shrug on my chiffon negligee gown.
> You know I know my stuff,
> And if daddy that ain't enough,
> I've got the deepest bomb shelter in town.

Her voice was burnt honey. Tom walked through it to the bar and ordered a martini.

"On the slate this evening, sir?" the bartender asked.

"I'm a guest of Earl Wall's. Put it on his tab."

The bartender's shovel chin grew an inch. "Today is the first, sir."

"Wait a couple minutes if you don't like it. It'll be the second soon enough."

"Mr. Wall generally settles his accounts several days before the new month."

"He hasn't been in?"

"Not this week, sir. Perhaps you'd care to . . ."

Tom laughed. "Nothing I'd rather do than pay Earl's debts. But no, not tonight."

"There are regulations, sir."

"About a bar bill?"

The chin receded. "Only the martini, then?"

"Yeah. Hold the vermouth."

Tom couldn't figure what the problem had been. Didn't matter. He let the martini and the music warm him. He was almost mellow, could almost let himself unclench. Not yet. Earl might still show. If he didn't, Tom would talk to Flight Lieutenant Rivere, ask around. Walk back Earl's treachery until he could walk no more.

CHAPTER
THIRTEEN

NIGHT, DECEMBER 1, 1941

AUDREY UNPINNED HER hair at the undressing room's mirror. She'd thought the man was Earl—the way he'd stood at the foot of the stairs, running his eyes over the tables and the bandstand and bar; the way he'd lighted a cigarette; the way he'd waited, in no rush, quietly confident the room would offer itself to him.

She'd detoured around the back tables to get a closer look. Grabbed Margaret's tray to serve, though she was meant to be onstage in twenty minutes. She'd simply wanted a closer look.

She laughed to herself as she removed her white gloves—she'd simply wanted to toss a glass of wine in Earl's face. She would have been discreet about waltzing in her sling-backs on his handsome head, about accidentally breaking his spine in seven places.

"What evil are you intending?" Imogene asked, applying rouge.

Audrey's hand paused on the top of her dress. "Thought I'd go starkers and prance about in public. You?"

"I've heard that evil chuckle before, Vee."

Vee for Venus, a long and silly tale.

"That was not an evil chuckle," Audrey said. "It was a girlish giggle."

Imogene curled a lock of auburn hair around her finger. "I've already gone gray"—which was nonsense, as Imogene was nineteen, three years younger than Audrey, and she oozed youth, standing naked in front of their mirror, frowning at herself—"so your laughing can do no further harm."

Audrey wriggled from her dress and shook out her hair. How her laugh had become a calling card was beyond her. She found things funny; that was all. Her laugh was just a laugh. Inch said it sounded like a cavalry charge thundering across a tin bridge, but she imagined he'd read that somewhere. He *could* read. He wasn't half the ass he pretended.

Rodolfo stuck his head in the room and said, "Get yourself onstage, girls. Three minutes for slap and cossy."

Neither she nor Imogene nor the Three Annes bothered covering, and none of them bothered rushing. Three minutes would be enough, given the costumes weren't much more than heels.

Imogene said, a little lower so the Annes couldn't hear, "Will you tell me, or must I bribe it from you with coconut ice?"

"Well, a man came in. . . ."

"Imagine that! A man, here."

"For a moment—he looked like Earl."

Imogene fluttered her eyelashes. "Incendiary Wall. He can drop a bomb on me any day."

"But it wasn't him."

The man didn't have Earl's overfed flush of good health. He

didn't have the blunt physical presence that had—momentarily—attracted Audrey. And had more permanently attached the Annes, Peggy, and Winnie. He didn't have the solid, heroic expression. Give him a helmet and a horse, and Earl would be Sir Galahad. But he was unable to make distinctions. About women at least. About women . . . well, he was subtle as an English country squire shouting "Yoicks" at the foxhounds.

She smiled, because that was what her mum would have said: "Subtle as shouting 'Yoicks.'" Maybe she laughed.

"That laugh is frightful," Annie sneered from the chair where she was unrolling her stockings. "Sounds like a Heinkel with engine trouble."

But there was no time for a tiff—in two minutes, they'd be onstage, the lights shining brilliant and broiling behind them. They dropped their robes and grabbed the props, and their shadows loomed and danced over the heavy black curtain. Audrey lifted the pitcher onto her head—it was meant to be a water jug—and held it in place with one hand, the other on her hip.

Rodolfo clapped. "A seraglio, not a train depot. Imogene—recline, abandoned . . . there! Annabel, not so much . . . Good." He squinted at their silhouettes. "The pose, Hester—ramrod-straight! Ser-a-gli-o! Chin up, Vee."

"Ramrod-straight" meant "Stick out your backside," and "Chin up" meant "Damn the torpedoes." Still, it was harmless fun, wasn't it? Audrey's mum would have thought so. It was only Da's staid values that still chafed, sometimes.

"Where has Winnie gone?" Rodolfo fretted, stepping offstage. "The screen, what has she done with the screen? . . ."

George, the piano player, had the loveliest bass voice, and it rolled over the stage: "From the Far East, beyond the mountains of Siam, past the rivers of the Middle Kingdom." A flourish of keys. " 'In Xanadu did Kubla Khan a stately pleasure-dome decree.' The Waterfall Theatre presents a living tableau. . . ."

The curtain rose, and the audience clapped—one or two wolf whistles—and the girls were absolutely still. It always felt backward to Audrey. The lights were shining full at the audience; she saw them clearer than they saw her—the smooth men who didn't glance at the stage more than once, the boys who couldn't look away. The nervous men who joked and the solitary men who drank, the boorish men, the intriguing men . . .

Where was he? There, at the bar. His suit was well cut and ill-fitted. He moved like Earl; he sat and drank like him. But he didn't have the gruff heartiness, the fair-haired assurance. His eyes were darker and deeper than Earl's.

Audrey's shoulder ached. Must be time for Winnie to cross the stage with the "screen"—a wooden panel on wheels. As she passed, each of the girls would assume a new pose, with no motion seen by the audience except perhaps a residual jiggle.

The man who wasn't Earl lighted a cigarette. His face was lean. If he'd been better dressed, better groomed, he might have been Byronic. Instead, he looked broken, a broken Earl.

And Audrey's disenchantment with Earl had always been with his soundness. He was so complete. It ruined him for women; he was untouchable in every important way. Ruined him for her at least. But the man who wasn't Earl . . . he was naked, there, in his suit.

She almost laughed. If he was naked, what was she? She smiled toward him instead. She sometimes suspected that life was trying to teach her lessons, lessons of caution and circumspection. Life gave her a small gift, then snatched it away. Well, life could soak its head. She was her mum's daughter.

The man who wasn't Earl—there was something about him.

TOM WAS FINISHING his first drink when the curtain parted and light streamed forth on a faux-Oriental tableau with a dozen naked girls striking poses around a mound of fake Aubusson rugs. All he could see were silhouettes, but those girls looked good in outline. He gestured for the bartender and ordered another drink. "Featherlight done for the evening?"

"Featherlight, sir?"

"The torcher." He didn't give a cold damn about the singer. "Voice like heavy sugar. You worked here long?"

"Quite some time, sir."

"You know Lieutenant Inch?"

The bartender nodded toward the dance floor. "Regular table."

"Swell." Tom stood and headed for the tables, but he wasn't sure which was Inch's. He paused to watch a girl in a see-through dress wheel a red screen across the stage, and a plummy Englishman's voice called his name from the corner.

"Wall? Is that Wall? I say!" It was a dapper young man with bright eyes, sitting at a table with two other men. There was a crutch propped against his chair, and he had his elbow on the crosspiece. "If it ain't the Earl of Wall, I'm an ape's auntie."

Tom raised his drink, approaching. "Tom Wall."

"Tom? I say!" The man blinked in disbelief. "I *am* an ape's auntie!"

"Earl's my brother. So you're half right, or—"

"Merely an aunt! Or merely an ape, what?" The man gestured to his companions, who were staring at the stage. "You know Jacko and Murch?"

"You're Inch Rivere."

"In the flesh. Won't you sit? Tommy Wall, is it? The Earl

110

never mentioned heirs or assigns, but of course you look entirely alike."

Tom sat and said, "Well—"

"Under the weather, are you? Your hand, I mean to say. My foot is the same." He wiggled the crutch under his elbow. "Bung us together, and what would result?"

Tom took a slug of martini, put the empty glass on the table.

"Well, either a single chap with two good hands and two good feet," Inch said, "or a chap with one bad hand *and* one bad foot. Or possibly you'd have two chaps, one with—"

"Have you known Earl long?"

"Long? My happy boy, forever! Eight months." Inch speared a carrot with his fork. "Call him *the* Earl, you know. Ought to stand for the House of Lords."

"You expect him tonight?"

Before Inch could answer, a girl appeared and placed a fresh martini at Tom's elbow. "Fancy more fags?" she asked, eyeing Tom's crumpled pack.

"Got anything Virginian?"

"Passing Clouds," she said. "And Fifth Avenue is toasted, American-style."

"A pack of Airmen for the second Wall," Inch told the girl. "And where is the wave-born ecdysiast? Promised she'd stop for a chatter."

The girl said Vee was onstage.

Inch peered at the tableau and nudged Tom. "There! Stage left, with the thingummy upon her prow."

"Listen," Tom said. "Is Earl—"

Inch gave a sudden start. "Did I say 'prow'? Meant 'brow.' Venus Pritchett is her name."

"You expect Earl tonight?"

"If he were coming, he'd be here already. Y'know why she's

111

called Vee? I refer to La Pritchett. Named her myself, so I take an interest—"

"When was Earl here last?"

"Earl? Am I your brother's keeper? Reminds me of the story about the two Irishmen . . ."

It was impossible; he'd learn nothing until Inch ran out of steam. But that was one of the benefits of insomnia: He could wait all night. He finished his drink, the girl served him another, and Inch babbled on: "Have a friend who longed for a Duesenberg J. He said, 'Inch.' He said—"

"Why 'Inch'?" The booze made Tom's voice rough. "Why do they call you that?"

"Full name's Eggert Miles Rivere," he said, as if that were an answer. "Mother disliked me. Ruined her girlish."

"When did you see Earl last?"

Inch's face moved into mystification. "When did I see her last *what*?"

"Earl. When did you see him?"

"Oh, the Earl! Yesterday, day before. Friday."

"Friday?"

"No, Friday was Boneless Bateman's orchestra. Wasn't here Thursday. Wednesday."

"You saw him Wednesday?"

"Not Wednesday. Think it was Tuesday."

"You sure?"

"Been lathered since October, Tom. I'm sure of nothing." Inch's face fell into melancholy. "Days bleed together since I was grounded."

"You expect him tonight? Tomorrow?"

"No expectations, that's the family creed." Inch downed the rest of his drink. "I was stuck with a Blenheim. Finally found a Jerry to shoot at, and met his Messy one-oh-nine head-on.

Sheared my wing. Landed in a field with barely a bump, and they shove me in a training unit."

"Did he mention—" Tom said between his teeth. "Did he say where he was going?"

"Back to Germany, one imagines. Mean to say, he was on fire and shot full of holes, but—"

"Jesus! Does Earl always sit with you?"

"Or upstairs, with company." Inch considered for the space of an eye blink. "But the girls wouldn't know. To the girls, Earl didn't speak so much as he . . . *spoke*, don't you know. *Spoke* spoke, not *speak* spoke."

A girl's voice from behind them, light with amusement: "Flight Lieutenant Rivere. If you're finished declining *spoke*, perhaps you might introduce me?"

"What?" Inch tottered upright on his good leg. "Declining? Never decline you, Vee! I mean to say!"

The girl put her hand on the back of Inch's chair and smiled at Tom.

She was the serving girl with the white gloves and the backward glance. She was the silhouette with the prow. She'd changed into a plain frock, a half ounce classier than cheap and the color of nothing. On her, it looked like sculpted velvet. Her black hair was wrapped in a scarf knotted at the top, and Tom figured she'd dressed down for some effect—the effect she got was of an oomph girl in a plain frock and a head scarf.

Tom rose and faced her. Her teeth were small and white, her lips wide and smiling. Her eyes were dark blue, wide-set and happy as her mouth. Something about her was naïve and exuberant, despite the chassis of a calendar girl.

"Any chap," Inch continued, "who declined your company would be no chap who— Oh, indeed! Miss Venus Floryville, may I present Mr. Tommy Wall."

"Audrey Pritchett," the girl said. "I thought you were Earl for a moment. I can't tell you how pleased I am that you're not."

"I'm his brother. Do you . . . know Earl?"

She laughed—a rowdy child's laugh. "I'm not one of his girls, if that's what you're asking."

"Not for his lack of trying, what?" Inch said. "Vee's captivating. Venus Flytrap. Ain't how she came by the name, but—"

"Hush, Inch." The girl put her slim hand over his mouth. "Let somebody else have a turn."

"I'm looking for my brother," Tom said. "I can't—"

"Aren't you curious?" she asked as she took a seat.

Curious about what? "As a dead cat," he said.

She laughed again, uninhibited and overflowing. A man could get lost in her laughter. "I do wish Americans would speak English," she said. "You're meant to be curious as to why I'm glad you're not Earl."

"Why are you glad I'm not Earl?" he asked.

She took her lower lip between her teeth. "I shan't tell. Not if you ask like that."

"You want me to set it to music?"

"Flight Lieutenant Rivere," she said, turning away. "How does this evening find you?"

"Better ask, old chap," Inch told Tom. "Or she'll pout all night. Well, an hour or two. Ah! Smiling already. Not a good pouter, our Vee. Has a temper, though. She hit one of the other girls once. Strong left jab. Nose bled for an hour." He swiveled his drunken attention toward the stage. "Fine tableau, by the way, Vee. Not so keen on it as I was on Gymnosophists of the Maharaja, but—"

Tom said, "You socked one of the dancers?"

"There!" she said. "Now ask why I'm glad you're not Earl, in precisely that tone!"

He smiled at the eagerness in her voice. "Why are you glad I'm not Earl?"

"Because I'd rather not have to accidentally break a table over your head."

"Yeah? When's the last time you saw Earl? You know where he is?"

She cocked her head. "Has Inch been afflicting you? He can be infuriating when not entirely sober. The last I saw Earl was—"

"I have not been afflicting the happy boy," Inch said. "Told him already that I saw Earl on Friday—except Boneless Bateman was Friday, so must've been Wednesday or Tuesday, but—"

"Inch is in a mood," she said as Inch rattled on.

"That what you call it?"

"Don't be fooled. He's terror in the skies. Completed his thirty missions in ten months, then a hundred sorties as a night fighter. Twenty-two confirmed kills. He crashed on number one oh two and is supposed to be instructing now. He can't stand the soft duty." She sneaked a bit of cheese from Inch's plate. "So you're looking for Earl?"

"Yes, Miss Pritchett, I—"

"Audrey."

"Audrey—I need to find him."

"You're not the only one. I've been meaning to accidentally stick a fork in his eye. He's not been home?" She nibbled the cheese as Tom shook his head. "Then Inch is the last person who saw him. Isn't that right, Inch? You're the last person to have seen Earl after he . . ."

"After he what?" Tom asked, seeing a blush color her cheeks.

The girl ignored him, and Inch said, "What? Didn't see Earl. *Heard* him. Of course, accent thick as American mash, one can't understand two words in ten. . . ."

115

"Inch hears no better than he waltzes, these days," the girl told Tom, with a glance at the crutch. "All the machine-gun fire."

"Said he was going to Hyde Park," Inch said. "Heard that well enough. I was passing by—a trifle ossified—when the siren sounded 'Raiders away.' The Earl was speaking and the siren cut out and he bellowed on about Hyde Street Misfits."

"Hyde Street Misfits?" Tom said. "What's that? Is it nearby?"

"On Hyde Street, one imagines." Inch shot the girl a triumphant look. "With his accent, and through the door, an elephant with an ear trumpet couldn't do better."

" 'Through the door'?" Tom asked. "What door?"

"Upstairs, I mean to say. Door to his room."

Earl's *room*? Tom stood. Harriet wouldn't allow him to search the house, but Tom would do better. Earl had a room here.

The girl put her hand on his arm. He turned and her face was a foot from his. She was young and her skin was silk and she glowed like a warm candle in a warm, dark room. She had eyes so blue, they were black. Her lips were wide and red and looked soft and eager to laugh.

She said, "Come."

AUDREY LED TOM upstairs. She was telling a story about Inch; he was thinking about Earl. Thinking about Crete and the farmhouse, about the warmth of her fingers on his arm.

She stopped on the landing and her face glowed in the light of the wall sconces. She smelled of jasmine, of a small white night-blooming flower. "You haven't heard a word," she said.

"I'm sorry," he said. "I was . . . thinking."

"Were you?"

"I haven't been sleeping."

"Nightmares?" she said. "Delirium tremens? Purple spiders on the ceiling?"

He looked at her.

"I can't abide not asking," she said, leading him toward the foyer. "But if you'd rather not say, tell me to shove in my clutch."

" 'Shove in your clutch'?"

"Earl taught me how to speak Yank in three easy lessons."

What else had Earl taught her? She was too open, too artless. The body of a showgirl and the manner of an ingenue. "You're two lessons behind, dollface" he said, exaggerating his accent. "And so's your old man."

She laughed, and the stairway grew five shades brighter. "Your brother sat through two hours of comedy without a chuckle. Not even at Peter Sellers."

"Never heard of him."

"He's just a kid—his parents do vaudeville. He did impressions and I split a seam, but not a smile from Earl."

In the foyer, the girl got the key to the Pugilist Room from the doorman. She slipped it into the beaded bag at her elbow and led Tom upstairs.

One flight up, he said, "After what?"

"After what, what?" She laughed again. "You're making me sound like Inch."

"You said Inch was the last person to see Earl after he did what?"

"He—he misbehaved." A tint of red started above the swell of her breasts and rose to the nape of her neck. "It's personal. It's embarrassing."

"So spill."

"Shove in your clutch, Tommy," she said.

On the second floor, a long corridor unrolled in front of

them. A dozen dark wooden doors lined the cream-colored walls. The ceiling was high and the carpet thick.

"Here," she said. "Hardly a shelter in a raid, but private as private can be."

The doors on the left side had pictures of flowers. The doors on the right had dogs: a poodle, a Yorkie, a bloodhound. At the end of the hall was a picture of a boxer. The Pugilist Room.

"Earl's room?" Tom said.

She nodded, and it hit him again. The Hun *knew*. Knew Earl was a member of the Waterfall, knew he called it the Rapids. Maybe even knew he had a room. The connection between them was real.

"You look ill," the girl said.

"I am."

"You need—" She unlocked the door. "I'll fetch a glass of water." She put a hand on his arm. "You should rest a moment."

He shook her off. "Wait outside."

"Don't be ridiculous."

She tried to enter, but he blocked her. "You heard me. My brother. My business." He took the key and dropped it in his pocket. "My key."

"You wouldn't know about the room if it wasn't for me. You wouldn't have the key. . . ."

He raised his hand to cuff her and she didn't flinch. She stared with her midnight eyes and set her jaw. He dropped his hand. "Stay out of my way."

She slipped past him into the room, switched on the light.

"Fuck," he said, following her.

She flopped onto the bed. "That is rather the notion, yes."

And it was. The room was a peach trap—big blue bed with big blue pillows and carpet thick enough to make a girl want to kick off her heels. There was a bureau, a night table, and a pair of cushioned chairs, which wouldn't look right unless draped with stockings. A walk-in closet with a chest of drawers. Blackout shades covered by ruffled curtains, a desk under a shelf of books with spines that matched the walls. A door half-opened to a bathroom. Another door, dull red, like a fire door, leading . . .

"Exterior stairs," the girl said. She had her shoes off and her legs folded under herself, reclining against the headboard. Her dress was rucked to her knees and her stockinged feet rubbed smoothly, slowly together.

He opened the red door, and it was cold and dark outside. There was a wide ledge with a half wall of brick extending along the building. It would have been used for hanging laundry if this were a tenement. He closed the door.

"That's what I meant by privacy," she said. "The outside stairs. What are you looking for?"

"Please," he said.

"I can help."

"You can leave."

He checked the bureau. It was empty. There was nothing under the bed. The bathroom was a bathroom. He tossed the chair cushions to the floor. He ran his fingers over the wallpaper. He walked into the closet—Earl's suits, shoes, hats, ties. There was an empty suitcase, which was only an empty suitcase. He grabbed one of Earl's ties from the rack, clumsily loosened the knot on his own loud tie, pulled it over his head, and tossed it on the floor.

"I'm starting to think it *is* delirium tremens," the girl said.

Tom pulled the new tie around his neck, but his bandaged hand gave him trouble. He struggled with the fucking thing. It was all falling apart.

The girl unwound herself from the bed and stood eight inches from him. She was small. He looked down at her glossy black hair, the tip of her nose. She fixed the knot, taking her lower lip between her teeth while she worked. He turned his head, told himself he couldn't smell the perfume of her hair, couldn't feel how warm she'd be to hold. Her fingers were clever and quick. She finished the knot and smoothed the tie. She put her palm on his chest and looked up at him. "Much better."

His eyes locked with hers. He moved to the desk and she returned to the bed. He heard the mattress sigh.

He checked behind the books and opened the drawer of the night table—lipstick, scattered change, a box of matches, a pen with a mismatched cap. He dumped everything on the tabletop, turned the drawer over to check the underside.

The girl watched him as he tossed the place as thoroughly as he knew how, without slitting cushions and snapping chair legs. It took forty minutes by the bronze windup clock used as a bookend on the shelf. He found nothing. Hyde Street Misfits, then? It was all he knew.

He threw a pillow back onto one of the chairs and sat. He needed to search the bed, but the girl was there. She had unwound her scarf, and her hair fell in perfect bedroom disarray.

"What was it Earl did?" Tom asked. "The embarrassing thing?"

"I'd rather not say."

He fumbled in his pocket for the silver lighter, snapped it open and closed. It reminded him of the smell of rum and ashes. By what dark magic had Sondegger stolen it?

The bronze clock clicked off two minutes. The girl said, "He spread word I'd been . . . He said we'd been sleeping together."

"Had you?"

"I can't imagine that's any of your affair."

"Whose affair was it?"

She laughed suddenly. "You're almost charming, Tommy."

"I'm almost a lot of things. Were you lovers?" Wrong word, if it had been commerce. "I mean, had he . . . Did you—"

"I know perfectly well what you mean."

"But you won't answer?"

"Why do you have trouble sleeping?" The girl smoothed her skirt. "The answer is no, we weren't lovers. He was taking the mickey out of me by saying we were. He's not malicious, just unable to draw distinctions."

"You'd be surprised," Tom said.

"A girl in a place like this can't afford gossip." She grinned. "Unless she's the one who starts it."

"Undercut your prices? He said he'd had you for free?"

"Don't be cruel, Tommy. It doesn't suit you."

He lowered his head. He was tired. His mind was dark as the streets outside. "Why are you here? What do you want?"

"Must I want something?"

"Everyone wants something." He heard bitterness in his voice. That didn't suit him, either. "What do you want, Miss Pritchett?"

The mattress whispered as she stood. Her feet made no sound on the thick carpet. She knelt next to his chair. She reached for his right hand, and he moved it away.

"My name is Audrey." She spoke softly, as if she were gentling a horse. "My father was killed early in the raids, and our house burned with him. He was a docker, a proud, poor man. I'd been an ambulance driver since County Office first asked for volunteers—because that's the sort of girl I am. Or was. I had no home, Tommy, no family, no savings, like ten thousand other Londoners, but more fortunate, because when they dug me out, Inch was there. He arranged the job here. I serve and I pose—and that's all I do."

Tom didn't know what to say. He still didn't know why she

was here, with him, in this empty dead-end room. "I need to find Earl."

"How long since you slept?"

"Forty days and forty nights."

"How much longer can you go?" She touched his forearm with her fingertips. "Come to bed."

He raised his head.

She laughed, and he almost smiled. "Alone. I'll tuck you in."

"Bring me a cup of tea?"

"Then to bed?"

"Sure," he said.

She stood and opened the door. "You're planning to lock me out."

"Why bother?"

"Give me your word."

"You wouldn't rather have half a crown?"

She moved toward him over the carpet. He looked up at her. She had a funny sort of face.

"You have my word I won't lock the door," he said.

She said something soft and rich, and left.

He stood. Turned the bed inside out, the pillows, the bed frame, the headboard. Felt for lumps. Checked the wall behind. Nothing.

He sat on the edge of the mattress. Glanced at the clock. His head was heavy on the pillow, surrounded by the scent of night flower. He closed his eyes. He heard a rush of water, the sound of a distant train.

CHAPTER
FOURTEEN

THE SOUND of a distant train.

There were no rail tracks on Crete. There was one airfield, a pitted concrete patch with no electricity, no equipment, no hangars. There was a single paved road, which ran almost 150 of the island's 170-mile length, from Kastelli through Canea and Retimo, then to Iraklion and a handful of villages whose names Tom had never learned. Then it faded to dirt.

It was a common trick of Cretan roads—well-packed dirt roads narrowed into foothill paths, finally dwindled to mountain trails fit only for goats. Half the bridges could carry military traffic. Half would crumble. Nobody knew which half was which.

In the south, the mountains rose ten thousand feet above the turquoise sea. In the north was civilization: a handful of homes with electricity and kerosene, and a few telephones. There was a scattering of taverns where GIs could buy what passed for beer, what passed for cigarettes, and ouzo and retsina and raki. Or wine like Tom had never tasted, and olives and strange dishes with strange names.

The terrain was rough—rocky outcroppings with patches of abrasive shrub, dry pebbled riverbeds subject to flash floods. Fields of grain and olive trees plunged into knife-blade ravines, and spiny trees rose above ancient crumbling walls. There was a village of stone houses, a church with a cemetery, and a three-span steel bridge over a dry river, crowded with oxcarts and peasants and supply trucks. The village was Máleme.

Beyond Máleme was the new airstrip, at the foot of Kavzakia Hill. Hill 107.

Tom's platoon had been attached to the New Zealand Oakes Force during the evacuation from Greece. The Twenty-second and Twenty-third pulled the defense of the air base, the Twenty-first was allocated as a mobile force to counterattack any pressing threat, and the Maori Twenty-eighth was in reserve at brigade HQ. They had rifles, a few light automatics, and a whole lot of nothing else.

Two battalions of Greeks and Cretans were deployed with them, on the western flank. Some of the Greeks and Cretans had rifles; the rest had curved swords, wooden axes, and flintlocks. It was cause for concern. Tom assured his boys he'd investigate the matter, so he got blind drunk with a handful of Cretans—fishermen and goatherds, as organized as a pile of leaves in a windstorm. Only two of them spoke broken English, but it didn't matter. The next morning, he had a deadly hangover, but he wasn't too worried about the western flank. The fishermen and goatherds would fight.

It was the first day of May. The platoon had seen enough action in Greece to be grizzled veterans at nineteen and twenty. They were better equipped than some, with blankets and utensils, beanpoles and mess tins. No banjos, though, so they dug slit trenches with their steel helmets and waited.

Lord Haw-Haw on German radio boasted nightly of the invasion of Crete. May second and third came and went, and there was no invasion, despite the steady drone of bombers. Except for the plumes of smoke over the harbor, the days were brilliantly clear.

They could smell the Germans coming.

On the way to Retimo, they were outmaneuvered by a flock of sheep. They stood on an unnamed hill in the shade of a gnarled tree, which would outlive them all, and looked over Suda Bay. Thick black haze hung between the sky and water, oozing upward from the sunken hulls that littered the bay. Only one out of three supply ships made it through—it was a graveyard of rations, of weapons and vehicles and men. Everything afloat was set upon by the Luftwaffe swarm, from wooden fishing boats to the HMS *York*, which had been shattered by dive-bombers and strafing fighters.

The next day, the bombing started in earnest. Burial efforts couldn't keep pace, and bodies rotted where they lay. By mid-May, only three Hurricanes and three Gladiator biplanes survived to repel the German air attacks. The Nazis attacked the antiaircraft batteries, but their attacks were not answered. The orders were clear: Do not return fire until the invasion by airborne troops begins, lest you reveal your position.

May sixteen, seventeen, eighteen . . . The Fliegerkorps, Goering's elite paratroopers, would spearhead the invasion. It was a Luftwaffe assault, not Wehrmacht or Kriegsmarine. Bowing to the overwhelming Nazi air superiority, the three Hurricanes and three Gladiators were withdrawn to another theater.

Permission to mine or crater the airfield was requested. Engineers arrived, explosives ready. Permission was denied: Máleme was the only airstrip from which recon flights could depart. Which was swell, except they had no recon aircraft.

There were rumors that the invasion would begin the next day.

"It fuckin' won't," Hanner the croot had said. "They got us on a dress parade tomorrow."

"That's proof," Rosenblatt said. "Twenty thousand Krauts coming for breakfast, they order a parade rehearsal."

Hanner glanced at Tom. "He shitting me, Sarge?"

Tom smiled and sat, started unlacing his boots.

Manny from Montreal wiped his face with his palm. "Then what the hell do we do now?"

"Don't need a big band to jitterbug," Tom said.

They'd stripped naked and leapt into the ocean, swimming and splashing, their constant escort of a dozen grimy Cretan children watching in astonishment. It was beautiful country, Crete. It was close to heaven.

The next morning, the locusts came.

CHAPTER
FIFTEEN

A SHARP NOISE startled Tom awake, his heart firing bursts like a grease gun in his chest. He reached for his Colt, but his Colt wasn't there. It didn't matter. The room was empty. The noise had come from his own throat. He checked the clock, saw he'd slept three minutes. Swell.

What else was in the room? Earl's clothing, two sizes too large. A suitcase. A bar of soap. A shelf of books with matching spines and a pillowcase with the scent of night jasmine. The girl's palm had been hot on his chest. She had clever fingers and bright dark eyes. He could crawl into bed with her and forget the past, forget the future.

No. Time to shove in his clutch.

He didn't lock the front door—his word was still worth that much. He cut the light, stepped through the back door to the exterior stairs. Without his hat and coat, two stories up, the cold wind slashed at him. He walked twenty feet, found the stairs. Three flights to the bottom, and he emerged in what could have been a parking lot or a cemetery.

He stepped between the dark shapes. There was a faint smell of engine oil—a parking lot, then. The street was quieter than it had been, and colder. He needed to get to Hyde Street, needed to find this tailor, the misfit shop. He'd head for Hyde Park, then find someone to ask. He tried to orient himself, and a gust of wind blew freezing air through his shirt. First, he'd circle around, claim his coat and hat. Keep the girl ditched, because he didn't trust her, because the desire for her warmth and scent and smoothness was a hard knot in his gut. He had room for only one desire: Stop Earl.

He kept the buildings to his right, circled the block, and the night lightened. It was the square. Tom crept forward, his lighter hooded by his hand, looking for Tudor's. He had to find the alley, the entrance to the Waterfall.

He heard a clatter of iron-banded wheels—the creak of wood against wood, a soft tune. Tom almost fell into the man's rubbish-heaped cart. The peddler swung around. He had an oil lantern banked to nothing. His face was obscured by a wild beard; his eyes were slits. Wearing a rough jerkin and a peaked cap, he'd walked off the streets of the eighteenth century.

"Lookin' ta buy summat, guv?" he said.

"Looking for Tudor's."

"Right where he's allus been . . ." The man raised a tattered arm and pointed.

Tom thanked him, headed across the square, back into 1941. Harriet had said he couldn't trust his own mind. Maybe so, but he'd trust his eyes—he recognized the awning, TUDOR'S DRY CLEANING AND PRESSING. He patted his pocket for the check ticket for his hat and coat. Get warm, get to Hyde Street, and get Earl.

"Oi," a high-pitched voice said, three feet from his ear.

"Pardon me, sir," another man's voice said. "Spare a light?"

The man leaned forward, into the glow of Tom's lighter. He was an inch or two shorter than Tom, and a year or two younger. He had wavy hair parted down the center, friendly eyes, and big teeth jutting out of his wide grin.

He didn't have a cigarette. He drove the dome of his forehead into Tom's face.

Tom stumbled backward, his lighter clattering in the darkness. A flashlight blinded him, and the man with the teeth slugged him in the stomach with two quick jabs, then two more. Neat work, fast and loose, with a lot of muscle.

Tom staggered to the side and hit a wall.

The wall was wearing wool trousers and a thick coat. The wall said, "Fookin' cank," and put a hand on his shoulder, like a raptor sinking talons into a soft-bellied fish. King Kong. He drove a fist into Tom's kidney and the blackout flashed white.

Tom couldn't breathe, couldn't see. Orange blotches spun behind his eyes. He went limp. He'd fall to the ground, curl up, and let them take his goddamn wallet—but Kong didn't let him fall. He grabbed Tom's good wrist and dragged him through the dark.

It was half a block before Tom regained his breath. He opened his mouth to shout, and the man with the teeth stepped up, one-two, one-two, one-two, leading with the left this time, in the man's favorite rhythm. Tom's mouth closed.

They stumbled onward, from dark to dark. Tom used his feet to keep upright, his weight borne by King Kong. His wrist was numb in the vise of the big man's grip.

"Bleedin' muck," Kong said. "Can't speck my own arse."

"Keep it in the cupboard," Teeth said.

"Sets me fookin' off."

129

Tom used Kong's grip on his wrist as a fulcrum, pivoted his knee up, and drove it into the big man's stomach.

Kong grunted and swatted him.

Tom went semiconscious, the dark streets and the dark of his mind flashing on and off. The clouds cleared. The moon shone. A misshapen skeleton projected against the sky, a building stripped by the Blitz—only the pipes remained, like the carapace of an insect, two stories tall. Then they were in a cratered field, amid a slab of granite, a pile of rocks, and an earthen mound. The man with the teeth pointed with the flashlight, and Kong tossed Tom at the heaped rocks. He fell hard. His chin was wet with blood from his nose. He wiped it away on his sleeve.

"Ten pounds," he said. "It's all I have."

Kong thrust a massive hand at him. "Give over."

Tom gave over. "I'll need a receipt."

"Visited by a ponce, weren't you?" Teeth asked. "In the old Rowansea."

"The fookin' lock hospital."

Tom shook his head. "That's all the money I have."

"Early this morning," Teeth said, "a ponce came calling on you."

"A ponce." Tom put his left hand behind to steady himself. Found a rock.

"You know bleedin' well," Kong said.

"You've got the wrong man," Tom said.

"Wrong yobbo," Teeth said. "So many Yanks wandering the streets, one hand bandaged."

"Are you gonna tell me?" Tom said. "Or you want me to guess?"

"What'd the ponce want from you, yob?"

"I got off the boat in Liverpool on Friday. Whatever the fuck you think—"

The big man slapped him. Tom rode with the blow and swung the rock. Left-handed, he didn't have the speed or the strength, and barely touched Kong, a gentle swat.

Kong slapped him again, and it was like being slapped by a frying pan.

His eyes watered and he faked right, moved left. If he could reach the darkness, he'd disappear—but the flashlight beam was a searchlight at a prison camp fence. Kong swung, and Tom stepped under and past him, moving toward Teeth. Take the smaller man first.

He went in fast and low, but Teeth caught him in the eyes with the light. Tom swung, and the man wasn't there. He stumbled, and Kong lifted him like a rag doll and slapped him again.

Then they got to work. Tom kept it together, silent and still. He rode the pain. Pain was an old friend, familiar territory. Take off his slippers and doze by the fire.

Then Teeth unwrapped the bandage on his right hand and pulled that arm from Tom's body like a kid snapping the wing off an injured bird. Tom couldn't look at his hand. An alien thing, ugly and writhing with nerves.

The big man put his heel on it and ground down.

THE NEXT MORNING, the locusts came.

Tuesday, May twentieth. The boys were shivering lumps under frost-stiff blankets. A nightingale called. One of the boys grunted and rolled and scratched at fleas. The whine of a Messerschmitt broke the stillness. Tom and the boys dived for the slit trench and Hanner, bleary-eyed, smacked Lifton on the back of his head.

While in Greece, Lifton had acquired the gift of remaining asleep while scrambling into a trench. He'd rest his head on an

131

outstretched arm, eyes closed and still snoring. Tom had established LR duty: Lifton reveille.

"I'm fucking awake," Lifton said.

They hunched as the fighter buzzed closer. The rattle of machine-gun fire sounded over the roar of the engine. Three bombers behind the Messerschmitt loosed their cargo with whistles and thumps and were gone.

"Good morning, Hitler," Tardieu said, giving a rude salute.

They waited for the all clear and then climbed from the trenches to the shithouse and mess tent, an ear cocked for Jerry. The anxiety of the previous night was gone; it was morning, and they were young. An hour later, they were shoving Compo rations and eggs into their faces, washing them down with goat's milk and raki, when there was a sudden roar of archie fire.

Halfway to the trenches, they knew it was starting. The sky was mottled with German planes: diving, bombing, buzzing, strafing. Then came the waves of silent silver gliders, moving slow toward Canea on long, tapered wings and landing with ghostly quiet in the scrub around Hill 107. A single Hurricane could have chewed through them like a wolf through kittens, but there wasn't a single Hurricane. There were no Allied planes—the Nazis owned the skies.

"Arms!" Tom heard himself shouting. "Stand to! O'Rourke, Corelli!"

Cooks, clerks—every man not attached to the field hospital or ambulance unit grabbed a weapon as the throb of the Nazi paratroop carriers sounded overhead. Black-and-yellow behemoths dropped green, pink, and black spores to the earth. The elite Fliegerkorps. Yellow parachutes, blue parachutes, they drowned the sky.

They died by the hundred, hanging in the air.

It was a game of fish-in-the-barrel, hide-and-seek. Take cover in a trench, behind a cactus, aim and fire. Parachute silk billowed from the barrage of bullets and caught fire. Distant paratroopers twitched and went suddenly stiff. Legs kicked downward, desperate for the ground; bodies jerked in harnesses and fell still.

The Bofors gunners at the edge of the airfield had been punished for weeks, and they were answering now with endless blind roars behind a haze of bomb-borne dust and smoke. A full fucking battalion was dropping from the sky. Another battalion to the west, out of range of the Bofors, was digging into the dry riverbed. Not Tom's problem, not yet. Slaughter them in the air—and if they set foot on his island, hunt the bastards down.

He could smell the sweat and fear, the burn of cordite. Tom's eyes stung; his hands ached as he fired and fired again. He heard the hoarse roar of his men, of his own voice, the machine growl of Bren guns and rifles, mortar shells, and the pop of automatic pistols. The sky was full. They killed and killed, but it didn't matter. The Nazis never stopped coming. They landed; they massed.

The Bofors boomed ineffectually now, the onslaught out of range, and Nazi light field and 20-mm antitank guns answered from the west. Machine-gun and rifle fire cut down Germans driving toward Hill 107. A bloody crossfire: Bodies tumbled down the slope; the wounded crawled beneath shrubs and into hollows.

A three-inch antiaircraft gun barked over a rise. A 40-mm hurled a hail of incendiary and tracer bullets skyward, barrel glowing dull red—and got lucky. A Junker transport plane exploded into a brilliant orange fireball. A cheer arose and was indistinguishable from the screaming.

The paratroops were machines. They dropped, shed harnesses, sprinted for the weapons canisters. With drill-field precision, they checked and loaded weapons, stepped around their dead buddies, and joined in the battle. The Luftwaffe pounded the Allied positions, covering the paratroops, buying them time to rally, dropping weapons and more men, always more men. . . .

The squad was on recon, skirting a field of barley. O'Rourke froze at a sound, signaled. Manny and Rosenblatt crawled into hollows and relaxed: Kiwi accents. A lieutenant was leading three dozen armed men—released prisoners—from Prison Valley. On a turkey shoot, he said, head-hunting Nazis.

Twenty minutes later, they found a Kraut whose parachute had caught in a tree. He was slumped in his harness, dead—until Hanner approached. The Kraut's gravity knife snicked open and Tom shot him without a pause in his sentence: "We're not fucking grave robbers. Weapons, yes, open season. Take what you can carry. And cigarettes. Leave the rest." The paratroopers were Christmas come early—chocolate and rusks, cigarettes and sausages and rubbers, hypodermic syringes of jump juice, and blankets and socks and vests. They carried 9-mm Parabellum Lugers and hand grenades. Their supply canisters were treasure troves of Mauser K-98s, Schmeisser MP-40 submachine guns, MG-34 light machine guns. And ammunition. Blessed fucking ammunition. "Manny, radio base and request—"

From a scraggly grove of olive trees came the *woof* of mortar shells. The squad moved, fired, moved, fired; stalked forward like one animal, preying on the ground troops and cringing from the air attacks. The sky was the enemy. The Germans bombed and strafed and fell in waves, an endless swarm.

Before the wireless failed, they heard that Nazi troop transport had taken the beaches; Junkers had crash-landed in the fields. The swarm was unstoppable. Nazis were on the bridge over the Tav riverbed. Farther south, they'd captured a handful of hospital ground staff, used them as human shields while pushing up Hill 107 toward the airstrip.

Farther south? Tom's squad was farther south.

They flanked the Nazis; the squad fired hesitantly around the white-faced Aussies and Brits, afraid of hitting an ally. The hostages were beaten forward but maintained composure, unwilling to panic. But the Krauts were taking the fucking hill. If they took the hill, they took the airfield. If they took the airfield, the island fell.

Tom couldn't shape the words, couldn't speak the order. His mouth moved into a snarl, he squeezed the trigger. His captured Schmeisser 9-mm spoke, and was silent. The boys mopped up.

Still they came. Waves of bombers, waves of men.

CHAPTER
SIXTEEN

THE YOUNG WOMAN who called herself Duckblind adjusted her burleigh hat to a more rakish angle. She smiled in the darkness of Mr. Pentham's garden—there was *never* a time when the angle of one's hat wasn't simply *vital*—and reached for her bicycle, which was propped against the gate.

They'd been lackadaisical, the Luftwaffe—halfhearted raids, scalded cats scampering quickly away. How she *did* wish they'd begin bombing properly again. She'd heard stories of the Blitz, fire raging at the docks, bombs falling in an endless hail, sirens shrieking, the chatter of bullets as fighter pilots dueled to the death in the sky above, like gladiators.

All she wished was the teensiest bit of pageantry and splendor, a spot of color in this gloomy city. Not that the people were gloomy. They were lovely. They made her laugh. They were too perfectly easy to deceive, the English. Of course, she was good at roles—sometimes she even fooled herself. It reminded her of playing dress-up when she was a little girl, clumping about in Mama's shoes, draped in ropes of pearls that fell to her calves. Mr. Pentham had some *divine* old trinkets, too, tobacco pouches and tiepins, lovely theatrical props.

Poor Mr. Pentham, so brave and bewildered. Duckblind hoped this new English gentleman, the one she was bicycling across the city to meet, would treat her as kindly. She'd been surprised when she'd discovered the request for a meeting in the dead-letter drop, surprised and wary, as the request had been imperfectly encrypted and the drop had been imperfectly marked. But then, after she retrieved the message, it wasn't so surprising after all. It was not the man she called Bookbinder who had requested a meeting in such a clumsy manner, but a lesser agent he controlled, an agent freshly recruited. An agent who did not know for whom he was working, but who had listened and learned and would heed his master's call.

Duckblind would meet him at the bomb site and learn the full text of Bookbinder's message. She propped her bicycle against a tumbling brick wall and picked her way over the wreckage to an observation point to wait. She settled into the shadows, her hand on a length of iron piping.

THE CHAIR SQUEALED as Davies-Frank put his feet on the desk. He held the phone to his ear and listened to it ring, watching Highcastle scowl at maps across the cramped office at Hennessey Gate.

"Mrs. Davies-Frank," he said into the phone when his wife's voice came on the line.

"Lambkin," Joan said, her voice pitched low and warm. The tone and the pet name told him everything he needed to know.

She forgave him the late hours, the midnight calls. She more than forgave him.

"Did the twins finish dinner without catastrophe?" he asked.

"Without undue catastrophe."

He felt himself relax. Not because he'd been worried about dinner; because he *could* relax, with Joan. "Excellent news."

Highcastle, across the room, ran a finger along the crease of the map on his desk, not bothering to listen, not bothering to pretend he couldn't hear.

"They're upstairs as we speak," Joan said. "Giggling under the blanket with a torch."

"Wasting batteries."

"You ought to speak sternly to them when you come home. I shouldn't wait up?"

"Not tonight, love."

"No. Well, do try to get some sleep, my sweet."

Davies-Frank told her something to make her smile, then returned the phone to the cradle as gently as kissing the back of her neck.

Highcastle spoke without looking up. "There ought to be a law."

"Jealous, old cock?"

The salt-and-pepper head rose. "Yes. You're a lucky man." He jabbed a thick finger at the map, where he was planning the capture of Duckblind. "Ten-fifteen. We need a minimum of six men. Better a dozen."

Outside All Souls Church at the rendezvous tomorrow night, at what Sondegger had called a 'treff.' Davies-Frank untangled the phone cord. "You're confident we'll make the arrest?"

"In the blackout?" Highcastle said. "No guarantees, even with a dozen men. Lethal force has been authorized. Better he's dead than free."

"There'll be clear skies and a moon tomorrow," Davies-Frank said. "Raid weather, but good visibility for us. We'll catch him."

"If he's there."

"Duckblind will be there." Because if he wasn't, Sondegger would be executed. It was the only reason Davies-Frank believed the rendezvous information was correct. Though why Sondegger had insisted on telling only Earl . . . "Why Earl? Sondegger could have told us the rendezvous information directly."

"Tom's holding back."

"Is he?"

"Not sure," Highcastle said. "Let the Americans worry that. We've too much on our plate already."

"Mmm. At least Sondegger seems to believe Tom is Earl." Davies-Frank rose to look at the map with Highcastle. "You're satisfied?"

Highcastle grunted. "You briefed Rippen?"

"Rippen won't be holding the white umbrella. I will."

A short sharp silence. "That's daft."

"I'm the only one with enough German to pass for native, if it comes to that."

"And if Duckblind draws down . . ."

"He's a wireless operator, not Commander Flash. I'll make contact, then withdraw."

Highcastle scowled at the map, his spectacles magnifying his eyes. "Thomas Wall," he said in disgust.

"What's he to do with anything?"

"Amateurs. The pair of you."

Davies-Frank flicked his lighter open, flicked it closed. "Making contact with an unarmed WT operator while surrounded by your men—it'll be a walk in the park."

"Or a minefield," Highcastle said.

IN THE SMALL ROOM under the eaves, the small man at the small desk removed his earphones with a jerky, nervous motion. Melville was pale—and as he stood and stepped close to the wall, he turned paler.

He lifted an ink-stained hand. He nodded to himself. Nodded again. He knocked on the wall. Two quick, two slow.

Farquhar, another transcriptionist, would relieve him in fifteen minutes. How time swept by so fast, and crept so slow! The duration of time came from the succession of ideas, from the speed at which thoughts formed and dissolved, a slick of petrol in a puddle of rainwater. Not only time but life itself flowed from the mind. Melville had learned a great deal. He knew so little. The message entrusted to him was in a language he could not decipher. It didn't matter. It was not for him to judge significance. He was merely a receiver—well, now a transmitter, too.

He returned to the small desk. He had fifteen minutes. He had never known conviction until tonight. He would never again be so brave as he was tonight.

"A MINEFIELD?" Davies-Frank stifled a yawn. "That's the way to buck up the old esprit."

"Ought to turn in," Highcastle said, talking of the narrow folding Plimsat bunks downstairs. "Tomorrow won't be short."

"One last briefing and I'm done." Davies-Frank checked his watch. "Farquhar's late."

Before Highcastle could respond, there were footsteps on the stairs. Farquhar arrived, all apologies, and Davies-Frank briefed him—the fire and its aftermath, the new terms and response keys—and escorted him to the transcription room. Pretending to escort him for courtesy's sake, but actually testing himself. He couldn't function properly, afraid. He monitored his heart as they passed the warder at the bulky desk, approached the whitewashed door. His heartbeat stayed level and smooth. Bless you, Joan.

Important to remember that one was not a superstitious primitive, that a man was never more than a man. Important to remember the reason for the dread, the lies, the nights away from home: all those who risked their lives, who risked even more than their own lives, to defeat the Nazis. He would never forget them.

Mr. Krajewski. The Pole who dragged a shattered collarbone from Lodz to the Baltic Sea by willpower alone, hijacked a fishing trawler with an empty pistol, trained with the SOE in England, and returned to Poland with a different name. *Mr. Vedel.* A soft-spoken Frenchman almost single-handedly responsible for the dozen pocket bombs that reduced the railroad in his *département* to a level of inefficiency so egregious, the Germans preferred lorry convoys, which traveled over bridges that Vedel then bombed.

And *Whiskbroom*, in Berlin. Whiskbroom wasn't merely a highly placed asset; he was a mirror. He was Davies-Frank's age and class; he spoke English as well as Davies-Frank spoke German. His wife was Joan's age, and almost as beautiful. He had three children. He risked his family to fight the fascists, braver than any soldier in the field. If the Twenty fell, he'd pay the ultimate price.

No, not too difficult to remember the reasons.

"Quiet tonight," Farquhar said as he followed Davies-Frank into the transcription room. He grinned at Melville. "Running low on steam, is he?"

"Well, nighttime," Melville answered with a weak smile. "He's most likely asleep."

Farquhar tapped the stack of notebooks. "Did some talking earlier, looks like." He turned to Davies-Frank with a mock sigh.

"Our guest always turns mum when I come on duty. I'm starting to think he doesn't approve of my handwriting."

"You'll have to type his Christmas card," Davies-Frank said. He locked the door as he and Melville returned to the hall. "He's sleeping nights now?"

"He may be awake," Melville said. "I really couldn't say."

"He was nocturnal last week—you were on night shift then, weren't you?"

"Only through Thursday."

"Of course," Davies-Frank said. "Bit of excitement today."

"Oh? Oh—the fire."

"Yes, the fire," Davies-Frank said absently, considering the various transcriptionists' output as they walked toward the office. Unless he was mistaken, Sondegger had filled two notebooks with his rantings when Melville was on duty, but only a dozen pages with Farquhar or O'Brien—as if he could distinguish between Melville and the others. Davies-Frank glanced at Melville, shuffling beside him. Ought to buck up the poor sod, bent under the weight of Sondegger's words. "Carefree bachelor, aren't you?"

"Afraid I am."

"Explains why you're given nights. Like Mr. Highcastle, you're a born bachelor. I caught Highcastle wearing a gold watch with a gray jacket, something a wife would never allow." He shook his head, grinning, but Melville failed to return his smile. "Had to speak sternly to him. One prefers silver with gray, of course. . . ."

Melville bobbed his head twice. He was a nervous one. Still, he'd been vetted and approved. Probably been tough as rock when he'd begun the work. They all grew nervy as the days wore on—too much at stake. Too much depended upon so little.

CHAPTER
SEVENTEEN

"HOME," TOM SAID. "Sweet home."

He raised himself from the pillow. His head was heavy and battered as a big brass gong. Took a week to lift it, but he persevered. That's how tough he was.

He hitched himself against the headboard and eyed the room. It was the sort of cubby he'd grown to know too well the past six months. A small impersonal room, with a small impersonal bed, upon which nothing could not be rendered small and impersonal. His skin smelled bitter and mixed badly with the close air. The curtains were open. Outside, black clouds were raining a torrent.

He didn't hurt much. He'd slept, but it had been doped sleep. Sleep without rest.

A railway man had found him an hour before dawn. "I didn't hear a bloody sound," the man had said. "Worked right through—

not a single sound." The railway man thought there'd been a raid. He thought Tom had been bombed.

Tom had laughed, spat blood, and said, "Rowansea."

He'd passed out, awakened, and passed out again. At the Rowansea, there was a commotion. Tom saw it in flashes: the front drive, the Court Room, the hallway, the stretcher too narrow for his shoulders.

The doctor tutted, said Tom shouldn't have done himself harm.

Tom said no, it had been muggers. Get Davies-Frank.

The doctor examined his hand, tutted again.

Tom told himself it was someone else's hand, nothing to do with him.

The doctor primed a syringe. Morphine?

"No," Tom said.

"Won't feel a pinch," the doctor said.

"No."

"You ought to be ashamed, sir, at your age, afraid of—"

The doctor tried to stick the needle in him and Tom bucked on the stretcher. Knocked one of the nurses away, laid a couple knuckles on the doctor's arm. Flashes of a struggle—one-sided, as Tom was strapped down. MacGovern pinned him, his hot breath in Tom's face.

Mrs. Harper appeared and shooed them away. Tom had wanted to fall weeping onto her wide starched bosom. Instead, he told her to get Davies-Frank. He needed to speak to Davies-Frank before the next set of gorillas killed him. Who the hell were Kong and Teeth? He needed to speak to Sondegger, needed to find Hyde Street Misfits. . . .

There was a prick in his leg and MacGovern grinned down, syringe in hand. Tom swung at him, hard as a butterfly closing its wings.

IT SET RUGG OFF, the servants' entrance at Burnham Chase. Him, a day laborer? Fookin' night, that's when he labored.

"You'll give the tweeny fits," Renard told him. "A face like that."

Rugg made a noise in his throat. It set him bleedin' off.

Inside was a cramped hallway, ceiling low enough to give him a crick in the neck. He yanked his fingers one at a time, heard the joints crack, and followed Renard into a low underground room, wooden tables and cabinets for ancient bloody hand-servanting, a scratch of window over a tin sink. The bleedin' boot and knife room.

Renard stood near the door. Rugg looked about for something to snap. Saw an old gent's shoehorn. He snapped it. There was a shallow pit in one of the wooden tables, from all the hands over all the years, polishing, sharping, polishing, sharping. Made a fine seat for his arse.

Chilton came and he and Renard chattered for a long space about nothing that needed chatting. Then Chilton said, "You had no difficulty finding the man?"

No difficulty? Ice-cold swamp-dark night. Near froze his eggs off.

"No difficulty at all," Renard said. "We caught him outside the Waterfall, and took him to a . . . a more private locale."

"He was forthcoming?"

"We convinced him cooperation was the wisest course."

"He is fragile and deranged—it cannot have proven too difficult."

"Fragile?" Rugg blew air out his nose. "Yank is fragile as boot leather. Took some bloody convincing."

"He told you what, exactly?"

145

Rugg shoved the heel of his hand against the cut on his cheek and let Renard talk. Renard liked talking.

"He was visited yesterday morning by a man from the Home Guard. David Frank. Frank wanted—"

"David Frank." Chilton's gray eyes glittered. "Is he a Jew?"

"Dunno about that, m'lord," Renard said.

M'lord. Be yanking his forelock next. Rugg snapped another bit from the shoehorn.

"What news of the American's brother?" Chilton asked.

"He doesn't know where his brother is," Renard said. "He's as keen to find him as you are. Now, this David—"

"—FRANK IS SOMETHING ELSE." Renard's teeth protruded in a feral smile. "The Yank was reluctant to chinwag about him. Close-fisted and par, par—what's the word?"

Chilton didn't answer. These men had their uses, but it was certainly not incumbent upon him to further their education.

Rugg shifted. "Parsimonious," he said in his womanish voice.

"Parsimonious," Renard said. "Our Mr. Wall gave nothing but tripe."

Which Chilton knew was correct. David Frank and the Home Guard—both lies.

"You could not convince him to speak?" Chilton asked, and then immediately regretted the question. He should demand, not inquire. To do otherwise diminished his authority, and authority was the reason fascism was "the wave of the future" as Anne Lindbergh wrote, while democracy was the withered fruit of a withered tree.

Sadly, the persons of fascism were rarely as exalted as the philosophies. These two men were regrettable specimens. Chilton imagined they would be most happy scrawling slogans—

"Christians Awake! Don't Be Slaughtered for Jewish Finance!" "Stop the War, Stop the Warmongers!"—if they were sufficiently literate to scrawl. Still, after the Public Order Act, there were few who could be trusted. Chilton's source had assured him of the pair's effectiveness, and discretion.

"Yank has his Achilles' heel." Renard's toothy smile widened. "His Achilles' palm. It got him talking. He saw some dustup in Greece. We heard about that, didn't we, Rugg?"

Rugg cracked a knuckle.

"And David Frank?" Chilton said. "I presume you have details."

The details were worthless—Tom had taken refuge in delirium. Still, enough remained to make Chilton a great deal more curious, especially given what he already knew.

The first call had come yesterday morning. Ponsonby had brought the phone to the breakfast table. "The Metropolitan Police, m'lord."

"This is Chilton," he'd said into the phone.

A police sergeant introduced himself and inquired as to Chilton's health.

"My health is sufficiently good that strangers have no cause for concern."

The sergeant asked if he was a relation of Thomas Wall.

"By marriage."

The sergeant said Tom had left the Rowansea and might be heading to Burnham Chase.

"Has his brother been informed?" Chilton asked.

The sergeant had been unable to contact Mr. Earl Wall. Perhaps Lord Chilton knew where he might be?

Lord Chilton did not. But Lord Chilton was curious. Thomas Wall had escaped again—and Earl was impossible to locate? Perhaps this would occasion a change in the fraternal relationship.

Perhaps Earl would reappear for his brother's sake. Chilton's best leverage against Earl was Tom, but it was no leverage at all while the two remained estranged.

He'd been in the library, letting his mind play over the possibilities, when Ponsonby reappeared. Busy day for the telephone.

"A Mr. Rowans, m'lord."

Chilton waited for the door to click shut before answering. "Chilton."

"This is the, er, man who you arranged to—"

"I know who you are, sir."

"I have, er, I have news about the man who—about the patient, the American."

"I have heard the news already," Chilton said. "And am disappointed it was not you who informed me of it."

"That he's gone from the hospital? No, this is new news. This is, er, news of a more particular interest."

Chilton bent over the phone. "The patient had a visitor?"

"He did, yes. He never met him, though. The patient was scheduled for an appointment this morning, but he'd gone by the time the visitor arrived."

"The visitor was a relation?"

"Not his brother, no," the caller said. "A man from the City. He secured Mr. Wall's temporary release. For the one day only. I've never heard of such a thing."

"What is the man's name?"

"Rupert Davies-Frank." He spelled it. "Claims to be from the Home Office, but there's some confusion on that count."

Curious. To Chilton's knowledge, Tom Wall was exceptional for one reason only: his relationship with Earl. If that relationship was repaired, Tom could be used to extract information from his brother and, through him, from both American and British intelligence. But who else would have interest in him?

He gave the caller his instructions, then had Jesper drive him to his club. He made a few discreet inquiries. Who was Rupert Davies-Frank?

The men he trusted couldn't say. The men he didn't, wouldn't.

After additional inquiries, he'd discovered that Davies-Frank had been educated at the right schools, belonged to the right clubs, attended the right events. His wife was a relation of Lady Bassington. Davies-Frank was not SOE. Didn't seem to be MI6. Davies-Frank was a cipher. And Davies-Frank had business with Thomas Wall.

It was excellent news. Events were proceeding apace. Chilton had been imposed upon by Rugg and Renard for too long, allowing them sanctuary on his land. They'd be his eyes and ears in London now—and his hands.

WHEN TOM WOKE, his hand was rebandaged. He was alone in the room. After two hours and six mugs of water, the door opened and Tom lifted his head, hoping to see Davies-Frank, but it was a PC with a clipboard of questions.

"Sounds like Rugg and Renard," the PC said after Tom told the story. "Rugg's the ape, Renard the ferret. A pair of likely villains—and buffers."

" 'Buffers'?"

"Fascists. Mosley's men, the BUF."

The British Union of Fascists. "You know who they are," Tom said. "Pick them up."

The PC nodded solemnly. "Eyewitness is Sgt. Thomas Wall. Resident in the Rowansea Royal Hospital. The odds of a supported complaint are remote. If it was Rugg and Renard, they make it easy not to find them."

"Exile the Duke of Windsor, but you can't slam a couple of likely villains?"

"We would 'slam' them, as you say, if they'd not gone quiet." The PC tapped his clipboard. "And if it were worth the effort to chivy them out."

"What's their angle?"

"Hoist boys, demanding with menaces. An injured man alone in the dark is meat and drink to them. They brought away how much?"

"They weren't after my wallet. I need to contact Mr. Davies-Frank; he's at the Home Office. Fire Control. It's urgent."

The PC tapped his pen against his teeth. "I spoke with a doctor. Funny vocabulary they have. *Excitation* and *acute sensitivity* and *fixation.*"

"Sure. I beat my own ribs against a wall to see what they'd sound like breaking."

"I understand they are only bruised, sir."

Tom didn't bother sighing.

More questions, more answers. The PC left and Tom watched the ceiling. Rugg and Renard were Blackshirts, and they knew about Davies-Frank. Who were they working for? Maybe Earl was Duckblind. Both were missing, both connected to Sondegger, both traitors. He had to warn Davies-Frank he was blown. He stood unsteadily and stepped into the hall.

Mrs. Harper took his elbow before he got five steps.

"I need a phone," he told her.

"I left a message for your Mr. Davies-Frank," she said. "Don't fret yourself on his account."

"Forget Davies-Frank. I want to talk to my tailor about a couple new suits."

When she finally allowed him the phone, he spoke with Directory Enquiries. The woman told him no Hyde Street Mis-

150

fits was listed. He asked for Hyde Street Tailor. Nothing. Asked for another misfit shop or tailor or haberdasher on Hyde Street.

She told him there was no such street.

"What?" he said.

"There's no street with that name."

He made her say it again. No such business, and no such street.

He'd thanked her and stared at the wall. Back at the Rowansea, back where he belonged. He needed Davies-Frank, needed Sondegger. He needed Hennessey Gate, a new lead on Earl.

He gathered what remained of his strength and sent Mrs. Harper off with his bedpan. He ruffled his bed, created a lump under the blankets. He edged himself behind the door and made a little noise. The new orderly with the walrus mustache stepped in, checked the lump of blankets, and Tom slipped out on stocking feet.

Straight into MacGovern's scarecrow smile. Back to bed again. Home sweet home.

CHAPTER
EIGHTEEN

CHILTON CUT ACROSS the grass toward the paved terrace and paused at the scalloped lily pond, the water still as glass, reflective as his mind. Renard had reported that Tom said "David Frank" was from Whitehall, and that he was from the Admiralty, that he had flown a Gladiator on Crete. That he was chained to a rock, lashed to a mast. . . .

Renard had repeated Tom's fabrications with relish, while Rugg scratched at a fresh scab on his chin, his mouth sour and skeptical. Still, despite the lies, much had been accomplished. They'd confirmed Davies-Frank's presence. They'd given Earl a reason to surface—to help his brother, who had been so cruelly mistreated. Chilton had done what little he could to mend the fraternal relationship.

He nodded to himself and turned onto the yew walk, unable to suppress a flush of pleasure at the rich verdigris of the hedge. The garden was his pride. It was also the strongest bond he shared with his daughter—their love of everything green and growing. What Harriet failed to understand was that one must ruthlessly prune in order to foster new growth—in society as in horticulture.

On the west lawn, he passed what would blossom, come spring, into a display of Darwin tulips with ground cover of aubrietia, alyssum, wallflowers, and polyanthus. Past the lawn, the blue spruce was looking well, though not so well as it would when the Japanese weeping cherry came into bloom. He surveyed the John Downie with its red-flushed yellow fruit; the early-flowering magnolia with heavy white cups; the row of clipped yew in parade-ground order.

Chilton ascended the sundial terrace steps and heard a low and distant mumbling—the *put-put* of an engine upon the front drive. His pleasure deepened. It was Harriet's MG. He'd greet her at her car today, instead of in the library. She would understand he was apologizing for his behavior when last she visited. It was a shame they argued, but she was too bright and too beautiful—too much like her mother—and her naïveté pained him. He could no more ignore her devotion to Churchill's cause than he could ignore cankers gnawing at the limbs of an ancient elm.

"My dear," he said as she stepped from her little MG. "What a lovely surprise."

"Father." She kissed his cheek. "I see from your shoes you've been in the garden."

"I'm considering building a ruined abbey on the rise."

"What folly!" she said, and they smiled as they always did. "Or are you really building it this time? I passed two men who could be builders, or—or what would one call a man who constructed ruins?"

"Ruiners, of course," he said. She must have seen Rugg and Renard leaving the grounds. Ruiners suited them as well as any title, and better than most. "A pair of men with a sad tale and an exemption from duty. I'll find something for them."

Harriet's tired smile brightened. She appreciated his efforts at employing those in need. It was very near an insult—as if she thought he could not be trusted to care for his people. Quite unfair; he might demand respect, but he knew his duty. One was impossible without the other.

"I am not an ogre," he said.

"Father," she said, "I need your help."

IT WAS TOO EARLY for tea, but Father insisted. Harriet knew he enjoyed watching her pour—it reminded him of her mother, whom he had bullied and cosseted and finally lost in childbirth when Harriet was eleven. She often wondered what sort of man he'd be now had her mother survived. She had blunted his sharp edges.

They were in his library, surrounded by leather-bound books. There was the clink of a spoon against the warmed Sèvres porcelain, the smell of steeping tea and of Mrs. Godfrey's scones. Rationing hadn't come to Burnham Chase.

Father sipped and visibly relaxed. "Now we can talk."

She pushed a lock of hair behind her ear. "Earl hasn't been home for days. Over a week, actually. I'm being alarmist, I suppose."

"You phoned the embassy?"

"They said there was no cause for concern. Precisely what they'd say if there were."

"Harriet, you knew his business when you married."

"Yes, I simply—I've an uncomfortable feeling."

"I see." Father's gray eyes were watchful above his teacup. "Tom visited you?"

"You heard he left the hospital?"

"The police called."

"Of course. He smashed a window. He was in the front room, waiting for Earl."

"Or you."

"Mmm. He told me Earl was gone. Not merely gone but missing, as well."

"Tom is hardly reliable."

"He said—he said Earl had evanesced. *Evanesced.*" She turned her teacup on its saucer. "It's not the sort of thing he'd say. It— I know it's ridiculous, but that one word . . ."

That one word had kept her awake past midnight, had awakened her from fitful sleep before dawn. She'd arrived at the office and worked for six hours before Mr. Uphill came. Another five hours, and she'd pleaded exhaustion and driven directly to Burnham Chase to ask Father for help.

"That word," she said. "And an uncomfortable feeling I can't seem to ignore."

"Feminine intuition, Harriet?"

"I'd like you to ask after Earl. If you know anyone at the American embassy who might quietly inquire. Just to know he's safe."

"Me? I'm sure your contacts are far superior to mine."

"Not among Americans of a . . . a certain type." She set her teacup gently down. "I know very well that you've been cultivating"—she groped for an inoffensive word—"*individuals* at the embassy."

"Of a certain type," he said.

"I'm asking for your help, Father."

"Which type? The honorable type? The patriotic type?"

"The fascistic type."

"You needn't say the word as if it leaves a sour taste in your

155

mouth. There is nothing to be ashamed of in supporting fascism. The Britons, the British Fascists, the Fascist League—British patriots all. The British Union of Fascists is fifty thousand strong."

"Hardly that any longer."

"And why not, Harriet? Because—"

"The Battle of Cable Street? The Blackshirt bullies who attacked protesters at the Olympia rally?"

"Because," he said, as if she hadn't spoken, "the Public Order Act made it illegal to wear the fascist uniform. Illegal to rally. Because Rothermere was frightened into inconsequence by the warmongers."

Lord Rothermere, owner of the *Daily Mail*, had initially supported the BUF. "Rothermere," she said, "changed his own mind, due to his ability to distinguish between conservatism and fascism."

"He was afraid, Harriet. Mosley was interned and the BUF banned." He shook his head. "And people have the presumption to say *we* repress dissident voices."

She didn't like that "we." She met her father's gaze; his eyes were precisely the same gray as her own.

"You admire the Americans," he said. "Yet you fail to emulate them. There are seven hundred and seventy fascist groups in the United States. Father Coughlin has fifteen million loyal listeners, the Bund half a million members. The most popular magazines—*Reader's Digest*, *The Saturday Evening Post*—endorse what you call 'isolationism.' The question is simple: Do you prefer fascists to Communists?"

"I prefer democrats to tyrants."

The conversation deteriorated further. Harriet had been wrong to ask for his help. Still, she couldn't ask the SOE, for which she worked, or the Americans. Such a thing wasn't done, and the Americans wouldn't help in any case. Two years of fighting, and the best they'd offered was the Lend-Lease Act, while the British and Soviets died fighting fascism. They could hardly be expected to help one worried wife.

She stood to leave. "I should be getting back."

"I'll ring you as soon as I hear," Father said.

"Hear?"

"About your husband—my son-in-law." He rose to escort her to the door. "Family is family."

"Yes," she said. "I suppose it is."

"Speak to Mrs. Godfrey before you leave. She's put steak and kidney aside."

"Father . . ." He knew she disliked his largesse as much as she liked—to his amusement at her low tastes—steak and kidney pie.

"Please, Harriet. It will do me good. The parcel already waits."

"As a favor to you," she said.

"Very kind." He smiled, and it lightened his face. "And Harriet—I'm concerned about Tom."

"Poor Tommy. He's a disaster. Safely returned to the Rowansea by now, I hope."

"Safely?" Father said. "Then you haven't heard?"

TOM WALKED a circuit around the room. Walking in a circle, going nowhere. He sat in the chair at the window and made no less progress. The door opened and the orderly with the walrus mustache stepped inside with the newspaper.

Tom read that the German thrust at Sidi Rezegh had failed. The Brits destroyed eighteen enemy aircraft. The Red Army abandoned Tikhvin on the Leningrad–Vologda railway but scored a victory at the Sea of Azov.

He folded the page, looking for news from home. Ah. TEN-SION IN THE PACIFIC — MUCH ACTIVITY IN WASHINGTON. Japanese envoys spoke with Hull and Roosevelt at the White House, said they'd continue negotiations for at least a fortnight. In Japan, the Tojo cabinet's decision to keep talking renewed hopes of a peaceful settlement, and the stock market soared. The next column told him the Japs still insisted on "Asia for the Asiatics, under the leadership of Japan" and rejected the American principles of nonaggression and the "open door."

Nothing he could do. He turned to the crossword puzzle. One down was "This lordling has very much the makings of a regal aunt." Ten letters. What the hell was "a regal aunt"? A queen ant?

The door opened and Harriet stepped inside. Not her day to be beautiful — her eyes were smudged, her face haggard.

"I heard you were attacked," she said.

"Mugged, if you believe it."

"You don't?"

He shrugged.

She walked around the room, touching the door frame and the wallpaper. Using her hand to see, like a blind woman. She touched the edge of the mirror. She touched the cold metal bed frame. She stood five feet from him.

"I heard it was serious," she said. "You look better than I expected."

He grinned. "Flatterer."

"Though still appalling. The nurse said all you need is one good night."

"Is that an offer?"

A spark of a smile flashed in her eyes but didn't reach her lips.

"They weren't muggers, Harry," he said. "Muggers don't inquire into your social life."

She said offhandedly, "Did they ask about Earl?"

He laughed, and two spots of color appeared on her cheeks. Rarely was Harriet so clumsy. "No, Harriet. They didn't ask about Earl. *You're* here to ask about Earl."

"That's one reason."

"You called the embassy."

"This morning."

"They told you not to worry your pretty little head?"

"Yes."

"Makes you wonder how deluded I am. Getting hard to tell. You checked Earl's club?"

She nodded curtly.

"He's not at the Waterfall, either. Hasn't been since Tuesday, maybe Wednesday." Earl had a room at the Rapids, had girls at the Rapids. Tom felt the words, the knowledge of Earl's betrayal, bright and hard on his tongue. "Why not ask your boss to— Oh. Can't mess with American intel. No, you spoke with your father and he told you to bugger off. So you want to know what I know about Earl. Is that why you came?"

"Certainly not for your irresistible personality."

He laughed, but it didn't sound like much. "I guess not."

"Who told you Earl was missing?"

"Man named Rupert. You do two things for me, I'll take you to him."

"Which two things?"

"One, get me out of here."

"You know I can't do that."

"I know you can."

"I won't, then."

"Your decision."

It was her decision, and she spent twenty minutes making it. She came back half an hour after that with the clothes from his duffel bag and a daily pass.

"You haven't asked the second thing," he said as he dressed.

"I'd rather not know."

"Ten letters. 'This lordling has very much the makings of a regal aunt.' "

"Fauntleroy," she said, unsmiling. "Come along."

THE SKY CLEARED before they were halfway to Hennessey Gate. Tom told Harriet there would be an old white church at the next junction, with a small graveyard. There was no church and no graveyard. He said perhaps the next junction. Wrong again.

She pulled into the drive of an ivy-covered building with a timber frame and a peaked roof. A sprinkling of golden leaves clung to the sycamore behind her, like the halo on a Russian icon.

"I'll ask inside," she said, opening the door. "Back in a kick."

He put his hand on her arm. "You believe me, don't you? That Earl is missing."

"I believe Earl knows where he is, and knows what he's about."

"Working for the COI."

"Of course," she said.

"With or against the Nazis?"

"You know Earl better than that."

"The United States and Germany aren't at war."

"It's not Earl who worries me. The nurse said you'd never get your rest at the Rowansea."

"He could be running a private party. With Wild Bill Donovan in charge of the place, gunslingers are encouraged."

"When you speak like that, Tom . . ." She shook her head. "Wild Bill and gunslingers and Earl's treachery. Your delusions help nobody."

"Earl betrayed me, Harry."

"More than I did?"

Tom turned his head. He was tired of talking. He looked out the window. The red-gold leaves were pinned to a latticework of bare branches. Harriet waited a long moment, then stepped out of the car for directions.

Tom called after her, "Hey, Harry. Why 'a regal aunt'?"

"Fauntleroy," she said. "F. Aunt Leroy."

Tom watched until she disappeared into the house. He slid behind the wheel, hit the self-starter, and drove off. He had to warn Davies-Frank about the Blackshirts who'd stomped him, had to get a new line from Sondegger to Earl. Three turns and ten miles, and there was the old white church. He turned left. The road was distantly familiar. He was watching for landmarks when a car gunned past, horn blaring.

He started, heart pounding, then realized he was driving no faster than he walked. He breathed, focused, and stepped harder on the accelerator.

He was tired; he was spent. The road in front of him blurred.

CHAPTER
NINETEEN

MAY 1941

STILL THEY CAME. In waves of bombers and waves of men.

The Mediterranean sun was dim behind the haze of smoke. The Krauts had rallied in the Tav riverbed west of the airfield. Their air superiority was unanswerable; they'd reduced the ack-ack batteries to blood and rubble. Nazi paratroopers who'd been surrounded signaled with white-and-yellow strips for bomb runs and machine-gun cover, for medical supplies, mortar ammo, reinforcements. The Krauts owned the sky. They would own the island, too, if they took Máleme. It all came down to Hill 107.

Communications were dead. Every move was watched from above; every thrust was parried. Half the defenders were pinned in trenches, low on ammo, low on hope. At least Tom's squad was mobile in the trees. . . .

Early evening. Tillotson wrestled a wild-eyed boy in an Aussie uniform to the ground. The boy said D Company had been decimated and there was another Nazi charge on Hill 107—the Fliegerkorps pressing a fierce attack on the opposite flank. Tom helped the boy to his feet, asked who was defending.

"What's left of the Twenty-second," the boy said. "Guess McCurcheon's company and—"

The boy stepped behind an overturned mule cart, and Tom never saw him again. They moved, keeping to the trees until hidden by the swirls of smoke shrouding the hill. Found a supply hut near an outcropping of rock. They had no mortars; they were out of grenades. They filled ration cans with concrete and nails, triggered them with gelignite.

Tom was working deaf and blind. There was no coordination, no strategy. Unseen pockets of the Twenty-second—lone men and clusters, maybe an intact platoon—beat the Nazis bloodily back. Metallic shrieks hammered the air; the smoke surged in overheated waves. Tom was numb and hoarse. When he spat, it was pink. His Schmeisser was long gone; he had a rifle and a handful of rounds. The paratroops were dug into slit trenches, signaling the planes. Tom's squad was in a trench, too. Someone was laughing. Two of the boys were singing a bawdy version of "With Plenty of Money and You."

More Germans came—they drove forward. The first Nazi rank was cut down by Staffo and Rosenblatt, behind a smoking Fallschirmjäger heavy machine gun juryrigged to a recoilless carriage. The second rank advanced. The gun exploded in Staffo's arms; the squad fired blind and panicked and stopped the advance.

The third Nazi rank swarmed the trench.

Tom heard himself scream orders, felt himself slash his bayonet across a man's face. He was knocked onto his stomach—rolled and stabbed a paratrooper in the back of the knee. He heard a shriek, pistol shots, and the slam of rifle butts. The boys were shit-terrified, fighting like animals in the blood-wet earth. The frenzy continued a full minute after the last Nazi was dead, like a hanged man's legs kicking at the gallows.

There was a lull. Staffo and Tillotson were dead. Two Brits and an Aussie he didn't know were dead. Corelli and Blondie needed stretchers. One of the Krauts was sucking air through a chest wound, drowning from the inside out. Tom rallied what was left of his squad to join C Company. The Nazis had established a toehold on Hill 107, dug in deep. The C Company lieutenant sent a message by runner to Creforce HQ:

HEAVILY ENGAGED ON BOTH FLANKS. AMMUNITION LOW.
NO MACHINE GUNS. NO HAND GRENADES. WOULD KINDLY
APPRECIATE HELP.

The sky was a soup of flak; the defense was FUBAR. One platoon, shit for weapons, and endless fucking Nazis. They fought until the sun set. With relative dark came relative quiet, and Creforce's answer:

REGRET UNABLE TO SEND HELP. GOOD LUCK.

The men laughed. "And God bless."

"We who are about to die."

"Hey, Sarge," Manny said, too quietly.

"Yeah, Manny?"

"Listen, Sarge." Manny's eyes were wet, his face caked with dirt. "The thing is, thing is . . ."

"I know, son," Tom said, his hand roughly on Manny's shoulder. "I know."

They heard shots across the killing ground. The Twenty-eighth Maori, reinforcing them? No way to tell. Then silence. Tom squatted beside the C Company lieutenant in the slit trench. "We have to counterattack, in the dark. Clear the hill. If the Krauts have safe landing on the airstrip, it's all over."

The lieutenant nodded. "Your men have hidden reserves of ammunition?"

"My men have hidden reserves of guts."

"Reinforcements will come soon. They have to." The lieutenant smiled an empty smile. "Your squad might scout for them. Establish contact, coordination. Use some of those reserves."

Tom roused the boys. They scouted along the Allied encampments and pieced together the news:

The Twenty-eighth Maori had come, and found B Company already withdrawn, found A Company wiped out. Captain Winchell's of the Twenty-third was nowhere. The command post of the Twenty-second was deserted; the Fifteenth Platoon had been decimated. The Maori had marched six hours to reinforce them, been immediately ordered to turn back toward brigade HQ.

There were no reinforcements.

At 0340, a runner found Tom at the northeast perimeter of the airfield; he and his men were ordered to withdraw. Hang their boots around their necks and creep away, hand Hill 107 to the Krauts. The order was bullshit. If they lost Hill 107, they lost the island. They could still hold. There were no airdrops at night. Retake Hill 107—all of it—and retrench. They'd killed twice what they lost, three times.

Tom led the squad back toward C Company to argue against withdrawal, but the camp was already abandoned. They were too late; they'd lost Hill 107. The Nazis would land Junker transports on the airstrip without opposition. They'd lost Crete.

Tom sat on a half-fallen stone wall. "Take off your Abners and hang 'em around your neck."

He bent to untie his shoes—and to keep the boys from seeing his face. A cloud shifted and the moon filtered through, illuminating a tarp that had been abandoned in the withdrawal. A tarp over a crate . . .

"Sweet holy fuck," he said.

"Sarge?"

Permission had been requested to crater the airstrip. Engineers had come, prepared the explosives: cratering charges, in 10-kg sticks of C4. Permission had been denied. The crate was five feet from him, barely visible under the tarp. He stared into the shadows. The crate had to be empty. Of course it was empty.

"Rosey, come gimme a hand."

They pried the crate open. It wasn't empty.

"The fucking engineers," Tom said. "The sloppy bastard engineers."

The boys were looking at him. There was something strange on his face: a smile.

"The RAF interservice mission to Greece," he said in an urgent undertone. "November 1940. The only fucking English-speaking groundhogs in a thousand miles." He paused, and the boys watched him. "Where," he asked them, "were you?"

"We were there."

"The advance on Valona," Tom said. "January of 1941. Where," he asked, "were you?"

"We were fucking there, Sarge."

"How about March? The asshole of the world, fighting twenty-seven guinea divisions on the Albanian front—where, pray tell, were you?"

"We were there, Sarge!"

"Think back to April. That filthy retreat through the pass—mauling the holy rosy fuck out of the Nazi Eighteenth. Where were you?" He answered with them: "We were there."

The night was still. They were bright-eyed children, eager to be roused, eager to be shaped and molded and used. They were young, they were tough, and they were his.

"We got our asses wiped off Greece," he said. "But we gave better than we got. Your orders—our orders—are to walk away." He patted the crate. "Tomorrow at dawn, if the Krauts have the airstrip, they land all the troops they want. *If* they have the airstrip."

They nodded. Their faces glowed in the moonlight.

"You lacy bastards," he said. "You wanna see tomorrow?"

"Hell no, Sarge!" they said.

"Hanner, O'Rourke, on point. Ammo? . . . That'll have to do. Someone shake Lifton; he's asleep. Tardieu, you better know how to detonate these things, or I'm pissing in the wind. Rosey, you and Manny flank left. . . ."

IT WAS OVER long before dawn. Tom was bleeding and shattered, but death wouldn't come. Rosenblatt dragged him off Hill 107, dragged him miles over pebbles and scrub to the field hospital, and smiled through his broken face and said, " 'Don't need a big band to jitterbug,' Sarge."

They patched Tom through the night. A bucket of blood, a yard of bandage, and nothing was wrong with him a Nazi enfilade wouldn't fix. He was in uniform again by noon. They gave him a rifle and told him Rosenblatt had died in the night.

He bloodied his bayonet on Cemetery Hill, fighting from

tombstone to tombstone. The Maori crossed Xamo Road, dying for every inch, and got as far as the base of Hill 107, when the sun rose and brought the strafing ME-109s. No Junker transports landed, though. Not yet. Too much debris on the Máleme airstrip. Tom heard that and smiled, and the man who had told him turned away.

Days later, Tom was fighting alongside the Greeks and Cretans. Hadn't shaved in a week; he'd added an embroidered Cretan waistcoat and baggy black pants to his uniform. A flock of sheep had been slaughtered by a bomb and Cretan women cooked the meat. A skinny man with a flashing smile offered Tom the eyeball. Tom dipped his cup into the pot of raki, popped the roasted eye in his mouth. Better than army chow. He was still chewing when the captain told him in halting English to report to HQ.

He had to find it first. Creforce Headquarters had been withdrawn from Canea, and withdrawn again. HQ staggered across the map like a wounded mouse from a playful cat. It was currently based in a cave. The floor at the entrance was packed dirt and bracken.

"A cave," Tom said.

The sentry grinned. "Better'n a grave."

Tom said nothing and was waved into a dim, rough-hewn office, tornado-struck by the chaos of retreat. Tom saluted the officer behind the desk and heard himself speaking with calm and comprehensive recall of events he didn't quite remember. He accounted for the loss of his squad. He offered his best estimate of the Nazi positions, strength, and movements.

A clerk called the officer away and Tom was alone. He rested his hip against a makeshift table, scattered some papers, and a poem caught his eye. No: a poem code. Earl had described poem codes to him, explained how to decrypt them. Frequency counts, tedious iterations of probability. This code, however, had already been broken and the poem that decrypted the message was attached. Some kind of security.

"Sergeant Wall." The officer was back.

He straightened. "Yes, sir?"

"Force Reserve's looking for volunteers."

"Give me a peashooter and a Kraut," Tom said. "I'm a happy man."

The next day, maybe the day after: They were facing a fresh Nazi division, bristling with equipment and ammo and Aryan superiority, fresh-faced from sleep, with Stukas and Sturmgewehrs. The general withdrawal had been sounded, the Allies abandoning Crete—except Force Reserve didn't retreat. Force Res advanced, unsupported and outnumbered, to buy time.

The Krauts moved on Canea and Suda, and Tom was in a killing fog. He couldn't die. His feet were bloody inside his boots; his tongue was a swollen slab. Then the noise stopped. He was lifted by God's hand and tossed through the air, smacked facedown onto the hard-packed earth. A snail's slime trail crept over twigs an inch from his nose. The silence was beautiful.

He was at a first-aid station, the medic shaking his head. He was on a stretcher, in a truck, being driven through a smoldering fishing village. His hand was shattered; his breath was a dying wheeze. He was in a boat, swathed in bandages, puking chunks of blood.

A white-blond limey gave him morphine shots for the pain.

"You're bloody lucky," the limey said. "Twelve hundred Force Reserve, and more'n a thousand coiled rope."

"Coiled rope?"

"Died, mate. Only a hundred and fifty left."

"Yeah. I'm a lucky man." Even his cigarette case had survived. Inside were a tarnished silver napkin ring, a buffalo-head nickel, and a poem. The poem code.

No decrypting required, and it still took three days to fill the gaps. There were two messages:

TO CREFORCE HQ: BE ADVISED THAT OUR AGENT IN PLACE, CODE EULT, SUGGESTS MÁLEME AERODROME WILL BE THE FOCUS OF STUDENT AIRBORNE INVASION. EULT HAS DETERMINED THAT NAZI MOUNTAIN REGIMENTS PLAN TO LAND HILL 107 FOLLOWING SEIZURE.

A response from Creforce HQ must've followed. No doubt saying they'd turn Hill 107 into an impregnable fortress. The reply to Crete command read:

PERMISSION TO REINFORCE MÁLEME AIRFIELD EXPRESSLY FORBIDDEN. UNDER NO CIRCUMSTANCES COMPROMISE SOURCE EULT. TAKE NO ACTION OR INACTION THAT COULD REVEAL INTELLIGENCE DERIVED FROM EULT. AGENT IN PLACE MUST NOT BE ENDANGERED.

They knew Máleme was the primary target. They knew, and did nothing. The boys had died for nothing. . . .

Tom was in the field hospital. More morphine. Courses of antitetanus serum against infection, blood counts to measure the secondary shock. The treatment of burns he hadn't realized he had, his body broken and his mind bent.

They knew the crosshairs were on Hill 107, but permission to entrench had been denied. Permission to reinforce, denied. Why? To protect the source. Protect the agent in place, code-named EULT. Sacrifice the squad to protect the source.

The source? The source had betrayed Tom before. The source knew poem codes, knew intelligence—knew sacrifice and denial. The poem itself revealed the source's identity:

Wrapped in war's perfume, the delicate banner.
Leaps and beckons from the fiery front.
Signs billow and plume—on anvil, on hammer.
Of flags like the eyes of a woman.

The poem was Walt Whitman, Earl's favorite. Protect the source? Protect the traitor, the turncoat. Protect Earl.

CHAPTER
TWENTY

TOM'S HEAD JERKED and he woke, driving on the wrong side of the road. He panicked, yanked the wheel to the right. Realized he was in England and shoved the wheel back, almost losing control. He slammed the brakes and the MG squealed, fishtailed. He blinked. The car was stopped in the middle of the road. He was steady. He was swell. His eyelids were heavy as gravestones.

He was driving again, and a panel truck loomed from nowhere and thundered past, hammering wind at him. The MG veered toward a ditch; he gripped the wheel, regained the road. He had to focus. The road was an endless curving ribbon. He hadn't been so near sleep in four days.

His eyes were burning. Focus. Keep the car on the road. Sedgeware Bury. Another left? The endless road, the endless weight of the past.

DAVIES-FRANK CLOSED the case file and stared at the ceiling.

Sondegger was in London for a reason. Every word he spoke, every gesture and expression served a purpose. He had not infiltrated England without reason, had not surrendered to the auxiliary firemen without reason. He had not given them Duckblind's rendezvous information without a hidden, deadly reason. If only they knew a single fact about the man. Who had he been before the war? What was his background, his training, his rank?

The door opened and Highcastle entered, mopping a handkerchief over his brow. He'd been briefing the men for tonight's action, and his briefings were more physical than verbal: explosive bursts of warning, threats, strategy.

"Have you terrified the men into shape?" Davies-Frank asked.

Highcastle grunted. "Just spoke to Farquhar."

Davies-Frank checked his watch. "He's still on?"

"Shift ended twenty minutes ago. Hasn't been relieved."

"Who's late?"

"Melville."

"Could be traffic," Davies-Frank said, unconvinced. "Another twenty minutes and I'll place the call."

Highcastle grunted again, and there was a knock and he said, "Come."

Abrams stepped inside. "Your Yank is in the drive. Motored up easy as you please. Claims he needs a moment of your time."

"He drove himself?" Davies-Frank said.

"Yes, sir," Abrams said. "He's alone."

"Send him in."

"Arrest him," Highcastle said, because Tom had pulled a sneak on the drive to the Rowansea, because he'd returned to

173

Hennessey Gate and compromised security, and because he was long odds in a short game. "The man's a wild card."

"Wild cards win games," Davies-Frank said. "Sondegger told Wall more in ten minutes than he told us in a week."

"More what? Lies?"

"We'll know tonight. The men are prepared?"

"All save one."

Meaning Davies-Frank. He ignored Highcastle.

"I don't like it, Rupert," Highcastle said when Abrams left. "Breach of procedure."

He meant for Davies-Frank to join the action tonight. True enough, but inevitable nevertheless. "*Es spricht nichts dagegen,* Highcastle," he said. "*Not kennt kein Gebot.*"

Highcastle didn't speak two words of German. Didn't speak four of English. Still, his scowl was eloquent.

The door opened and Tom Wall stepped inside. He was wearing a pea green Billsby jacket with square black buttons and a light blue shirt open at the neck. His brown trousers were half-bunched and half-cuffed over a pair of general-issue army boots. His hair was tousled and one side of his mouth was swollen; his face was raw and abraded.

"You should see the other fella," he said. "You get my message?"

"Your message?" Davies-Frank said.

"Nurse Harper left a message for you at the Home Office, at Fire Control. Wherever the hell you claim to be."

"I've no idea what you mean," Davies-Frank said. "Or what you're doing here. I thought you understood security."

"Security is why I'm here." Tom eyed the map on Highcastle's desk. "Two men gave me the business last night."

Highcastle grunted and folded the map closed.

Tom grinned. "The Metropolitan Police say they're muggers."

"You were robbed," Davies-Frank said.

"A couple gorillas named Rugg and Renard wanted to know about"—Tom attempted a Cockney accent—" 'the fookin' toff what paid you a visit at the crack flat.' "

"Two men attacked you?"

"Yeah."

"They mentioned the Rowansea by name?"

"And they knew you were there."

"They asked about me?"

"At length." Tom raised his bandaged hand. "Persuasive lads."

Highcastle spoke with uncharacteristic softness: "You told them what?"

"Fuck if I know. I'm just a fainthearted nancy boy, remember?"

"Names?" Davies-Frank asked. "This location?"

"I didn't mention Hennessey Gate," Tom said. Which didn't matter. The words *Hennessey Gate* weren't on any map. "I told them about you—told them you were Fire Control. You were an old friend, I told them . . . I don't know. Told them about Greece."

"What are you holding back?" Davies-Frank asked.

Tom hesitated a moment, then shook his head. "I trust you with your deceit—you trust me with mine."

"Sit," Highcastle said. "From the beginning."

Davies-Frank took notes. Had the "gorillas" truly asked about him? If so, it was a serious breach. Probably linked to the Rowansea, but who would be surveilling the hospital? How deep did Sondegger's purpose flow?

For all the drama, Tom didn't have much to say. Harriet Wall had directed him to the Waterfall, told him Earl was often there.

He'd had a few drinks and stepped outside into a beating and interrogation. Davies-Frank glanced at Highcastle. Fifth columnists with a line on Sondegger, or at least on Davies-Frank, were extremely dangerous. Still, it was secondary to Duckblind, secondary to All Souls Church.

"I hitched a lift back to the hospital," Tom said. "Got patched up. Then Harri—Mrs. Wall sprung me. Here I am."

"Mrs. Wall?"

"She lent me her car."

"You told her what happened?"

"Don't worry about her. She's cleared—she's SOE."

Another glance at Highcastle. Tom knew about the SOE?

"Intelligence runs in the family," Tom said. "Like beauty and wit."

"So you breached security to—"

"It's fucking breached already—that's what I'm telling you. It's split in two—ask Rugg and Renard. They knocked shit out of me, and I talked." He looked to Highcastle. "You think you could've done better?"

Highcastle didn't respond.

"So I talked," Tom said. "I fed them what bullshit I could. That's why I came, to tell you. Fair warning. More than you gave me. Plus, I have a— There's something else."

There was a long silence. Tom looked at his hands, and Davies-Frank wondered if he'd lost the thought. It was impressive that he'd come this far, shocked and battered, and still had the guts to admit he'd talked.

Tom lifted his head. "I need to speak with the Hun."

"Do you?"

"To double-check the meeting tonight."

"No," Davies-Frank said. "You hope he'll tell you where Earl is. How can he, when he thinks you *are* Earl?"

"He might let something slip."

"Sondegger?" Davies-Frank pinched the bridge of his nose. Tom was volatile, but they might need him again. The closer he got to Sondegger, the better. "Do you remember the man I mentioned, code-named Whiskbroom?"

"In Berlin. The highly placed asset."

"If Duckblind blows the Twenty Committee, they'll kill his family. Think about that, Tom. We have a lead now, thanks to you; maybe we can stop the transmission. Maybe we can save Whiskbroom, save a hundred other agents, save the entire Double-Cross System. But don't think about that; think about Whiskbroom. You take a wrong step, Tom, his children die."

THE SMELL OF BONFIRE still hung in the air. Inside the room behind the white door, the wooden desk was bare and there was no trace of the fire beyond the smell. The paper had burned bright and quick and been easily extinguished. Tom remembered the heat on his face, felt it merging with the ache of the beating and the weight of his fatigue.

He patted his pocket for a cigarette as Davies-Frank settled into the upholstered chair. He had to remember they thought Sondegger believed he was Earl. It was the only way to maintain access, the only way to track his brother. He straddled the chair at Sondegger's table and faced the mattress in the corner. Sondegger lay on his back. His hands were clasped at his stomach and his eyes were closed. His cheeks were rosy. The chain snaking from his ankle to the bolt was heavy and still.

"In ancient Athens," Sondegger said, "ostracism was used to prevent tyranny. They'd hold an election, and the winner—a leading politician—would be exiled for a decade. The Greeks understood politics because they understood drama." His eyes remained closed as he spoke. "In the Inquisition, a minor heresy was punished with a flogging or a fine. More serious crimes were punished with the yellow cross of infamy—social ostracism. The fundamental deprivation, Mr. Wall, is deprivation of human contact. Even a monologue requires an audience. Come closer."

"I'm close enough."

"There are obligations of polite conversation."

"Is that what you have in mind?"

Sondegger's eyes flicked open. "You'd do well to treat me with at least the pretense of courtesy. Please, join me." Sondegger patted the mattress at his hip. "Today, I cannot even offer rum."

Tom stayed in the chair. "Next time, I'll bring kerosene."

"You investigated the contents of the cupboard in the hall?"

"Gum boots and slickers. A couple hatboxes."

"To lie well, Mr. Wall, one must believe. You would do well to study Ibsen. You have an inquiry? A request?"

"Yeah."

Sondegger sat cross-legged against the wall now. His round moon face was untouched by wrinkles. "Sit with me, if you have something to say. I see no reason to include Rupert in our conversation. I will not ask you again."

Tom stood, stuck an unlighted cigarette in his mouth, and tossed his lighter to Davies-Frank. He sat on the mattress next to the Hun. Felt ridiculous, which must be why Sondegger had demanded it.

"Do you remember the third most erotic opera?" Sondegger said. "*Tristan und Isolde.*"

"I remember the fire."

"Whoever beat you applied more enthusiasm than science." The German glanced at Tom's bruised face almost flirtatiously. "Wondrous is the work of the untutored man. No? Two men. Ah. Savvy enough to avoid doing real damage. Who did this?"

"Muggers."

"Of course." He pitched his voice lower. "Did they get what they wanted?"

"They got ten pounds."

He chuckled almost inaudibly, then said, too softly for Davies-Frank to hear, "Your brother left the Rapids."

"Where is he?" Tom asked equally quietly.

"Waiting in the wings."

"Maybe I should beat it out of you."

"You could try." Sondegger unbuttoned his shirt, and there was a flat white bandage on his chest. "Electric current. A modified wireless, in an attempt at dramatic irony."

"But you're too tough to talk."

"I talked at length—yet remained in character."

"What the fuck are you saying? Where is he?"

"I'm not convinced Earl is your first concern. Your hand was hurt in combat? It's not just surgery that pains you, Thomas. Is it love? Memory? Sleepless nights and . . . treachery? Yes, always treachery."

Something unwholesome crept up Tom's spine. "He left the Rapids."

"I don't know where Earl is. But I do know how to find him."

Tom couldn't focus. Exhaustion was like a bad drunk, blackstrap bourbon tasting of burnt sugar and iodine. Audrey Pritchett's voice: *Delerium tremens?* Harriet's smile when she thought he was Earl, and Sondegger's suffocating presence.

"How much?" Tom asked. "What's your price?"

"Give me your hand."

Tom offered his left.

"The other one. You won't find your brother without me. Give me your hand. You won't know, Thomas, unless I help you. You won't sleep." The air was heavy with smoke and the sun-

179

drenched gold of Sondegger's voice. His breath was hot on Tom's ear. "You won't sleep until you find him. You will not heal. You'll never recover what you lost—unless you give me your hand."

Tom gave him his hand.

Sondegger enfolded it between his palms and bent over the bandage, a chubby blond boy inspecting a dead dove, snow white and frozen still. "It must be tender." Sondegger stripped the stiffened gauze from his flesh. "A good man, your surgeon. First-rate, but not brilliant. Shrapnel? A half inch lower . . . Are you familiar, Mr. Wall, with Laurence Sterne?"

"Laurence Sterne," Tom said, from a distant place. "No."

"He wrote *The Life and Opinions of Tristram Shandy, Gentleman*. A seminal work, a comic masterpiece—an extraordinary and self-reflective investigation—a repository for the information you seek."

"What the fuck are you saying?"

Sondegger tightened his grip. "In the spine, Thomas. In the Pugilist Room. In *Tristram Shandy*." Then, more conversationally, though no louder: "Surely you're not unaware of the marvels of microphotography."

Microfilm? In the spine of a book in Earl's room? "Bullshit."

Sondegger released his hand in disgust. "Believe what you like. There *is* microfilm in the book, and within ten days a surprise attack *will* be launched against your country."

"The Fallschirmjägers are gonna drop on D.C.," Tom said. "And you're telling me because you're a true-blue American patriot."

"I'm telling you because it is in my interest to tell you. Remember *Tristram Shandy*, Thomas," Sondegger said. "It, at least, is not spineless." He raised his voice, Davies-Frank now permitted to hear. "Your aversion to your own right hand is biblical, Mr. Wall. 'If thine hand offend thee, cut it off.' Does your hand offend? Are you frightened of what it might do, or sorry of what it has already done? You failed in love, Mr. Wall. You failed at war. You are a man of many parts, none of them whole. You stumble, you fall. You fail . . ."

CHAPTER
TWENTY-ONE

TOM OPENED the car door, reached for the wheel that wasn't there. He slid to the right side, hit the self-starter, and drove. The MG smelled of Harriet. Her scent enveloped him—her scent, Sondegger's voice, Earl's betrayal, his own fatigue. Highcastle had searched him, debriefed him until there was nothing left: What had the Hun said? Was the meet tonight confirmed? Where was Earl?

Tom had lied, and for nothing. For the fantasy of a microfilm in one of Earl's books . . .

The car wouldn't stay on the road. The sun was red and mis-shapen. Wispy clouds stretched over the horizon like gray gauze tinged with blood. He was on a narrow country road. The car jolted over a grassy hillock; he wrenched the wheel. His face ached; his hand was numb. He was on a busy wide street. Car horns blared. He was stopped at a traffic light in a city square. Someone banged on the window. The little MG jerked forward.

He was standing on the sidewalk. He threaded through a line of parked cars toward a stairwell. There was no stairwell. He asked a man for Tudor's Dry Cleaning—the shop near the Waterfall—and found himself standing in an alley with a set of double doors and a half moat of sandbags. Inside, the foyer had high ceilings and cream walls and red-and-gold carpet that faded out of focus.

"Jacket and tie required, sir," the doorman said.

"I haven't—" Tom said. "I'm Earl Wall's brother."

"Yes, sir."

Tom looked toward the narrow stairway. "My jacket's in Earl's room."

"Not upstairs, sir. Perhaps you might speak with Miss Pritchett?"

"With Audrey."

"Yes, sir."

"No. I'll run upstairs, get a jacket and tie. . . ."

The doorman was smooth and deferential. He said "Yes, sir" and "Of course, sir" and led Tom to the door on the left side of the foyer. The wrong door—it didn't lead to the stairs. Led to another door, to what the doorman had called "the small flat."

A languorous redheaded girl answered Tom's knocking. She wore lounging pajamas, which emphasized more than they concealed. "Vee has all the luck," she said, softly sarcastic, and stepped aside.

In the entrance, there was a white coatrack adorned with brightly colored scarves and wraps and a dark fur. There were three pairs of Glastonburys lined neatly at its base. There was a long narrow table and a half-open door, through which Tom saw a tiny, tidy kitchen. Through an archway was a small room papered sky blue. An India-print davenport was angled in the corner, crowded by two low armchairs overflowing with round cushions. There was a delicate tea table and a sturdy piano with no bench, and a jade plant and gewgaws and curios. It was a comfortable, welcoming, haphazard room.

There was a love seat the color of rubies, and Audrey was curled like a cat into its overstuffed embrace. She was dressed like a man, in dark trousers and a white shirt and someone's old school tie. Her hair fell untidily around her face; her little white teeth nibbled on the cap of her pen as she frowned at the pad of paper in her lap.

Her wide mouth moved into a vivid smile as Tom entered, then immediately turned downward in anger. Her eyes darkened, her lips narrowed, and she cocked her head and the anger was gone, replaced by forgiveness. A flicker of impishness chased that across her face . . . and was itself replaced by concern.

Two seconds. A dozen emotions. Tom smiled.

"Your face!" She stood from the chair, knocking her notebook to the floor. "Oh, you poor bunny."

"Told you Earl was the handsome one," he said.

She traced his lip and the bruise on his cheek with her fingertips. "Mum always said, 'Handsome is as handsome does.' Shall I wet some tea? We have a nice thick soup—and the bottled gooseberries I won in a raffle. Have you slept? Here, sit. It was very wrong of you to leave."

He told her to hush. "The doorman told me—"

"First sit," she said. "Then eat. Then speak."

"I'm finished sitting."

"Then I am finished speaking." She put her palm on his chest and backed him into one of the low armchairs.

He sat. He wanted soup. He wanted comfort. He wanted a

woman's care—a pipe and slippers and Audrey to curl into his lap. The soup was parsnip. It was sweet and thick. He ate a bowl, and asked for another. Audrey disappeared into the kitchen and he grabbed her notepad from the floor.

Her handwriting was looped and tidy: "Anticipation of the raids combines resignation and fear with a great part of relief. To be engaged again, rather than merely waiting. To be on the front, in the war, rather than merely . . ." He flipped toward the front of the notebook: ". . . Young people of the 'faster' set scoff at those who seek shelter, perhaps because they enjoy a sense of community in nightclubs and . . ."

The hell was this? It read like an intelligence report.

"Mass Observation," she said, from the archway. "They send a directive—a questionnaire—once a month."

"Who does?"

"Mass Obs, silly, to gauge the public mood. We answer questions about rationing, transport, war work. How people feel about coupons, about air raids and ack-ack flak."

It reminded Tom of the COI's propaganda branch, the Foreign Information Service, and he was struck by a sudden suspicion: The Brits must have a similar arrangement. The girl was too good to be true. Too interested and too generous and too beautiful. "You work for them?"

"You're as bad as Inch! You hear nothing at all. They send a directive, and I answer."

"Mass Obs," he said. "It's based in Whitehall?"

"We're volunteers," she said. "Three thousand civilians, keeping the muck-a-mucks informed. I know it isn't much, but one does what one can."

"Does one entertain the troops? Aid the war effort? Stiffen morale?"

She ignored him. "It's an opinion survey, really. They were

happy to have me because I'm in a unique sort of position. I've access to a public most volunteers haven't."

"You mean pillow talk?"

She slammed the notebook on the piano. "Why, Tommy?"

"Money, I suppose."

"Why be cruel? Have I been anything but kind?"

It was her kindness that frightened him. "The doorman wouldn't let me in the club. I need a jacket and tie." He needed that fucking book, *Tristram Shandy*. He needed to play Sondegger's game until he learned the rules—and found his brother. "I need to go to Earl's room."

She turned to the wall. Her bare feet peeked underneath the cuffs of her trousers. She lifted her arms and gathered her black hair in her white hands. She spun it into a loose bun, a shining black tiara. "His clothes are here. In the flat."

"I thought— You said you weren't one of his girls."

"He was late on rent, so they cleared his room. Michael told me you didn't want to pay, so I—"

"He said I *what*? Who the hell is Michael?"

"The barman."

Who had the shovel chin, saying Earl settled his accounts before the last of the month. "And they cleared Earl's room."

"There's a queue for the upstairs rooms. I took his clothes"—she turned to him, her face expressionless—"as a favor to you."

"You took his books, too? Are they his?"

"This isn't a lending library."

"Audrey, listen—did you take his books?"

"No."

"The trash—the rubbish—they cleared his room? I need— Show me where they threw the trash."

She lifted her chin. "I would rather not."

"Miss Pritchett—Audrey. Please."

She curled into the love seat and flipped through her notepad. She traced her finger down the page, pretending to read. She took the pen in her hand, and a moment later between her wide unsmiling lips.

Tom clawed himself from the chair. As long as he was motionless, he didn't feel it, but the moment he stood, the world spun. The floor slid from under his feet and he grabbed the back of the chair. He had to find the book. He'd check the Pugilist Room, then the garbage. He thanked Audrey. She frowned at the notepad. He let himself out.

HE WAS IN THE FOYER. The doorman approached and Tom brushed him aside. He removed the chain at the stairway and climbed to the second floor. Last room on the right. He worked the key he'd pocketed last time he was here.

Inside, there were no clothes. No hats, no ties. No lipstick, matches, change, pen. No books.

He'd failed, then. A dead end. He wouldn't get another chance at Sondegger. He wouldn't find Earl. He stood with his shoulders slumped, his mind barren. After a long, dark, empty pause, he heard something behind him.

Audrey was in the doorway. She was wearing a semiformal frock, which made her look young and sweet, the same dove gray as Harriet's eyes. She shook her head. She'd been there for some time, watching him lost in the middle of the room.

"Yeah," he said, trying to smile. "I also jitterbug."

She laughed and took his hand, then escorted him downstairs. A crowd of young bloods with bright girls on their arms made a noise coming in from the street. Tom and Audrey waited at the foot of the stairs until the crowd faded into cigarette smoke and expensive perfume.

Audrey asked the doorman what had happened to Earl's books.

"Sold for late payment. You know the policy."

"Sold to whom?"

"A scrap jobber—don't even know the bloke's name—a tattered old man with a tattered old barrow. He stops in when he has cash and inclination. He's often about."

"Swell," Tom said. A tattered old man, in blackout London.

"It doesn't matter, Tommy."

Did Audrey know why he wanted the books? Did she care? Did she think he was crazy?

"We'll find them," she said.

Instead of answering, Tom watched Inch enter the foyer from downstairs, lean elegantly on his crutch.

"Tommy Wall and Venus Lovingsly," Inch said, "arm in arm. How goes the day, my cherubim? Ghastly mouth, by the way, young Tom."

"I accidentally hit him with a cricket bat," Audrey said, rising on tiptoe to kiss Inch's cheek. "Seven times."

"They sold Earl's books," Tom said. "To a jobber."

"What? What? His boots?"

"His books, Inch. To a scrap jobber." Audrey spoke clear and loud. "Earl's books, from his room. They sold them for the December rent."

"Sold his books to a copper, eh? Didn't sell *all* of them, though." Inch tapped his fingers on his crutch. "Earl squirreled away bits of the old library last month. Took 'em home. The moth-eaten tome and the dog-eared incunabulum, the—"

"Wait, stop," Tom said. "He took books home?"

"At least one. Remember most distinctly."

"Like you remembered Hyde Street Misfits."

"Memory keen as an eagle's beak."

"There's no such place," Tom said.

"Rubbish! You think they eat with their claws?"

"Hyde Street Misfits—no such shop. No such street."

"Never said there was. Don't scowl, Thomas. You'll frighten young Vee."

Audrey squeezed Tom's arm so that he wouldn't grab Inch by the throat. "So what *did* you say?" she asked.

"Gent's apparel on Hyde. Remember distinctly. I mean to say, he probably said 'Hyde.' Definitely 'gent's apparel.' Hyde Street might've occurred to me on account of Pongo McCormick. He does a bit about misfit shops. Had the Earl in stitches. Ha! Ha-ha! In stitches! I mean to say! What? Tommy? Where's he off to now?"

DUCKBLIND TINKLED her bicycle bell at a group of soldiers manning an antiaircraft battery. One of them whistled, and she waved and wobbled on her bike. Not yet dusk, but the Luftwaffe would be calling tonight, and the thrill of anticipation tingled on the back of her neck: the *crump-crump thoom* of high explosive, the smoke and dust glowing in a green haze over the city, spotlights veering crazily, the panic and the fear and the courage.

The air-raid sirens would rise and fall over the sound of aeroplanes straining against the sky. She cared little for the bland thrum of the engine—it was nothing to the abrupt shattering release of explosive, the short, sharp shriek of a young man, the groan of a broken building about to collapse.

She found a lonely spot—a row of narrow brick buildings that had been leveled, behind which was a stone wall disinterred by the archaeology of explosion. She brushed the stones carefully and sat, watching the skies.

There were hours and hours before she needed to be in place

for her first action of any importance in England. It would be her third action, if one counted settling Mr. Pentham so that she might have his house, and meeting the silly little man in the shiny waistcoat at the bomb site. She didn't count them. They hadn't been prepared and— Oh! Or fourth, if one counted gathering intelligence on Tom Wall, as Bookbinder had requested in the shiny waistcoat man's message.

Tonight was different. Tonight was cat and mouse . . . and nobody knew which player had been given which role. She slipped off the wall and brushed her skirt clean. She wasn't perfectly happy with her plan for the meeting tonight. Oh, it would do—it was utterly adequate. But how tiresome adequacy was.

The sun finally set, and the raid began. She jingled her bell at a Messerschmitt burping overhead and circled the meeting point. She spiraled closer, and there was a *thoom* behind her ear. She was shoved aside by an invisible hand. She hit the curb and fell off the bicycle, sprawled on the road.

Another *thoom*, and another! She stood and craned her neck skyward. The earth rumbled beneath her. She was still and silent and safe—she was the audience for whom the raid had been orchestrated. First the HE bombs, to rip the roofs from buildings, then the incendiaries, to burn what was exposed. . . .

An idea flickered on *Schmetterling* wings, a far more dramatic plan. The ack-ack shells flew and burst. She smiled and righted her bicycle, then rode toward the wreckage. The fire was red-yellow; it breathed hot billows of hazy smoke and silhouetted the rooftops and chimney pots. It glowed over firemen, over ambulance drivers with stretchers and rescuers digging in the rubble.

She rode and rode, and all the people were so solemn and frightened and driven and brave . . . and *oh!* Green folds of silk looped over a garden wall.

The parachuted bombs were modified sea mines, weighted so

190

the trip wire faced downward, to explode on the surface with maximum damage. But sometimes a parachute caught in a tree or on a chimney, and the trip wire didn't quite touch the ground. It wasn't *at all* what she needed, but curiosity grabbed her. The house beyond the garden wall appeared empty, the owners in the shelter, under the stairs, or gone to the country. She wheeled her bicycle into the garden. The mine was dangling six inches from a wooden bench. It swung in the breeze. Six inches and it would trigger. How *perfectly* exciting!

Of course, it did her no good at all. Far too large to lift, and . . . She almost clapped when she spotted the familiar colors in the rosemary bushes: the field gray body with a stripe of yellow on the wings, crossed by a stripe of red.

The *Splitterbombe* would do divinely well. The rotating vanes had failed on release, and the arming pin hadn't been withdrawn. The little bomblet was perfectly inert, its pin in place.

Back on her bicycle, Duckblind arranged her green leather coat over the lump in the basket, placing the fur collar just so. She led her bicycle toward a crowd of onlookers watching a fire with appalled fascination. They were asked to disperse, so she dispersed. She *always* did what she was asked.

CHAPTER
TWENTY-TWO

THE DRAWING ROOM of Puveen's club was plush and wood-paneled, and so Edwardian that Chilton half-expected to see the glow of oil lamps through the foggy London streets outside.

"I trust," Chilton said, sitting at the hearth, "that your news will be worth the inconvenience. I dislike coming to town even when a night raid is not anticipated."

Puveen swirled his brandy and studied the slow-falling logs. "Trust is fundamental."

"As is brevity." Chilton rose from his chair. "If you'll excuse me."

"Ought to hear me out, old chap." Puveen's florid face was alive with self-satisfaction. "Family business."

"Family business is yesterday's business. I must attend today's."

"Regarding your son-in-law. His name arose in peculiar circumstances."

Chilton had expected, when Peevy invited him for a drink, that he'd be wasting his time—but this was quite promising. "My son-in-law?"

"Peculiar circumstances," Peevy said. "Starts with a body, a man who died last night at a bomb site."

"I heard there were no casualties."

"Three raiders of the Luftwaffe, the greatest airborne force in the history of man." Peevy's eyes brightened. "I've half a mind to—"

"This man," said Chilton. "He was struck by a bomb?"

"Not at all. Died at a bomb site—slipped on the wreckage, or a roof fell on him. Can't tell you how often it happens. However, you suggested I take heed of any unusual investigations or activities that—"

"I know what I suggested."

"Well, more notice was given this man than he warranted. I engaged my own investigation. You've never thought me clever, but I had my office compose a letter. . . ." It took him twenty minutes to explain that the dead man had a pocket diary in his waistcoat, which Peevy had diverted to his office. "Couldn't read the gibberish, myself. Shorthand stenography, you know. Still, the names in proper spelling leapt out. Chap named 'E. Wall' was mentioned. Thought of you."

"That's all you could decipher? Where's the diary now?"

"Returned it. Wouldn't do, being caught sneaking the—"

"This, then, is the sum of your knowledge?"

"Should say not!" Peevy grubbed in his pocket for a piece of paper. "Other chaps were mentioned, 'T. Wall' and 'Sonder.' Doesn't your son-in-law have a brother?"

"What else?"

"There was an acronym. At first glance, I thought it was RAF. Not an *A*, though; it was a *D*. R Defence Force? Rural? Romanian? Haven't a notion. RDF."

The shadowy Rupert Davies-Frank.

Chilton spent half an hour attempting to pry additional information from Peevy. He learned only two things: the dead man's name, William Melville. And his home address.

TOM SWUNG OPEN the gate at the Shepherd Market mews and weighed Harriet's keys in his hand. Inch had said Earl took books home. Was there microfilm in the spine of *Tristram Shandy*, microfilm that would lead him to Earl? No idea. But the Hun knew everything else—why not this? So he'd find the book and prove to Harriet that Earl was a traitor. Show her what her choice had been.

The house was dark. He fumbled at the door, and a woman's voice said, "Back again? Oh, pardon me!" The elderly neighbor was holding a paintbrush, dripping white paint into a bucket. "I didn't mean to startle you, Mr. Wall."

"You know my name."

"Mrs. Wall mentioned you were visiting."

"Why are you— Is there something you want?"

"Oh, I'm struggling along nicely, thank you." She raised a paint bucket. "Touching up the keyhole. I have terrible trouble finding the lock in the blackout."

The door in front of him swung open and Harriet stood before him in dark green trousers with wet patches at the knees and muddy gardening shoes and a blue quilted jacket. He knew without looking that her fingernails were dirty, her hair tangled. He knew without looking what he'd see in her eyes.

He looked anyway.

"Good afternoon, Mrs. Turnbull." Harriet took the key ring from Tom's hand and disappeared back into the house without closing the door.

"Oh!" the neighbor said. "Didn't you know she was home?"

"There's a lot I don't know." He stepped inside. "Harriet?"

"In the kitchen."

He followed her voice, leaned against the table, and watched her watch the kettle. "I'm sorry."

"You're worse than sorry."

"Earl not back yet?"

She didn't answer.

"I spoke to the man. As far as the Brits know, the COI lost him."

"Have you ever known Earl to be lost?"

"Never heard him admit it."

She almost smiled. "How about you, Tom?"

"I've been lost so long, it's starting to feel like found."

"Stay for dinner." She opened a cabinet. "I've fresh spinach, and steak and kidney in the fridge, if they haven't gone off."

Just the two of them at the kitchen table, a candle burning, a bottle of red wine half-empty. "I can't. I can't stop."

"You will stop, Tom, and soon. I was very frightened today—in your state, behind the wheel of a car."

"The car is fine. A few grass stains."

She reached for something on the top shelf. The seat of her trousers stretched tight across her ass. He remembered her moving beneath him, the slap of skin against skin. He looked away. And he sat.

She placed a yellow ceramic mug in front of him. Steam twined upward and the mug was hot on his hands. The tea was sweet and creamy and had an alcoholic bite.

"Someone accidentally spilled milk in this," he said. It was a joke they'd had, about milk in tea. Not *accidentally*, though. That was new. He sipped and listened to the silence. "I need sleep, Harry," he said when he'd finished. "I haven't slept in days."

She led him upstairs. She showed him the bathroom, the guest room. Gave him a towel and a bar of soap. The sheets were turned back on the guest bed. There were cut flowers in a vase. There were ruffled curtains.

"Cozy." He wanted to throw her on the bed, wanted to please and to punish her.

"No," she said. Her heels tapped down the hall, down the stairs.

Swell. At least he could still chase a woman off in one word or less. He removed his shoes and searched the upstairs. Many books. No *Tristram Shandy*. No microfilm. In her bedroom, he sat on the bed. On *their* bed. He rummaged in the bureau. The bottom drawer held a lavender bag and dressing gowns, which Harriet called "undressing robes." The memory stopped him for a moment; then he moved the gowns aside.

Beneath them were two guns, four boxes of ammunition. They were illegal in London, but that was Earl. There was a Colt .25 ACP auto with a custom ivory grip and a Webley .455 revolver. Tom figured Earl had bought the .25 for Harriet, then overcompensated with the .455 for himself—heavier, more serious than Harriet's toy, a pound and a half loaded, while the .25 would be lost in the palm of his hand.

Tom closed the drawer and finished searching the upstairs. Nothing. Back in the guest bedroom, he grabbed his shoes and sat in darkness. It could've been ten minutes or two hours before Harriet's heels sounded on the stairs. Her bedroom door opened and closed. Time passed.

Tom crept downstairs. Found the flashlight and searched.

No *Tristram Shandy*. No comedic masterpiece, no fucking repository for the information he needed. The window he'd smashed was covered with a tacked-up board behind the curtain.

Nothing else was out of place. Frustration shaded into anger and faded. He couldn't—

"Tommy?" She was in the front hall, looking in.

"Harriet. I couldn't sleep."

"You never could tell a proper lie."

"Not to you."

"Air raid purple has been called," she said. "I looked in to wake you."

He stepped forward, and was inches from her. He was going to kiss her.

"We're to have an air raid," she said. "At any moment."

He felt her breath on his face. He was going to kiss her.

She pressed a finger to his lips. She said, "No, Tommy," and the siren sounded.

"Goddamn," he said.

"Come, I've a shelter beneath the stairs."

"No Anderson?"

"And dig up what little garden I have?"

He smiled, and a bomb exploded outside.

There was a *whump-whoom* and a shriek of brick and timber, the gliders swooping silently from the sky—Hill 107 at Máleme, his boys firing staccato bursts through clouds of cordite, and there was blood on his face and in his mouth, the taste of blood in his mouth.

"Tommy," she said, and he slammed the front door behind him.

DUCKBLIND TROTTED FAST, her eyes wide with manufactured fright—hunched over the bicycle's handlebars, a timid girl rushing home to the safety of mother.

197

She glanced at the lump under her bunched coat. The adjustments had been made. She was stupid, mechanically—she could barely use a hair grip!—but she'd learned what they'd taught her. She still needed a trigger, though, and couldn't think how to arrange one. Perhaps the *Splitterbombe* wouldn't work. Of course, she could follow Bookbinder's instructions in any number of other ways, but it would be such a pity to waste the windfall!

She lowered her head as a fire truck sped past. The sky was moonlit behind a shroud of smoke. She walked without swinging her hips, frumpy and overwrought. Her heels went *clip-clip-clip*. Nothing to see here.

On Bookbinder's instruction, she'd kept busy. Meeting the man with the shiny waistcoat, locating Tommy Wall, and arranging tonight. Plus, she and Bookbinder had been given three names to investigate—three trusted agents of the untrustworthy Abwehr. Well, Bookbinder had been given three names. She had only one: a man who went by "Digby" and had been told to infiltrate the BBC. She'd pinched a schoolgirl uniform and adopted a sullen sulk, and nobody at the BBC had raised the slightest eyebrow at her petulant questions. She'd located Digby without difficulty.

She'd observe him properly beginning tomorrow. He *seemed* at liberty, so either he hadn't turned or had rotated fully. Could he be a traitor to the Abwehr? She'd suck her bottom lip and inquire. It wouldn't be hard. He was a man, and men were—

"Give over!" A child's voice sounded at her elbow—a darling boy, no older than twelve, got up as a proper ragamuffin. "It's mine. Give *over*."

"I shan't!" a girl said, slightly younger but equally darling. Missing two of her front teeth, fiercely clutching an orange. "You stop or I'll—" She fell silent at the jingle of Duckblind's bicycle bell.

"Look here, you plaguey things!" Duckblind said. "You ought know better than being out in this weather. Where do you live, then?"

They examined their shoes, scuffed and black, with colorless socks bunched around their ankles. The boy mumbled something inaudible; the girl peeked up from behind an uneven fringe. A breeze wafted past, carrying the fragrance of incendiary fire and airborne brick dust. Two planes grumbled overhead, solid specks of light glimpsed through the shifting veil of haze.

"German aeroplanes," Duckblind said. "This is no place to be playing."

"Square-headed Jerries," the boy said. "Couldn't hit a barn from inside."

"Come along." She attempted a governess's sternness. "There's a shelter two blocks back."

"Don't like the Underground," the boy said.

"Well, if the Tube isn't good enough for the likes of you!" Duckblind said. "Where's your Mum, then?"

The children muttered and shifted.

Poor precious poppets. "Well, the Tube *is* rather stinky." The Tube also had mosquitoes and lice and masses of sweaty *Untermenchen*. Duckblind shuddered. "We certainly can't subject you to that! Come along. The wardens will sort you—"

The girl shook her head. "Don't want to."

"The wardens stinky, too?" Duckblind asked. "You make me worry that even *I* have gone off."

"Not you, miss," the boy said. "You smell nice."

"Well, from the mouths of babes!" She held her hand out to the girl. "We'll find a warm little cranny, safe and snug."

"Not a *surfie*," the girl said, holding her hand tight. "George fancies the surfies."

"What's a surfie, then?" Duckblind asked.

"*You* know," the girl said. "Made of brick."

"Oh! A surface shelter." Brick constructions the size of a bus, with a door at each end shielded by a blast wall and a concrete slab for a ceiling, apparently designed to collapse at the slightest impact.

"At his school," the girl said. "For lunchtime, they line up boys on one side, girls the other. They pass through the surfie and snog their way down the line."

Duckblind gave the girl's hand a squeeze. "Don't worry, love. I know a shelter that smells like roses, and no snogging allowed."

"NO, THEY'RE SURE it's Melville," Davies-Frank said. "They're calling it a raid casualty."

"Weren't a dozen raiders last night." Highcastle was in the driver's seat of the parked car, chewing on an unlighted cigar. "Not half a dozen."

"He had a concussion injury to the head, compression to the throat. . . ."

"Finger marks?"

"No finger marks. No defensive wounds, no burns, his clothing undamaged. Fell on a bit of piping perhaps. He wasn't bombed." Explosions sounded faintly through the lowered window—tonight there were far more than a dozen raiders. "Unlike us."

Highcastle grunted, and Davies-Frank tapped the white umbrella in his lap. Poor timid Mr. Melville. Wandered into a bomb site and caught his toe in rubble. It wasn't uncommon—bomb sites were dangerous. Like the Queen's Hall, at which the secondary meet with Duckblind had been set. Davies-Frank had peered inside. Within the buckling walls, a cross-section was visible—there the third floor, there the second, there the dank basement glowered through a hole. And there, on the ground floor, squatted an EWS static water tank. Twenty thousand gallons for the fire brigades. Children climbed in for a swim and drowned; they played in the rubble between crumbling walls and sinkhole cellars. They hoarded jumble, and prized nothing more highly than UXB, unexploded bombs. Bomb sites were dangerous, but Mr. Melville was no child. Caught his toe in rubble, hit by a falling wall . . . but why had he been there?

"Scavenging?" Highcastle said, echoing Davies-Frank's thoughts. "Not our Mr. Melville."

"Rescuing a stray dog."

Highcastle grunted. "It wasn't an accident."

"No. I'll have the body sent to Dr. Wheeler for postmortem. Illingworth will investigate. There's nothing more to do."

"There's always more."

Highcastle scowled at the near-deserted street and Davies-Frank followed his gaze. A man in his middle years escorted his elderly father over the road. A gentleman in a lounge suit and a mud-colored trilby strode past. A young mother guided her children along the pavement.

"Five to nine," Highcastle said, consulting his watch.

"Shall I step outside?" Davies-Frank was suddenly nervous, though all he needed was to allow Duckblind to make contact, and to signal the men.

"Patience," Highcastle said. "Soon."

CHAPTER
TWENTY-THREE

THE AIR-RAID SIRENS faded for a moment, and hoofbeats sounded behind Tom, echoing down the narrow street. The sky was lighted by the moon and the flush of a hundred fires. It was beautiful. It had been beautiful on Crete—the ocean, the hills, the blue sky above the dying boy clawing in the blood-damp dirt with the stump of his arm.

Hoofbeats. A dappled horse trotted across an empty intersection, an elegant animal, glossy and well muscled. A woman rode astride. She passed out of view, leaving nothing behind but the clip-clop of hooves.

The sirens drowned out the echoes, and Tom saw a Beaufighter whining above. A dark speck against the moon, it arced in a graceful half circle, closed with one of the German raiders, and was lost to Tom as a cloud of smoke drifted overhead.

Tom followed the smoke, and across the city the blacked-out

streets were wreathed in flames as the Luftwaffe loosed their bombs. "The sparks," a bald man told Tom, his face raised to the sky. "Feel like snowflakes on your skin."

A furnace blast of heat exploded from the paint factory across the street as something flammable ignited. Tom's face was dripping sweat; his shirt was soaked. The roiling flames consumed the building, and a tin of paint burst and rocketed skyward in a Fourth of July display.

"I was working late when the raid came," the bald man said. "I ran downstairs, and old Sandy's sitting in his chair, calm as you please. I clap a hand on his shoulder—" Three Roman candles burst from the factory. "One side of his face hadn't a hair out of place. The other side," the bald man said, "was charred black."

A flock of pigeons circled above, drawn to the flame or the heat. Tom watched them and felt snowflakes brush his face.

Fire trucks arrived. There were jets of flame and jets of water. An AFB screamed that there were engineers trapped in the pit under the buses. He shouted, "Drive the buses out! Get the bloody buses!"

The bald man said, "Shall we?"

A spray of water hammered them, and they were behind the wheels of neighboring buses. The noise was an unbearable clangor, the heat buckling metal and burning Tom's eyes. They drove to the street and Tom lost the bald man. He collapsed on the curb and watched the slicks of clear varnish rippling with blue flame.

Hours later, Tom stood beneath a lamppost that had wilted from the heat, bowed low to the ground. On the corner, a heap of rubble swarmed with rescue and ambulance workers. Filmy wafts of smoke reeked of fish oil, and a woman's high-pitched keen rose and fell above the din.

A soot-covered woman—a FANY, a WAFS—told Tom they'd been digging for hours. The keening woman was at the bottom of a ten-foot shaft. They'd uncovered her head, but her body was trapped. There'd been a man, earlier, who'd fallen silent.

"She'd have, too," the WAFS woman said, "if not for her dog."

"Fallen silent?"

"Scrappy little mite scratched for her when the first lot fell," she said. "He was standing over her when the roof came down. Saved her life, didn't he?"

Tom said, "It's hell being man's best friend," and a wall collapsed and the woman's keening stopped.

The rescue workers paused a moment, then began again.

TEN O'CLOCK. Davies-Frank ran his fingers through his hair, brushed his cuff clean of a speck of ash, and almost smiled. He was being ridiculous. No reason to become overwrought, especially about an imaginary ash on gray cheviot after sundown. He'd be home with Joan and the twins in two hours. He'd creep into the girls' room, watch their sweet faces closed with sleep, and feel his heart expand in his chest.

He checked his watch. Four minutes after the hour. He tapped the tip of the umbrella against the side of his shoe. The street itself was quiet, though the bombers and night fighters battled in the skies above the other end of the city.

Ten-oh-eight. An elderly man staggered from a side street. Why was a man that age abroad on a raid night? Innocent perhaps. Or Duckblind. Davies-Frank stayed relaxed, and the elderly man passed, trailing a whiff of liquor.

Davies-Frank casually swung the umbrella in a half circle, propped it against his left shoulder—silently telling Highcastle's men to stop the man for questioning.

It was thirteen minutes after ten. The moon was bright, and the night busy with muffled explosions, the distant rattle of anti-aircraft batteries. The wind rose, and storefront signs swayed and creaked on their chains.

"Here, mister!" Something tugged his sleeve.

"Good God!" Davies-Frank almost hit the grubby little girl with a reflexive jab of his umbrella. "You'll be the death of me, a fright like that. Have you lost your mum?"

"I've a message." She glanced at the umbrella, ghostly white in the gloom. "For you."

He swung the umbrella jauntily across his right shoulder. "A message? Well, now—is it a singing telegram?"

She looked dubious. "No."

"Pity, that. I've always fancied a singing telegram. Do you know what those are?"

"Message is you should come along and follow me."

"The gentleman is not born," he said, "who could refuse such a charming invitation as that."

She headed away from Queen's Hall, and he saw no option but to follow. Duckblind was too important. The Twenty Committee was too important. Still, what the devil was he meant to do with this child? He walked slowly, giving Highcastle time to react. Not cricket, Duckblind using a child as a contact. . . .

But his nervousness was suddenly gone. His fear had evanesced and the night air warmed him. Any positive activity—even this—was an antidote to the endless Sisyphean strategizing. He'd been too long chained to a desk, to the painstaking ground-work. It was simple: The XX Committee trumped all other considerations. What was there to fear? Sondegger might outwit him, but he could never undermine him. Tomorrow, he'd stride down the hall at Hennessey Gate and throw open the white door without fear. Look into Sondegger's eyes and reveal nothing but contempt, contempt and the satisfaction of tonight's job well done.

"What sort of chap gave you the message?" he asked the girl. "Skinny or fat? Taller than I?"

She shook her head.

"Shorter than you?" he asked, attempting to charm her.

"I'm not s'posed to say."

"Will you tell me for half a crown?"

They turned onto a narrow street and she scratched her nose, considering the offer. "Must I share with George?"

"George is the skinny bloke with the message?"

"He's my brother. He thinks he's clever."

"Half a crown for you, half a crown for George."

"*She* says she'll give a crown each."

So it was a woman. "Has she brown hair? Blond? Is she—"

"She says the Tube smells awfully. She's taking us to tea tomorrow—with cake and oranges. There's George."

She lifted a chubby hand. Over the road, next to a newsstand, a boy straddled the front wheel of a bicycle. He jingled the bell as they approached.

"What ho, George," Davies-Frank said. "I hear you've a message for me."

"Yes, sir." The boy patted a fur coat in the bicycle basket. "It's right under—"

TOM READ A NOTICE in a shop window—NO CHOCOLATE, NO SACCHARINE—and saw flames gleaming over rooftops, and a thousand-pounder burst down the street. He dropped onto his face and groped for his rifle as an avalanche of glass and plaster swept over him.

"Reggie?" A woman in a white gown staggered past, cupping her elbow in her hand. "Reggie?"

"Get down!" he shouted. "Get goddamn down!"

Behind the woman, the churning air parted like a curtain, revealing a lanky man with sandy hair standing in the street, hip cocked. No rifle, no helmet . . . A shaft of firelight flicked over his face.

Earl.

Tom scrabbled for his Colt. Earl was here, twenty yards away. He grabbed a length of metal, a faucet with a bit of copper pipe attached. It was wet and cold and heavy enough for a cudgel. He angled over the rubble but couldn't see ten yards through the murk. Earl was gone. . . . No, there—between the fire pump and the wall. Behind the crowd of shouting men in their steel helmets.

Tom ran low over fire hoses squirming like fat worms through the debris. Earl slipped away. Tom stalked past an old man weeping outside a burning draper's shop. Caught glimpses of his brother, too far ahead—a blurred figure moving with Earl's unmistakable grace. He passed a teenage lad fashioning a splint from bits of shattered trellis, passed two dead cats on an overturned wardrobe.

Earl slipped wraithlike into the shadows and was gone.

Tom shouted. "Earl! It's me!" No answer but the roar of bombs and the roar of fire. "It's Tom. Your brother."

There was a brick wall where Earl had vanished. He was nowhere. Tom wiped his face. *It's Tom, your brother.* Remember the summer in Maine, teaching me how to stick a worm on a hook? Remember ruffling my hair, telling me slow and steady wins the race? Remember the jazz clubs, the dance halls, the cramped, smoky bars?

He dropped the copper pipe. Earl was gone.

He trudged through the darkness, toward the Waterfall.

There was nowhere else to go. He almost felt his rifle webbing biting into his shoulder, almost smelled the Cretan night, almost saw the parachutes blooming like lesions overhead. Almost heard a tune he knew, in a sudden break in the noise, a mumbled hymn. It was the shambling peddler with the tattered cart and the wild beard and yellow teeth—the jobber. The man was squatting behind his cart, eating a tin of sardines, his woolen mittens unraveled, revealing grimy fingertips.

"Fancy a chew, guv?" the man asked, offering the tin.

"You buy books. You're a scrap jobber."

"Chapman's what I am." The man guffawed, his beard rippling like an animal's pelt. "Rags and bones and the old goat's teeth."

"You buy from the Waterfall? Near Tudor's?"

"Part of my itinerary. Linens past mending and wore-out bits to sew into patchwork."

"And books."

The man shook his head. "No books from them."

"You bought a stack of books"—Tom lifted the canvas half-covering the cart—"yesterday. At the Waterfall."

"Never did, guv."

Groping under the canvas, Tom found brass fittings, bottles of tonic, a musty leather bag stuffed with fabric scraps. . . .

"Those'll fetch me a few," the man said, pointing to three typewriters. "Taylor's on Chancery pays honest."

Tom dug beneath a bag of seed, a thick bundle of dowels tied with twine—and found a stack of books. There was a math primer with a water-stained cover, and Willa Cather's *The Professor's House*, but nothing of Earl's.

"Got any lighters?" Tom asked.

The man wiped his greasy mittens on his pants. "That I do.

Know a bloke works munitions—turns out petrol lighters when he has the time. Three and six."

"How about cigarettes?"

The man rummaged in his pockets, emerged with a handful of half-smoked butts. "Help yerself."

Tom didn't. "Got a torch? I could use—"

He saw a flash of familiar color in the cart, under a cracked ceramic lamp: the spine of a book. It was the poetry of Robert Burns, same color as the Waterfall peach trap. Tom pushed the lamp aside and found six more books, poetry and literature and philosophy. None of them was *Tristram Shandy*.

Tom turned on the shambling man, stepped close.

"Ain't mine!" The man raised his mittens in fright. "Ain't mine. Didn't buy that lot—took 'em on assign. I'll cart 'em round, ask if the bookmen have a need. Bring 'em to Cubby's and—"

"How many?"

"Them there."

"You sold the rest?"

"On assign, guv. To Cubby." The man put a nervous hand on the six books remaining. "Not these. It was on assign. You ask Cubby, he'll tell you."

Ask Cubby. Walk back through the damaged dark city, the fire and the fear, and find Cubby.

AN HOUR LATER, Tom flicked the petrol lighter, put his face to the glass of the small bookshop. Cumberson and Sons Booksellers. The jobber said Cubby had stacked Earl's books on the desk, but Tom couldn't see the desk.

He tapped at the door. Nobody came, so he tossed a rock through the window, then wrapped his jacket around his forearm and cleared the glass. He'd heard looting was a problem during the blackout. It wasn't a problem for him. He stepped inside and found Earl's books, but no *Tristram Shandy*. He crumpled a sheet of paper into an ashtray and set it on fire for light. He found a letter opener in the top drawer and slit the spines of Earl's books. There was room for a microphotograph. There was room for a fucking loaf of bread. There was room for all his delusions, and all his failures, too.

What the hell was he doing?

There was no Earl, no book. Should he try to find the jobber again? If he hadn't sold it, and he didn't have it, then what? Harriet had it. Or Earl had hidden it. Or Sondegger was pulling an invisible string, and Tom was dancing to the rhythm of his narcotic voice.

TOM COULDN'T FIND the jobber. He found the back stairway to the Waterfall instead. Climbed to the third floor—the Pugilist Room. Fumbled in the frigid dark until he fit the key to the lock. It was warmer inside. He flicked the light and sat in the chair.

There was a folded note on the table: "Dear Tommy, the room is yours for another month. Please see me—after you sleep! I have something for you. Dream sweet, A. Pritchett."

The note smelled of her perfume. Clean white flowers, plain and pure.

He washed his face in the bathroom. His clothes were mud-splattered and flecked with ash and splinters. There was a slash on his jacket, from the window at Cubby's. He bathed and picked through Earl's clothes in the closet. The best looked like a zoot suit on him, all he needed was a knee-length key chain and a big bow tie. And a strong drink.

Downstairs, he stepped onto the parquet floor and wished he

had a cigarette. A band was playing and a dozen couples were scuffing the dance floor. He sat at the bar, nursed a double scotch, and watched the dancers. Audrey wasn't among them. Inch wasn't at his table. He flagged a cigarette girl and bought a pack of Gold-flake on Earl's account. He asked if there'd be a tableau tonight, but the girl said he was hours too late.

He didn't ask the time. He didn't want to know.

The band took a break and a comedian had a set. One more drink and he'd try Audrey's flat, see what she had for him. Maybe news of Earl. What he wanted was to dance. He used to know how to swing.

Someone tapped his shoulder. He turned, and Highcastle spun him violently off the bar stool.

"Jesus!" Tom tried to twist away, but Highcastle clamped his arm at the small of his back. Tom slammed down hard with his heel and Highcastle made a noise and stepped away. Tom hit him in the stomach and moved closer to hit him again, but one of Highcastle's soldiers appeared between them.

It was Ginger—the granite-hewn redhead who'd driven Tom from the embassy to the Rowansea. He hadn't gotten any smaller. "Not here, mate," he said.

Another soldier jerked Tom's arm behind him before he could answer, then frog-marched him up the stairs.

"I know how to walk," Tom said, struggling free. "You fuck."

Highcastle shoved him across the foyer. "Rupert's dead."

CHAPTER
TWENTY-FOUR

TOM AND THE GUARDS waited in the car as Highcastle trudged up the front steps of Davies-Frank's town house. They waited as he stood motionless at the closed door, as he lifted his hand to the bell. Tom recognized the set of his shoulders: *The adjunct general desires to express his deep regret that your son was killed in action. . . .*

After a cold hour, Highcastle returned to the car and they drove toward Hennessey Gate. Halfway there, Highcastle said, "His daughters—Rupert's daughters—they heard my voice. They thought I was their father. They come downstairs in their pajamas, shoving and pushing. Little hooligans. They knew it was past bedtime; they wanted a good-night hug." He stared silently at the dark countryside. "What was left of her husband? Joan wanted to know. Was there enough to bury? A pair of shoes with feet still in them. Bits of two dead children and a gold cuff link.

212

All that remains of Rupert Davies-Frank, God have mercy on my soul."

It was dawn. Tom was back at Hennessey Gate. Back at the beginning, talking to Sondegger one last time. Highcastle wanted Duckblind's location, or an excuse to hang the Hun. He'd rather have the latter, he said—and he'd get it if Sondegger didn't produce Duckblind.

Upstairs, in the room at the end of the hall, Sondegger sat erect at his desk. Blood from split lips tinted his teeth red. "Have you heard of the Japanese ambassador general, Oshima Hiroshi?" he asked Tom, his voice silken. "He's a boon companion of Foreign Minister von Ribbentrop, a right-thinking man. Right-thinking, Mr. Wall—a pun for your benefit."

"Not in a laughing mood, Hans," Tom said. "Tell me about Duckblind."

Tom dragged an upholstered chair next to Sondegger's bolted wooden seat. There was pressure in his ears, the rushing of water. He was tired; his mind was slipping gears. He watched Highcastle pace at the far end of the room, his knuckles raw and his yellow eyes worse.

Sondegger ran his tongue over bloody lips. "Oshima is a member of the Führer's inner circle, a linchpin of German-Japanese relations. He is the man who—"

"I need a description and a location. You don't give Highcastle a reason to keep you alive, he'll be a very happy man."

"Oshima informed Tokyo of the invasion of Russia weeks before it occurred. He—"

"You have daughters," Tom said. "There was a little girl, ten years old—Duckblind killed her."

"I was asked for Duckblind's location. I gave it."

"That girl was somebody's daughter. Your wireless man is killing children."

"I acted in good faith." Sondegger glanced at Highcastle. "Am I to blame that your tradecraft is inadequate?"

Highcastle lowered his head and stepped forward. Tom raised his hand—they'd decided he'd speak to the Hun before other steps were taken.

"Duckblind was warned," Tom said. "He knew they were coming."

"Duckblind is a professional." Sondegger took the pencil from behind his ear and stuck it in his mouth like a cigarette. "Give me your hand."

"You don't feel like talking, don't talk. Highcastle could use some good news."

"Oh, I'll talk. There are facts I'm willing to share. But I never rush my lines. Your hand, please."

"My hand's the same it was yesterday."

"It is vulnerable, Mr. Wall, as am I. I feel a certain empathy. You sustained the injury how many months ago? Four?"

"Six."

"It was infected? If you don't change the strapping soon, it'll happen again. Lend me your hand, Mr. Wall."

Tom looked across the room. Highcastle was gripping the back of a chair. He needed that information—needed Duckblind stopped and Sondegger executed and the Twenty saved. And the only road to Duckblind was through Sondegger.

"Swell." Tom placed his hand on the table.

Sondegger picked at the bandage with the blunt end of his pencil. "Duckblind is twenty years old," he said, too low for Highcastle to hear. "Did you locate the book?"

"They sold it to a jobber."

"Duckblind has blond hair—unless it's dyed. Is it lost to you?"

"I'll find it."

"Duckblind has green eyes, a scar behind the left knee,

crescent-shaped, two inches in length." Sondegger spun the pencil in circles, the bandage coiling round it. "The microphotograph contains proof of the surprise attack against your country—partial proof—sufficient to stop it, if you act in time. You can enlarge the photograph?"

"Yeah."

"Of course—with the help of your brother's wife."

Tom glanced at Highcastle to be sure he couldn't overhear. "Yeah."

"Duckblind spent years in London. There are those in the chain of command who believe a more appropriate trade name would be 'Butterfly.' " Sondegger inspected Tom's hand. "The surprise attack will claim thousands of American lives. What would you do to prevent it?"

"If you're against it, I'm all for."

"You led men in battle. You lost men. Five men? Ten? Imagine a thousand. Five thousand of your comrades dead, and you'd do nothing?"

"Not on your word."

"Have I misled you? Did Earl have a room at the Rapids? Was Duckblind at the rendezvous? Is there a microphotograph in *Tristram Shandy*'s spine? Yes, yes, and yes. Imagine a group of loyal citizens in my homeland, Thomas. We are few, but well placed; we can do nothing officially. Still, we wish to prevent this surprise Japanese attack—without exposing the source of the warning."

"Swell bunch of Nazis."

Sondegger's swollen lips moved into a smile. "We became aware of the attack plan only last month. Our attempt to stop it combines improvisation and desperation—based upon my chance acquaintance with your brother." He twirled the pencil between his fingers. "That, and what few personal resources I myself possess."

"You met my brother where?"

"You can prevent this murderous ambush. Only you can."

"Duckblind," Tom said. "Give me a name. Give me a—"

"Find the book, Thomas. Get the information to your people. If your government knows of the attack, it will be stopped. Do you understand? If you show them what is planned, it will not happen."

"Sure. I'll give them a jingle."

"The proof, Thomas"—Sondegger's eyes twinkled—"is well within your grasp."

"Unlike any information about Duckb—"

Sondegger stabbed the shiny lead of his pencil hard into the seam of Tom's palm.

SONDEGGER HAD TWO primary motivations. His first was to deny the United States a pretext to enter the conflict, as the Republican Senate would not allow Roosevelt to join the war without one. The American people had no desire to sacrifice their boys for the British, the Jews, and the Communists. If they were not forced to fight, they would not.

His second goal—which some in the SD believed was his sole purpose—was to determine if the Abwehr network had been compromised. It almost certainly had. All he required was a modicum of evidence, which would easily be secured, once he escaped this dreary theater.

He missed performing. He missed intoning, missed the timbre of his voice reciting ancient lines: *Maledicant illum sacrarum virginum chori, quae mundi vana causa honoris Christi respuenda contempserunt.* May the holy choir of the holy virgins, who for the honor of Christ have despised the things of the world, damn him.

Poor damned Thomas Wall, with his bluster and his sad eyes.

Sondegger had grown fond of him. He burned so brightly. He howled when the pencil dug into his hand.

Maledictus sit in capillis, maledictus sit in cerebro. May he be cursed in his hair, cursed in his brain, in his *vertice*, in his temples, *in dentibus, in guttere*, in his cheeks and jawbones, in *pedibus et in unguibus*.

May he be cursed in his hands.

An upwelling of dark blood coated Tom's palm, and Highcastle vaulted forward, fast for a stout man, and struck Sondegger a glancing blow. Sondegger fell, grasped Highcastle around the waist, and was kneed in the chin. His head snapped back and he dropped to the floor.

The door flung open. The warder rushed inside and grappled with Tom. Might as well grapple a feral cat. Poor Thomas, a bit player forged by heat and the clang of metal upon metal into something intriguing.

Thomas swung his right hand, and an arc of black blood hung in the air. Highcastle swept a meaty forearm across the back of Tom's head, and the warder tackled him and clamped handcuffs on his wrists.

Sondegger lay on the floor, clutching his stomach. He slid the metal nubbin he'd snapped from Highcastle's spectacles into his nostril. Was Tom still the best route to the U.S. embassy? Yes, he was indispensable. Soon Sondegger would join him on the stage of London. He'd hover in the wings, offer what prompting was necessary.

THE LIFT WAS DISABLED, so Chilton walked the four flights down from the suite in his London club—without the slightest loss of wind. He did not suffer fools and he did not suffer weakness, not in others, not in himself.

"Is a raid still anticipated?" he asked the head porter upon reaching the front door.

"There is some uncertainty in that regard, m'lord," the porter said. "Gas masks and tin hats are available, if your lordship will be dining out."

"I will not be going far, nor for long."

The porter was a good man, of the old school, deferential without being obsequious. The old school was best: One was obedient to one's God, loyal to one's class, the master of one's family, and pleased with 4 percent for one's money.

He stepped into the early evening and headed toward Waterloo Place, a handsome block of insurance companies and banks. They would remain, long after the troubles of the day were a memory. As to the rest, he was confident of his God, concerned for his class and his family. Harriet was the image of Lady Chilton—though with Chilton's eyes, and an alien temperament. Earl, however, was no blood relation. His brother, Tom, was more distant still. Tom was merely leverage. Earl could not be approached directly, as one struck at weakness, not strength.

At Leicester Square, Chilton paused to inspect the statue of Shakespeare. Once, the square had been called "the pouting place of princes"; now it was merely another drab wartime garden, a place to linger while Rugg and Renard determined if he'd been followed. They materialized, as if condensed from the darkening gloom, at the corner of Gerrard Street. They fell into step with him and walked quite openly down Wardour Street, pausing at an unlighted display of film posters.

"Now here's *Fantasia*, sir," Renard said, pointing. "With the wizard, the apprentice. It's . . . it's—the word's on the edge of my teeth. . . ."

"Apropos," Rugg said. The big man's eyes were narrow and

porcine, absent any gleam of intelligence. Chilton would have to watch Rugg carefully.

"Apropos!" Renard said. "Knows his words, Rugg does. Now, tell his lordship your favorite picture—*Dr. Jekyll and Mr. Hyde*, with Freddie March."

"You have something to report?" Chilton asked.

"That we do, sir. Late last night—or early this morning—we were at the Waterfall, your other errand set aside for later still. Our Mr. Wall, it seems, was enjoying the nightlife too well." Renard grinned toothily. "He was booted from the Waterfall."

"Scruff of his bleedin' collar," Rugg said.

"He was forcibly ejected from the Waterfall?" Chilton asked. He was primarily concerned with the "other errand," but he'd not wheedle for the information. He'd demand it in good time.

"Blokes who did the booting were Yard," Renard said. "Special Branch, or something in that line. Not ejecting him, either. They were inviting him elsewhere."

"Inviting him." Another meeting with Davies-Frank? "Where?"

"Haven't a hunch. They grabbed him and were gone."

"Very well. Return to your observation of the nightclub. Have you sufficient funds?" He arranged the financial details. "Do not mislay Wall again. A message at the Lion will find you?"

Renard said it would. "But sir? We fixed that other errand, too."

Excellent. "You managed Mr. Melville's flat?"

"The lock on his door was easy as kiss my hand." Renard's sharp face quivered around his protruding teeth.

"You found something?"

Rugg thrust a meaty fist forward, offering a crumbled wad of paper. Chilton smoothed the paper between his hands, but he couldn't read the writing in the evening light. "Stenography?"

"Tiny letters is all."

"You found nothing else?"

"Just that one scrap. It's what you might call . . . What's the word? Cryptic. 'Herr Sonder contra Abwehr,' it says. Rugg reckons this German bloke, Sonder, he's working against Jerry—"

"Fookin' bleeder."

"Bleedin' bleeder," Renard agreed complacently. "This Herr Sonder has something for Earl, a parcel, Rugg says. Study on it yourself. With Earl gone, Tom Wall's the chap. S'pose that's no surprise to you."

IT WAS FOUR FLIGHTS up to his suite. Chilton wasn't breathing heavily, but his heart pounded in his chest. He locked the door, lay the paper on the escritoire, pulled the chain on the hooded lamp, and bowed over the wrinkled sheet.

Rugg and Renard hadn't done badly deciphering Melville's confusion of personal notes. Chilton did better. He spoke the words aloud as he deciphered the dead man's scrawl: "Defector, Herr Sonder, sequestered at farm . . ." He turned the paper to catch the light. "Intelligence? In Herr Sonder's possession. Wary of British, of RDF. Wrong element might suppress intel."

Chilton rubbed the back of his neck. His hand was shaking— not from exhaustion, but excitement. One loose thread would enable him to unravel the Churchillian tapestry of lies and deceit. The scrawl continued: "Intel released to an agent of the U.S. Identify. E Wall unavailable. . . .

There was a knock at the door.

"I'm not to be bothered," Chilton called without raising his head from the paper.

He read the rest silently, then stared unseeing at the paper. Thomas Wall was to be contacted in his brother's stead. This

Sonder had information that would undermine the Abwehr, destroy the network. There was some gibberish about drawing a line in the zero of 309. . . . Chilton lifted the brass paper knife and turned it over in his hands. A German agent named Sonder had defected with information, a parcel, which could be used against the Germans. He distrusted the British, so sought contact with the Americans? Melville had passed the parcel to Tom Wall? Who was Melville? Why Tom? Whatever the reason, Tom had information that would injure the Abwehr.

"At long last," Chilton said.

At long last he could act. He must locate Tom, secure the parcel. Was it remotely possible that any of this was true? It was hardly likely, except for two things: Davies-Frank's mysterious visit, and Melville's mysterious death.

Chilton would secure the parcel and destroy it. There was no other course.

THE CEILING WAS TWO INCHES above Tom's head. His hair caught on the rough planks as he paced. Five steps, and turn. There was a bed and a bucket and seven stairs leading up to a locked wooden door, his cell having been converted from a coal cellar. Five steps, and turn. The floor was packed earth. His hand throbbed, but the bleeding had stopped. He'd refused medical attention. Lines of light glowed above him, cracks in the planking of the kitchen floor.

He lay on the bed. Shut his eyes and couldn't sleep. He couldn't trust what he thought. Fear drove him. . . .

There was a shaft of light from the door. A man entered with a bundle of clothes. They'd taken Tom's to search. He dressed and bandaged his hand. Upstairs, Highcastle spoke with him. Highcastle's skin was tight, his eyes brittle. He wanted Duckblind—

more detail than blond, twenty, and green-eyed. He wanted Sondegger. He had to protect the Twenty, protect Davies-Frank's legacy. He wanted to jail Tom.

There was a silence.

Tom said, "You came to me."

An hour later, Ginger, the red-haired guard, was driving Tom to London. The sun was bright. The car stopped outside a first-aid station. It drove away, and Tom was standing on the sidewalk in the cold wind. He stuck a butt in his mouth and flicked a match with his thumbnail. It didn't ignite.

He needed Harriet.

It was early evening. Tom was swaying on his feet, standing outside the fire door at the Waterfall, three frigid stories up. There were no cigarettes left in his pack. His hand ached. He worked the lock and stepped inside to the warmth of the peach trap. He sat on the bed. He wouldn't sleep: It didn't matter. There were dark clouds at the edges of his vision.

He lost time. His eyes hurt more closed than opened. He stared at the swirls of nap on the carpet. The door handle moved and Tom straightened. A hallucination? No. It moved again.

He hefted a brass lamp in his good hand and switched off the overhead light. Had the handle really moved? How long ago? A heartbeat? An hour?

He waited.

THE STAGE UPON which Sondegger performed was not bound by twenty-seven iron links terminating in a locked cuff. He was surrounded by props, not trapped by shackles. He expelled the length of metal from his nostril.

He sang *Ein deutsches Requiem* to cover any noise. Working blind, his hands clasped behind his back, he molded the metal into functional form. *Selig sind, die das Leid tragen.* Blessed are they who mourn. The lock smoothed open and the chain fell away.

He was free.

He killed the warder. He killed the transcriptionist and stripped him. There was a wardrobe change. He could not find matches or a lighter, so he set fire to a scrap of paper with a light-bulb filament. He blew, and the flame quickened and caught. Downstairs, he stood in the farmhouse kitchen and waited, his face smudged with ash. A wisp of smoke made itself seen and a man's voice called, "Fire," but the warders maintained the perimeter, were not diverted.

A shot sounded within the house—the fire touching one of the bullets Sondegger had removed from the dead warder's gun. There were two more shots, almost simultaneous.

He was humming. *Denn alles Fleisch es ist wie Gras.* All flesh is as grass.

Three warders advanced. He slid a knife sharpener—the narrow gritty rod and the comfortable handle—into his sleeve and stepped into the cupboard until the footsteps sounded up the stairs. Another bullet fired.

He ran outside, waving distraught arms, playing the part of a panicked transcriptionist for an audience of one. Yet the warder was well trained, and as Sondegger closed, he raised his sidearm.

Sondegger pushed the knife sharpener into the man's eye.

The third movement of the requiem introduced the baritone, pleading to God—as he drove across the English countryside, Sondegger's voice swelled within the confines of the car he'd stolen. At the Gough Square drop, he found money and a message from Duckblind: The Abwehr agent known as Digby was at liberty. His loyalty was still in doubt. Thomas Wall would likely be found at the following locations. . . .

Sondegger smiled. Superlative work. He expected no less, but still—he was proud. He tendered her a message in return. Duckblind should secure the proof of Digby's loyalty while he evaluated the other two Abwehr agents, Kruh and Gerring.

First, Gerring. He was a barrister, employed in London and instructed to report on the public shelters. Sondegger wore an officious expression and a Metropolitan Water Board armlet, and visited the shelters of the legal district. He asked intrusive questions. Hours passed. Then he had a stroke of luck; he found Gerring.

As evening shaded to night, he identified Gerring's British control. Gerring was now in the employ of British Military Intelligence. He was a traitor.

Ihr habt nun Traurigkeit. And ye now have sorrow.

Sondegger vanished into the city. One Abwehr agent, Gerring, had turned traitorous. One—Digby—was in Duckblind's capable hands. Kruh, he had yet to investigate. If there was treachery, all who had been touched by the Abwehr would be destroyed.

Establishing the loyalty of the Abwehr agents was simple, an uncomplicated entr'acte before the curtain rose. But now that he was free, the show would begin. The spotlight would shine on Thomas Wall.

CHAPTER
TWENTY-FIVE

TOM HELD HIS BREATH as the door cracked and light fanned across the carpet. The brass lamp was heavy and cold in his hand. A head moved inside the room, wavy dark hair parted in the center.

Renard?

Tom's lips moved into a frozen grin as he swung, and a bare shoulder followed the head. Tom jerked up his arm, and the lamp crashed against the wall.

"Sweet lord!" Audrey said. "Tommy?"

He turned on the overhead light.

"If you want to be alone," she said, "you need only say."

Ten minutes later, he was sitting in the chair and the girl was curled on the bed, saying, "Two weeks ago, I ran into Miss Boyd at the market. She's a neighbor, from when Da was alive. She asked after me, very polite. The evil cow. You know the sort."

"Sure," Tom said, having no idea.

"I told her I was working as an ecdysiast. Inch taught me the word. I expect—I expect you think I'm ashamed of what I do."

"Are you?" He had the idea Audrey was leading somewhere.

"Da wouldn't approve. Oh, he'd not *disapprove*. He'd say I was my mum's little girl. He'd say that, but he'd think what you think."

"I don't know what I think."

She fixed him with an arch stare. Her neck was ivory. "I do," she said. "Da would blame himself. He took responsibility for things beyond his control. Mum, for example. Poor man, he'd rather die than see me—well, he *did* die, didn't he?"

Her eyes were downcast. Her hair was piled high. One hopeful black curl twined down her neck. She breathed deeply, at the edge of some emotion, and her breasts rose and fell. He stood and looked down at her body, curled catlike on the bed.

She reached smooth white arms behind her head and unpinned her hair. There was a spray of freckles on the inside of her right arm. "Even with me in tow, my mum accidentally captivated men—fiddling with the strap of her shoe on the street, she'd break three hearts." Audrey placed her hairpins on the bedside table, one at a time. "They wrote odes to her eyebrows when she was young, to her ankles—she saved the silliest."

Tom sat on the bed. The mattress shifted, and her thigh moved against his hip. Maybe she wasn't leading somewhere. Maybe she was drunk. She didn't look drunk. She looked eager and afraid.

"She'd tell Da she could've married a gentleman who likened her earlobes to pink pearls. She had no regrets. She never had a single regret."

"Life treated her softly, then."

"She lost her family, Tommy, after she married Da. She lost

two children before me. She grieved like a Sicilian. Then she finished grieving, and no regrets."

"Just like that."

"It's not so simple. You try it."

"I wouldn't know where to start."

"Start," she said, "here." Her hand was hot on the back of his neck. She drew him close. They kissed.

He thought, *Harriet*. He gently disengaged.

She watched his face and weighed what she saw there. "My mum wore bobbed hair and fringed skirts and Peter Pan collars. One night, she drank too much and fell in a fountain. Da saw, and escorted her home. He disapproved of her plucked eyebrows and her lipstick, her drinking and smoking. He was decent and upright and *too perfectly* dull—or so she informed him, at drunken length."

He nodded. Whatever Audrey had been moving toward, she'd nearly arrived.

"Now listen, Tommy. The next day, she knew she loved him. You think it's silly, but she *knew*. No questions, no regrets. She spent two weeks finding him, two more seducing him. She told me once. She said, 'You'll know. Not from here' "—her hand on Tom's heart—" 'nor there' "—her eyes flicked downward—" 'but here.' " Her hand was hot on his stomach. " 'In your tum. You'll know,' she said. And I do."

"I don't know your middle name, Audrey. I don't even know the color of your eyes."

"Liar."

Midnight blue. "Hortense?"

"Elizabeth. And I *know*, Tommy."

"You know Earl."

"You're very like him—hush, you *are*. But you're not him, and

I . . . I'm trying to seduce *you*." She laughed again, but there was a sad note in it. "I expected it to be easier."

"I can't."

"You won't."

"I can't."

"Because of your brother's wife."

"What do you— What about her?"

"Earl," she said, "is not the most discreet of husbands."

His skin pricked for no reason. "You didn't—"

"*I* didn't. Winnie told Anne. Imogene told me. I didn't. I *haven't*." She raised her chin. "I never have."

"But you . . . you don't mean—"

She said, "I never *knew* before," and turned her face away.

He said, "The first time I saw her was at a dinner party. She was wearing a white dress. I don't think knowing is silly, Audrey. By the time she reached for her soup spoon, I *knew*. She likes chocolate in the morning. She's plain. You're far more beautiful. She never—"

"Shut up, Tommy. Please do."

She cried and he stroked her hair. He lay beside her, the weight of her head in the crook of his arm.

Eventually, she slept. He listened to the ticking of the clock. An ache gripped his elbow, his arm cramping under the weight of her head. He rolled to his side. There was a dark freckle on the nape of her neck. She made a noise in her throat, like a purr. His arm draped over her hip.

Tom dozed.

Hands tugged at his neck and he opened one eye. The girl was working the knot of his tie with her clever fingers. Her lower lip was caught between her teeth. Her cheeks were flushed and her hair was a glossy black halo in the lamplight.

"Lift your head," she said, and slid his tie from his collar.

He closed his eye and felt her lips against his forehead.

"Sleep, Tommy."

He said, "Harriet." And slept.

"WOTCHER, MATE," Renard said, smiling with all his teeth at the doorman in the Waterfall lobby. "I've a message for one Mr. Thomas Wall. He in residence?"

The doorman said he'd see the message was delivered.

"Personal delivery," Renard said. "This Mr. Wall, he below?"

The doorman said he couldn't say.

Rugg knew it was fookin' wrong, chatting at the pinstripe doorman. Still, a muscle in the man's eye twitched, maybe toward the stairs roped behind a fancy brass chain. Rugg tugged on his little finger until the knuckle popped.

The doorman greeted a couple toffs with a groveling welcome. He lifted the cream blue phone and murmured words, and told the toffs if they'd proceed downstairs, they'd find everything in readiness.

"I'm just an honest bloke doing an honest job," Renard said as the toffs punted off. "Like yourself."

The man licked a finger and opened his book, and a corn-haired bird came from nowhere. The doorman told her to be quick. She waved past, saying, "ta."

"Hard for an honest man, these days." Renard slid one of Chilton's notes across the doorman's desk. "You'll be doing me a favor. Doing Mr. Wall a favor."

The corn-haired bird missed a step at the words, batted her lashes at Renard before she pushed out the front door.

"Doing your own self a favor," Renard said.

The doorman said thank you kindly, if that was all, but no sir.

Rugg wrung his hat and shoved off. It was cold outside, and

not yet dark. The corn-haired bird was crossing the square. A quarter of the way down the street, he laid a hand on her arm, stopped and spun her.

"I'll scream," she said, cool as sweat. "Leave off."

He bowed his head and said, "'Pologies, miss."

"Naff off my arm." She tried to jerk away.

What'd the pinstripe call her? "Don't mean nothing, Miss Anne."

Her eyes narrowed. "You overheard."

"Mr. Wall told me," he said.

The bird didn't miss a step this time. Her face softened. "Earl?"

"He told me." Rugg's grip was loose on her arm. They were almost alone. "He said, 'Fetch Miss Anne. Tell her.'"

"Earl said that? Tell Miss Anne what?"

He pulled her between the building and the brick. "Tell Miss Anne to sing."

She started to scream, so he knocked her in the stomach, held her while she retched, then cuffed her proper.

"I know fuck all," she finally said. "Fucking Earl."

"Ever run a stick against bricks? Scrape it on concrete?"

She didn't say a bleedin' thing.

"Carves wood right off." He pressed her face against the wall, blond hair falling everywhere. "Pretty bird like you."

She sobbed it all: her fookin' hopes and dreams, and Earl Wall. Our Mr. Wall's brother. Some slag, name of Venus, was paying on a room for the Yank upstairs, the bleedin' Pugilist Room. Wasn't there now, the corn-haired bird thought. She didn't know, but he should be back later. Please. Please, no.

THE TICKING OF THE CLOCK woke Tom. The bedside lamp cast a dim glow like dawn, but with the blackout curtains closed, it could be any time. Didn't matter. The pressure was gone from his temples. It was a new day.

He'd finally slept.

There was a book under the lamp, with a folded note obscuring its cover and five half-smoked cigarette butts in a semicircle at its base. Groping for the note, he put his weight on his bad hand and swore. It was more sensitive than ever, dipped in acid and throbbing.

He'd slept and was still half-sleeping, could barely read the neat, looping hand:

> Dearest T—
>   Another offering. This one I insist you accept.
>   (The fags were the jobber's idea. I tucked a pack of Players in your jacket pocket, if his aren't to your taste.)
>   I remain,
>   Always yours

The book was leather-bound, the title printed in gold: *Tristram Shandy*. Tom turned it over in his hand. He couldn't believe it. He'd slept, and the book had appeared. When had Audrey found the jobber? Finally, he'd caught a break—

A club struck him in the back of the head. A light flashed and the room upended and he was facedown on the carpet.

CHAPTER
TWENTY-SIX

DUCKBLIND FOLLOWED MR. DIGBY, the Abwehr agent whose loy-alty was in question, to the *most* darling café, a hop and a skip from Broadcasting House. It was tucked under a too-lovely striped awning and had the cutest patterned tablecloths. Had he truly defected?

Even if he hadn't, it was cruel of Digby to take his warm and woolly ease while she stood glum-faced at the motor-bus stop, pretending to wait for the 53a or the 88, whichever didn't come. It had sprinkled early that morning, and the rain wetted the city like an old-time cyprian damping her skirts. But now, at half past eight, the streets stank of people, too much cologne and too little soap.

An ugly man walked toward Digby and sat two tables away. He was joined by an ugly woman and they ate an ugly breakfast.

Digby ate alone. There wasn't any indication of his disloyalty, but it was early yet and—oh. *Oh!*

She wasn't the only person with an eye on Digby.

Digby raised his napkin mockingly toward an older man in a careful blue suit. The older man ignored him. Poorly done! If he didn't want to be associated with Digby, he should have pretended confusion. Ignoring the gesture was terribly bad tradecraft.

After breakfast, Duckblind followed Blue Suit as he followed Digby—not to Broadcasting House, Digby's ostensible workplace, but to a bland brick building. She sucked the knuckle of her thumb. So Blue Suit was Digby's British minder? He *had* turned traitor. *Schmetterling* indeed. Flighty and frivolous and only a WT operator, yet she'd uncovered the traitor!

She must learn the whole story. She must confirm that mocking wave hadn't been merely a gesture to a coworker, and the bland brick building not simply a reassignment.

She returned to Mr. Pentham's house and changed clothes. She applied a touch of rouge to her cheeks and kohl to her eyes. She wore silly wedge sandals—utterly wrong for the season but cute as a caterpillar. She strapped Mr. Pentham's oversized watch on her wrist—deliciously outré—and her disguise was complete.

The family next door had a darling curly-haired dog, and she put it on a leash and returned to Digby's building. She entered directly, chattering to the dog, whom she called "Loochie." He was a scruffy thing of uncertain parentage, but full of pride. He stuck his nose in the air and strutted around her ankles.

The lobby was bare and institutional. Governmental. Her heels echoed, and her voice—pitched high and fussy—echoed, as well. She told Loochie not to get underfoot, and to please attend Mummy, or she'd take a tumble, and then where would little Loochie be?

A man with stubby black shoes asked if she were lost. There were two businessmen waiting at the lift, and another stubby black shoe man at a desk. Both the men in black shoes were armed. It *was* a secure building, and she had confirmed Digby's treachery!

She flittered and flustered and said, "Me? I? *Lost?*"

He said yes. Could he please see her identification?

She tossed her hair. "Oh, don't be ridiculous! I've been coming once a week for months! Where's Albert?"

She dropped the leash and gave Loochie a swift kick in his fuzzy little tum. Loochie yelped and dashed away. She shrieked for help in catching him, and almost fell out of her dress chasing the beast. She lunged, Loochie fled, and the men attempted assistance. It was dreadfully comic. Finally, after she'd committed the layout of the building to memory, one of the men cornered the ravening hound behind a drooping potted plant.

She gave him a firm scolding. The dog, of course, not the man! Him she gave a vacuous smile and a barrage of gushing gratitude. There were four basic approaches. Most agents relied on stealth and all sorts of surreptitious sneakiness. But stealth was tedious, and nobody expected an agent to call the greatest-possible amount of attention to herself. Nobody suspected a scatterbrained young lady making a spectacle, especially after Loochie pooped in the lobby.

The first man ignored the odiferous offering and said he suspected she had the wrong building, and she said, "*Yes, of course,*" and launched into a flustery explanation as she clattered back outside. She waved to the men and escorted Loochie on a long and aimless stroll to ensure she wasn't being followed.

She was soon back at Mr. Pentham's street. She gave the dog a peck on the muzz and returned him to his garden. So Digby *was* a traitor. She had caught him, though, and all his double-dealing would come crumbling down. She hoped he took a long time hanging.

She retrieved her transmitter for maintenance and tests. She'd notify Bookbinder at the next letter drop: The Abwehr network—one agent at least—was compromised. Bookbinder would investigate the other two agents, and they'd transmit the information to the SD. Shouldn't be long now.

TOM WAS FACEDOWN on the carpet. He rolled to his side and touched the back of his aching head. Kong and Teeth—Rugg and Renard—were standing over him. Renard was wearing a too-bright plaid coat, Rugg a shapeless raincoat.

Tom said, "Swell."

"Heavy sleeper, yobbo," Renard said.

"I'm out of practice." Tom winced as his fingers found a tender spot.

"You've something we want."

"My boyish good looks."

"Bollocks," Rugg said, his high-pitched voice not unfriendly. He extended an oak burl of a hand. Tom took it and the big man hoisted him back onto the bed.

"You could've saved yourself the trouble," Tom told him.

Rugg shrugged a massive shoulder.

"A parcel's what we're after," Renard said.

"A parcel of what?"

"Haven't a hint."

"Sure," Tom said. "Wait here. I'll get you a parcel."

Renard smiled a malicious smile. "Sharp as a snail's tooth, our Mr. Wall."

The clock said it was a few minutes after seven. Tom's mouth was stale from sleep. He'd slept, and woken, and ended facedown on the floor. He needed a plan, needed a Colt, needed a miracle. "You mind if I brush my teeth?"

"Bugger your blinkin' teeth."

"Brush 'em every morning, just like Mother told me."

"Every *morning*—you hear?" Renard asked Rugg. "Playing the pennywhistle is our Mr. Wall."

"Come hold my hand if you're afraid I'll slip down the drainpipe." Soon as he said it, Tom realized Renard meant something else. "It's seven o'clock. It's—what day is it?"

"It's night."

"Christ." He stood. "I slept eighteen hours."

Rugg shoved him back onto the bed.

"Eighteen hours, I need to take a leak." He stood again, and Rugg preceded him into the bathroom. He brushed his teeth. Pissed and washed his hands. There was no plan. There was no miracle. And short of his .30-caliber BAR, what did he need? A hand grenade.

In the other room, Renard was sitting in the chair reading Audrey's note. "Nice bit of quiff, is she?"

"Try to take me, Renard." Tom grabbed his lighter and the pack of Players. "Without lover boy here helping."

Renard frowned, maybe realizing Tom was different now. Nothing like eighteen hours of beauty sleep. "You talk tough, yobbo, but I've seen you fold."

"Just you and me." Tom stuck a cigarette in his mouth and flicked the lighter. "One hand tied behind my back."

He inhaled and offered the pack to Rugg, who shook his head. Tom could make a play, but the room was too small and Rugg was too big. Keep them talking, then. Sure, that was a plan.

"We got all the time in the world," Renard said. "Even know which bird is yours, black hair and high explosives. Don't expect she'll come knocking; it's dinner below. All the time in the world."

He flicked one of the jobber's spent cigarette butts onto the floor. "What're these, then?"

"British cigarettes."

"Girl named Venus." Renard glanced at the note. "She remains always yours. What's the nightly?"

He couldn't let them drag Audrey into this. "Girl leaves a note for all her customers."

"What's the blinkin' nightly?"

"Told her I had half a crown. She said no worries, she had change."

"Old joke, that," Renard said. "Now, your teeth sparkly, Mr. Wall? Fancy combing your hair?" Renard flipped idly through *Tristram Shandy* as he spoke, and Tom wondered if he knew what it contained. "Cleanliness and godliness, yobbo—where the fuck is that parcel?"

Renard slammed the book shut, and Rugg tapped Tom in the stomach.

Tom folded and his cigarette flew across the room. Rugg eased him onto the floor. Tom's breath came in wheezes. He watched the cigarette smolder on the carpet and tried to form words. No luck.

"We'll waste more than tobacco," Renard said, "you don't pass along that parcel, Sonder's parcel. You know Sonder."

"Never heard of it."

"We know you have." Renard removed his plaid coat and folded it carefully onto the desk. "We blinkin' well know."

"Oh, Sonder. Sure."

"He gave you something."

"Fashion tips. Told me only weasels wear plaid."

"Corridor's empty." Renard ground out Tom's cigarette with his toe. "We got a sign propped, end of the passage. What's that say again?"

"Fookin' maintenance."

"All alone, yobbo." Renard grinned toothily. "Good thick doors."

"He gave me nothing."

"Who is he?"

"A neighbor, an old neighbor. We used to play poker."

"That right?"

"I knew him in the States. In D.C."

"D.C.," Renard said. "A Yank, then, is he?"

"American as apple pie," Tom said.

"Apple a day." Renard took a steak knife from his pocket—six inches long, the blade mottled with rust. "Found this in the gutter. Bit of everything caked on here."

"I don't know any Sonder."

"He knows you. American as *Wiener*-bloody-*schnitzel*. Rugg."

Rugg clubbed Tom on the temple with an open hand. Tom's knees buckled and he almost fell. They knew Sondegger was German, but they didn't know his full name. Knew about the microphotograph—it had to be the "parcel"—but didn't know it was in the book on the table. If it *was* in the book on the table . . .

Rugg shoved him into the chair and tied his wrists to the chair arms, palms up.

"Blinkin' disgraceful," Renard said, looking at the bandages. "Seeping through. That's nasty foul, that." He yanked at the gauze. "You ought to take better care."

Tom saw without looking: The hand was puffy and streaked red. The fingers clenched and unclenched. *Sondegger had driven the pencil into the seam of his palm.* . . .

"Nasty foul," Rugg said.

"Pain don't bother you, does it, yob? Old boot leather. Time we got civilized. I'll go gentle with the cutter." Renard tightened his grip on the blade and brought it toward Tom's hand. "Like a surgeon."

"Stop," Tom said. "I'll tell you."

"'Course you will. Only question is when."

"Sonder's German. He's in London. He's working for the COI, the Americans. It's a new agency. He—"

Rugg grabbed Tom's head from behind and twisted. "When we get done blotting you, we call on your girl."

Tom felt his neck bones strain. His bound arms spasmed; he was on the verge of blacking out. At least his teeth were clean.

"Fuck he care for the girl?" Renard said.

"He cares," Rugg said. "Don't you, Wall?"

Pain flared at the base of his skull. He was almost gone. He tried to say, Don't need a big band . . .

Rugg released him. "Do his other hand, squit. Do his left."

"His other hand? Oh-ho. Right you are." Renard twirled the knife until he held the haft in his fist. "You've one good hand, yobbo, till I pin it to the chair, infect it worse than that mess you've already got. No hands, stumps for wrists. Give you six seconds. Five. Four . . ."

HARRIET SUPPRESSED A SIGH as Mr. Uphill's shadow fell across her desk. She was busy and hadn't time to spare.

"Officially, Mrs. Wall, you are what?" he said. "The coordinating officer of WIT."

"Days like this, I hardly remember."

"You may take my word on the matter." Mr. Uphill tapped an open folder on her desk. "You've been here since . . . I believe you arrived at five this morning?"

"Surely not five."

"You signed in at seven minutes past. It's now twenty-one minutes after five in the evening. Twelve hours is sufficient for a single day."

"There's a good deal still to be done," she said, gesturing at her cluttered desk. "That dispatch minute we received is alarming. I really ought—"

"You really ought to tend the home fires before the blaze, Mrs. Wall."

She bit back a sharp retort. "Yes, Mr. Uphill. There are only a few final things. . . ."

The dispatch had arrived that morning, sent from an ALBANS authorized source to select offices that ran agents into occupied Europe. There had been a serious breach: A Nazi agent was at liberty in England and could fatally compromise their agents, *her* agents. Governess had been tortured; Mathilde, executed; Nanette, missing. Now a single Nazi agent could kill the rest. The dispatch instructed Harriet to evaluate all documentation according to the eight specified guidelines. It was work enough for two weeks. She had three days. She could not save her young ladies; she could only ensure that their loss would cripple nothing but themselves.

"Mrs. Wall?" Uphill said.

"I'm very nearly finished," she said.

"No, my dear. You *have* finished," Uphill said. "You're no good to us exhausted. Mistakes will creep in, and we're better safe than sorry."

She bristled at the cliché, but she knew he couldn't help himself. He spoke as he thought. And on the rare occasions he "put his foot down," he was immovable.

She tidied her desk under his watchful gaze, and was too soon home.

The house was empty. Her worry for Earl mingled with her

fear for her young ladies—though she worried far more for them. He'd gone to ground for reasons she couldn't imagine, and would surface for reasons she'd never learn. He was Earl, untarnished by fear or failure, untrammeled by imagination. Unlike Tom, walking into the raid to find the death that had eluded him on Crete.

There was a knock at the front: Mrs. Turnbull from next door. "I'd have you in, Mrs. Turnbull, but—"

"Oh, I've no time myself. Mr. Pomfret's come for dinner. But a young woman came this morning and asked that I give you this." She handed Harriet a sheet of paper folded around a small weight. "You wouldn't have a trickle of tinned milk to spare?"

Harriet waved Mrs. Turnbull toward her kitchen and unfolded the note. A key was inside. In neat girlish script the message said Mr. Wall was in difficulty and needed Mrs. Wall. It was a matter of grave importance. If possible, please go to the following address. . . .

The note was unsigned. The address was the Waterfall. She'd never been. She'd never wanted to know. But if Earl was there, if he needed her . . .

"FOUR. BLINKIN' THREE . . ." Renard rested the tip of the blade on Tom's palm and hefted *Tristram Shandy* to pound down like a hammer on a nail. "See he don't yell too long, Rugg. The door's thick, but it ain't—"

"I'll talk," Tom said. "I'll fucking sing."

"First tap won't do a jot of harm, yob. Was I at two or three?"

There was a scratching at the door.

"Police!" Tom bellowed. "Get the pol—"

Rugg shut him up and yanked the fire door open. "We'd best sod off. One exit, and this ain't our town."

Renard swore and grabbed his coat, still holding *Tristram*

Shandy, and Tom gripped the chair with both hands and kicked. Caught Renard on the back of the thigh and knocked him off balance. Renard dropped the coat and book and turned on Tom, his face murderous. He swiped the knife at Tom's hand, and Tom bucked in the chair and took a shallow cut on the forearm. He yelled again, and Rugg grabbed Renard and dragged him into the darkness, slamming the fire door shut behind them.

Tom collapsed into the chair, and there was another scratching at the door. The lock snicked open, the handle turned, and he half-laughed. "Harriet?"

"Tom? I heard— Good Lord! What on earth?"

"Rough couple days. Untie me. No—lock that door first," he said, gesturing toward the fire door with his chin. "Now, Harry! Drag the chair and prop it— Harriet, just fucking do it. I didn't tie myself. Now the other door. Lock it. . . . Good, thank you. Now untie me."

She inspected him as she loosed the knots, noting the cut on his arm, his sweat-slick face. Her gray velvet eyes revealed no disgust at the ruin of his palm. "You need medical attention, Tommy. It's quite horrific."

He looked at the scratch on his arm. "Needs to be cleaned is all."

"Don't be an idiot. You know what I mean."

Rugg grinding into his hand, Sondegger's pencil piercing the tissue with splinters and lead. "I need a shower."

"It's infected, Tom."

He opened a drawer and grabbed a fresh shirt. "It's fine."

"Tommy, you have to— That's Earl's shirt." She looked in the drawer. "That's all Earl's."

"I borrowed a few of his things. After I rented the room."

"The room."

"Yeah."

"It's yours?"

"Sure. Don't look like that—I didn't decorate it. I just needed somewhere to sleep." He never could lie to Harriet, but she wanted to believe him. "Needed some clothes."

"Earl . . ." she said. "He didn't—"

Tom shut the bathroom door before she could ask. He started trembling. What if they'd done it? What if both hands were cut and infected? The trembling slowed, then stopped. He'd finally slept. He was okay. Not quite four-oh, but he'd do. He washed the new cut. Put his unbandaged right hand under the water until it ached. Dried himself and rebandaged his right hand and dressed.

"Help with my tie?" he asked, opening the door.

Harriet was holding Renard's coat at arm's length, watching the bright fabric sway. She was far away. Her lips were down-turned and the faint lines at her eyes had deepened.

"Not your size," he said. "And drape-cut plaid does nothing for you."

She was paler than usual. She was sublime. She'd come for him.

"Harriet," he said.

"Mmm?"

"How'd you know I was here?"

"I didn't. I expected Earl."

"Swell." Then he realized. "You heard from him?"

"I was given a message. I was afraid . . ." She folded the coat over her arm. "The note said it was urgent."

"Who sent it?"

"Mrs. Turnbull—my neighbor—said a young woman claimed Mr. Wall needed me."

"True enough," he said.

"The room key was—" She caught some expression in his face. "Who is she?"

"A friend."

The girl had laid her heart at his feet, and he'd walked away. She'd told her story and she'd wept in his arms, and he'd . . . Had he called her Harriet?

Yeah, he had.

He'd refused her kindness and laughter and her open heart, and she'd still brought Harriet to his side. The girl knew he ached for Harriet, knew he wanted Harriet instead of her. So she'd given him Harriet. She was some kind of woman.

"A friend," he repeated. "Are you happy with Earl?"

"I'd be happier if he were here."

"Sure, but—are you, do you . . ."

She said, "I am and I do, Tommy. I love my husband."

Tom fiddled with his lighter. "I ever tell you about the summer in Maine? He taught me to fish, taught me to sink or swim."

"Which were you doing just now?"

He tried to grin. "Dead man's float."

"More new friends?"

"Rugg and Renard," he said. "They do odd jobs. Used to be Blackshirts."

Her mouth tightened. "They're political?"

"In their charming homespun fashion."

She went paler and slumped into the chair. Hearing about Rugg and Renard hit her harder than Earl's absence, harder than seeing Tom's hand. She was tough, but something pained her. Tom didn't know what. He looked at her, and she just shook her head, so he took the rusty knife into the bathroom and rinsed off the blood and grime.

Back in the room, he said, "Toss me that book."

She tossed him *Tristram Shandy* and he sawed carefully at the spine.

"Whatever are you doing?"

"Eighteen hours of sleep, Harry. I'm a new man." He ripped the binding away. Nothing inside. He ran a finger down the spine, felt a crease, and picked at the leather. Something was lodged inside. He caught it with a fingernail, a tiny square of film—a microphotograph.

"Is that microfilm?" She came closer. "That's microfilm, Tom. What on earth . . ."

"I'm not sure. Something to do with Earl."

"We'll take it to Inter-Services."

"Earl is COI," he said. "This is American."

She objected. It was her husband's; it was found in London. They were allies. Even if the United States refused to fight while Europe fell, she knew her duty.

Tom knew duty, too. "And *my* loyalty," he said, "doesn't change with the weather."

Her voice went cold enough to burn. "If you're suggesting that I cannot be trusted— I assure you, Thomas, I can be trusted with things of *value*."

He said some hard words, and she returned them, fighting like an old married couple. The thought made him smile. Her face cleared and she brushed her hair behind her ears. "We seem to have misplaced the subject," she said.

They decided to compromise. First, they needed the microphotograph enlarged. It could be nothing, a flat waste of time. Or it could be the key to Earl, the key to Sondegger and the Double-Cross Committee. Could be the key to a sneak attack on the States, or a checkmate in the chess game he was playing with the Hun—playing blind, and running out of time.

CHAPTER
TWENTY-SEVEN

THE FLOWERPOT THEATRE was small and old and closed; bomb-damaged. The stairs were roped off and a statue had been shattered and lay facedown in the rubble. There was a dusty plaque on the wall. Highcastle rubbed it clean with his sleeve and read WE THAT LIVE TO PLEASE MUST PLEASE TO LIVE.

The author's name was obscured. Rupert would know, but Rupert was dead—and Sondegger was free. Highcastle had failed.

He'd stopped at the Flowerpot en route to the Metropolitan Police. He had his men combing the streets for the Hun, had them roused to a panic. There was no lead they wouldn't pursue, and it wouldn't achieve bugger all—there were no leads to follow. Sondegger's only trail was the bodies at the safe house, and his knowledge of Earl Wall.

Highcastle needed help. The Special Branch, the Home Guard—hell, give him the Housewives Service and the Boy

Scouts. He'd beg help from anyone. Not enough time, not enough men . . .

Yet he found time to stop here. They'd come last year for an evening show, he and Davies-Frank and Mrs. Davies-Frank. It had been the first overture of real friendship outside the office, and it revealed the depth of trust and fondness between them.

Well, that was over. Highcastle brushed the dirt from his sleeve and turned away. Dead was dead, and now he'd mourned for Rupert, and his men murdered at Hennessey Gate. He hadn't time for guilt. Hadn't time for anything but finding Duckblind and the Hun and seeing them hung.

Get the Yard on board—and the bloody Salvation Army, for all the good it would do. He'd speak to Harriet Wall himself. Her husband was the only lead they had.

TOM AND HARRIET stood on the dark, drafty street outside the photographer's flat. Tom lighted a cigarette while Harriet rang the bell. There was no answer, so they spent some time knocking. They needed that microdot enlarged.

A girl with her hair in a net opened the next door and said there were those trying to sleep. Harriet asked for help, her tone warm and her accent clear as cut glass. The girl clutched her robe closer and told them where to find the photographer.

It was midnight when they arrived at the Underground station. Harriet told Tom that during the Blitz, after the Tube stations were opened as raid shelters, the walls had wept moisture, and sewage ran in rivulets underfoot. The air was alternately a freezer or a blast furnace, thick with clouds of mosquitoes, which thrived underground. The platforms were crammed with children in hammocks, scratching from lice, babies crying, prostitutes touting for business.

"There was panic about pickpockets and public fornication," she said.

"Public fornication," Tom said. "Disgusting."

She glanced sharply at him, and he said nothing about the picnic in Virginia, the lemonade and sandwiches, the sugar cookies. . . .

They descended into the shelter. There were triple-layered bunks with thin blue-and-white-striped mattresses and gray wool blankets. Suitcases and wicker baskets had been stacked neatly under tables set with watercoolers and pitchers and cups. There was a stove in the corner, and a gramophone, and the ladies' WC had been festooned with Christmas decorations. A couple of little girls giggling under a blanket were hushed by a sleepy mother. An old couple shared a top bunk under a frilly counterpane.

Tom glanced at Harriet. Where was the sewage and misery?

"That was during the Blitz," she said. "They've become quite neighborly."

They soon found Harriet's tame photographer—a wiry man with fleshy lips that expressed nine degrees of disapproval within a minute of his being awakened. Harriet soothed him, and he grumbled back to his studio, unlocked the door, ensured the blackout curtains were closed, and switched a light.

"Darkroom," he said. "Entire city's one big darkroom." He subjected the microfilm to a cursory inspection. "Can I do it? Of course I can *do* it. Need a projection reader, though. I've a Recordak somewhere in this tumult." He went directly to the box he wanted and slid the microphotograph into the projector, placing it between two sheets of glass. Showed Harriet how to work it: "Beware of glare points and hot spots." He pointed out the projection bulb and the heat filters and the screen. "Some prefer blue-white, but amber-gold's better for eye strain. Any problems, adjust here. . . ."

Harriet thanked him and shooed him into the back room, asking him please to remain on hand, and then bent over the reader. "Yes. There's writing. . . . It's in German." She brushed her hair from her face and groped for pen and paper. Tom provided them, and she translated as she transcribed.

QQ: PREV. TO HAWAII, ISLE OF KUSHUA (PEARL HARBOR). IMPERIAL JAPANESE NAVY, ADMIRAL YAMAMOTO. VICE ADMIRAL NAGUMO.

NAVAL STRONG POINT PEARL HARBOR

1. BOMB PLOT GRID OF FIVE AREAS UPDATED TO NINE. NOTE NEW DESIGNATIONS.

2. STATE WHARF—PIER INSTALLATIONS. PETROL INSTALLATIONS, SITUATIONS OF DRY DOCK NO. 1 AND THE NEW DRY DOCK.

3. SUBMARINE STATION PLAN AND LAND INSTALLATIONS.

4. TORPEDO PROTECTION NETS DEPLOYED? AVERAGE SPEED REDUCTION WHEN IN USE? DETAILS OF CONSTRUCTION.

5. STATION FOR *MINENSUCHVERBÄNDE*. DREDGER WORK—

"*Minensuch verboten?*" Tom asked, reading over the shoulder.
"*Verbände.*" Harriet didn't raise her head. "Mine-search formations."

She continued translating.

DREDGER WORK AT THE ENTRANCE AND EAST AND
SOUTHEAST LOCKS. WATER DEPTH. NUMBER OF ANCHOR-
AGES. PRESENCE OF A FLOATING DOCK IN PEARL HARBOR.

She rubbed her eyes. "Pearl Harbor?"
"Big navy base," Tom said. "In Hawaii somewhere."

1. NAVAL INFORMATION: ENEMY SHIPMENTS, MATERIAL,
   CONVOYS. NAMES OF SHIPS AND SPEEDS.
   ORGANIZATION OF STRONG POINTS FOR E-BOATS
   AND DEPOT SHIPS.

2. HAWAII: AMMUNITION DUMPS AND MINE DEPOTS.
   AMMUNITION RESERVE AT THE ALIAMANU CRATER.
   PUNCHBOWL CRATER MILITARY WORKS?

3. AERODROMES: NAVAL AIR AND HANGARS KANEOHE,
   ARMY HICKAM AND WHEELER FIELDS. JOHN
   RODGERS AIRPORT. ARMY/NAVY. PAN AMERICAN
   AIRWAYS WIRELESS STATION ON THE MAKAPPU
   PENINSULA.

"There's a break," Harriet said, "after number three. The film
appears to continue from another source."

"Wait—wait. Hawaii? The Hun said a surprise attack. By the
Japs? Against *Hawaii*?"

"I could write a note saying the Chinese were invading
Greenland. Doesn't make it true."

02530-JN: TWO FLEET AND TWO LIGHT CARRIERS. TWO
CARRIERS CONVERTED FROM BATTLESHIP AND CRUISER.
TWO BATTLESHIPS, TWO CRUISERS, A DESTROYER
SCREEN, TEN SUPPORT SHIPS.

111 BOMBERS, 44 TORPEDO BOMBERS, 142 DIVE-BOMBERS, 97 FIGHTERS. SIXTEEN I-TYPE SUBMARINES, FIVE TYPE A MIDGET SUBMARINES.

DEPART KURE NAVAL BASE 18 NOVEMBER. STRIKE FORCE TO ASSEMBLE ETOROFU, KURILE ISLANDS.

ALSO NOTED, PER DOCNUM 23A-881-UH-I: "IF, PROCEEDING EASTWARD FROM HITOKAPPU BAY, FORCE SHOULD BE DISCOVERED, TURN BACK AS THOUGH NOTHING HAPPENED; HOWEVER, IF SUCH DISCOVERY IS MADE ON X-1 DAY OR LATER, PROCEED TO RESOLUTELY CARRY OUT ATTACK."

"November eighteenth," Tom said. "What's today? December fourth?"

"The fifth—since midnight."

"When the hell is X-One Day? We need an almanac. We need a map. How do we confirm any of this?"

"First we finish. Two more sections. This one's in English. They both are."

EAST WIND RAIN.

PER AMBASSADOR OSHIMA. RIBBENTROP QUOTED AS: "SHOULD JAPAN BECOME ENGAGED IN HOSTILITIES AGAINST THE UNITED STATES, GERMANY WOULD DECLARE WAR IMMEDIATELY. THERE IS NO POSSIBILITY OF GERMANY ENTERING INTO A SEPARATE PEACE WITH THE UNITED STATES UNDER SUCH CIRCUMSTANCES."

"The last section is a single sentence," Harriet said. "It says that confirmation proof is provided in the accompanying microdot."

" 'Accompanying microdot'?"

"That's what it says, Tommy. Read it yourself."

She stood and he took her place. Read the final paragraphs, both in English: "East Wind Rain" and "Confirmation proof of previous available in accompanying microdot. 670-AT7-08597."

Another microdot, an accompanying microdot. And an attack on Hawaii? A destroyer screen and— No. He couldn't let himself think about the message. First find the confirmation proof microdot. Then take action.

He dug in Harriet's bag for *Tristram Shandy*. "Why the hell not show the proof in the same message?"

"SOP for sensitive initiatives. Neither microphotograph is sufficient without the other. It allows operational flexibility."

" 'Operational flexibility.' How small do microdots get?"

"Speck of dust. This one's fairly large, as if concealment wasn't the first concern. These tend to be no smaller than a freckle."

Tom remembered a spray of freckles gracing smooth white skin. Harriet's bare arm? Or Audrey's? "We need a clean surface," he said, opening the book. "Some tools, like dental picks."

Harriet called the photographer back into the room and told him what they needed. "And prints of the microphotograph. Nothing fancy. Legible is all that matters."

The photographer told her the prints would take time, and gave her tools and two clean tin trays. He pursed his fleshy lips and disappeared into the back room. The door didn't quite slam behind him.

Harriet sat next to Tom. They slit the binding and dismantled the book. Inspected every thread of leather binding, every fleck of dust, every period that seemed too three-dimensional. . . .

"We ought to report this immediately." Harriet looked up from the jumble of paper in her tray. "Even if it is only a hoax."

"It's no hoax."

"Then we ought—"

"It's the middle of the night, Harry. It'll wait till dawn. I want to be sure. Sondegger plays a deep game." He sifted one-handed through a few loose pages. "Least it's not in code. I saw a poem code once." *Permission to reinforce Máleme airfield expressly forbidden. Under NO circumstances compromise source EULT.* "My squad—Lifton and Manny and Rosenblatt, they were sacrificed to protect one man, a covert source. Headquarters knew the attack was coming, knew where and when, but wouldn't let us reinforce. My boys—they died for . . ."

"For what, Tommy? For Earl?"

Yeah. Tom rubbed his eyes. Earl betrayed me. He stole you. He was EULT, the source on Crete, protected at the cost of my boys and— *No.*

"No," he said, surprising himself. "Earl had nothing to do with Crete."

THE TYPEWRITER MECHANIC had fair hair and a clubfoot. Sondegger observed him until he could identify the role he was playing: a variation of Gundlach, the proud cripple who would neither beg nor bend, a performance presented with a great deal of flair and personal interpretation.

Late afternoon turned to early evening. The mechanic returned home, then departed for the local. He stumbled on the front steps.

Sondegger extended his arm. "Need a hand, mate?"

The man stiffened. "No. Thank you."

"Right enough," Sondegger said. "You need a foot."

The man stared, then snorted a laugh. "Cheeky bastard."

A few words, and the mechanic bought Sondegger a drink. A profitable evening already, and Sondegger hadn't yet inquired into the man's knowledge of Kruh, the Abwehr agent whose loyalty was in question.

"A toast," Sondegger said, lifting his glass. There was a noble history of cripples in literature: King Lycurgus had amputated his own foot while chopping grape vines, trying to destroy the cult of Dionysus. "To the sacred kings."

The mechanic drank, and was distracted by a hubbub in the corner—a dart tournament. He nodded toward the boards. "Fancy a go?"

Sondegger said he'd like nothing better, and the mechanic bought another round while they waited. Telephus, lame king of the Mysians, had been set adrift on the sea as a baby, but he'd survived. Cripples were a hardy folk, and proud. Pride was a useful tool—Sondegger told a tale of his adventure with a delayed action bomb during the Blitz. He was modest and smug.

The mechanic said he'd had a bit more excitement than a time bomb.

Sondegger, carefully patronizing, said of course he had.

"Honest to Christ I have."

"I'm sure you have. And how lucky was I that the bomb didn't—"

The urge to upstage was universal: "Wasn't I there when three Heinie spies floated down? Parachutes dropping overhead—I thought the invasion had begun. I half-expected they'd be got up as nuns, but nothing like—"

"Not a wimple among them?"

"Tell you what was among them. A unit of Security Service, like a fox among chickens. Security Service or some lot who knew their business."

Sondegger considered the hue of his porter. Aegisthus, exposed as an infant, was suckled by a goat and lived. Hippothous, son of Poseidon, was suckled by a mare. The son of a god was

254

nursed at the bosom of a beast. Had the Abwehr agent Kruh, a son of the Fatherland, been captured and nursed to the bosom of British counterintelligence?

Sondegger looked toward the dartboards. "What's the prize, then? Set of six darts—Unicorns? Wouldn't mind a bit, winning those."

"I bloody saw it," the mechanic insisted. "The Security blokes shot two of the Heines dead as donkeys."

"And the third?"

"The third?" Belated wariness crept into the mechanic's red-rimmed eyes.

"The third parachutist. Another round? Oh, that reminds me why I'm celebrating. Industrial market gone to pot, but the brewery group's strong as ever. Fremlins advanced to thirty-two shillings three pence, and Benskins to seventy-five shillings on the report. . . ."

They stepped up to the dartboard, and Sondegger spoke until the defensive hunch smoothed from the man's shoulders. He didn't believe a word the drunk cripple spoke, and he would rather talk about the Exchange than Nazi spies: "Shanghai Banking dropped off sharply. . . ."

The mechanic said, "If you'd only bloody shut up—"

"I've been watching the price of rubber, too."

"The third Heine pissed his breeches and was taken into custody, and I never heard peep from the papers."

Sondegger murmured something about the advance of Indian Iron and tossed a dart into the bull's-eye. So Kruh was captured, and had been transmitting from a British safe house or prison. Gerring and Kruh both turned: The Abwehr network had fallen. Half his purpose in England had been achieved. Perhaps the other half, as well. If Tom Wall had acted as expected, Sondegger's operation was an unqualified success.

"EARL HAD NOTHING to do with Crete," Tom said again.

Earl wasn't EULT, wasn't the agent in place on Crete. Tom had been wrong, because of the morphine, the insomnia; he'd confused a personal betrayal for a professional one. He'd been deluded and drugged, the code name EULT looking like Earl to his misfiring mind, and that poem code looking like Walt Whitman. But EULT wasn't Earl, and the poem wasn't Whitman. Tom had slept, and he'd healed; he knew what treachery Earl had done and what he hadn't.

"Welcome back, Tommy," Harriet said.

"I still hate the bastard. Steal his brother's woman." But his heart loosened; Earl hadn't killed his boys. "Goddamn Earl."

The photographer bustled in with the prints. He instructed them on locking up, and the door jingled softly behind him when he left. The room was suddenly intimate. Tom and Harriet worked quietly side by side. They'd always worked well together, played well together. It hadn't been enough.

It was slow work with two hands, slower with one. Tom's back ached. His mind was numb from the tedium. He felt Harriet's gaze, and looked up.

"I find it offensive," she said, "that you blame Earl and not me."

"*You're* offended? You left me."

"I'm not speaking of leaving, I'm speaking of blame."

"He seduced you."

"He made his wishes known. I decided. It was my decision. Not his. Not yours. Mine."

Tom gestured toward the dismembered book. "You tired of working?"

"You hate him, but I'm merely a victim?"

"I don't—"

"I'm not worth hating? I'm a bagatelle, a bone between two dogs?"

"I spent some time trying to hate you, Harriet. Never could pull it off."

Her eyes softened and deepened.

He was afraid of what he might say. "Let's get this done."

He bent back over his tray. A moment later, she did the same. They picked the book apart with tweezers and magnifying glasses. His world shrank to the tray and the chemical smell of the photography studio. He found a page of asterisks—rows and columns of asterisks—and his heart leapt. But they were ink, not film. Harriet slept on the photographer's camp bed for three hours. Tom slept for four. They continued the dissection. His hand pulsed with his heartbeat. They finished after dawn. There was no second microdot.

"Doesn't matter," Tom said. "You report to your office. I'll visit the embassy." He shrugged into his jacket. "Again."

"Wait, I've a call to make first." She found the phone and spoke to the operator.

Tom read his copy of the notes. A Japanese attack on Hawaii? The Philippines, he could almost believe, but Hawaii? It was crazy. And if the U.S. had advance warning, would the attack be withdrawn? Maybe. You couldn't ambush a prepared force—not if your plan called for surprise. Made sense they'd have a cutoff date, this X-1 Day. He couldn't believe it, but had to act as if it were true. Too much was at stake.

Harriet hung up. "The aerodromes mentioned do exist, the craters, as well. The codes check—oh two five three oh-JN and East Wind Rain. Pan American has a wireless on the peninsula. If it's a fabrication, it's a professional fabrication."

"Kure base?"

"The Kurile Islands are northeast of Japan. An extensive naval base."

"How long from—"

"Two or three weeks to Hawaii. Depending on a great many things."

"The strike force left on November eighteenth," he said. "Today's what? Early morning, December fifth."

"Must be still the night of the fourth in Hawaii."

"That's two and a half weeks. If this is true, we have no time." He grabbed his print of the microphotograph and the notes. "I need a few pounds, Harriet, for a taxi to the embassy and— Shit, they'll never believe me. Not after the other day."

"They won't be open for hours. We'll stop at my office; I'll file a report, and leave a copy. We'll go to the embassy together."

"Yeah. Good," he said, pleased at the prospect of her company. Then he realized she wasn't doing him a favor. She was working: She wanted to check on Earl and the COI, and was using him to open unofficial embassy channels. "Great."

"Then shall we?" She slung her bag over her shoulder and hung Renard's plaid coat through the strap.

"What're you doing, collecting for the church jumble?"

Her eyes froze. "Perhaps I am."

THREE CRIMSON PETALS clung to the flower with the crooked stalk. One lay on the glossy desktop, clenched like a tiny fist at the base of the green glass vase.

"We expected Bloomgaard," Tom said. He needed Bloomgaard. Needed *someone*—anyone—to act on the information about Pearl Harbor. Even if the microfilm was sham, it meant something. And it came with a deadline.

"Mr. Bloomgaard hasn't yet arrived." The man in Bloomgaard's office had tufts of white hair and a blushing pink scalp. "I'm Mr. Palk, the deputy diplomatic consul. Well, *one* of the deputy diplomatic consuls."

He emitted a nervous laugh, and Harriet laughed with him, trying to put him at ease. She said it was a pleasure to meet him.

Palk assured her the pleasure was all his. "Now then, how might I be of service?"

"We have information," Tom said. "It's red-hot; it's military—it's gotta be seen, and fast, by someone who can act on it."

"And from me you want . . ."

"We want it passed along, to Military Intelligence, the COI. We can't vouch for it. It looks McCoy to me, but I'm infantry. Either way, it needs to be checked. It's—it says . . . I don't know where to start."

"It claims that a Japanese attack force is currently under way, approaching U.S. installations at Pearl Harbor." Harriet summed up a few of the points. "It's not entirely clear, however—"

"Yes, but—Japanese troops?" Palk smiled weakly. "I don't understand how you came upon this, er, bombshell. . . ."

"My husband is Earl Wall." She slid the print and her translation across the desk.

Palk reluctantly read them and said, "Hmm."

They waited for more. There was no more.

"Perhaps," Harriet said, faint spots of red appearing high on her cheeks, "my husband's coworkers might be interested in seeing this?"

"Oh, certainly, certainly. And, er, the proof mentioned, at the bottom here?"

"We haven't found the second microdot."

"Then this is an enlargement of a note that came from where, exactly?"

Tom sat back in his chair. They couldn't expose the XX Committee to embassy workers, especially not in Bloomgaard's office. Harriet planned to meet Highcastle later that day—if she could contact him—but until cleared, they couldn't mention Sondegger or Hennessey, Abwehr agents or the SD. They'd hoped it wouldn't be necessary, that the document would speak for itself.

"It was among my husband's belongings," Harriet said.

"Take the film," Tom said. "Take the notes. If it's true, we don't have time to chew gum. The strike force is moving as we speak."

"The strike force, yes," Palk said. "If one only knew the source . . ."

"Listen to me," Tom said. "If it's bullshit, fine—they'll can it. But if it's true, it must be dealt with. I don't wanna hear Kendall did it. I want to hear you'll fucking do it yourself."

The man bent a disapproving eye at Tom. "I hardly think it necessary to use such language in front of the lady."

"You'll have to excuse Thomas," Harriet said. "He oughtn't to speak as though he were raised in the fucking gutter."

The door opened before Tom could laugh. He turned: Bloomgaard.

"Don't bother standing, Mr. Wall," Bloomgaard said, his pleasant expression a transparent veneer. "Mr. Knudson is on his way; he'll help you from your chair."

Tom attempted a chagrined smile. "I was out of line the other day. The surgery . . ." He raised his bandaged hand, looking for a spark of sympathy. "Wounded on Crete. I want to apologize."

Harriet stood and offered Bloomgaard her hand. "Mr. Bloomgaard, Lady Harriet Wall. I hate to intrude, but I asked Tom to accompany me this—"

"I heard." Bloomgaard tapped the intercom box on the desk. "Red-hot information."

"It's quite alarming. I'm not certain if my husb—"

"Who found the microfilm?"

"Does it matter? If you'll take a moment to read the—"

"Who found it?"

"Tom," she said, "made the initial—"

"Ex-Sgt. Thomas Wall, of the Commonwealth infantry." Bloomgaard extracted a cigar from a case. "Of the Rowansea and the Red Army. He magically—"

Harriet tried to interrupt, but Bloomgaard spoke over her.

"—magically discovers top secret information and convinces his brother's wife to sell it to me. Is this correct?"

"Nothing *I* have is for sale, Mr. Bloomgaard. Check the information. Check the codes. November eighteenth is the date mentioned."

"Mentioned by whom, one wonders." Bloomgaard was too adamant. Of course, he was a Hitlerite—and thought Tom a raving Commie.

"My husband will no doubt explain. Where, exactly, is my husband?"

Bloomgaard inspected his cigar. "Elsewhere."

"I didn't imagine he was hiding under the desk."

"He's unavailable. On assignment." Bloomgaard turned to the door as Knudson and one of his men entered. "Ah, Mr. Knudson, escort my guests outside, and see they don't return."

Knudson and his man led them downstairs, away from the entrance. He opened a side door and Harriet stepped out.

Tom didn't. "Knudson. You served in Haiti?"

"I work for Bloomgaard now."

"In the Marine Corps—you know Franklin Berry? He'll vouch for me. All I ask is—"

"Not a chance, pal."

And Tom was outside, blinking at the morning light, as the door behind him closed and locked.

Harriet said, "We'll speak to my people."

"Good luck."

"They'll go over Bloomgaard's head. They'll have the document examined."

"Without proof? When? There's no time. This is just something mad Tom Wall found. And not being able to reveal the source . . ."

"I'll speak with your Mr. Highcastle. I can't think what else we might do."

Tom could. There were powers beyond the political. He left Harriet promising she'd find Highcastle, and slid into the taxi. He told the driver his destination: Ed Murrow at CBS. The driver pulled into traffic, fuming about the firemen who'd taken over a third of the city's fleet to tow trailer pumps, and Tom let the man's words roll over him. He saw yesterday's paper crumpled in the foot well, ripped and grimy, but the headline caught his attention:

U.S. CALLS FOR AN ANSWER

Japanese Forces in Indo-China
Plain Speaking by Mr. Roosevelt

He brushed the paper halfway clean. The Japanese were massing in Indo-China. Roosevelt called them on it, and the Japanese envoy said it was nothing; they still wished to avoid war if possible, as war wouldn't settle anything.

That was news to Tom. In his experience, war settled plenty.

The article ended at a long, jagged rip, and he scanned the next legible page. Tinned herrings were reserved for the armed forces, there'd been a big potato crop, and Noël Coward's new play *Blithe Spirit* was a smash hit. The paper said he'd written it in six days, a couple weeks after the Luftwaffe blew his London office to splinters—a genial farce about death, in which the dead return to haunt the living.

Tom snorted. He knew all about farces. Was the microphotograph genuine? His gut told him it was. But his gut had been telling all sorts of lies. . . .

He read that two German POWs had escaped from a hospital on Tuesday and been recaptured on Wednesday. Lord Derby's stallion Hyperion had won £25,836. Then he saw a headline: CHALLENGE TO U.S. ISOLATIONISTS. A new newspaper, the *Chicago Sun*, was being published in "the heart of isolationist America," to challenge the circulation monopoly of the leading organ of anti-British opinion, the *Chicago Tribune*.

"That's yesterday's news," the driver said. "For mud, not reading. You want a newsagent?"

Tom told him he was in a rush. The driver shrugged and dropped him outside the CBS building. If he couldn't get Ed Murrow, any newsman would do, anyone to take this news and shout it from the rooftops.

The receptionist listened to his story and wasn't impressed. He turned on the "Aw shucks" charm, angling toward Earl's easy conviction, and she rang an assistant just to be rid of him. He waited while the strike force sliced through the Pacific. Forty minutes later, the assistant arrived. Tom showed him the print and notes.

"How confident are you of this translation, Mr. Walt?" the assistant asked.

"Extremely."

"Translated by whom?"

"A freelance contractor."

The assistant tapped his desk blotter. "We'd have to clear it with the languages staff, of course."

Tom told him that was fine, as long as it happened today.

"And you have corroboration, of course."

"Sure. Yeah. That's on the way."

The assistant nodded. "When it arrives, call me."

"We're working against a deadline here."

"In the absence of substantiation—"

"Run it as speculation."

"We're a news organization, Mr. Walt, not a gossip mill. Without verification from a second source, we wouldn't run a sentence about the sun rising."

They went back and forth for ten minutes, and Tom accidentally lost his patience.

Back on the street, he trotted around the corner before reinforcements could arrive. He couldn't walk away from this. He wasn't going to watch dive-bombers turn Pearl Harbor into Hill 107. But whom could he trust? Try another newspaper? They'd never believe him without proof. He spent a couple of hours trying to track down Ambassador Winant, but couldn't find him— and if he did, what the hell was he going to say? Sure, Ambassador, I was bughouse yesterday, but you can trust me today.

He needed proof. He needed that second microdot. Which meant he had to go back to Sondegger, or after Earl.

CHAPTER
TWENTY-EIGHT

SONDEGGER INTERCEPTED THE MAID as she exited the greengrocer. He struggled beneath his load of groceries, he wavered, and he failed. The onion dislodged from a bunch of carrots, thumped heavily at the maid's feet. He bent to retrieve it, and lost a radish. He offered her an expression of overwhelmed good nature, and a genuine smile. He ensured she saw the stolen clerical collar he wore round his throat.

The maid lent him a hand with the errant onion. He'd discovered, earlier that morning, that she worked at the American embassy. She could confirm that Tom had whispered the microfilm's message into the right ears.

They sat together at tea. Poor innocent girl, she imagined herself a sinner. He sighed at her confessions, as if in disapproval, and she looked at her feet. Despite the improvisation he'd been forced to perform, the scene was set. The new script was as com-

265

pelling as the original. More compelling perhaps: The replacement of Earl Wall with his understudy Tom only increased the odds of success.

Sondegger spoke sternly to the maid. He understood she was employed by the Americans, but it was incumbent upon her to ensure she did not relax her own sense of probity. The girl didn't understand *incumbent* or *probity*. She was new to England and English. It didn't matter what she understood—as they spoke, *he* understood perfectly: No intelligence bombshell had been dropped at the embassy. Tom had gone to the embassy. Tom had spoken. But his message had not been heeded.

Sondegger's mission was at risk.

He disentangled himself from the maid and engaged in anti-surveillance, tutting unhappily, still in the role of the village priest. Tom had delivered the warning and been ignored, so the second microphotograph must be used; Tom must deliver that, as well. The only difficulty was time.

They would transmit tonight.

Sondegger bought a sheet of cheap paper and wrote a semiliterate letter, as if to an ailing sister. He discussed the weather at length. Plumbed the depths of his delicate digestion. Mentioned last Saturday's rugby results with great enthusiasm and little accuracy: Westminster Bank, 9; Old Paulines, 10; Gwyn Bayliss XII, 0; Rosslyn Park, 30, with Knapp, Steel, Ward, Huxley, and Gallaher.

He was telling Duckblind, first, to ready the wireless, prepare and secure the transmission location. Second, in the remote possibility that he himself would be unable to do so, locate Thomas Wall and alert him to the location of the confirmation proof microphotograph.

The streets of Shepherd Market held nothing for Sondegger. The Rowansea Royal Hospital required too much time, as did Burnham Chase. He'd go to the nightclub, then. If he failed to locate Wall there, he'd obtain a pressure asset—Earl's wife perhaps. He must find Thomas Wall and reveal the second microphotograph. Wall would return to the embassy, and this time they'd be unable to ignore the message; they would be forced to act.

"GOOD MORNING, good morning." Mr. Uphill bustled toward the hat stand. "Might a spot of tea be forthcoming? I must say, Mrs. Wall, you look perfectly . . ." He paused for a moment as he opened the door to his office, and Harriet smiled to herself. She looked dreadful. "Delightful. I see the night's rest agreed with you."

Harriet told him it had, and slid the paperwork she'd just completed into the file—another record reviewed per the ALBANS dispatch minute. Another agent to live or die from this security breach.

She fixed Uphill his tea. She'd left messages at various offices, indicating she wished to speak with a Mr. Highcastle but knew no other way to reach him. Nothing else to be done but pour the tea, add a dollop of milk. The small comforts of daily routines—the tea, the garden—helped her carry on. Unlike Tom, who was no small comfort. She'd grown used to thinking of him as a broken Earl, a weak or second-rate Earl. Seeing him whole again reminded her how wrong that was. If Earl was a lion, Tom was a panther, dark and loose and swift. Earl was the King of Hearts, true, but Tom was the Jack of Spades. He was—

She clattered the teapot onto the Chinese lacquered tray. What on earth was she thinking? She couldn't allow herself to become distracted, especially now—but anything was preferable to thinking about Father.

Tom said they were called Rugg and Renard, the men who'd

fixed him to the chair in that detestable love nest above the Waterfall. The plaid jacket Renard had left behind was folded discreetly in the bottom drawer of her desk. She'd seen it before. The man—the builder, the "ruiner"—she'd seen approaching Father's house had been wearing one precisely like it. He'd been walking with an overlarge tough who matched Rugg's description exactly. And Rugg and Renard were known sympathizers of the British Union of Fascists, as was Father.

She couldn't think of the contents of that drawer without making herself physically ill. So she would not think of it, not until she knew what must be done.

She entered Uphill's office with the tray, and he said, "Just rung off from the oddest call. You've been asked to a pressing meeting with a gentleman downstairs."

"ALBANS?"

He inspected his tea moodily. "I've no idea."

She collected herself and went downstairs. In the corner room, a squat, bullish man with gray hair and a rather vocal tie strode forward to meet her.

"Mrs. Wall," he said, taking her hand.

"Mr. Highcastle. Tom described you well."

He grunted. "Need to ask a few questions."

She sat, straightened her skirt. "I was hoping to do the same of you. You heard I was making inquiries?"

"Needed to meet you in any case. Regarding your husband."

"You'd do better to speak with the American embassy."

"Already did. Got a chilly reception."

"I know little of Earl's work, but of course I'll tell you what I can."

Highcastle grunted again, then asked about Earl's movements, about his friends, about his recent behavior and his current whereabouts.

She told him what she knew, which was essentially nothing. "Why now?" she asked. "Why speak to me now? Because Earl is missing?"

"Not sure he is."

"Because of the document Tom and I found?"

"Only landed on my desk an hour ago." He patted his attaché case. "Skimmed it, nothing more."

"From what Tom tells me, it hardly comes from a trustworthy source, but—"

"You know the source."

"Only what Tom told me."

"You trust your father, Mrs. Wall?"

She was suddenly parched. "What has he to do with this?"

Highcastle said nothing.

"He's my father."

Highcastle waited. His eyes were yellow-brown, sharp as thorns.

"I . . . No. No, I don't trust him."

He made a noise in his throat. "Man I'll call Sleet was an engineer with an Admiralty subcontractor. . . ." He rested his hip against the desk and told her a tale, abbreviated but compelling, about the Twenty Committee and the Double-Cross System. He spoke steadily and without inflection: "Now my partner is dead. The Hun is free. Your husband is the only link."

"I'm not sure I agree," she said. "You reviewed the documents? The Japanese fleet moving toward Hawaii?"

He nodded. "They appear to be sanctioned codes. Assumption is, it was passed from the Hun to your husband."

"Precisely. So that is a lead, too. Sondegger has some interest in this microfilm."

"Impossible to follow it without Earl. We have no time."

"But you'll notify the Americans?"

"And tell them what? Unconfirmed information was planted by an enemy spy? It's absurd—Hawaii? Rudolf Hess is locked in the Tower of London with a better story. My concern is Double-Cross. The Hun passed the microdot for a reason. I'm not going to act until I know what he's after."

"If it's true, we've an obligation to—"

"I know my obligations, Mrs. Wall. Give the Hun his head, he'll return the favor." He sat, as if suddenly exhausted. "You brief our girls, don't you? Before they drop?"

"Yes."

"If Double-Cross is blown, none of them will be coming home. Did your husband ever mention the name Melville?"

"Not that I recall."

"Farquhar? O'Brien? Transcriptionists? Stenography?"

"If it was work-related, I heard nothing from him."

"Your husband enjoy the opera?"

"Earl? Heavens no."

He fired dozens of questions at her. Then: "He belong to any clubs?"

She listed Earl's clubs.

"That all?"

"The Waterfall. He calls it 'the Rapids.' "

Highcastle grunted. "Friends there?"

"He likes the comedians."

"The shows?"

"I presume so."

"Takes lovers?"

She tried to say "No," but the word wouldn't emerge.

"He rents a room," Highcastle said.

"Yes."

"Has a special friend?"

"He would hardly have told me."

"Collect books?"

"He rarely even reads them."

"Microprint was in a book."

"In the spine, yes. Not bound in. Tossed inside, almost haphazardly." She told him everything she'd seen, then asked, "Did you find the men who attacked Tom? Rugg and Renard?"

"I've a man on it. They're cunning brutes, but we'll get them." He asked what Tom had told her of their attack, asked about Earl's movements again. Just then there was a tap on the door.

"Come," Highcastle called.

A young woman stuck her head in, said Mr. Wall was at the front desk.

Harriet's heart constricted. Earl had finally returned. Then she realized: "Tom."

Highcastle snorted. "Bloody toadstool after the rain. Send him in."

The young woman nodded and Harriet stared toward the door, looking at nothing. Of course it wasn't Earl, finally returned. But why not? Where was he? With a woman? Hiding? Dead?

It wouldn't be a woman. Earl wouldn't inconvenience himself so completely for a woman. Could he be dead? No. When Earl died, his passing would not go unnoticed; he would not ease like autumn to winter. Might Earl die young? Certainly. Might he die quietly? Impossible.

He was hiding, then, but from whom? Why? Earl had always been too fond of shell games on city streets.

Tom entered and stood in the doorway. He had an unlighted cigarette in his mouth, stubble on his face. His hat was under his arm and his eyes were dark and wounded and warm. The bruises on his face had faded. She caught a glimpse of how he might look to a stranger—to a woman.

"Cozy," he said, looking from Harriet to Highcastle. "Got a light?"

Highcastle tossed him a book of matches.

"You told him?" Tom asked Harriet.

She said she had. Everything except that she thought Rugg and Renard had visited her father.

Tom looked to Highcastle. "You've seen the print?"

"Forwarded to my desk this morning."

"Some reason, the embassy won't take my word it's genuine." Tom struck a match one-handed. "Can't think why."

"The Hun told you where to find it."

"Yeah."

"You failed to mention that. Slipped your mind?"

"Wasn't the only thing." The match died before Tom brought it to his cigarette, and he threw it at the ashtray and struck another. "My mind was slipping."

"What else?"

"What else did Sondegger say?" He lighted the cigarette and told them the German had known he wasn't Earl from the start. Had known about the Rapids, about Earl's room and *Tristram Shandy* and this potential surprise attack on the United States.

"Why?" Highcastle said.

"Why tell me?" Tom asked.

Highcastle grunted.

"Because Earl's evanesced. Because I'm American. I don't know."

Highcastle closed his eyes and rubbed the bridge of his nose.

"Yeah," Tom said. "Me, too."

Harriet didn't understand. She lifted an eyebrow at Tom.

"A man named Davies-Frank," he told her. "I wish he were here."

She looked from him to Highcastle. They had an affinity. From the moment Tom had entered, it was clear they enjoyed one of those male relationships based not on words or affection. Based on something less and more than friendship. Understanding perhaps.

"He escaped," Highcastle said.

Tom went still as a hunted animal. "Sondegger? No."

"Killed three of my men. He's free."

Tom felt the floor shift. He ground his cigarette into the ashtray to steady himself. Sondegger was free.

"The Twenty Committee . . ." he said.

"Hanging by a frayed thread."

"And Duckblind? No leads from the bomb that killed Rupert?"

Highcastle shook his head. "We presume he's gone to ground until transmission."

"How long will that be?"

"Could be an hour, could be a week—though the microdot is heartening. Means he's not only checking Abwehr agents; he has another initiative running, and—"

"That's heartening?" Harriet said.

Highcastle nodded. "Won't dare transmit twice. They'll wait on both initiatives before transmitting. Buys us time, unless the microdot's only meant to muddy the waters."

"You think it's a diversion?" Tom asked.

"You think it's the truth?" Highcastle snorted. "It was written in German and delivered by Sondegger. What odds that it's true?"

"The codes check; the information checks. Yeah, the SD are professionals. But why lie about—"

"Real question is, Why tell the truth?"

They kicked questions around for twenty minutes. "Maybe a screen for the SD investigation," Highcastle said. "Internal Nazi politics, to keep the Abwehr off balance."

"Elaborate screen," Harriet said.

"It's not a goddamn screen," Tom said.

"Hawaii," Highcastle said. "Why bother? Can't establish a base there. Japanese negotiators are still in D.C., after they launched an attack force on the eighteenth?"

"That's what makes it surprising," Tom said.

Highcastle grunted. "My first duty is clear. Save the Twenty."

"Your first duty," Tom said. "Not your only."

"Today, we control the Nazi network in England. Tomorrow, whenever Duckblind transmits, the whole thing is blood and rubble. How many lives hang in that balance?"

"Mr. Highcastle's right," Harriet said. "There's nothing more important. We subverted an entire network—it's extraordinary—it could be the key to Europe."

Tom stood at the window and didn't see the street outside. "You'll inform the COI about Pearl Harbor, though. You can't do otherwise."

"Inform them what?" Highcastle said. "Six months ago, Rudolph Hess flew himself—"

"I know the goddamn story, Highcastle. Hess came—and you told the Americans."

"Hess wanted an audience with the king, or so he said. To negotiate a treaty against the Soviets, or so he said. You think we took his word for it, drove him to Buckingham Palace? No. Good thing, too, because he's off his trolley. First we learn what's going on; then we act."

"There's no time to fuck around."

"You want the Hun's parcel wrapped in a bow? No proof but his good intentions?"

"There's no time, Highcastle. There's no time."

"Then go. Find the second microdot. Find proof."

OUTSIDE, TOM PAUSED at a telephone box for a tram to pass. "We need proof, so we need Earl. First we check the last place he was seen. The East End."

"The East End?" Harriet crossed the road beside him, her pale hand firm on the brim of her dark hat. "You saw Earl in the East End?"

"Yeah."

"Where?"

"I wasn't consulting Baedeker." Past the crowd of shouting firemen, the burned-out draper's shop. "I'll recognize it."

"When was this, Tommy?"

"During the raid the other night."

"You were in Shepherd Market."

"I was, yeah, when it started."

"And you went east? Toward the bombs?" Her voice was sharp with disbelief. "You followed the raid."

"I didn't follow it. I happened to be . . ."

"To be what?"

"Going that direction?"

She laughed. He'd forgotten what her laugh sounded like. "You were a little overwrought."

"I'm better now," he said. "I saw him, Harry. I was ten yards away."

"You're certain it was Earl?"

"You couldn't mistake anyone for Earl."

An unreadable expression clouded her face. "Couldn't I?"

"I saw him."

"We'll start at the Rapids. The last location at which he was reliably seen."

" 'Reliably'? I'm telling you—"

"Do you think I want to go? Do you think I'm a fool, I don't know my own husband? Well, I can bear the sniggers and the coy superior looks. I can bear the presence of his tarts, because I must." Her jaw was clenched into a sharp, bloodless curve. "My agents are facing such dangers that worrying over a husband's infidelity would be a welcome relief."

He knew Harriet well enough to keep silent. They walked a block, crossed the street. She slipped her arm through his. She was wrong about the Waterfall: It was a dead end. Tom had seen Earl in the East End, had followed him for ten blocks.

"We'll go to your house," he said. "Get a recent photograph and knock on doors. He's in Stepney or Wapping, maybe the docks—in the warehouses, the bombed-out buildings. . . ."

She didn't respond. She fit perfectly on his arm.

"Once I recognize the neighborhood, we'll knock on doors," he said as they threaded through a group of soldiers on the corner. "We'll talk to boardinghouses."

Harriet held him close, didn't speak.

"We'll check evacuated apartments. We'll talk to food vendors. Even Earl has to eat."

Her fine brown hair moved in the breeze of a passing bus.

"Fine," he said. "The Waterfall."

CHAPTER
TWENTY-NINE

THE WIRELESS was in *super* condition, safe as houses in Duck-blind's baby blue straw bag with the lemon ribbon curling prettily round it. The transmitter was ready, Mr. Pentham's house was neat as a pin, and she was breathless from dancing.

She'd bought a few trifles at a darling this-and-that shop off Threadneedle, and though Mr. Pentham's gramophone hadn't seen a great deal of use, it bore up mightily under the strain of "You Can't Stop Me from Dreaming" and "It's De-Lovely." She spun herself giddy as the song ended. She'd found simply the *perfect* spot from which to transmit. She expected they'd be sending tonight or tomorrow, depending on Bookbinder—and one could *always* depend on Bookbinder.

She tucked the straw bag into the wicker pram and checked herself in the mirror, modeling one of Mr. Pentham's silly old shirts. It cried out for his clunky cuff links, but one of the links had popped from the cuff yesterday. It took her quite another ten minutes to pick a new pair and leave the house.

The next scheduled drop to contact Bookbinder was Ebury Square. There were days and days of scheduled locations, no two repeated. She took the Tube to Sloane Square, where she found a lovely tea shop. Ebury was hardly a stroll away. After her tea, she came out into a drizzling soft mist and a very handsome old gentleman asked if she wasn't getting too wet. She flirted happily but with a great deal of decorum. She did enjoy the English. If only they weren't so *stupid*! Unwilling to admit the new Reich was rising as their own empire fell.

Ebury Square had a scattering of benches under leafless thick-limbed trees. In the center was a modest fountain, and the park was surrounded by blocky, tentatively modern buildings. Two women were pushing prams, and a horse clattered by, pulling a cart. Duckblind cleared the area, then checked the fountain.

The base had been marked! Bookbinder was free. Her heart beat a little faster. He'd been right here.

She fiddled with her shoe, as if she had a pebble in it, while she checked the mark on the fountain. She sat on the bench indicated and fiddled a bit more. Then she rose and departed, the note safely tucked in the heel of her pump.

At a distant street corner, she read the letter. His delicate digestion indeed. She laughed. *Rosslyn Park, 30, with Knapp, Steel, Ward, Huxley, and Gallaher.* She checked the order of the names against the newspaper, deciphered the remainder, and was beyond pleased.

They would transmit tonight. And her secondary instructions were to keep an eye on Tommy Wall. Well, she'd been eyeing him for some time, since the little man in the waistcoat had passed his name. Oh, but what a very *funny* place to hide the microfilm. How silly Tommy would feel when she told him.

AUDREY DUSTED THE FLAT and noticed the furniture needed a good polish. She polished, which brought out the dinginess of the floor, so she swept and mopped, then rolled the rug into a cylinder, hauled it outside, and thrashed it savagely. The room looked better, except the blackout curtains trapped filth terribly. She cleaned the windows, swept the floor again, and ate a tin and a half of Woolworth's sweet biscuits. She straightened the lamp shade, tidied the kitchen cabinets, scoured the sink and the fridge. Finally, she took up her knitting bag and mangled a bit of yarn.

The front door sounded and Imogene wafted in and lifted an eyebrow at the spotlessness.

"Whatever it is," she said. "It can't be *that* bad."

"Or that good," Audrey said. She hadn't seen Imogene since yesterday, and the redhead was glowing with satisfaction. "You look like the cat who—"

"That canary was delicious. I—" Imogene noticed the knitting bag. "Knitting, too, Vee? Tell me all."

"I don't like living in a rubbish heap."

"The new Mr. Wall, I presume?"

"The rug was filthy. The kitchen was worse."

Imogene inspected the misshapen cobweb Audrey had knitted. "What could he possibly have done to deserve this?"

"Oh, Genie . . ." Audrey told her she'd thrown herself at Tom as brazenly as she knew how, and been rejected. She'd left a message for Harriet Wall, whom Tom loved despite everything. She'd finished an entire tin of biscuits. . . .

Imogene started to interrupt, then stopped herself.

"What?" Audrey asked.

"Your Tommy is in the lobby. With a woman who must be his brother's wife."

The biscuits turned to cement in Audrey's stomach. "Now? I mean—*now?*"

"They're asking after Inch. Russell's on the door; he was saying Inch would arrive momentarily, if they'd wait."

"What sort of looking woman is she?"

"The sort a man would love for her manners, her mother, or her money."

"Truly?"

"Horse-faced. Utterly Newmarket."

Audrey stood and brushed dust from her sloppy joe sweater and turned to Imogene. "How am I?"

"Disastrous. You've a smut on your nose and no lipstick. You can't think—"

"I'll only peep round the door," she said, rubbing her nose with her sleeve. "She won't see me."

"Pull on your green shirtwaister."

"But what if she's gone?" she wailed. "I'll only peek."

"If you must, Vee, but remember—" Imogene grinned. "Ramrod-straight, and chin up!"

Audrey laughed shakily and ran down the corridor. She took a slow, calming breath at the door to the lobby. None of the girls but she and Imogene had a flat in the building—because, as she delighted in telling the Three Annes, the management had standards. She exhaled and the door swung open before she could lay a hand on it.

Tom was there with a posh woman in a floral frock and a fur coat. She was taller than Audrey, and slimmer—a neat, boyish figure—and older. She had a strong face, a good complexion, striking light eyes, and the sort of carriage one is born with, or never attains. Lady Harriet Wall was a graceful swan. Audrey Pritchett was a fat, waddling duck.

"Aud—Miss Pritchett," Tom said, and she spared him a

glance. He hadn't even the grace to appear abashed. He looked different, though. No, he looked the same, only more so.

"Mr. Wall," she said.

"You going out?" he asked. "We need to find Inch. I thought you might— What? Oh. Miss Pritchett, Harriet Wall."

Audrey liked that she was rated first in the introduction. Didn't like that she was wearing an old sweater and baggy slacks and her hair was a shapeless lump. She said she was charmed to meet Mrs. Wall. Lady Harriet said likewise, with a perfectly posh accent, and smiled as if she meant it. Her eyes were warm and clear, but Audrey saw a hint of wariness. Good. Lady Harriet offered her hand and Audrey resisted the urge to curtsy. She laughed at herself, and Lady Harriet's wariness sharpened into suspicion: afraid of what she'd learn of her husband during her visit to the demimonde. The graceful swan was afraid of the waddling duck!

"Take no notice," Audrey said. "Excess levity is a failing of mine—one of masses."

"I cannot believe that, Miss Pritchett."

"Oh, ask anyone. Ask Tommy."

They turned to Tom, who feigned interest in his matchbook.

"You have lovely hands," Audrey said. "Do you salve them?"

"They're my only passable feature, and all I do is neglect them shamefully."

"Well, I suppose"—Audrey was careful not to look at Tom— "I suppose one is sometimes best treated by those things one most neglects."

"Or one most neglects those things that treat one best."

Audrey managed an agreeable smile, unsure if Lady Harriet was speaking of Tom or his brother, although entirely sure she'd not win a duel of wits.

"We need Inch," Tom said. "You know where he is?"

"Your husband is a member here," Audrey said, making pleasant conversation.

"Yes." Lady Harriet's eyes grew a shade tighter.

"How lucky you are! All the girls are terribly jealous. He's quite dashing."

"I've always thought so."

"And a novelty, as well. An American gentleman, I mean. Well, there are two of them now." Audrey glanced at Tom. "No longer so unusual."

"I'm not sure I agree," Lady Harriet said. "Tom continues to surprise."

Audrey gritted her teeth into a smile. "Isn't that the loveliest thing about very *old* friends?"

"Christ," Tom said. "You can chat later."

Is that what he thought they'd been doing? Chatting? Even the brightest men could be so stupid. "You're looking for Inch," Audrey said.

"Harriet spoke to his commander. They've no idea where he is. Thought he'd be here, but the doorman's blowing smoke."

"Tom said you might help us find him." Lady Harriet's gaze was suddenly calm and direct. "It would mean a great deal. It's more important than we can say."

Beautiful, smart, and sincere. Awful cow. Still, Audrey owed Inch. Would he want to be found? If it were just Tommy . . .

"He mentioned he was taking his niece on an outing," she said. "The Sickert Exhibition? Do you have the address of his family home?"

Lady Harriet said she'd already rung.

There was one other address that Audrey knew. She tried to rise above the pettiness. She failed. "Terribly sorry," she said. "I've no idea where he might be."

THE TURBOT WAS MERELY ADEQUATE, but the duck and plum pie was excellent, and the *poulet à l'estragon* better still.

Chilton dabbed at his mouth with the linen napkin. He did not, as a rule, enjoy coming to town, but the business of politics required sacrifice. Sadly, the club offered only marmalade dumpling with clotted cream to finish—closer to Harriet's taste than his own.

Chilton smiled into his wineglass, thinking of his daughter. She was an eccentric, but he enjoyed sending her home with parcels of steak and kidney in order to satisfy her "low cravings." It was, however, problematic when her eccentricities intruded into the realm of the political. Lady Chilton had known better, and he'd hoped Harriet would emulate her mother. He'd hoped her flirtation with politics would have ended long since. It hadn't, and now they both must pay the price.

Chilton had meditated on dead Mr. Melville's note at some length. Herr Sonder was apparently a German defector who intended to damage the Abwehr network, using the parcel he'd given Tom. Chilton did not have a clear idea of this turncoat's plans, of course, but he could not allow any such antifascist initiative to proceed. He had instructed Rugg and Renard to secure the defector's parcel from Tom . . . at any price.

"You may suppress Tom Wall," he'd told them. "To prevent the parcel being delivered."

" 'Suppress'?" Renard had asked.

"If need be, to prevent him from damaging our interests— Tom Wall must die."

They had understood that at least, and brightened with malignant purpose. A pity, but the business of politics required sacrifice. Chilton finished his wine and stood from the table. No time to dwell on it. He had his own task to perform, which would brook no delay.

THE BELL JINGLED as Sondegger entered Tudor's Dry Cleaning and Pressing, from where he might observe the Waterfall. The bell was precisely the same pitch as the intermission bell at the Munich Kammerspiele, which he took as a propitious sign for his upcoming performance.

Performance and intelligence were as closely twined as life and breath; espionage and theater were the same. As a young man, Sondegger had traveled to Russia to study at the Moscow Art Theatre, to become one of Stanislavsky's "knights of culture." After the outbreak of the Great War, the Abwehr—the Nicolai Abwehr, not the current, contemptible organization—had approached him following a production of Chekhov's *The Cherry Orchard*. Was he loyal? Was he able? Was he willing?

He'd seen the potential immediately, and from that moment lived in two worlds, both of them stages. There were no lessons more apt for the world of shadows than those taught for the spotlights. Stanislavsky's new Method was Sondegger's inspiration: Truth cannot be separated from belief, nor belief from truth; the actor uses words to instill his inner vision in others; success requires complete surrender, passionate desire.

Following the Great War and the fall of imperial Germany, the Nicolai Abwehr had been briefly disbanded. But Sondegger's service had not been forgotten, and when he was called upon again to trod the boards in the service of his country, he did not consider refusing. An actor was only as great as his parts, and there was no part greater than this.

He stepped farther into Tudor's and closed the door gently

behind. He identified two viable exits—stage right and stage left—and waited in the queue to speak with the clerk. He needed to find Tom immediately. Once informed of the location of the second microphotograph, Tom would faithfully deliver it.

In the mirror behind the counter, perfectly on cue, he caught sight of the American, who was walking past with a woman who could only be Lady Harriet. Sondegger did a little business with his borrowed briefcase and exited the shop in time to see them enter the Waterfall.

He was more than pleased with the serendipity. The Waterfall, however, was not the place for a delicate operation. He would wait for Tom to exit, then act.

Three locations recommended themselves as observation points. At the least of them, a sharp-faced man slouched against a lamppost, picking his protruding teeth with the folded edge of a newspaper. At the best, between a newspaper van and a wine bar, a matronly woman watched a chalk artist draw on the pavement as a large man cracked his knuckles nearby.

Sondegger secured the third point. He would whisper into Wall's ear, ensure the proof was delivered. He would meet Duckblind and they would transmit. One report to the SD—to destroy the tainted Abwehr network—the other a code within a code, to his own cohort. The Americans would not intrude further in the war. Not, at least, until the British and Russians had been safely defeated.

HIGHCASTLE SAT AT HIS DESK, head in his hands, and ran his weary gaze over the map between his elbows—Hennessey Gate, Tipcoe's boardinghouse, Melville's deadly rubble, the street where the bomb had killed Rupert and two unidentified children. . . .

Sixteen points on the map, mute and meaningless. Highcastle's sole duty was keeping the Double-Cross System safe. He'd failed. He'd flooded London with direction-finding vans, trebled security for the turned agents, even sent Tom Wall and Lady Harriet after Earl, with Ginger tailing them in case of contact. Long shots didn't come any longer.

A secretary tapped at the open door, carrying his lunch. Highcastle waved her away. There was an angle he was missing. He was missing Rupert, too. It was in memory of Rupert that he'd passed the microfilm to the Americans, despite his fears—and the Americans were frankly unimpressed. Didn't make any sense, so Highcastle made inquiries and learned the Yanks had already received the bulk of the information several months ago.

One of MI-6's double agents, a Slav code-named Quadrangle, had been sent to the States last summer with a microdot of his own. His microdot didn't mention Ambassador Oshima, or the composition of the strike force—or the November eighteenth date of sail—but it contained exhaustive questions about the Pearl Harbor base. The similarity to Tom Wall's microdot was striking, almost word for word.

Quadrangle had met the head of the Yanks' domestic intelligence agency, the FBI—man named Hoover—after being kept waiting a month. Always the playboy, the Slav had passed the time living the good life in New York, with blond twins in his bed and FBI microphones in his lamp shades. When Hoover finally condescended to meet, he said he had no use for foreign spies. He confiscated Quadrangle's funds, almost arrested his German contact, and threatened him with violating the Mann Act when he took an unmarried woman to Florida. Not a word about Pearl Harbor. As far as Highcastle could tell, the information died on Hoover's desk.

Highcastle couldn't figure it. Had Wall's microdot been based—by the Hun or his masters—on Quadrangle's microfilm, in an effort to deceive? Or did the duplication of the data mean it was correct?

The phone rang. It was Illingworth, saying the bomb that had killed Rupert was a BD2 *Splitterbombe*, no doubt a salvaged dud. And he had news about Mr. Melville.

"Melville, the transcriptionist who died in the rubble? It wasn't an accident."

"No, sir," Illingworth said. "A pocket diary was found among his effects, and—"

"No diary in the original report."

"The coroner's office overlooked it. It wasn't logged until last night."

Highcastle grunted.

"Mr. Melville apparently established a relationship with Sondegger and had been, er, unduly influenced by him."

" 'Unduly influenced'?"

"Melville had been turned, sir."

"From the other room? By voice alone?"

"So it appears. He apparently believed he was acting for king and country. That Sondegger was working *against* the Germans."

"Go on."

Illingworth told him the diary mentioned Sondegger and Wall, mentioned a parcel for Tom and a meeting with Duckblind. "Melville used a highly personal form of stenography; we've had trouble deciphering it. However, if you recall the air-raid warden?"

"Who found Melville's body?"

"He claims the body was warm when he found it. No lividity. No rigor."

"And?"

"There was a young person on the scene, a young woman."

"A witness? Tell me he got a name."

"I'm afraid not, sir."

"Bloody hell."

"Yes, sir."

"Description?"

"Average height, slender, light hair, knee-length skirt. Likely in her early twenties. Nicely turned ankles, good accent."

Something about Illingworth's tone tugged at Highcastle. "You don't peg her for a witness."

"The warden thought he'd heard scuffling. When he saw the woman, he thought lovemaking. Then he saw the body."

"She killed him? Bloody hell, Duckblind's a woman! Blond and young, and I'd wager green-eyed." It fit with what the Hun had told Tom, and Highcastle's heart pounded with the chase. "I need every incident report checked for mention of a young woman. We need a general call." He scribbled notes as he spoke. "Well done, Illingworth."

"I took the liberty of authorizing the incident reports examined, sir. Not yet finished, of course, but there was one curiosity. A young woman wandered, by apparent accident, into Kingsway-F. She—"

"Which one is Kingsway-F?"

"The office building, sir."

Bloody code names. It was a secure building, from which they ran some of the more trusted Double-Cross agents. "And?"

"Mr. Digby's LCO is stationed there. Digby is, I believe, one of the names on the list you sent of Abwehr agents likely to be targets of the Hun's investigation. It's just possible that—"

"How long ago? Any distinguishing marks? Tell me something. Anything."

"She had a dog, sir."

"What about the bloody dog?"

"The men believe it was a Pekingese."

Highcastle snorted. "She's disposed of it already. Still, try notices about lost dogs. Paper the city, we might stumble on luck."

"Yes, sir."

"What else?" There had to be something. Something to scratch the itch at the base of Highcastle's scalp, telling him he missed an angle.

"I'm afraid that's all I have."

Highcastle put his head back in his hands. A young woman with a well-turned ankle and a Pekingese, abroad in London. Impossible.

"I'VE REALLY NO IDEA where Inch might be." Audrey pretended her cheeks weren't flaming red, pretended she didn't feel Tom's disbelieving gaze. "You might ask Jacko and Murch, or his sister. Inch pretends to dislike her, but don't believe it." She was babbling, and unable to stop herself. "He dotes on his niece. He—"

"Audrey," Tom said.

"Well, I haven't any nieces," she said desperately. "Or nephews. And I haven't any idea where he might be, except— Oh!"

Inch was at the door, leaning on his crutch. "Hullo-ullo-ullo, what?" he said to Russell. "You rang and, like whatshisname's hounds, I froth."

Russell murmured something and gestured toward the three standing outside the door to Audrey's flat.

Inch lurched forward. "The Duke of Wall and— Well! What divine creature do I see before me?" He bowed to Lady Harriet, playing the buffoon. "I have not had the pleasure, the honor—"

"Harriet, Flight Lieutenant Inch," Tom said. "Inch, Mrs. Wall."

"Lady Harriet! I say!"

She extended her hand. "Pleased to meet you, Flight Lieutenant."

Inch leaned on his crutch, kissed her wrist. "Pleasure's mine."

"We have a couple questions, Inch," Tom said.

"What?" Inch blinked. "I mean to say, a couple Hessians?"

Audrey almost laughed. Inch had a hard enough time with an American accent without being dazzled by Mrs. Wall. They'd be lucky to get a single coherent sentence from him.

"Questions about my husband," Lady Harriet said. "Anything you might have inadvertently overheard. Perhaps about Hyde Street Misfits."

Inch understood *her* well enough. "Hyde Street Misfits? 'Course it don't exist. No such street. Chimera of an unbalanced mind." He winked at Tom. "By which I mean yours, old boy, not my own."

"We need to hear it again," Tom said. "All of it."

"Shall we go downstairs, then," Inch said, "to table and chair and pianoforte? Nothing to offend the refined sensibility, Lady Harriet—least not this early, what?"

"A fine idea," Lady Harriet said.

"I should be getting back," Audrey said, gesturing to her flat. Because she could take no more. "Pleased to meet you, Mrs. Wall."

"We need you as well," Tom said.

"Me?" Dressed like this, with Lady Harriet Wall present? Not unless Tom had a very good reason.

"To translate," he said, eyeing Inch.

Not good enough. She preferred to sulk in her room.

"Charming outfit, Venus, by the by," Inch said. "Oliva Twist, don't you know, always so enchantingly waifish."

Always? Curse Inch. Lady Harriet would think she didn't know how to dress herself. "I'll meet you downstairs in a jiff." She slipped into her flat and yelled for Imogene. "Genie, help! I need—*everything*!"

Imogene's voice floated from the back of the flat: "In the bedroom." She'd already laid Audrey's dusky rose wiggle dress on the bed.

"You angel!" Audrey said, pulling her sweater over her head. "It's not too early for this?"

"There isn't a man alive who'd care."

"Tom won't even notice." Not even the wiggle dress, which was so tight that it made her walk with one foot directly in front of the other. "It's horrid. They're perfectly comfortable with each other."

"Good," Imogene said. "After comfort comes boredom. Not those stockings—these."

"You think?"

"Men don't want the comfortable, especially when horse-faced."

"She's beautiful, not horsey."

"Stupid girl." Imogene brushed Audrey's hair fiercely. "She has the sort of beauty only women notice, and who cares for that?"

"Inch noticed."

"There is nobody more womanish than he," she said, pinning Audrey's hair.

Audrey laughed. "I'll tell him!"

"Do." Imogene stepped back to survey her work, then pinched Audrey's cheeks. "Glowing on the outside, as well. Now go dazzle. And Vee? Be nothing but yourself."

TOM STUCK an unlighted cigarette in his mouth and listened to Inch natter. Tea came. A comedian delivered unfunny lines from the stage and Inch delivered unfunny lines at the table. Tom should be in the East End, knocking on doors. . . .

"I was upstairs," Inch said. "The siren suddenly stopped and Earl was yelling in my ear."

"From the hallway?" Tom asked.

"Wasn't in the hallway—was upstairs. My room's the Maltese. Needed a place in town, away from . . . Well, a bird with clipped wings sharing a cage with—"

"You were outside," Tom said. "And the door wasn't quite closed, and you heard what, exactly?"

"Told you seven times."

"Tell me eight."

"Heard Earl bellowing about gent's apparel. Always dresses to a snap, the Earl. Man could wear a Turkish rug to Mouflet's."

"That's all? Nothing about Hyde Street Misfits?"

"Gent's apparel, told you seven—"

"With whom was he speaking?" Harriet asked.

"Haven't a notion. Imagine it was one of the girls." Inch blanched. "The chars, I mean."

Harriet's gaze was steady. "I know why he took a room, Flight Lieutenant. This is more important than my injured pride. He said nothing about Hyde Street Misfits?"

"Joke of ours, Hyde Street Misfits, but the Earl said 'gent's apparel.' Thought he was addressing me. Then realized he'd been talking to the, er, char, and slunk past quiet as a velvet church mouse. Days later, Vee was storming about, looking to boil him in paste. Then you came asking—"

"Why did she want him?" Harriet asked.

"Venus? Well, could be for one reason, could be for another. Could be for— Oh!" Inch nodded toward the red-and-gold stairs. "Horse's mouth, I mean to say."

Audrey descended the last two steps to the floor. It hadn't

been fifteen minutes, and she was transformed. Her glossy black hair was a silken crown, and her face was flushed, her lips ripe. Her breasts were high and full, her waist was a hand span, and her hips flared beneath her tight dress.

Tom caught himself staring, and realized that Inch had finally shut up. The two men rose and watched the girl approach. It was better than any show on the stage, but Harriet didn't rise and didn't stare. She asked Audrey why she'd been looking for Earl.

Audrey said she'd been upset with him.

"About what?" Harriet said.

"A personal matter."

"And what personal matter might that be?"

"A personal matter of the sort that will remain personal," Audrey said.

"Well!" Inch said, casting nervous glances at the women. "I heard the Earl say 'gent's apparel.' Didn't catch more than that."

" 'Gent's apparel . . .' " Tom tapped a finger against his glass. "And nothing else?"

"Wait," Audrey said. "Wait. 'Gent's apparel'?"

"Brought to mind Hyde Street," Inch said, "on account of Pongo McCormick."

"Remember my lessons, Tommy? How to speak Yank in three days?" Audrey put her hands over Inch's eyes. "I've an idea."

She leaned to Tom and whispered in his ear. It took him a moment to realize what she was getting at. He shook his head. "It can't be that simple."

"And mumble," she whispered.

"That's swell, dollface," Tom said, his voice coming from somewhere in Brooklyn. "But I gotta see a man at Regent's Canal."

Audrey removed her hands from Inch's eyes. "Sound familiar, Inch?"

" 'Gotta see a man at gent's apparel,' " Inch said. "Odd moment for the Earl to repair his wardrobe, but I applaud the intent. Would you mind terribly, telling me what you're on about? I mean to say, my pleasure, charming company, happy to oblige, but you're all barking mad."

"Regent's," Tom said. "Canal."

SONDEGGER ENGAGED in cursory antisurveillance when Tom and Harriet Wall emerged from the Waterfall. The chalk artist was gone, chased by the rain. The large man remained, as did the man at the lamppost, picking his teeth. They drifted after Wall in a loose pincer. Sondegger followed the followers. He would whisper, and be gone.

CHAPTER
THIRTY

TOM TIGHTENED HIS BANDAGE as he and Harriet crossed Baker Street. Something was wrong with his hand, the dull ache now a sharp burn, but he didn't have time to stop. The sky was feature-less, gray and drizzling, a hopeless sky for a hopeless task.

Regent's Canal ran nine miles, through three tunnels dug under the city streets, through a dozen double locks with resident lockkeepers at every pair. Hundreds of thousands of tons of cargo a year were transported by horse-drawn barges and steam chain tugs, and old-time boatmen. The route ran from Paddington Basin through Regent's Park, where it split, one branch curving south into a cargo basin surrounded by the houses and shops of Cumberland Market, the other running east past Islington, skirt-ing Victoria Park, and heading south to Stepney and Limehouse and Regent's Canal Dock.

"Nine miles." Tom stepped off the curb into a puddle. "It's

almost two weeks since Earl headed for the canal—if he did. And we're supposed to pick up his trail?"

Harriet brushed a wet strand of hair from her cheek. She'd hardly spoken since the Waterfall, withdrawn into herself; more than worried, she was afraid.

"Earl's a cat," Tom said, to reassure her. "He always ends on his feet."

"It's not him that worries me."

"What, the Japs?" Cutting through the water toward Hawaii, if they were attacking. If it wasn't a lie . . .

"Highcastle asked that I join you, Tom, and I'm happy to. From loyalty to you, not because I believe the microfilm."

"You and your loyalty."

"Despite what you pretend to think," she said, "I never stopped caring."

"Like the Fliegerkorps cared for Crete."

The drizzle thickened and Harriet opened her umbrella. She didn't ask Tom if he wanted to share. A rivulet streamed from the brim of his hat to his shoulder. A bus spat a billow of damp exhaust as he and Harriet headed toward Broad Walk—classic Regency houses, terraces shored up by rough timbers or reduced to a rubble of Bath stone and scraps of bronze. They entered Regent's Park, where fat gray squirrels chittered in chestnut trees and wood pigeons beat the air with startled wings.

They passed flower gardens and barrage-balloon sites, and cricket fields converted to Home Guard training grounds. Harriet put her hand back on his arm and stayed close on the bridge over the canal. The water was sluggish and reflected the gray of the sky. Drizzle pocked the surface.

"Nobody knows him like we do," Harriet said.

"Why was he here, then?" Tom said.

"Perhaps to disappear."

"He'd been given the microfilm, right? He didn't take it to the embassy; he hid it in a book. Why? Say he arranged to meet his runner here." He shook his head, sending droplets of water in an arc. "Nix that. The microfilm was still in his room. Why come here?"

They turned left onto Prince Albert Road and Harriet said, "For the confirmation microdot."

"Had to be. Earl would get the whole story before reporting in. So who was he talking to in his room?"

"One of his women."

"Say it was Sondegger. He'd already given Earl the first microfilm, and they were setting a meet to hand over the second."

"Why?"

"Operational flexibility."

Harriet considered. "Possible. Sondegger meets Earl, gives him the bait but withholds the proof."

"Yeah. Earl got the first microdot and came here for the second. . . ."

"If it was Sondegger in his room."

"Say it wasn't. Say it was . . . No, it doesn't matter. The only lead we have to Earl is here."

So they checked. They showed Earl's picture at warehouses and the public gymnasium and a depot for spare parts for buses. They asked at the block of recently constructed residential flats. They talked to the women running the boats, called "idle women" for their IW armbands. None of them had seen Earl, but more than one, eyeing his picture, said she wished she had. They spoke with a man watching the brush turkeys in the zoo, and another pushing a handcart past the empty zebra cages. They finished at the zoo offices, with nothing. They'd given too much weight to Inch's memory, because there was nothing else.

A DOZEN WRENS sat around the table, young girls with fresh faces. Rupert would have charmed them speechless before he said a single word, but all Highcastle could think was that Duckblind wasn't much older, and held a thousand lives in the palm of her unlined hand.

He cleared his throat, and the room went silent. He gestured at the stacks of incident reports. "It's not glamorous work. Airless room, hard chairs. Tea like pond water. Nobody'll ever thank you." His voice deepened the hush in the room. "Lives depend on you today. I depend on you. Read each report; look for any mention of a young woman—a young woman, or a small dog."

There was a titter from one of the girls, and the others strained to remain serious.

"I know," he said, thinking what Rupert would say. "Sounds like *The Wizard of Oz*. But do you have a brother fighting? A father, cousin, a lover?" The girls laughed, and their warrant officer cleared her throat in warning. "You think the war's fought far away? It's fought here, today, at this table."

He wanted to inspire the Wrens, to rally them. He gave them the details instead, and they got to work. Another long shot, but he'd take every shot available. He was still missing an important angle; he felt it in the hollow of his stomach.

Back in his office, Illingworth reported that the woman with the dog—possibly Duckblind—had walked a block or two, waited at the bus station, and then vanished. His men were speaking to the drivers.

"Anything else on Melville?" Highcastle asked.

"Nothing new, sir." Illingworth slid a copy of his report across the desk.

Highcastle patted his pocket for his spectacles. Learned nothing, except that his bloody spectacles were broken again. "Started with the Hun turning himself in, to infiltrate counterintel. It worked, but he was stuck at Hennessey. So he sent Melville to Duckblind. That's how she knew to rig a bomb."

"Pardon me, sir—Melville was thoroughly vetted."

Highcastle grunted. "Can't vet for the Hun. Melville was recruited through a microphone, sight unseen. The Hun has . . ." He caught a thread of thought: "Melville was turned. Tipcoe's arrested. Rupert's dead. Who else listened to him?"

"The other transcriptionists?"

"Right." Highcastle scribbled a note—Farquhar and O'Brien were to be brought in immediately, under guard. "Question is, Why the microdot? Why Tom Wall? Say the Hun is using Wall the same as he used Melville. To send a message."

"What message?"

"Damned if I know. That bloody microphotograph. I'm still not sure if I was playing the Hun's game, taking it to the Yanks. But can't do more than—" He stopped. It was the angle he'd been missing. "Bloody hell."

"Sir?"

"Did you see Rupert before he—before—"

"No, I—"

"He was wearing gray. A gray shirt. The cuff link we found? It was gold."

TOM AND HARRIET passed Blow-Up Gate, talked to an old Hungarian man with a young boy, selling bread and bangers from a cart. The man had seen a dozen gentlemen who looked like Earl's picture; the boy had seen none. Harriet bought a half loaf and they cut up to the canal, where they stood in the waning drizzle and extravagantly tossed crumbs to the ducks.

Tom was aching again, his face and hand. If the microdot was genuine, he needed someone to send a message to Japan, saying that they knew a strike force was sailing east toward Hawaii. The Japs could abort, or be met with a prepared force. If there was time to prepare. If it wasn't yet X-1 Day.

He watched the ducks in the canal squabble over a crumb. Lucky bastards—at least they knew what they were after.

Harriet broke a long silence: "Earl really hasn't any imagination, has he?"

"Never needed any." Tom tossed the ducks another crumb. "When we played hide-and-seek, he hid the same place every time."

"Did he?"

"In the linen closet with Maribeth Carlisle."

"No imagination." She tilted her umbrella back to reveal her pale face. "I have plenty, too much. I thought I needed someone solid, someone with no doubts, no fears. Someone impervious."

Tom tapped a cigarette out of his pack and it was freckled by rain before he brought it to his mouth.

"Someone to dismiss my fears, to tell me"—Harriet almost smiled—"not to worry my pretty little head. An anchor. Earl's that way, but you . . ."

Tom ruined two matches, trying to light them one-handed, and tossed them into the canal. The ducks drifted toward them and pecked disdainfully.

"I love Earl," she said. "For what he is—and what he isn't."

Tom finally struck a match that caught fire. He let it die without lighting his cigarette and threw it after the others. The drizzle was ticking the ground; the sky was smudged and smelled more of earth than rain.

"But I wonder." A lock of hair was plastered to Harriet's forehead and she wiped it away. "I wonder what kind of frightened little fool chooses an anchor over a sail."

The rain slowed, then stopped. A wisp of fog rose from the canal.

"He loves you the best he can," Tom said.

"Yes."

Tom watched the water wend through the canal, a sluggish snake.

"There are men, Tommy," she said, "who know how to love."

"Harriet—I've been shot; I've been drugged. I've been beaten up and locked up and walking this city forever. There's no time for crossword puzzles."

The city noise was muffled in the damp gray world. Harriet bowed her head and was silent, and the fog rose around her. When she finally spoke, her voice came from a great distance: "I'm not sure I'd make the same choice again."

He let it lie between them for a moment. "Because Earl takes lovers?"

"I never expected he'd do otherwise."

No. She wasn't that sort of fool. "I only ever wanted you," he said.

She watched the mist rise from the canal. "Is she his lover?"

"No," he said, knowing she meant Audrey.

"He pursued her."

"Yeah."

"We won't find Earl, Tom. Not here. Not like this."

"We have to."

But the haystack was too big, and the needle made of straw. There were too many questions without answers, and the Japanese attack force was closing on the undefended base at Pearl Harbor, to kill young sailors who could have been his squad.

"Come home," she said.

"I'm not Earl."

"I know who you are, Tommy." She lifted her face to him, rain-streaked and striking. "Does anyone know you better?"

Nobody did. "Then you know—I can't."

She put her hand on his cheek. "No," she said. "You can't."

She left. He was alone. Without Harriet. Without Earl.

FINDING THE YANK was no trouble. Shepherd Market, the Waterfall, and he was found. But it set Rugg off, Tom Wall crossing the square with his fancy bint on his arm, not looking behind, not worried, like he was on holiday. He didn't have the wit God gave herring. It set Rugg bloody off.

The chalk man had left an hour ago. His portrait of the dome was bleeding over concrete in the cold spitting rain, veins of color seeping into cracks and the gutter. Rugg stood still as a statue and watched without raising his head. Wall's bint had a death white face against her black gamp, eyes like frost.

Rugg specked Renard push himself from his doorway and wait a long count for Wall and the woman to cross the road. They turned the corner, and Rugg moved to where he could watch them, went still again.

Grab Wall and slip the parcel, take him by the neck and snap the bone. But the couple was never alone, first in the zoo and Albert Road, then knocking on doors and talking to shopkeeps. Walking the canal as if on parade, tossing bread for the ducks in a rainstorm.

Then the rain slowed, the bint left, and Wall was as alone as he'd ever been, standing near the wooden bridge at a meeting of two footpaths. There was no canal traffic, nobody walking the trails. The rain stopped. Fog rose from grass and gravel.

Rugg caught Renard gawking at him, and he scratched his chin. Renard nodded—he couldn't speck nobody about, either. Rugg watched him fiddle his cuff, slipping his cutter into the fold of his newspaper. In one flash, the blade could cut through paper, through skin and meat, and nick bone.

Rugg and Renard angled in slowly through the pea-soup mist.

TOM TOSSED a spent butt into the canal. It swirled in the water, trapped between the bank and a cluster of broken reeds. He'd search in the East End, then. Earl couldn't stay hidden forever. If only Tom knew how much time he had. It was eleven hours earlier in Hawaii, early morning. Sondegger was loose in the city; Davies-Frank was dead. Highcastle had to stop the Hun and Duckblind before they transmitted.

The cigarette butt broke free of the reeds and drifted in a lazy circle. What was Sondegger's game? Hell, what was *Harriet's* game? Something was gnawing at her, something more than she'd said. Well, it would have to wait. Everything could wait but finding that second microdot.

"Tommy?" Harriet's voice sounded from the other side of the canal. "Tommy!"

Maybe it wouldn't wait. He lifted his head and saw Audrey, not Harriet, enveloped by a ring of fog on the far embankment. She was waving or throwing something. No, she was pointing— at a man walking fast toward the narrow bridge lofting high over the canal. Renard. Who dropped the newspaper he'd been holding, revealing a sliver of metal in its place.

"Audrey!" Tom yelled. Where the hell was Rugg? "Go back! Run!"

She pointed more energetically, and he saw Rugg behind him. Thirty yards away, two paces off the path, his back to the city.

Tom's hand reached for the Colt he didn't carry. The canal was behind him. There were no boats. Could he swim? Not with the banks so muddy, the water so cold. Not with one hand he couldn't use. Not and leave Audrey behind.

He'd have to take one of them. It was an easy decision, even if Renard had a knife. Tom felt a sudden rush of warmth. All he wanted was to stand and fight. He was tired of wrestling ghosts. He glanced at Rugg to be sure the big man was far enough away before he tangled with Renard. He had no weapon, not a shattered brick or a length of wire. He wanted to finish this.

Audrey's scream rose and wavered and Tom spun back toward her, his stomach twisted with the fear that Renard's knife was pricking her throat, but she was nowhere near him. She was standing under the dripping canopy of an oak, arms held straight at her sides, hands in fists, mouth open and color high—a one-woman air-raid siren.

Renard glanced toward her, must've decided she was too far to silence, and continued toward Tom, holding the knife by his leg.

The bridge was narrow, with a low rail. Tom had never killed a man off the battlefield. He removed his jacket and wrapped it around his right forearm, tight enough to set his hand burning. There was always a first time.

A long way off, a car roughly shifted gears. Tom put a foot on the bridge and stood sideways to Renard, watching Rugg from the edge of his eye.

"Sad blinkin' yobbo," Renard said, the knife casually at his side. "Should've given us the parcel when we asked."

"You got a first name, Renard?"

"Not for the likes of you."

The planks of the bridge were slick under Tom's feet. If he

could toss Renard into the canal . . . "Never killed a man whose name I knew," he said.

"I have." Renard spat over the railing. "He got just as dead."

Tom lifted his swaddled right arm and dropped into a crouch. He heard Audrey screaming and saw Rugg stop and clasp a hand to his shoulder, as if he was soothing a sudden injury. Renard was watching Rugg, too—distracted—and Tom sprang forward, leading with his wrapped jacket. He needed to let Renard cut him, to trap the knife in the cloth and toss Renard into the water. One more slash wouldn't kill him.

Renard feinted, then hit Tom's bandaged right with a backhanded swipe. Pain jolted up Tom's arm and his eyes watered as he jabbed Renard in the face with his left.

Renard stepped back. "Bastard!"

"Must be tough"—Tom faked left, but Renard didn't bite—"fighting a man with one hand."

Renard circled. "No hands when I'm through."

Tom raised his jacket-wrapped right arm to try to catch Renard's knife in fabric instead of flesh and finish this.

"Rugg's shot," Tom said.

Renard glanced toward the big man, and Tom tossed his coat at Renard's face and aimed for his throat with the edge of his left arm, but he hit him high on the chest. Renard sliced with the knife as he fell backward, and Tom felt the blade pass an inch from his cheek. He stepped forward and hit Renard in the throat with his right fist. The pain was a spike through his palm. Renard gagged and swung wildly as Tom ducked and lunged in a football tackle—lost his footing on the wet boards of the bridge and slammed to the ground.

His vision blurred and cleared, and he saw Rugg, twenty yards away, shaking his head like a bee-stung bear. Heard him cursing toward a dark copse of trees, and saw a flash in the air, glimpsed the outline of a well-dressed man throwing something at him.

Renard moved forward in a crouch, and Tom kicked and connected with nothing firm, but the clatter of metal on wood told him he'd knocked the knife from Renard's hand.

He bared his teeth. Now they'd see who'd walk away.

He rolled, and out of nowhere Audrey leapt at Renard. She shrieked and clawed his face, her eyes blank. Holding her shoes like brass knuckles, she stabbed at Renard's neck with the heels. He grunted and swung an arm, flung her away. She fell against the railing and slipped on the wood. Tom grabbed Renard's leg and yanked. Unbalanced, Renard stumbled past and scrambled for the knife.

Tom rolled backward, put the railing behind him. He would take the cut to his arm and use his legs to push Renard into the canal. But Renard was gone. Tom was alone with Audrey on the bridge. She knelt next to him, wet and shaken. She said something that didn't quite form words.

He said, "Are you hurt? Audrey, are you hurt?"

She shook her head. "I saw that man. He was following you. *I* was following— You're bleeding."

He said he was fine and she started crying. He held her, looking over her tangled black hair for Rugg and Renard, and saw four men approaching, attracted by her earlier screams.

"Get your shoes on," he told Audrey. "Keep your head down! Time to go, quick and quiet."

She reached for the shoe lying beside her, the heel she'd swung at Renard. "There's blood—"

"Put it on, love. Let's go."

"I lost the mate." Her eyes were wet. "Over the side."

"Time to go, Audrey."

"I saw that man—I thought you needed me."

306

"He's still out there. I still need you." Tom grabbed his jacket and stood. "Let's go."

He helped Audrey to her feet. She weighed nothing. Without heels, she barely reached his chin. Hitting Renard, spitting and hissing, she hadn't done more than scratch him, but it didn't matter. Maybe Renard ran because he'd lost his knife, maybe because he was afraid for Rugg, maybe because of Audrey. But now she was paying the price in shock. He brushed a twig from her hair. "It's good, Audrey. You did good. We have to go."

"My shoes . . ."

"I'll buy you another pair."

"I . . . I ruined these."

"That's what happens, love," he said. "When you accidentally stick your shoe in someone's neck."

Her laugh was weak, but definitely hers. "I came after you because—I know where you might find Earl."

Someone was stalking through a dense patch in the trees—a big man with a gun. Tom grabbed her hand and ran.

RUGG WAS CLOSING on Tom when something jabbed his shoulder, then hung there, sharp and deep. He put a hand out, and it was a dart. Then another pricked the back of his neck—he felt the weight of it dangling—and a man dressed as a headmaster stepped out of the fog.

Rugg cursed him, and the headmaster said, polite as a parlor maid, that the next dart would be in his eye. Rugg had bowed his head and charged. A fookin' dartboard don't move when you're aiming, does it?

The dart scratched his cheek, but he'd done worse shaving, and the headmaster backed into the trees. Rugg specked him sneaking behind a shuttered kiosk and went the other way round.

Slid behind the kiosk, and walked into a swinging shovel blade. Made a fierce clang on his forehead. He staggered and fell to his knees.

The headmaster swung the shovel again, and Rugg blacked into darkness for a spell. When he came to, he was still kneeling, hadn't even time to fall over. Another swing, and Rugg lifted his hand—slower than a tree grows—and caught the shovel and flung it away. He grabbed a fold of the old man's trouser and a voice behind them yelled, "Don't, bastards! Stop! First one goes in your knee!"

He looked at the headmaster and the headmaster looked at him, and they both turned and looked at a ginger-haired man with a great bleedin' gun in his hand. He had to be police, or near enough to make no difference.

"Step away," Ginger said, the barrel steady as a steeple. "Hands behind your head. On your knees, if you want to keep them. On your knees!" To the headmaster: "Been lookin' for you, mate. You too, Rugg. Where's your little friend, then?"

Rugg put his hands behind his neck. Want to know where my little friend is? He's creeping behind you, Ginger, through the pea-soup fog. Renard was a squit, but he knew how to handle a man with a gun—from behind.

The headmaster was rattling on, keeping Ginger from hearing as Renard moved close. Rugg popped a knuckle behind his head, Ginger pulled at a pair of cuffs, and Renard stuck him, twice, snake-fast, under the shoulder blade, into the heart.

Ginger sprawled forward, the gun flung from his fist. Rugg watched it drop to the brick and waited for the gunshot. It bounced, didn't fire, and he lunged for the headmaster while Renard stuck Ginger again. The headmaster stepped sideways, bowed, and came up holding the gun, pointed somewhere between Rugg and Renard.

"I'm better at firearms than pub games," he told Rugg.

"Go your way," Rugg said. "We go ours."

"You chased 'my way' into the night. You put a great deal in jeopardy." He inspected Rugg. "Can you stand?"

Rugg stood.

"You have an impressive constitution."

"Fookin' shovel," Rugg said.

Headmaster smiled. "Though a meager vocabulary."

Renard inched away to flank the man, but Rugg glanced at the squit and said, "Piss off it."

Renard stopped, and the old man nodded. "You know what you're about, Rugg," he said. "I had you cast as the mindless brute, but you know what you're about. However, I couldn't allow you to dispose of Tom Wall."

Rugg popped another knuckle. 'Course they were all after Wall.

"To kill him now would be disastrous," the headmaster said. "He has a dramatic purpose still to serve."

Rugg said, "Has a parcel, too."

"I should hope he does. I gave it to him."

"You're Sonder?"

"Very nearly. So, you know who I am." He touched Ginger's body with his toe. "And I know what this chap is."

"What he blinkin' *was*," Renard said.

"Fair point. But I'm not entirely certain what you are." The headmaster cocked his head at approaching footsteps. They faded, and he smiled. "Ah. Blackshirts? Yes, British Union."

"That's right—when there bleedin' was one."

"Excellent. You were sent to search for the parcel in Tom Wall's possession?"

Rugg palmed his forehead where the shovel had hit. Chilton had said Sonder was a coward and traitor, but with that voice and that calm? Not fookin' likely. Sonder was bone-tough.

"Ah, discretion," Sonder said when they didn't answer. "Well, it was in service of the Führer that I gave Tom the parcel." He dropped the gun in his jacket pocket and extended his hand. "Pleased to meet you."

Rugg took the headmaster's hand. Could snap him in quarters without raising a sweat, but when he looked in the man's eyes, there wasn't a stain of fear. Hard as a hammer, Sonder was. Not a dress-up fascist like Chilton, but a proper man.

"A pleasure," Sonder said. "Yet now we must find Tom Wall."

"*We?*" Renard said.

Sonder talked on, but it wasn't like Renard or Chilton nattering. He spoke truth, his voice smooth and thick as clotted cream. Looked you in the eye, too, and didn't flinch or fidget. Strong and straight, and saying again they had to find Tom Wall.

"He's long gone," Renard said.

"He's looking for his brother. If he fails to find him, he'll return to Shepherd Market."

"What if he blinkin' succeeds?" Renard asked.

"Then he'll do the same." Sonder stepped over the dead man. "Will you join me? We have much to do."

CHAPTER
THIRTY-ONE

"IT'S WINTER," Tom said. He didn't have time for this. The Japanese strike force had launched almost three weeks ago.

"Spring's around the corner, Tommy." Audrey eyed the shoes in the window—dark red, with pleated leather around open toes—and the sight seemed to calm her better than anything he'd tried. "It's never too soon."

"You said you know where I might find Earl."

"Shoes first," she said.

After the dustup in the park, they'd trotted—her in stocking feet—to St. Mark's Square and Princess Road, then followed the canal toward Camden Town. Every ten steps, Audrey had half-turned, wanting but afraid to look behind. She did again now, dragging her attention from the display window.

"There's nobody there." Tom hoped he wasn't lying. "We lost them at the park."

"We've time for shopping, then." She pulled him into the dress shop. "My toes are ice."

Inside, he grabbed the nearest pair of shoes. "Here."

She wrinkled her nose. "Revolting."

"What about Earl, Audrey?"

"He'd agree. Revolting."

"Jesus. I don't have time for this. If you know something, spill."

A rail-thin woman asked if they needed assistance, her eyes darting disapprovingly toward Audrey's laddered stockings. Audrey beamed and asked for a pair of the T-strap flats in size four.

"Hyde *Road*, Tommy," she said when the woman disappeared into the back room. "The canal barely meets Hyde Road—in Hoxton, or Islington."

"There's a Hyde Road?"

"Of course there is, silly. Didn't I just say?"

Not Hyde Street, but Hyde Road. "It intersects Regent's Canal?"

"Barely, Tommy." She took the shoes from the woman and wriggled her feet into them. "Too small. May I see the wedgies in the window?"

"They're fine," he said.

"They pinch. I need—"

"They're fine." Tom tossed a couple bills at the woman. "Let's go."

HYDE ROAD INTERSECTED three other roads in a wide junction just south of the water and ended in a bridge. It didn't touch the canal, but you could toss a rock from the sidewalk and hear the splash. What had Inch actually overheard? Earl talking about

312

Regent's Canal . . . and Hyde. Hyde Park, Hyde Street, Hyde Road. This was it. As close as Tom had come.

He handed the taxi driver an extra note. "Take the lady home."

"Rubbish!" Audrey said. "Of course I'm coming along."

"I'd rather you—"

"Tommy!"

He helped her from the car and pretended he wasn't pleased.

Inch had been right about one thing: She wasn't able to maintain a temper. A brawl in the park and a forced march through Camden Town, and she begrudged none of it, not even canvassing the neighborhood around the canal, wearing a pair of too-tight shoes. She followed as he knocked on endless doors, and smoothed his approach to wary shop owners and warehouse workers—but all for nothing until they spoke with a middle-aged woman smoking a cigarette outside a hairdresser's shop.

She looked at the photograph of Earl and said, "Haven't seen him, more's the pity."

"That helps," Tom said.

"Your young man," the woman told Audrey, "could stand to learn his manners."

"You'll have to excuse him. His mother is *that* worried, poor dear."

"Is she? Well . . . it's your brother, you say?" The woman inspected the photograph more closely. "No, I've not seen him. Poor woman, your mother. I've buried two, and two more fighting."

Audrey expressed her condolences.

"One in Norway," she said. "One not ten blocks from here. He wasn't fourteen—wanted to be a pilot. They all do, don't they?"

"Nobody loves the infantry," Tom said.

The woman looked at him for a long moment. "It's hard days we've been given. All we can do is carry on. . . ." Her thick eyelashes fluttered away tears. "Happy to be near water at any rate. I like the sound, even if it's naught but the Grand Union, with the weeds and clutter."

"The *what*?" Tom said.

"The weeds, dear."

"The Grand Union? This isn't Regent's Canal?"

"It's the Grand Union now," the woman said. "Hasn't properly been called the Regent's for ten years."

"I thought Grand Union was a train station." What had Highcastle said the first time Tom met him? ". . . *two auxiliary firemen heard a commotion over Grand Union, behind the stable.*" It had come full circle. Hyde Road and Grand Union, Earl and Sondegger. "The stables. Where's a stable?"

"Isn't one," the woman said. "Not anywhere near."

"There's got to be."

She said there wasn't, and he pulled Audrey away.

"Norway," the woman said behind them. "So far from home."

HARRIET COULDN'T FACE the empty house in Shepherd Market, not even for her garden. She returned to the office instead—there was work to be done. She understood the ALBANS dispatch memorandum now. The agent was Sondegger, and if he blew the Double-Cross, her girls would die.

She settled into her desk without informing Mr. Uphill she'd returned. The door to his office was closed, and she had a moment of privacy. She opened the bottom drawer and looked at the plaid check of Renard's coat. She must confront Father. She'd speak with him tomorrow. Today had been long enough, and it wasn't half over. Oh, Tommy—

314

"Mrs. Wall," Mr. Uphill said. "I wasn't aware you'd returned."

"Tidying up," she said too brightly.

"I'm sorry you came. I was told to expect you Monday next."

"Yes, I meant to—"

He said perhaps she ought to return home. He didn't phrase it quite as a question. Thirty minutes later, she unlocked the front door and hung her coat and Renard's on the stand. She dropped the keys on the kitchen table, splashed water on her face, and dried with a tea towel. Put the kettle on, then opened the door to the garden. Thin pink worms lay on the path, naked and vulnerable.

She stood over the fresh-planted bulbs and bowed her head. Let them live. Please, Lord, let them live. Her girls were too young to be sacrificed, too young to serve and too young to die. They were too willing, but please, Lord, do not allow them to die without cause and without gain. Amen.

The kettle was whistling in the kitchen. She went inside and made a cup of tea but could not abide the idleness. The house was cold and drafty. She sat at the table and realized she'd not prayed for Earl. She hadn't expected him. She ought to ring Highcastle again, inform him they hadn't found Earl. Of course they hadn't. If he chose to hide, he would remain hidden.

And the microphotograph? It had to be a ruse. There was no reason for a loyal German agent like Sondegger to betray the Japanese to the Americans. Why tell the United States that a surprise attack was coming? Why bring the microphotograph to—

"Oh," she said, softly. "My."

It was so simple, so obvious. She hadn't taken the time to sit and think. She knew what Sondegger wanted, realized what he planned.

She reached for the phone and in two minutes was connected. "I need to speak with Mr. Highcastle immediately. It's a matter of critical importance."

"He's not in the office at the moment, ma'am. Perhaps I could—"

"Where is he?"

"I couldn't say, ma'am."

"Tell him he must return my call immediately. My name is Harriet Wall and I can be reached at—"

"Mrs. Wall," the man said. "I see. From where are you speaking?"

"My home."

"I'll ring back in one moment."

They hung up and Harriet stared at the phone for two minutes before it rang. Highcastle's voice came over the line: "With a gray shirt, Mrs. Wall—what sort of man wears gold cuff links?"

"I beg your pardon?"

"Gray with gold—not the done thing, is it?"

"Mr. Highcastle, I have information that won't wait upon you learning how to dress."

"But it's not, is it?"

She sighed. "Gray with gold is perfectly appropriate, and has been since Beau Brummel passed away. What is this about?"

"We found a cuff—"

"No—I retract the question. I don't want to hear it. I know what Sondegger is doing with the microfilm."

Silence on the phone.

"Mr. Highcastle?"

"Continue."

"It's simple. Too simple to see. Why would a Nazi warn the Americans about a Japanese attack?"

"Because it ain't true. The Hun has more angles than a wrought-iron fence. He's trying to infiltrate the COI, with or against your husband. Have you found him?"

"We haven't," she said. "But that's not—"

"Tom with you?"

"He's still searching."

"Is he well?"

"Do you care?"

Highcastle snorted. "The ghost of Davies-Frank cares."

"The microfilm information is true, Mr. Highcastle. I can prove it's true without the second microdot. Why would Sondegger give the microdot to a private American? Why not use official diplomatic channels? Because Japan would learn what he'd done, of course. Tom said Sondegger was acting on behalf of a small and semiofficial group, correct? This group believes, and I think rightly, that an attack on Pearl Harbor would—"

"Other phone. One moment." His voice faded, but she could still hear him faintly. He was saying, "You found him? Keep him there. Well bloody done. Tell Nichols and Filterma—"

There was a click and the phone went dead. Harriet rang back immediately. The man who answered apologized and told her Highcastle had left the office.

She used a phrase that Tom had taught her, then said, "Have you located Sondegger?"

"I'm afraid I'm not familiar with the name."

"You bloody well are."

"Well," he finally allowed, "I suppose I am, at that."

"Has he been located?"

"Not that I'm aware."

"Tell Highcastle this: The Hun is the key to America entering the war. This second microdot—it's the key to everything."

She hung up and paced the kitchen. She needed Tom. Was he still at the park? No, probably the East End. She'd have to—

A draft pricked the back of her neck. There was a hush of sound upstairs. A footstep? Yes. And another. She lifted the phone to ring for help. The phone was dead.

HIGHCASTLE PUT A STEADYING HAND on the dashboard as his driver took a corner at speed. The cuff link was *gold*. He remembered Davies-Frank rabbiting on about wearing silver with gray. Some rule of fashion he'd inherited from his mother, who was old enough to know better.

The gold cuff link found on the body hadn't been Rupert's, hadn't been found on his body, either, but in the young lad's pocket. There were any number of ways a child could end up with a gold cuff link—a memento, a gift, a bit of scavenging. Could mean nothing. Could mean everything. Could be the answer to Highcastle's prayers.

The cuff link was custom-made, gold, with diagonal black enamel bars. The maker's mark was visible under a microscope, praise all heaven's hosts. Highcastle had sent his man Abrams to track the jeweler down, and—wonder of the world—it had been easily done.

The jeweler was a burly, bespectacled man. "That's my design, yes." He nodded, setting the loupe around his neck bobbing. "Prettily done, if I say it myself."

"Who ordered it?"

"Years ago, it must have been." He pulled a ledger from the lowest drawer of a glass-fronted cabinet. "Office retirement, unless I misremember." He ran a finger along pages of sketches and scribbles. "I've a notion it was spring. . . ." He pulled another ledger, and another after that.

Highcastle didn't breathe.

"Well, fancy that!" the jeweler said, tapping a sketch. "It wasn't retirement at all. The customer bought it as a gift for himself. Friendly old chap."

"His name? Hurry up, man."

"One Mr. Pentham. Have his address right here."

TOM GLANCED AT THE CLOCK: almost 4:00 P.M. In Hawaii, it was 5:00 A.M. December fifth. There was no time. He had to find the stables, find Earl, find proof. He cut through queues and interrupted conversations as Audrey left apologies in his wake. The seventh person he asked knew of the stables. An old man with a cap and a cane said, "Stables? Don't reckon there's three buildings inside a mile I couldn't name."

"And these stables?"

"Used to be a warehouse for goods barged up the canal—back in my day."

"It's near the canal, then?"

"Any nearer, it'd be afloat. Ain't a stable, though," the man said, a glint in his eye. "Still, they offer a man a good working mount."

A whorehouse. Swell. "Where is the bloody place?"

The man pushed his cap back on his head and pointed with his cane. Five minutes later, Tom and Audrey found it: a sturdy stone building divided into half a dozen shops along the canal. Stables & Co. Automobile Repair was at the far end, with clean windows, a neat pile of sandbags, and a shaggy black mutt drowsing on the step.

Tom shook his head. Sondegger broke into an auto-repair shop before turning himself in? It didn't follow. He walked around back to the canal towpath. There was an overgrown bramble and a small brick structure twice the size of a telephone booth, built to house a canal winch. Its thick wooden door creaked open on sturdy iron hinges when Tom worked the handle. It was empty but for desiccated weeds struggling from the packed-dirt floor, a fire pit surrounded by a circle of stones, and a cobbler's bench overturned in the corner. Gray light trickled in through a rusty metal grating facing the towpath.

Audrey peeked around his shoulder. "Have we found it?"

"Might have."

"Oh, *good*! What is it, then?"

He crouched next to the fire pit and stirred the soggy ashes with a twig. "Could be nothing. But say Earl met Sondegger here—it's private enough."

"Who's Sondegger? And what's her first name?"

It was a light switching on inside a dark room. He'd never told her why he needed Earl. He'd told her nothing, given nothing, shared nothing. He looked at her face—eager and pleased, her black hair falling messily, wrecked by the rain. She was fearless and beautiful, and he'd treated her like a kid sister he didn't much like. She deserved better.

"I haven't thanked you," he said. "I haven't told you—"

"Oh no!" she said. "Don't you thank me. That's the first step, isn't it? Thanks very much, and fare thee well. You said you needed me."

"I do."

She bit her lower lip, looking ready to say something he'd regret.

"Get out of the door," he said, his voice thick. "You're in my light."

He finished stirring the ashes. Checked the floor, the walls. There was no cigar stub, no telltale bloodstains, nothing but an insignificant scratch on the grating, a stripe where the rust had been scraped smooth. He ran a fingertip along the metal as he looked through the grating to the canal beyond.

He went outside. The embankment was muddy and steep, a

five-foot drop to the water. There were marks in the dirt. "You see those?"

"Which?" she asked.

"The marks, there and there."

"Where the rainwater dripped down?"

"Yeah." So maybe they weren't scrape marks. He removed his hat and flicked his finger against the brim. Put his hat back on, looked at the small brick building. A coat of paint had peeled from one wall, leaving a dirty beige crust. There were two struggling trees and half a dozen pilings along the narrow towpath.

A woman came around the main building. Blond and plain, ten years older than he, with a hawkish face. "Find what you're looking for, then?"

"Give me a minute," he said, "maybe I'll get lucky. You live nearby?"

The blonde glanced from Tom to Audrey in disbelief.

"He grows on you," Audrey said, woman-to-woman. "And he really does want to know if you live nearby."

The blonde half-smiled. "I live over the shop."

"Stables and Co.?" he asked.

"It's as good a place as any, and better than most. My father is Bert Stables."

"There was an incident, almost two weeks ago," Tom said. "A couple fellows from the AFS found a man and—"

"Oh-ho! AFS *fellows*, was it?"

"Wasn't it?"

"I'm no beauty," the woman said. "But I'm not often mistaken for a gentleman."

"I could say the same," Tom said. Audrey's laugh echoed off the canal, and the woman smiled. "You found him?" he asked.

"Auxiliary Fire Service," she said in disgust. "Four thousand women, assigned to cook and wash and scrub. If I want to do the

washing up, I'll stay home. The AFS wouldn't even let me drive."
She looked to Audrey. "You're employed?"

"I'm an ecdysiast."

"And make a better job of it than any man, I don't doubt."

"Two weeks ago?" Tom said.

The blonde said there'd been a commotion. "Some yelling
out back. Well, we've had trouble on the path, so I took up a bottle and the boys crowded out after me. Heard a man singing,
pretty as a songbird. Some rummy who'd managed to lock himself in the—"

"*What?* It was locked?"

The blonde jiggled the latch on the wooden door. "Tight as a
drum."

"He was locked inside?"

"People'd been using it as a WC before we had the lock
installed."

Highcastle never mentioned a lock. If Sondegger had been
locked inside, maybe his surrender wasn't as voluntary as Tom had
assumed. "So you unlocked it and . . ."

"We never did," the woman said. "The key turned up missing,
months ago. But the latch here locks on closing, if you jiggle it."
She closed the door and fiddled a metal bar into place.

"And the man locked inside?"

"The rummy? He had no papers and a shiner on his eye, like
he'd been hit with a brick. Ned said he'd have to wait for the
Yard."

"He didn't try to get away?"

"Couldn't have made it to the door. He wobbled fierce, just
standing when they came for him. Whoever blacked his eye did a
job."

Tom could almost see it. The sudden noise from the brick

322

building, the motley procession led by Joan of Arc wielding a bottle. Sondegger hurt . . .

Tom entered the small brick structure and rattled the grating. It was solid. He went back out and considered. It was five feet to the embankment. He checked the grating from the outside. It didn't tell him anything. He went inside for the cobbler's bench and brought it into the London half-light. There was a smudge of rust along one edge.

Yeah. He looked at the canal, shallow water, running smooth. He patted his jacket for the picture of Earl and showed it to the woman. "Look familiar?"

She flushed and lowered her head. Yeah, Earl looked familiar. He stole her key, bruised her heart, and disappeared.

Tom stared beyond Audrey at the sluggish water. "We found Earl."

HARRIET GRABBED an iron frying pan from the hook. Heard the creak of a stair. She slipped her shoes off and started running water in the kitchen sink. She crept into the hall. There was a misshapen silhouette descending the stairs.

Her breath was ragged. She pressed her back into the nook between the stairs and the tallboy and held the pan in both hands. Her arms were shaking.

The shadow hesitated. Listened. The water in the kitchen splashed with merry unconcern, and the shadow descended. If it turned toward her, she'd swing and race for the garden. If it turned away, toward the front door, she'd remain cowering in the nook and pray the intruder would slip away entirely.

The shadow turned toward the door.

She didn't allow herself to exhale in relief. She peeked around the tallboy and saw the intruder was wearing a suit and walking boots. He pawed at the cloth of her coat on the stand, and something twisted in her stomach—it was a violation, his hands on her coat. She stepped from her hiding place and swung the frying pan; with all her fear and anger, she swung it too fast and missed the man by inches.

Tennis, Harriet—backswing. The man half-turned and lifted his hands to ward off her second blow. It was Father. He had Renard's plaid jacket folded over his arm. The frying pan fell to the floor with a clang.

"I'd intended to tell you," he said conversationally, "if something of this nature occurred, that I'd found myself in town without a room. That the club is renovating, and I'd used your key to let myself in, to rest before returning to the country."

"You bastard," she said. "You come into my—you slink like a coward into my house, to find what?"

His face closed. His bones and his blue blood—she despised them. Everything of his that she shared, she despised.

"You used me," she said. "My position, my trust, my husband. For what?" She snapped off each word as she spoke it: "Why did you steal into my house?"

He drew himself straighter; perfectly bloodless, perfectly patrician.

"The coat?" she said. "For your creature's coat? No—you were upstairs. You've been watching, listening. You have no interest in me, only in what I might reveal. You've never seen me, as you never saw Mother. Oh, you foul *thing*."

"You will speak of your mother with respect."

"Don't use that word. You have no right to it. Tell me you haven't been using my position to further your own." She looked into his eyes, so like her own, and saw the insufferable self-satisfaction. "You've caused me to betray everything I hold dear."

324

"Pap and pabulum, Harriet, is what you hold dear. I am your father, and I have—"

"An accident of birth."

"I have never shirked my duty. I supported you even in your fatuity—*Mrs. Wall.*"

"Sneaking like a thief into my home—"

"Your home. If it weren't for that accident of birth, you would be shelling peas in Covent Garden Market."

"Worse than a thief." She raised her hand to him, the first time in her life. "If you've betrayed any trust I was given, so help me God, on the grave of my mother, I will see you pay."

"*I* betrayed nothing. I know what I am; I know whence I come."

She pushed past him up the stairs.

"The strong rule the weak," he said, putting a hand on her elbow. "It is in your blood."

"No, Father. My blood is in *me.*" She pulled her arm away. "I will be placing a call. Defence Regulation Eighteen is still in force. If you wish to—" She suddenly realized what he'd done: "The phone upstairs—you listened."

What had she said to Highcastle? That Sondegger was in London, that Tom was searching for Earl. Something about the Japanese, about keeping the United States from the war? Father could not have understood. Yet there was a triumphant light in his eyes. . . .

"Ring who you will," he said with imperial disdain.

What did Father know, and why had he come? "Renard's coat," she said. "Kind of you to fetch for him."

"So you know his name. I was assured he was discreet." But he wasn't concerned with the coat, nor with concealing his employment of Renard. "Do not pin your hopes on the Americans, Harriet. They are unwilling to die for your crusade. They'll not send their boys to be slaughtered in a foreign war. Not without cause."

Her grip tightened on the railing. "No cause is foreign which casts its hungry eyes upon your shores."

"Oh, bravo, Harriet, how prettily said. But shall we stop playing charades? I came because I heard Tom was given a parcel in your husband's stead, a parcel that would damage the fascists. I'd hoped to find it here, and destroy it. But it appears I was misinformed." He chuckled, the sound of dry leaves underfoot. "Happily, I had the great good fortune to overhear your conversation with that gruff fellow on the telephone. The parcel will not damage my allies, only aid them."

"You heard," she said.

"Herr Sondegger, who has news of a Japanese attack on the United States, came to London to warn the Americans. A wise approach. Roosevelt is slick—he'll manipulate his people into the wrong side of a bloody war unless he is stopped. It seems Herr Sondegger is not betraying his fatherland, but protecting it."

"I pity the man with whom you will share a cell."

He waved away the threat. "You'd testify against your own father? I know you better than that. Is the parcel here? . . . No? Then I'll take no more of your time." He glanced at his watch. "I'm late for an appointment I expect to be quite informative."

"When you are in prison, I'll close Burnham Chase. I'll auction the paintings from the walls. Nothing will remain of what you love."

"And the gardens, Harriet? Will you burn the fields and salt the earth?"

"I'll do what must be done."

"None of us can do otherwise." He opened the front door and walked into the colorless dusk.

CHAPTER
THIRTY-TWO

THE MORGUE ANNEX was housed two streets from the borough hospital, in what had once been public baths. Inside the front door, a mosaic arrow on the wall pointed left under a hand-lettered sign reading INQUIRIES. Tom and Audrey followed the arrow into the blue-green light of a drained pool area used as a mortuary. Their footsteps echoed off the mildew-stained tiles as they passed rows of cots, empty now but sagging with meaning and grief.

They found a woman in a small reception room, sitting at a cluttered desk under a motionless ceiling fan. They told her their business and she ran to fetch the doctor.

Tom dropped his hat on the edge of the desk and kneaded his right forearm. The pain had faded, but was coming back hard. He turned toward Audrey, wanting to see her smile. She was standing with her hands clasped, her face a dull mask.

"You should wait here," he said.

"I'll go with you." A door slammed down the hall, and she startled.

"Stay here, love," he said. "It won't take a minute."

She shook her head, and a man entered. He had receding hair and a birthmark under his left eye that looked like a drop of blood.

"I'm Dr. Masaccio," he said. "Close as we come to a coroner at present."

"Close enough," Tom said, and told him what he wanted.

"Fellow in his thirties, in the canal?" the doctor said. "An open verdict, most likely. The water confuses matters somewhat. . . ."

He led them downstairs and then into a cool basement room with a row of file cabinets and a set of swinging doors. He checked his records and brought out a wheeled stretcher. He said no identification—nothing at all—had been found on this poor soul, which was not surprising, as some people lightened a body before reporting it found. He drew back the covers to reveal a face: fish belly white with a spiderweb of veins. The eyes were empty slits and the hair a thatch of stiff wire.

Audrey clutched Tom's arm as he shook his head. "It's not him."

"You're certain?"

Tom looked at the doctor.

"Well, there is one other candidate." Dr. Masaccio pulled the sheet over the dead face. "I'll have him brought out."

He wheeled the body away, leaving them surrounded by the chill and the echo of the swinging doors.

"Do you know why they call me Venus?" Audrey asked.

"I have a theory," he said, trying to make her smile.

She didn't. "I was at home during one of the first raids."

"You were hit."

"Half the roof gave way. Da was buried, but he . . . I wasn't even scratched. The gas lines broke; everything was flames and dust. I heard him calling." She stopped, and the echoes of her voice faded to silence. "He was a long time dying."

Tom wanted to hold her. Wanted to stroke her hair.

"Then I was billeted with a family," she said. "Living in the West End, I thought I was lucky, but it wasn't a month before another bomb hit. I was in the bath, having my five inches. The basin flipped upside down and I was trapped under, in a little cave, when rescue workers came, and I tapped a pipe for them as they dug. They shifted the basin and hauled me up a long shaft of rubble. It was dawn, and Inch was there. He gave me his coat. He said I was like Venus rising from the surf." A smile rose and broke and then died on her face. "I wasn't a bit of use anymore. In the Ambulance Corps, I couldn't face it, all the death and people buried and dying and dead. You think I'm a coward."

"I think you're a beautiful idiot," he said. "Wait upstairs."

She looked at her new shoes: "I don't want to be alone anymore."

The squeak of wheels preceded Dr. Masaccio into the room. "Excuse the wait," he said. "Now, then. The body was in the water for a time and it's possible a barge, er, impacted the—"

Tom flipped back the sheet. He put his hand toward the lifeless face and felt waves of chill. The seeping cold of refrigeration, the cold of empty flesh. Earl was dead.

Masaccio spoke from the end of a long, dark tunnel. "—wallet presumed stolen. Perhaps this isn't the best time?"

"Tell me," Tom said.

"The lady appears—"

"Tell me."

"His collarbone was broken," Masaccio said. "There's a puncture wound just under his floating ribs, not a fatal injury, possibly caused by airborne debris. Mostly likely he lost blood, fell in the canal. The shock of the water and the blood loss . . ."

"Take me home," Audrey was saying. "Tommy, I want—I'm cold. It's very cold."

"How long ago?" Tom asked.

Masaccio drew the sheet over Earl's face. "Difficult to say, with the water, this time of year. The official cause of death is drowning, but—"

"It's murder," Tom said. He could picture every motion, that night on the canal behind Stables & Co. "He was pushed."

Tom didn't know what Earl's game was, but he'd put the first microfilm in *Tristram Shandy*, then met Sondegger at Regent's Canal, off Hyde Road. Had there been a betrayal? A trap? For some reason, Earl and Sondegger had fought, and Earl had won. He'd locked Sondegger in the brick building on the canal towpath for safekeeping.

But Sondegger wasn't much for losing. Locked and injured, he'd drawn Earl close to the rusty iron grating with his honeyed voice. He'd asked for a light for his cigar, and Earl couldn't resist playing along. He'd leaned close and flicked his lighter. And Sondegger, barely able to stand from the blow to his head, had smashed the cobbler's bench through the grille into Earl's face and driven him into the canal. Earl had slid down the muddy bank, weak from blood loss, and unable to use one arm because of a broken collarbone. He'd sunk in the numbing current.

Yeah, Tom could see exactly what had happened.

"Please, can we go?" Audrey said.

"Mr. Wall?" the doctor said.

Earl was dead. He'd been dead since the night Sondegger was found. Why had Sondegger been singing? To cover Earl's cries, to cover the splashes, and to draw attention. At that point, with Earl dead, Sondegger *wanted* to be captured. Because there was no other way to get to Tom—and he needed an American to run with the microfilm. He'd sent for Earl, knowing they'd bring Tom, knowing they had no other choice. Before Davies-Frank had even entered the Rowansea, Sondegger had known.

It was worse than Crete. Tom had been pressed into service by Sondegger, drafted into Hitler's army.

"Tommy, I want to go." Audrey put her hand on his arm. "Please."

"Then go."

DUCKBLIND HAD CONSIDERED doing both her errands at once— wheeling the pram with the transmitter along while she stole a battery, then heading directly to the transmission location for a site check. Her *Schmetterling* self whispered in her ear: If you do that, you'll have time to locate Tommy Wall! She squashed the urge firmly. She was simply bubbling with excitement—they were *finally* transmitting—but still, security was paramount. She'd first filch the battery, then check the transmission location.

She left the pram safely at Mr. Pentham's, and a mile from the house she appropriated a bicycle. She needed a twelve-volt battery. Well, that or domestic voltage, but using domestic voltage was silly, as the Brits could pinpoint the area of transmission within a block using their DF equipment. They would turn off the mains to each of the buildings until the transmitter went off the air, and discover her precise location.

It was far better to take the minimal risk of securing a battery. She'd have bought one, but the black market was risky. Plus, pilfering was more to her taste.

They'd quizzed her silly on the matter of her wireless transmitter. The sender had a variable-frequency master oscillator that covered 5MHz to 16MHz in two switched bands, and a side-

331

contact based triode with a top-cap grid. Actually, the wireless was plain as a pumpkin. Easy as filching the battery itself.

Duckblind had first spied a lovely car, a Darracq, all alone under a spreading tree. Darracqs had twelve-volt batteries, ripe for the picking in a hinged panel in the valence. Nobody was about—but there was no hinged panel! The battery was under the driver's seat instead. She reached into her bag for the spanners and bent down to inspect the battery.

Six volts, not twelve.

Footsteps sounded behind her, and a man cleared his throat. She dropped a scrap of paper on the floor of the car and remained bent over the driver's seat. He cleared his throat again. She wiggled excessively as she rose. She stammered and blushed and finally admitted that a very important address—here, on this little slip of paper—had taken flight and then landed in his car. She'd merely been retrieving it, but he must think her the *lowest* sort of motorcar thief!

He jollied her gallantly and gave her and her bicycle a lift across town. She asked, wide-eyed, about his lovely car. A 1923, he said, which explained the cursed six-volt battery. Darracqs didn't go to twelve volts until 1924 or 1925.

She bade the gentleman farewell, then biked a short distance for countersurveillance. She'd have to bustle. In fifteen minutes, she passed a Sunbeam, an Alvis, and a Bentley. All would do nicely, but none were properly situated.

Oh, *lovely!* Over the road, she spied a Bedford lorry, with a pair of twelve-volt batteries mounted on the outside. She slipped behind the lorry and undid the connections. The battery was a little lamb. It leapt into her arms and thence into the bright pink paper she'd set in the bicycle basket. She headed down the alley behind the post office, rode past the viaduct, and took a circuitous route until finally she abandoned the bicycle at the station. She'd been associated with a bicycle already, and it wouldn't do to become predictable.

The battery was awfully heavy, but she carried it as if it weren't, hopped aboard the Circle Line, switched to the Northern, and got off at Moorgate, cradling her bright pink parcel close. She'd tied it more securely and added a bow. She passed the Insurance Institute and the handsome Gothic facade of the church and then entered the damaged churchyard. An old Roman wall had been exposed by the bombing.

She climbed the stone steps. At the top, concealed by a half wall, were two planks. Her secure entrance. She edged one of the planks into the blasted-out window of the priory next door and scuttled across. The priory was a burned husk, with no windows or doors remaining—and only one set of easily watched interior stairs up to the second floor.

She completed her site check, removed the pink paper wrapping, and left the battery hidden and protected from the rain. She gazed about one final time. The exit routes were arranged, the entrance clear. She could see the top of the Guildhall through a bombed-out window. It had been hit last summer, and there was a water-storage tank on the premises now, and a long, lofty antenna sweeping into the sky—a transmitter that would camouflage, at least for a time, her own transmission.

Descending the Roman stairs, she almost twisted an ankle. She really must take more care. She caught the motor bus and headed back to Mr. Pentham's, her home for today, though she'd not return after tonight.

HIGHCASTLE BARKED INSTRUCTIONS at Illingworth into the jeweler's phone. He had an action to plan and five minutes to plan it. He needed three teams. Each would split into two units: Alphas would control the roads encircling Mr. Pentham's house, and Betas would sweep forward to flush Duckblind if she slipped past the forward team.

She would not slip past. Highcastle himself would command the forward team.

"All for a misplaced cuff link, sir?" Illingworth said.

"No," he replied. "All for a bloody hunch."

He gathered the men and briefed them in twenty words— that's why it was called a bloody "brief"—and commandeered a direction-finding lorry, muddy brown, with dull green letters saying it was a Pearson & Eliot goods van. He wished he hadn't wasted Ginger on minding Wall and Lady Harriet, but no matter. This was his one break.

Highcastle told the driver not to arse around, and the lorry sped across the city, skidded around a corner, and screeched to a halt. Ahead, traffic was nose to tail in a sea of bloody exhaust; they'd missed smashing an Austin by inches.

"Back it up." Highcastle looked behind. Cars already there. Boxed in.

They were stuck.

CHILTON DETESTED WAITING, particularly for the likes of Rugg and Renard. He'd been wandering Central Hall for twenty minutes, pretending interest in the mosaic pavement, but the hall was open only until dusk, and he needed to speak with the two hooligans before it closed. He'd arranged this rendezvous to learn if Rugg and Renard had secured the parcel from Tom, but there was more at stake now. He must tell them that Sondegger was not a turncoat, not a defector. He was a patriot, and they must aid him.

Chilton paced between the statues of Street and Blackstone, his walking stick tapping the floor. There wasn't a moment to waste, and his urgency fueled his anger with Rugg and Renard for their tardiness, with Harriet for speaking so disrespectfully. The day would come when she'd thank him, when she'd understand that he had acted not for himself, but for her. She'd regret how she'd spoken, how she'd raised her hand to him. To *him*!

A cough echoed in the hall. Chilton glanced toward the tower flanking the public entrance and saw a wiry form flick around the corner: Renard. Chilton left the building and headed toward the market. As he stepped past a phone box, Rugg and Renard appeared beside him. Four blocks farther on, they drew him under scaffolding and into an abandoned stall. It was dark and cramped and stank of unwashed vagrants. Chilton could almost feel the fleas crawling onto his trousers.

A voice came from the darkness: "Get yer own bloody squatter."

His eyes adjusted, and he saw three boys—fourteen or fifteen—sitting on upturned crates. Filthy young vermin, with bad posture and worse teeth.

"Get out," he said.

"Bugger off, you old shitworm."

He struck the nearest boy across the face with his walking stick.

The boy yelped and stood, and Rugg said in his queer high voice, "Go on."

The boys looked past Chilton to Rugg and Renard, their dim eyes sullen. They shifted and scratched and shuffled outside, trailing a wake of stale sweat.

Chilton moved farther into the room, putting his foot in a smear of ooze. He suppressed a shudder as he turned to Rugg and

Renard. "Imbeciles. You were meant to arrive thirty minutes ago. Have you no notion what is at stake?"

"We've news," Renard said. "Took a bit of getting, but—"

"You may speak when I'm finished," Chilton said. "We work for an ideal founded on authority; you cannot pursue our goal while you undermine it. Do you understand me?"

"We have a blinkin'—"

"Do you understand me?"

Renard nodded, his eyes hot with insolence. "Thing is, sir, we met Herr Sonder."

The back of Chilton's neck pricked with alarm. "Tell me you didn't injure him."

"Not a bit." Renard opened his coat to show Chilton a pistol. "He set us to buying guns. Said we should fix that before we met you."

"You took instruction from him?"

"He ain't a traitor like you thought. He's true loyal."

"Do you understand nothing?" Chilton said. "You take instruction from me. You do not—you are not empowered to decide, on your own whim, to whom you report. Even my deluded daughter understands duty. Even she—"

Rugg interrupted: "Sets me fookin' off."

"Even my daughter," Chilton continued, "would never disregard the direction of a superior."

Renard glanced at his companion, then drove his right fist into Chilton's stomach. Chilton doubled over and his stick went skidding across the stall. The pain was hollow and barbed, expanding in his center, and his vision narrowed to a dark field swimming with stars. He gasped for breath, heard a harsh wheeze and a high whine.

Rugg clamped his throat in an iron grip and straightened him. "Fookin' endless natter. Set me off."

Chilton's mouth moved, but no sound emerged. His knees were liquid and his mind could not comprehend. Rugg flung him across the stall. He crashed into a rough wooden surface and fell to the foul ground. He tried to stand but couldn't. He heard Rugg's womanish voice outside the door of the stall, talking to the three young hoodlums. Chilton lifted his arm and watched his hand, a parched white claw, scramble for purchase on a splintered crate.

A shadow fell over him and the youth with the welt on his face said, "Now we'll see, won't we?"

THE NEIGHBORS were a lovely old couple. They thought Duckblind was Mr. Pentham's niece, and they waved her close as she made for the house. She hadn't time to gossip, but politeness was so very important, so she stopped. They told her about the factory fire at Huddersfield as Loochie scampered around her ankles in an ecstasy of wagging. She tickled him behind the ear, and the neighbors asked if she'd heard about the German spy. Her heart leapt, but her smile didn't waver as she said she hadn't.

"Well!" the woman said. "The Dublin police arrested one Hermann Goertz—five years of penal servitude."

She said, "Oh! I must be off," and gave Loochie a farewell pat as she straightened. Hermann Goertz be hanged. So long as Bookbinder was safe.

In Mr. Pentham's house, she checked the wireless one last time. The earphones, the aerial wire, and the spare valves were all safely swaddled in the pram. Even the Richter leather—beautifully executed in red and black—was in perfect nick.

They would transmit tonight. She felt like a bride proceeding down the rose-strewn aisle, so elegant and cool as she trembled inside. It all resolved upon her transmission tonight. Of course,

Bookbinder knew radiotelegraphy, too. He had a dreamy light "fist"—his transmitting signature—but tonight it would be she who transmitted.

She went through the house one final time. Everything in order. She thanked generous Mr. Pentham for his hospitality, told him she'd not be returning, and closed the door to the coal cellar firmly.

Like a *Schmetterling*, she was shedding her chrysalis. Tonight, she would fly.

HIGHCASTLE GRUNTED at the traffic. "Clear it."

"We can't, sir."

"You bloody will. Drive them onto the pavement."

"They say it's a UXB, sir."

Unexploded bombs. Highcastle cursed. The teams were assembled, waiting for him. "Clear behind, then." He consulted his mental map. "We'll cut down, cross the bloody depot, and—"

"The depot, sir? It's not—"

"Move!"

The driver reversed down the half block. The lorry scraped along the alley and shot across traffic to the depot, horn a steady whine. Bumpy ride. This side of the depot, the road was theirs. Breathless, they pulled to the rendezvous site, coordinated, and moved.

The forward team split on the fly, Beta for the rear, Alpha for the front. An old married couple sitting by their fence gawked and shrilled. A dog barked—a little mutt, might as well have been a Pekingese. Thank God. His hunch wasn't a waste of hours and twenty men.

The old marrieds said yes, Mr. Pentham's niece was staying the month, and a lovelier girl—

The men shot forward, smooth as clockwork. And four minutes later, Highcastle stood at the open door of the coal cellar as Abrams told him Mr. Pentham was dead. In the back parlor, the needle was skipping on the gramophone, a record playing static to an empty house. No wireless. No women's clothing, no money, and no papers.

Duckblind was gone.

BACK IN SHEPHERD MARKET, Rugg cracked the door next to the haberdasher's shop. The stairs were narrow and as crooked as the devil's tongue. Two flights up, the room was small and square, with a worktable and long-view windows facing the street. Lady Harriet Wall's street. Renard knew every nook in the city. He'd found this haberdasher's room, made for watching over Shepherd Market—just as Sonder had asked.

"No trouble at Central Hall?" Sonder said from the window, his voice syrup.

"Not a sniff," Renard said. "Left Chilton behind, too."

Fookin' right. Sonder had said there wasn't any reason for Chilton, that he was a complication and better left behind. Plus, the old ponce set Rugg off. Weak little man behind his fancy suits and grand house.

"And the weapons?" Sonder asked.

Renard opened his mack and showed the guns.

"Ah, fine examples of Mr. Roosevelt's Lend-Lease. Smith & Wesson, at a dollar apiece." Sonder smiled, warm like summer. "This is an excellent observation post, by the way. Well done. Best seats in the house."

Rugg stood next to the headmaster, bowed his head to watch the street below. "On with it, then?"

"Not long now." Sonder clasped his shoulder like a father

might've done. "Tom Wall will make his entrance shortly. However, if you'd be so kind as to ensure that nobody else awaits his arrival?"

Rugg went outside, staying in shadow and glowering at the Shepherd Market streets, cramped alleys in the middle of Mayfair. Nobody was about who shouldn't be. He bought a pack of Abdullahs at the corner—Renard's reward for hoisting a car, even if it was a Riley Ascot, a two-fookin'-seater, with the three of them to sardine inside. Renard said he fancied the green. Fancied smoking Abbies, too, though they were meant for birds.

Halfway back to the haberdashery, a young girl tapped past, all heels and stockings. Rugg eyed her and she eyed him back and turned toward Wall's street in a waft of sweet apple blossom. Wasn't right, how she looked him over. No young girl, slim and sweet as she, eyed him bold as that. He rambled in her wake and she passed him going in the other direction. She'd headed toward Wall's house, then circled back, playing like she was deciding if she should keep a date. What was the bleedin' word? *Vacillating.*

Two of the mews had second floors hanging over a narrow alley—closing off the sky. He caught the girl in the passage and said, "Oi."

She turned as if surprised, white teeth happy in the darkness, but when he stepped forward, her eyes turned to slits and she slashed at his face with a hat pin. He clouted her on the cheek and knocked her against a rubbish bin. She mewled like a cat, and he grabbed the hand with the hat pin and lifted her off her feet. She kicked him in the shin and opened her mouth to scream help.

He cuffed her, and bone snapped in her neck.

She went slack. No sweet apple smell now. He shoved her behind the rubbish bins and opened her bag. She wasn't bleedin' official, wasn't nobody. Some fookin' cow, too quick to call rape.

340

He took what bobbins she had and went back upstairs to the haberdashery. Found Renard in a hopping fit. "He's just come. Tom Wall. He's there now."

"We go on, then?"

"Not yet. Neighbor woman's on her step. Moment she scarpers, we push in."

CHAPTER
THIRTY-THREE

EVENING, DECEMBER 5, 1941

IT WAS DUSK. Tom headed for Shepherd Market but couldn't find a taxi or the Tube. A metal post jutted from the curb at a skewed angle, and there was a bridge on the road ahead, a series of arches under a low-peaked canopy. A man was bedding down in an alley under a ripped poster reading DON'T BE VAGUE, ASK FOR HAIG.

The man told him where to find the Underground.

"What about Haig?" Tom said.

The man didn't laugh.

Tom didn't feel much like laughing himself. He'd done nothing right—there was nothing right to do, nothing but tell Harriet that Earl was dead. He caught the Tube and lost himself in darkness—his failure and loss, a pawn in Sondegger's game. The train slowed and swayed at Green Park. He steadied himself with his right hand and swore at the pain, a thick-gauge needle pushing through his palm.

He left the train and headed for Shepherd Market. He stopped at the corner, cradled his hand to his stomach. Fucking Sondegger. It wasn't enough to use Tom as a distraction while he blew the Double-Cross System; he had to drive a pencil through Tom's palm. Blood and lead poisoning . . .

Lead? A memory sparked.

"Holy hell." Tom went breathless. "Sweet holy hell."

He took off running. Get to Harriet's and— No, not yet. What did he need? A photographer. There wasn't one in the market, but maybe the optician was still open. He cut across the street; a bus screeched behind him, and a man yelled. He shoved past a group of office girls. The penny dropped, and he *knew*. Lead poisoning. He ran into Shepherd Market, with its narrow streets, spun round a corner. There was the antique shop, the dentist . . . the optician!

Closed. *Fuck*. He'd break in. No, there were too many people on the street. The dentist next door was open. Tom barged past the receptionist, and after ten minutes—begging and threatening—he just took what he needed: a magnifying sheet from the X-ray view box.

Now to Harriet's, for privacy and tools and a place to bleed. He jogged to the little mews and swung the gate open. Harriet's neighbor with the red kerchief was talking with an elderly man outside her front door. "Good evening, Mr. Wall."

"Not yet," he said. He knocked on Harriet's door, but there was no answer. He jiggled the knob—the door was unlocked—and called her name, but there was no response, so he slipped inside. He was in the kitchen before he realized he wasn't alone. Harriet was sitting in the dark room, staring at an iron frying pan on the table.

"Harriet?"

"Tell me what you know of loyalty, Tom."

343

He snorted a laugh. "Me? Nothing."

"You're the most loyal man I know."

"I'm a sap." Dancing to Sondegger's pipes. "Loyalty doesn't excuse stupidity."

"And family? What does family excuse?"

"Your father? What's he done?"

She didn't answer. She traced the edge of the iron pan with her fingertip.

He put the magnifying sheet on the table and rummaged in the drawer.

"What is that?" she asked. "What are you looking for?"

"It's a magnifying glass—for X rays. Where are your tweezers? Or a sharp knife, a paring knife."

"Tommy— Knives are in the block. You haven't . . . You aren't . . ."

"No, I'm fine." He found a thin boning knife, lighted one of the gas rings on the stove, and sterilized the blade over the flames. "I have something to tell you, Harry, and there's no time to do it right." He removed the knife, placed it on the table to cool. "I'm the last person who should be telling you."

"Is it Father?"

"No."

Her gray eyes were sharp, then soft. "Earl. He's dead."

"I came from the morgue."

She became very still. "When?"

He told her. "Do you need—is there anyone you can call?"

"Almost two weeks," she said. "I think I knew. I've known for days he'd not be back. It seems forever. . . ."

Tom switched on the overhead light, stacked tea towels on the table, and began unwrapping his bandage. What else did he need? Nothing. Do it fast. Get it done.

"Have you rung your mother?" she asked. "The embassy?"

344

"I came straight here." His right hand was naked on the tea towels, the skin puckered and the incision inflamed. "I'm sorry, Harriet, I have to—"

She finally saw what he was doing. "What on earth?"

"The last thing Sondegger said was that I had the proof in the palm of my hand. Then he stabbed—right into the stitches. I saw it, in slow motion. I saw the shiny lead of his pencil."

"Tom, stop."

"His pencil had no lead, Harry. It was snapped off." Tom took the boning knife in his left hand and caught his breath. "He put the pencil in his mouth. It happened so fast, I didn't realize. Don't you see? I've had it with me for days."

"Stop, Tom. Please."

"Will you do it?" He saw from her face she wouldn't. He tried to smile. "You used to like playing doctor."

He dug the blade into his palm and it caught against something through the pulp of his flesh. It wasn't the microfilm. It was the blade scraping bone. He closed his eyes. His right hand was a tight knot of agony. His left probed deeper and he felt something shift inside. He levered the blade under and lifted a small furl of plastic from the bloody mess.

It rolled from the knife blade onto the blood-wet towels. He lay the knife aside, hands sticky and trembling. He was dimly aware that Harriet rose, ran water at the sink, and returned to the table.

When he could breathe again, he lifted his head. The microfilm was sitting in a bead of water in the iron pan. "Proof," he said.

"Tom," she said. "I know it's true. The attack on Hawaii. I know."

"It's proof. Take it to the embassy. Read it, Harriet. Now—unroll the—under the glass."

"Tommy, what if it *is* true? You still don't know why Sondegger gave it to you."

"Tomorrow's December sixth. We have no time. Read it."

She unfurled the microfilm into a strip and arranged the magnifying sheet and a lamp. She squinted and brushed her hair behind her ears. "It's too small; I can't make out . . . Oh, here. It references the other microfilm. It says . . . I can't . . . Oh, yes. It claims proof of provenance will be established by Lord Haw-Haw's broadcasts."

Tom closed his eyes as the pain ebbed. Haw-Haw was a Brit, had been a member of the British Fascist party and the BUF before fleeing to Germany in '39. He broadcast propaganda on his radio show, a perfect way to send information.

Harriet puzzled over the magnifying sheet. "Yes, I see. It lists statements he'll make on air, and dates, running through to the fourteenth. I can't make them out, not with this."

It didn't matter. They'd get a print from Harriet's photographer, then match the text with a broadcast. It meant the microfilm came from people who could put words into Haw-Haw's mouth. And yet . . .

"It proves where the microdot came from." Tom stood unsteadily, washed the blood from his hands in the sink. "Doesn't mean it's true."

"It means they'll have to act. And Tommy—it *is* true."

He wrapped his bandage tightly around the cut. "Why?"

"You need a doctor."

"Why, Harriet?"

"Don't you see? There's a Japanese strike force within days of Hawaii. Why would the Nazis inform the Americans?"

"Because there's not enough time. X-One has already passed." Tom looped the bandage and tied it off. "No, nix that. It was meant to go through Earl, with plenty of time, but then something happened—they fought—Earl got himself killed. . . ."

Harriet's eyes deepened, but she showed no other reaction. "Sondegger approached the only other American he knew how to reach, Tom—you. He'd researched Earl's family, or Earl told him. But why?"

"To stop the attack on Hawaii. Because if Japan attacks, Germany declares war on the U.S."

"And why do the Germans want the States in the war?"

They didn't. That's what she was saying. The Germans didn't want the States in the war. "So if the Japs *don't* attack, the States stays neutral. Roosevelt had to twist arms to get the Republicans to send dried milk—"

"And he had to promise to stay out of foreign wars, to get re-elected," Harriet said.

"It's not a *foreign* war if Japan attacks—"

"Exactly. If Sondegger's microfilm stops Japan's attack, the States will remain neutral. If Japan doesn't attack Pearl Harbor, the States won't fight."

The only sound was the dripping of water in the sink. The room was still and small. "We still have to stop the attack," Tom said. "You don't let your own men die while you watch. You do what you can, with what you have. That's all you ever do."

"You sound like your brother."

"Thank you."

Her breath caught. "He's really dead, then."

"I'm sorry."

She stood and slipped the microfilm into a pillbox. "Disturbing Mr. Bloomgaard, at least, will be a pleasure. We'll drive to the embassy. Fix your revolting bandage."

"It's fine," he said, following her down the hall. "It can wait."

She took her coat from the rack at the front door. "Father was here, Tom. He's working for the Germans." She turned the doorknob, and Rugg and Renard burst inside, pistols in their clenched fists.

"Not one blinkin' word." Renard gestured with his gun. "Get back."

Sondegger entered and closed the door gently behind himself. "Lady Harriet, this is a great pleasure."

"I gotta tell you, Hans," Tom said. "I'm starting to dislike you."

"A pity," Sondegger said. "I'm rather fond of you. Shall I tell you a tale?"

"I have a tale," Harriet said as they were herded into the parlor. "I this moment got off from the police. If you would rather not meet them—"

"How very theatrical," Sondegger said, his voice warm and rich. "But as King Shahrayar never told Sheherazade: Do be quiet. We have pressing matters to discuss. Your husband—"

"Whom you killed," Harriet said as she backed against the piano.

"I'd hoped my business with Earl would be congenial. He preferred otherwise." Sondegger turned to Rugg. "Would you be so kind?"

Rugg nodded and stepped from the room.

"You're aware," Sondegger asked, "that there were *two* microdots smuggled from Germany? The second is in a most curious location." Sondegger glanced at Tom's freshly bandaged hand. "Ah. Did you already find the matter was within your grasp? Excellent. The story itself is simple. Earl was contacted by an agent, a certain Monsieur Galland, who'd stolen the— Oh, the chain of events is too tedious to recount. But of two stolen microphotographs, one was passed to Earl, and the second, the confirmation proof, I managed to secure. May I ask who has it currently?"

Sondegger glanced at Tom, then looked with more interest at Harriet. She kept her face blank, but the Hun examined her with an owlish stare and nodded. He knew she had the microdot. And Tom could see in her face that she knew he knew; she put her hand on the piano behind her, as if to steady herself.

"With Earl dead," Sondegger continued, "I passed my microdot to Tom. It was—"

"Step back, yobbo," Renard said when Tom patted his pocket for cigarettes.

"Couldn't touch me with a blade, Renard." Tom brought the pack to his mouth. "You think the gun's enough?"

A knife appeared in Renard's free hand. "More than blinkin' *touch* you. Stick you in the heart and watch you bleed."

"Mr. Renard," Sondegger said. "If you please."

Renard flicked his hand again, and the knife was gone.

"Thank you. I handed my microphotograph to you, Tom." Sondegger chuckled. "Another pun, for your pleasure. *Handed* indeed. I was obliged to—"

"I got empty hands now." Tom lighted his cigarette. "Think you can touch me?"

"Bloody wait," Renard said. "I'll gut you like—"

"I was obliged," Sondegger said, his voice gentle as the dawn, "to give you the microfilm, Tom. One inspection of my mouth, and all would've been lost. I was sent—as I'm sure you're aware—to destroy the microphotographs."

"Then why not swallow the fucking thing?" Tom said. "It was stuck in your gums for a week."

"Leverage," Sondegger said. "It was an unwise solution to a difficult situation. I had hoped—"

349

Tom glanced at Harriet and saw her hand on the open lid of the piano, saw the glint in her eye as she caught his look. He knew that glint. He nodded slightly—and she slammed the piano lid down.

Renard and Sondegger swung toward the noise, and Tom flicked his burning cigarette at the German's face, kicked the end table at Renard. "The window! Harry, move!"

The microfilm was in Harriet's pocket. She had to open the boarded window behind the curtain—the window Tom had broken days ago—and scramble through and run to the embassy, alert the Americans, show them the proof. But first she had to get away.

Renard was entwined in the table, struggling to right himself, so Tom swung at Sondegger with the base of a lamp. Didn't connect, but the German flinched away from the window as Harriet slipped behind the curtain, her fingers scrabbling at the edges of the board. Renard tossed the table aside and lunged for Harriet, got a handful of curtain, ripped it from the wall. Tom side-armed Sondegger and saw Rugg standing massively in the doorway. Harriet screamed as Renard grabbed her coat. Tom stomped the back of Renard's knee and took Harriet by the shoulders and shoved her through the window. He heard her thump to the street outside and clamber to her feet.

It was done. It was over. Nothing he could do about the Twenty Committee. Harriet's girls were dead, and the man known as Whiskbroom was dead, and his family was dead. But the Jap sneak attack would fade into the Pacific mist. There would be no massacre at Pearl Harbor.

He blocked the window to buy Harriet more time. "It's over," he said as he watched Renard lift his .38.

Sondegger laughed. "And you still have no idea what *it* was."

"His bird's off and running," Renard said.

"Cover Mr. Wall closer, if you please, Renard."

Renard circled behind Tom. In a moment, Tom felt the gun barrel on the back of his neck. It was cold and small, a pin-prick.

"I asked Mr. Rugg to allow Lady Harriet to escape," Sondegger said. "Though I'd intended she use the front door at a time of my choosing."

"Allow her?" Renard said. "What's this, then?"

"All in the service of motivation, Mr. Renard." Sondegger smiled at Tom. "I hope you didn't believe a word of Monsieur Galland and his 'stolen' microphotographs. We needed to prompt Lady Harriet to deliver the information; she couldn't think I *wanted* it delivered. What was it her father said, Mr. Rugg?"

" 'She knows her duty,' " Rugg said. " 'Born and bred.' "

"She is far more reliable than you, Tom."

Tom wiped blood from his mouth. Bullshit. The Hun was still playing games.

"I am in complete earnest, Tom. I was afraid you'd prefer that your country fight in this war at any cost. But I've heard Lady Harriet is of unimpeachable character. She will deliver the information. And she, they cannot ignore. Of course, if she—"

"If she calls the police," Rugg said. "We ain't elsewhere."

"Patience, my friend. We have"—Sondegger consulted some inner timetable—"three or four minutes. We are well armed and will exit the rear. The police are hardly a threat. And think of poor Tom."

"Kill him and be gone."

"He shouldn't leave the theater knowing so little of the plot. It began, Tom, with those of us in Berlin who thought Japan's attack an egregious mistake. Invite the United States into a war we are winning? We could not—"

351

"Time's wasting."

"Point taken, Mr. Rugg." Sondegger cocked his head. "In brief, your brother was the best-placed American we could approach. He agreed to pass the microphotographs to his embassy, as was his duty. But at the last moment, he mentioned going directly to Washington, via the CIO. You see the difficulty?"

Tom saw nothing, felt nothing but the gun at the base of his neck. "Roosevelt?"

"Yes, I worried your president would ignore the information. He'd allow the Japanese to attack, use it as a pretext for war. I stabbed Earl when he mentioned the change of plans, but he was quite resilient. He locked me in a shed near the canal. You've seen the place? Well, I had to improvise to get what I needed: the only other American who'd have clearance to meet me. You. It's now December fifth in Hawaii. It'll be the sixth, soon. Lady Harriet has hours before X-One Day officially begins."

"Fookin' hell."

"Quite right, Mr. Rugg. I'm sorry, Tom. You were a good man." Sondegger nodded at Renard over Tom's shoulder. "Quiet, if you please—with the knife."

"Renard couldn't stick a dead horse with a pitchfork," Tom said.

Renard swiped at Tom's head with the gun barrel. It cracked against his temple and he fell and hit the carpet rolling. He moved fast and lifted himself into a crouch before an iron hand clamped around his neck. Rugg lifted him off his feet as Renard came at him with a predatory smile.

"Kill him," Rugg said.

Renard hit Tom twice in the stomach, two sharp jabs. "Work him first."

"No time."

Renard flicked his knife into his hand. He looked at Rugg over Tom's shoulder. "Go on," Renard said. "Me and him."

"Fookin' berk." Rugg shrugged and tossed Tom through the open door and into the hall.

He hit the wall hard, barely standing, his head still throbbing from the blow of the gun barrel. The tallboy teetered next to him; the stair banister veered crazily.

"Dance for us, yobbo," Renard said from behind him.

Tom stumbled toward the kitchen, knocking off the walls. He struggled out of his jacket, the only defense he had.

"Cut you good," Renard said. "Watch you bleed out. . . ."

A line of fire slashed down Tom's shoulder. He felt his shirt sticking with the warm wet of blood. He was through the kitchen door, his jacket wrapped around his bad arm. He stumbled into the table, tossed a chair back at the door.

Renard kicked the chair aside and Tom turned to face him, backpedaling past the fridge as Renard flipped the knife in his hand and slashed at Tom's stomach.

Tom threw open the refrigerator door. It swung hard, missed Renard, and crashed against the cabinet. Food burst from shelves—margarine and tinned tomatoes and a cabbage—a pot clanged, and a porcelain cup shattered on the floor. Tom slipped on a tin, the cut across his stomach burning, and fell onto one knee. He clawed at the fridge door, pulling it between himself and the knife, bundling his jacket in front of him and trying to move farther behind the safety of the door.

"All good things," Renard said, swinging the door open, out of his way, "end bad."

Tom's back was on fire; his outstretched hands throbbed from gripping his jacket, keeping it between him and the blade. Renard faked left, then drove the knife directly through the jacket. The blade cleaved the fabric and struck flesh.

Pain clawed Tom's chest and he slumped back. His hands clutched the jacket to his heart, the knife handle jutting between them. The refrigerator blew cool air on his neck.

CHAPTER
THIRTY-FOUR

"TIME'S WASTING," Rugg said from the kitchen door.

"Keep it in the cupboard." Renard flashed a cheeky grin. "He's finished."

Wall was slacked against the fridge, bloody knife handle sticking out of his chest, his breath short and sharp.

"Go on," Rugg said. "He ain't dead yet."

Renard pointed his ferret nose and sniffed. "Nicked his insides. He's dead and don't know it."

It was true. Rugg couldn't mistake that smell—innards sliced, exposed to air. "Stop cunting around, then. Where'd you leave the car?"

Renard smashed the refrigerator door on the Yank. "Told him I'd watch it bleed out."

Rugg grabbed Renard by the scruff. "The car, you squit."

"Over near Hertford—his nibs said none too close."

355

It wasn't so bad, the two-seater Renard had hoisted. Sonder sat behind the wheel, with Rugg in front and Renard bent like a corkscrew in the dickey seat. Sonder drove casually, no hurry. He talked that way, too, like a news announcer. They passed Ludgate Circus and the Old Bailey and Newgate, and Sonder was saying, "—men done to death at Pentonville and Wandsworth, I believe. Puts me in mind of Titus Oates, who was stripped to the waist, tied to the tail of a cart, and whipped from Aldgate to New—"

They drove past Cripplegate and swung to a stop. They'd hoof it from there, Sonder said. They could hear the hum of traffic, a brace of soldiers laughing drunk, a car door closing, the chirp of some night bird.

Sonder led them to a knacker's yard. Gravestones stuck up like broken teeth, the bones and bobbins planted deep in the dirt. Beyond the stones were old ruined steps and a wall.

"Our day for crumbling Walls," Sonder said. He flicked on a blackout torch, so dim it was shadow.

Up the steps, there were long planks for stepping over a drop to the next building, a bombed-out shell with half floors and less walls and no roof. They drew the planking after them. The building smelled of sodden coal and the moon shone up black shapes burned on the walls by fire. Sonder read a bit of squiggle on the rubbled floor and they crossed to a corner room that was once an office.

Sonder paused in the door, his face split in smiles. "Hannalore?" he called out.

Not ash stirred.

Sonder stepped in, dug under a three-legged desk, and found a red case and a bunch of yellow flowers. He put the case on the desk and a flower in his lapel.

"Waiting on a jane, then?" Renard asked.

"Sadly, Mr. Renard, we haven't time to wait." Sonder pulled

the case closer, cracked the clasps, and revealed a wireless. "All is in order. She must have judged herself needed elsewhere. Poor girl—she'll hate to miss this."

HIGHCASTLE RODE with the direction-finding lorry. Bugger regulations. Let Illingworth handle Central; nothing to be done there, nor anywhere. The moon was a flat gray. The DF vans were everywhere, and London was alive with wireless waves—searching for a single transmission was searching for one grain of salt in the wide bloody sea.

Highcastle sat behind a man with a headphone shoved like a hearing aid in his ear, the man sweeping the radio antenna and fiddling with the volume control. He was nervous, or desperate. He should be desperate. He should be terrified. Highcastle was.

The antenna was linked to a compass-bearing indicator, to give a position line on which an illegal transmission would lie. Two lines would give them a point. If they got bloody lucky, if they found the one rotten fish in all of Billingsgate. But the odds were 108 to 1 against. There was nothing to keep the Nazis from transmitting.

Should have hung Sondegger when he had the chance. Duckblind would be transmitting, but Rupert might still be alive. So many were set to die: Whiskbroom and his family. Lady Harriet's girls, all the agents still working, still breathing. And worse than the agents, the Twenty Committee itself was dead.

TOM SHUDDERED against the refrigerator. His chest was wet with blood, and the smell of his sweat mixed with something rotten and visceral. His harsh breath was the only sound.

They were gone.

He pushed the jacket from his chest. The knife was pinned through the cloth, embedded in the paper-wrapped package he'd shoved inside—thick steak and wet pig kidney. The blade had still cut into his chest, but only an inch. Bless Harriet and her steak and kidney pie. The butcher's parcel was foul, cold, and viscous. It dripped with blood and stank of offal and, wrapped in his jacket, had blocked the brunt of the knife thrust.

The cuts across his shoulder and stomach burned and his head throbbed. He peeled his wet shirt away from his skin and looked at his chest. A thin slice below his breastbone, bleeding freely, but not too deep.

He got to his feet; swayed but didn't faint. Upstairs, he dug in the drawer for the Webley revolver and the little Colt with the ivory grip. Finally, he had a gun in his hand again. The weight of it anchored him.

What had they said? Hertford Street. He staggered down the stairs and pawed at the cabinet for the keys to Harriet's MG. Hertford Street. Going to Park Lane or Piccadilly? He chose blindly. There were half a dozen cars on the streets, the sun a weak glow under the horizon. Was he too late? No, there—he spotted a convertible Riley, the three of them packed like clowns inside, with Sondegger driving slow and steady.

Tom drove slow and unsteady. He upended an ammo box in his lap; round-nosed lead scattered all the hell everywhere, but he managed to hand-load the Webley without blowing off his kneecap. His luck was changing.

He drove the dark streets. Saw soldiers on the corner—should he call for help? No, there was no time for explanations, no room for error. The Riley stopped at an intersection and Tom pulled behind a boarded kiosk. His eyes were heavy; he wanted to slump into the passenger seat and sleep and never wake. But Sondegger drove on, and he followed, scanning the black night with need and fear.

After a disjointed time, Sondegger parked. Tom pulled over and watched three dark shapes cut across the intersection; then he lost them. He backed onto the joining street and found them again, wraiths slipping over gravestones. He parked in the middle of the street. He couldn't work the car door. He was light-headed, losing blood.

He messed with his bandage, readied his gun, and dragged himself from the MG. He staggered into the cemetery and climbed a dozen stone stairs to a ledge. It ended nowhere. Back the other way, there was an opening five feet from the neighboring building, a gaping bomb-blown space in the wall. Swell. His grip tightened on the gun. The pain was a distant thing. Hell, he was on borrowed time anyway.

He jumped to the next building, crashed to the floor. The Webley was ten pounds in his left hand. He crept forward, cat-silent now that stealth was useless.

Sondegger's voice echoed from the charred walls and the sooty floor. "The happy news, Thomas, is that you're in precisely the right place. The happier is, I'm preparing to transmit as I speak. You have vanishing little time."

Tom followed the footprints scuffed on the floor, his Webley raised. He needed to stop the transmission. The scuffs led to a room at the corner. He entered the room next door, intending to approach from their flank, and heard the intake of breath an instant too late. A pistol cocked six inches from his ear. He froze, the Webley useless. They weren't in the corner room. The scuff marks had been a ruse.

Renard was to his left, knife in hand. Rugg to his right with a .38. Sondegger was standing over the transmitter.

"Lower your weapon," Sondegger said. "I'd rather not have noise, but I'm merely a player upon a stage. Mr. Rugg, shoot him now if he doesn't—"

Tom dropped the Webley and raised his hands. "Where's Duckblind?"

"Not to worry, I'll transmit myself." Sondegger tapped a rhythm on the transmitter. "It's in perfect working order."

Tom's left hand was as empty as his mind. His right was looped in bandages, which dangled from the lump of his fist. He glanced at Rugg, his bad hand throbbing and itchy and ten inches below the big man's chin.

"If you'll excuse me," Sondegger said. "I have a message to transmit. Perhaps you'd be interested to hear it. It seems the Abwehr network in England has—"

Tom fired the .25 Colt in his right hand. The *crack* was loud, even muffled by the bandages. The bullet caught Rugg under his jaw and punched toward the top of his skull. Tom pivoted, blocked Renard's knife thrust with his left forearm, and fired twice into Renard's side. Still twisting, he saw Sondegger raise an Enfield .38 with the grace of a crack marksman on a target range. Tom wrenched his arm rightward, against his spin, and fired until the .25 clicked empty. Two shots went wild before a dark hole appeared an inch off the bridge of Sondegger's nose.

Tom's legs tangled together and his vision darkened. Rugg leapt on him and bore him crashing to the ground. He fired the empty .25 until he realized Rugg was deadweight, killed by the first shot. He'd fallen on Tom, not leapt at him.

But Tom couldn't shift the body. He collapsed, his legs trapped under Rugg's unbreathing chest. The wireless was humming faintly, transmitting dead air.

CHAPTER
THIRTY-FIVE

THE SKY WAS TWO SHADES DARKER. Tom's legs were numb. He rolled Rugg's body off and tried to stand. His feet wouldn't stay under him. He lay on the floor and lighted a cigarette. Finally, he dragged himself upright, almost tripping over his bandage. He tore it from his hand and left it behind. He found the stairs, wide and muddy, like a riverbank. He was done standing, so he sat.

Time passed. There was noise outside, traffic and men. Tom swung the front door open and was on the steps of a gutted church building. There was a delivery van across the street. Men were running; one spotted him and shouted.

He tried blowing a smoke ring, but his cigarette was dead.

Highcastle stepped around the van. He came close and his

face loomed hugely in Tom's vision. He asked something, Tom replied, and Highcastle's bullet head disappeared. Then he was back, smiling. He said, "You bastard. You great bloody bastard." His face was shining and there were tears in his yellow eyes. "Sergeant Wall. Good show."

Tom heard Harriet's voice, and said her name.

By magic, she was there, ranting about her car. She'd had a call; her MG had been abandoned in the middle of the road. She'd been at home with the police, waiting for— "Oh, Tom!" she cried, spotting him. "Good Lord. An ambulance! Highcastle, where's a bloody ambulance?" She was in front of him. Her hands were soft and warm. "Oh, God—Tommy—you look like death."

"I'm swell," he said. "Never better."

"Oh no. Not you, too. I won't have it." She clutched him as he swayed, and then he was on a stretcher, with her leaning over him and the night sky whirling past. "Tommy? Can you hear me?"

"The microfilm," he told Highcastle, his voice a mumble. "We found proof."

"You famous bastard—you did what?"

"Confirmation proof." He felt his lips moving, couldn't hear a sound. "Harriet has it."

"The second microfilm?" Highcastle said. "Proof of the Japanese attack?"

"I believe that's what he's saying." Harriet's voice was clear and bright and wrong. "You found something, Thomas? I'm not sure what he's trying to tell us. . . ."

"In my hand—the message."

"I can't quite make him out," she told Highcastle.

"The proof! Harriet, tell him. . . ."

362

"He's not talking sense." She squeezed his hand. "Let him rest. Poor man. It takes him this way, since Crete. . . ."

She wasn't going to warn the Americans. "Harriet," he said. "Please."

"Poor Tommy, done to death . . ."

The fog rolled in.

CHAPTER
THIRTY-SIX

TOM WOKE FROM A DREAM, a memory of laughing. The room smelled of jasmine. They'd been at Café Society in Greenwich, with Benny Goodman blowing the clarinet. She'd been spinning around him with her outrageous laugh and her devil-may-care eyes. He said, "Audrey?"

"No." Harriet was standing by the bed. "It's me."

He waited, but she didn't speak. "I woke before," he said. "They wouldn't tell me anything."

"I brought today's news." She handed him the paper, folded in half.

"What's today?"

"Monday."

Two days gone. He didn't want to look at the newspaper. He didn't want to know. "Earl? Have you . . ."

"I spoke to your mother." She sat in the slatted chair. "They'll bury him in the States."

Tom felt the hollow of loss for the first time. Good-bye, Earl. May the fish always bite and the women always nibble. "To a volley of rifles."

"He'd have liked that."

"He wanted cannons."

She smiled softly, and her gray eyes lost their film of sadness. "They found Duckblind, a block from my house. Her neck had been broken."

"They found— Duckblind is a woman?"

"She was. Mr. Highcastle imagines it's more of your work."

"Me?"

"So I told him. It was a blessing from above, whoever is responsible."

There was another silence and the sadness returned, like a seep of cold air. He had to know. "Will you be at the funeral?"

She brushed her hair behind her ear. "I won't. Tell your mother I'm sorry."

So it was true. She hadn't informed the embassy, hadn't warned of the strike force. The Japanese had attacked, and the ambush had succeeded. She'd not visit the States after having cost his country so many lives.

"Father's been arrested," she said. "I offered testimony."

Testimony. Her husband was dead, her father had been arrested, and she'd done nothing to stop the slaughter in Hawaii. What was she saying, that she'd lost enough?

She sat straight and fragile. "You've no reason to believe me, Tom, but I love you. Earl is— Earl was . . . Well. I came to tell you. And because I shan't hide from what I've done." She lowered her head and watched the play of light over her fingers. "I'll dirty

365

my hands, Tom, because we fight the war America won't—
because as Europe falls, as my girls die, America will not fight.
How many more would've died while you watched from across
the sea? Fifty thousand British civilians killed, and you want me
to weep for three thousand American soldiers?"

He said nothing. There was nothing to say.

She stood. "Will you wish me well?"

Silence.

She walked to the door. Her heels echoed on the floor for a
long time after she was gone. When the echoes faded, he said her
name.

JAPAN AT WAR WITH U.S. AND BRITAIN

Hostilities Begun in the Pacific
Several Naval Bases Bombed
MOBILIZATION ORDER IN AMERICA

The Japanese, without any formal declaration of war,
yesterday attacked American bases in the Pacific.
While the White House has officially announced
Japanese attacks on bases in Hawaii and Manila, news
of the operations remains fragmentary.

The enemy forces, which were all apparently based
on one or more aircraft carriers, began their attack at
7:55 A.M. and continued it until 9:25 A.M. (Hawaiian
time).

Reports to be received with reserve say that 3,000
American servicemen and civilians were killed, and that
"untold damage" has been done to the naval base and
the city of Honolulu.

President Roosevelt has ordered the United States
Army and Navy to take the necessary action and has
mobilized all forces throughout his country. . . .

Tom closed the paper and set it aside.

He would heal. He would mend. There was a war to be

fought, and he was a soldier. He closed his right hand into a loose fist. The pain was fading. There was a war to be fought, and an old uniform to be worn again.

But first, he'd stop at a nightclub for a beer and a floodlight show. Maybe do some dancing. There was this funny little girl with open hands and an open heart. She was some kind of woman—with laughter and love and maybe forgiveness. He'd like to swing out with her on his arm, teach her the Sky Dive and the Mess Around. Yeah. Nothing he'd like better.

The only answer to the past was the future.

CHAPTER
THIRTY-SEVEN

AUDREY WAS AT THE MIRROR, arranging her hair into the right sort of disarray. Imogene was beside her, but the Three Annes were gone. They'd refused to share the undressing room since Audrey accidentally upset a dustbin on them. A dustbin and a mop bucket.

Rodolfo opened the door and clapped. "Three minutes!"

Audrey slipped into her heels as Genie drifted toward the corridor, wearing a transparent shift and an impish smile.

"What?" Audrey said.

"I'm *that* eager to be onstage," Genie said, and slipped from the room.

Audrey turned and saw Tom in the doorway. His suit fit, for once. His shoulders were broad and his eyes were warm and worried. He was holding a dozen red roses and a pair of peep-toed shoes.

He closed the door and her breath caught. *He'd come.*

"I've been sleeping," he said, "and I've been dreaming. And all I've been dreaming of is you."

"You brought me shoes," she said.

He tossed them on the counter and touched her cheek.

"I don't want to be alone anymore," she said.

"You aren't."

AUTHOR'S NOTE

ON DECEMBER 7, 1941, Japan attacked Pearl Harbor.

On December 8, 1941, the United States declared war on Japan.

On December 11, 1941, Germany declared war on the United States.

Over the next three years, the XX Committee maintained complete control of the Nazi spy network in England. The Twenty Committee, using agents of the Double-Cross System, kept 3,500 square miles of ocean clear of U-boats. It undermined the accuracy of the German V-weapons, and persuaded the Germans that the Allies would strike at either the Balkans or Sardinia after the liberation of North Africa, instead of the real target—Sicily.

And in 1944, it convinced the Germans that the Allied invasion force was poised to merely feint at Normandy in preparation for a massive attack elsewhere. The Germans, acting on tips from Double-Cross agents, moved huge numbers of troops first to Norway, then to the Mediterranean, then to Pas-de-Calais—and back again.

After midnight on June 6, 1944, British and U.S. paratroopers landed on the beaches of Normandy. D-Day had begun.

Within three weeks, the paratroopers were followed by almost a million more men. The Allies shattered the walls of Hitler's Fortress Europe—and the XX Committee misinformation was so convincing that even well after D-Day, the Germans still expected the "real" attack in Norway.

On May 8, 1945, Germany surrendered.

ACKNOWLEDGMENTS

THANKS TO Henry Morrison, Phyllis Grann, Kevin Morrissey, Kara Kugelmeyer, Chris Wagoner, Peter Prictoe, Lynn Nichols, and Mark and Helen Ross.